THE DRAGON LEGION COLLECTION

Kiss of Danger
Kiss of Darkness
&
Kiss of Destiny

Part of the Dragonfire Series by
Deborah Cooke

Dear Reader;

As many of you know from my blog and newsletter, I like to plan ahead and I love to make lists. Whenever I write a book, I always know the ending. In fact, it's pretty common for me to write the final scenes of the book before I write the middle, just so I know exactly where we (the hero, the heroine and me) are headed. Writing an ongoing series is no different: the process is just a little more complicated. There are more plot threads to be resolved and more details to be addressed before the big finish. Dragonfire is the longest series of linked books I've written to date, so as I start to wrap up the Dragonfire cycle, I'm making lists, trying to plan for all the details that need to be resolved.

Currently, there are eight Dragonfire paranormal romances available, as well as three books in the spin-off Dragon Diaries trilogy of paranormal young adult books. **The Dragon Legion Collection** is Dragonfire #9, and it comprises three paranormal romance novellas—*Kiss of Danger, Kiss of Darkness* and *Kiss of Destiny*. Dragonfire #10 is entitled **Serpent's Kiss** and will be Thorolf's book. Dragonfire #11 will complete this part of the story of my dragon shape shifter heroes and will be Sloane's book. (Maybe you already guessed that the Apothecary of the *Pyr* would have to be the one to heal the world.) I'm not done with dragons by a long shot, but these books will finish the Dragonfire cycle.

In planning for Thorolf's and Sloane's books, I had a long list of unanswered questions. Within the ranks of the *Pyr*, I was curious about Drake and his men. What was going to happen to the Dragon's Tooth Warriors? Would they have firestorms in our time? What about the Dragon's Tooth Warriors who had already found their destined mates in the past? Were they doomed to be unhappy *Pyr*, separated from their partners forever? Outside of the *Pyr* themselves, there were even more questions. What role does that last darkfire crystal play in the battle against the *Slayers*? I've only accounted for two of the stones so far. (Actually, I knew the answer to this all along, but had to create the Dragon Legion Novellas to share it with you!) In **Ember's Kiss**, we met the first mate who was an Elemental Witch—Liz is a Firedaughter. But is Liz really the first Elemental Witch to pair up with a *Pyr*? Are there Airdaughters, Earthdaughters and Waterdaughters? If so, what role do they play in the resolution of the Dragon's Tail War? Then there are my questions about the *Slayers*. Who—and what—is Viv Jason? Why does she hate the *Pyr*? What does she want to achieve? What happened to Jorge after he was drawn down into the earth by Pele in **Ember's Kiss**? Do the *Slayers* have a plan to win their fight against the *Pyr*? Their ranks are dwindling, so they need something big to turn the tide in their favor. What could it be?

These questions (and a few more) were answered in the writing of the Dragon Legion Novellas. I really enjoyed exploring the characters of three of Drake's men, as well as ensuring that they had their firestorms. It was great to have the opportunity to add more dimensionality to my Dragonfire world, too, and put the pieces in motion for those next two books. As with all of the Dragonfire novels, it's probably best to read the novellas in order, since the stories do build on each other. That said, I've tried to ensure that you can pick up any story and enjoy it without having read all the earlier titles first. In this edition, I've also added a couple of new resources for you: there's a list of continuing characters as well as a glossary of terms for the world of Dragonfire. There's also an excerpt from Thorolf's book, **Serpent's Kiss**.

In other news, I'll be republishing my urban fantasy romance series, The Prometheus Project, this fall. These books are set in a gritty dystopian future and feature fallen angel heroes who have voluntarily shed their wings in a quest to save humanity. **Fallen**, **Guardian** and **Rebel** were previously published and will be available in new editions. There will also be a new fourth title in the series called **Abyss**, which is Tupperman's story. These are Claire Delacroix books, so please visit my website at www.delacroix.net to read excerpts and learn more.

I hope you enjoy the Dragon Legion Novellas! Until next time, may you have plenty of good books to read.

All my best—
Deborah
also writing as Claire

More Books by the Author

Writing as Deborah Cooke

Paranormal Romances:
The Dragonfire Series
KISS OF FIRE
KISS OF FURY
KISS OF FATE
Harmonia's Kiss
WINTER KISS
WHISPER KISS
DARKFIRE KISS
FLASHFIRE
EMBER'S KISS
THE DRAGON LEGION COLLECTION
(including Kiss of Danger, Kiss of Darkness, Kiss of Destiny)

Paranormal Young Adult:
The Dragon Diaries
FLYING BLIND
WINGING IT
BLAZING THE TRAIL

Contemporary Romance:
The Coxwells
THIRD TIME LUCKY
DOUBLE TROUBLE
ONE MORE TIME
ALL OR NOTHING

Writing as Claire Delacroix

Time Travel Romances
ONCE UPON A KISS
THE LAST HIGHLANDER
THE MOONSTONE
LOVE POTION #9

Historical Romances
THE ROMANCE OF THE ROSE
HONEYED LIES
UNICORN BRIDE
THE SORCERESS

ROARKE'S FOLLY
PEARL BEYOND PRICE
THE MAGICIAN'S QUEST
UNICORN VENGEANCE
MY LADY'S CHAMPION
ENCHANTED
MY LADY'S DESIRE

The Bride Quest
THE PRINCESS
THE DAMSEL
THE HEIRESS
THE COUNTESS
THE BEAUTY
THE TEMPTRESS

The Rogues of Ravensmuir
THE ROGUE
THE SCOUNDREL
THE WARRIOR

The Jewels of Kinfairlie
THE BEAUTY BRIDE
THE ROSE RED BRIDE
THE SNOW WHITE BRIDE
The Ballad of Rosamunde

The True Love Brides
THE RENEGADE'S HEART
THE HIGHLANDER'S CURSE

Urban Fantasy Romance
The Prometheus Project
FALLEN
GUARDIAN
REBEL
ABYSS

THE DRAGON LEGION COLLECTION

The Dragon Legion Collection
By Deborah Cooke

These novellas have been previously published in digital editions. This collection is also available in a digital edition.

Cover by Kim Killion

The Dragon Legion Collection

Table of Contents

Kiss of Danger

They will sacrifice anything to regain the loves they've lost...

Alexander knew he had to fulfill his duty to his kind, the dragon
shape shifters called the *Pyr*, even at the price of abandoning his
new wife and young son. After he and his fellow warriors were
enchanted for centuries, then finally set free in a future long after
their own time, Alexander feared he would never return to his love.
Against all odds, the darkfire crystal makes his dream come true,
flinging him across the centuries to the world he left behind. Is this
his chance to regain the life he lost? Has his Katina waited for
him? Or has the darkfire crystal cast him back in time for some
mysterious purpose of its own?

PROLOGUE

Salvatore dreamed.

As he dozed in his elegant apartment in his son Lorenzo's home, the old dragon shifter dreamed of the future, the present and the past. He dreamed of possibilities and roads not taken, of chances lost and opportunities seized. Whether speculation or fact, his dreams melded together into a coherent whole.

Salvatore understood that he had entered the realm of the Wyvern, a mystical dimension in which all possibilities existed simultaneously. He wasn't sure how he had done it or why it had been allowed, but he was entranced. In every moment of his dreaming, he was aware of the steady pulse of the darkfire trapped within a large quartz crystal. Salvatore knew the gem in his dreams was secured in the hoard he shared with Lorenzo.

Darkfire was said to have the power to turn everything upside down for dragon shape shifters like Salvatore and Lorenzo, dragon shape shifters called the Pyr. *Darkfire introduced uncertainty and possibilities, challenged expectations and was a force for change—however unwelcome that change might be.*

Salvatore assumed it was the darkfire that had taken him to this dream place. The darkfire, after all, illuminated all he witnessed.

Though Salvatore had known little of darkfire in his life—save the rumor of its existence—in his dreams, he glimpsed its past and its future. He understood that there were three similar crystals, and he saw the locations of them all. He saw the destiny of the one in Lorenzo's hoard and understood his role in all of it. The gem had been entrusted to Lorenzo for safekeeping, but the darkfire had a will of its own. It awaited Salvatore, demanded that he play his role to ensure that the stone's destiny was fulfilled.

Salvatore followed the behest of his dream. He sent a summons on the wind of dreaming, a whisper lower than old-speak, a command that he knew would be obeyed. He slept yet more, awaiting the moment that would come.

One morning, Salvatore awakened from his slumber, confident his summons would be answered that very day.

He rose from his bed with purpose.

He had to fetch the darkfire crystal to send it on its way.

Las Vegas, Nevada. December 10, 2010

Erik, the leader of the *Pyr*, was only moments away when Lorenzo's security system began to sound. Someone — or something — had entered the courtyard secreted in the midst of Lorenzo's house. The only entry was from above. It had to be another *Pyr*, but which one? Lorenzo paused and inhaled deeply, disliking that he had been surprised.

It wasn't Erik.

The arrival wasn't a *Slayer*, either. Lorenzo knew the dark scent of decay and darkness carried by those dragon shifters who had turned evil. The lack of vitality that clung to the scent of *Slayers* was part of the reason he didn't want to join them. He feared that the cost was higher than they preferred to admit.

And Lorenzo adored being vital and alive.

This scent was faint, difficult to perceive. It was so strange that he couldn't quite place it. He chose to mull it over, keenly aware of Erik's increasing proximity.

Definitely *Pyr*, but ancient. More like the old perfumes that had been sold in Venice centuries before. Frankincense. Myrrh. Ambergris. Scents that could not be precisely described by anyone but which, once smelled, were never forgotten. This scent awakened something in Lorenzo that he would have preferred to have left slumbering.

Lorenzo returned to the atrium and pulled back the blind with a single smooth gesture. He hid his surprise that there was not just one *Pyr* there.

There were seventeen.

It was strange that their individual scents were not as readily distinguishable as those of the other *Pyr* Lorenzo knew. They must have arrived in dragon form. Together. Acting as one. The courtyard was open to the sky and all other windows to the house were locked against the heat.

But the arrivals were in human form now, and he was struck by the similarity of their appearance. They were all dark-haired with dark eyes. They all carried themselves with the impassivity of warriors, and they were all fit. They might have been in uniform, so closely did each one's choice of khaki garb resemble that of the others.

They could have been one of his own illusions, a single *Pyr* mirrored over and over again to look like a crowd.

One man stepped forward when Lorenzo opened the door to the courtyard, his gaze steely. That he alone moved was evidence that this was no illusion.

There was a bit of silver at this *Pyr*'s temples and determination in the line of his lips. "I am Drake, leader of the Dragon's Tooth Warriors. We have come, as summoned."

Lorenzo hadn't summoned anyone. He spared a glance to the upper window and wasn't certain whether he saw the blind move.

No. It was a trick of the light.

His father, Salvatore, slept. Hibernated really, his strength fading with every breath.

Aware that his glance might betray his secret, Lorenzo met Drake's gaze steadily. "I didn't summon anyone. You've made a mistake." He moved to shut the door, but Drake stepped forward quickly, blocking its path with his booted foot.

"We will have what was promised."

Annoyance rose within Lorenzo. "I promised you nothing."

"We will have it."

It? Lorenzo arched a brow, not troubling to hide his irritation. "You will leave."

A ghost of a smile touched Drake's lips. "Not until we have it." He put out his empty hand, expectant.

Lorenzo knew that Erik was only moments away. He had an illusion to stage for the leader of the *Pyr* and it must go flawlessly. He hated to be distracted before a performance, particularly a challenging one.

He had beguiled Erik before, but wasn't entirely certain that he could do it again. Erik might have learned something in the interim.

That uncertainty was part of what made the trick interesting.

He didn't need this interruption.

"I can't help you," Lorenzo said flatly, pushing on the door again. "You'll have to leave."

Drake stepped across the threshold, his defiance tempting Lorenzo to shift. "We will not leave." Drake spoke with resolve, and a faint ripple passed through his men. Lorenzo was aware of the glitter of their eyes, the way that they stood at the ready. He was outnumbered, in his own home, which did nothing to dispel his irritation. "We have been summoned and a promise has been made." Drake stretched out his hand again. "Keep the vow."

"It wasn't mine."

Drake didn't move or blink. He waited.

Lorenzo heard Erik's car at the gate. He heard the chime that echoed in the house whenever a vehicle was allowed to enter the compound. He saw the slight flare of Drake's nostrils.

"Leave," Lorenzo insisted.

"How timely," Drake said instead. "I can appeal to the leader of the *Pyr* to take my side. Erik is fond of promises kept."

"I made you no promise!"

"Promises must be kept."

"It *wasn't* my promise."

Drake held Lorenzo's gaze, his own unblinking. His warriors had moved when Lorenzo wasn't looking. They stood at attention in rows just outside the door, their gazes as flinty as that of their leader, closer than they had been before. There was a slight shimmer in the air around them, that pale blue light warning that they hovered on the cusp of change.

Shit. The last thing Lorenzo needed was a fight over a promise he hadn't made. As he did, Lorenzo was sure Drake heard Erik being ushered into the house, courtesy of his sharp *Pyr* hearing.

Drake didn't move.

He seemed to smile slightly, as if anticipating triumph.

The sight infuriated Lorenzo. "I must see to my guest." He gestured to the men in his courtyard, indicating that Drake should rejoin them. "You will wait together until I return."

Drake held his gaze for a long moment, as if wanting to ascertain whether Lorenzo was lying. If Erik had not been waiting, if he had not needed every bit of his strength, Lorenzo might have tried to beguile the leader of the Dragon's Tooth Warriors.

Just to find out whether it could be done.

But as it was, he was annoyed and surprised, precisely the way he did not want to be before a performance. Perhaps his irritation showed. Perhaps Drake knew that Lorenzo was more like Erik than he would have liked others to believe. Perhaps Drake recognized that Erik was close enough to aid his cause if necessary.

Because it took only a moment for Drake to incline his head and step back to join his men. He folded his arms across his chest and fixed his stare on the sliding glass door when Lorenzo locked it.

They both knew that Drake could rip it open if he so chose, that he could break into the house and take whatever the hell it was that he thought was owed to him. They were all dragon shape shifters and it was courtesy that made Drake step back, not fear.

Because he wanted something. What?

Who had summoned Drake?

If Lorenzo hadn't known for a fact that his father was clinging to the last tendrils of life, he would have known where to find the answer.

As it was, he wondered who had set him up.

An hour later when Lorenzo returned to the courtyard, the angle of the sun had changed.

And the courtyard was empty.

He unlocked the door, just to check. There was no sign of Drake and his men, not even a faint whiff of their peculiar scent in the air.

Even though Drake had been determined to have whatever it

was he believed he was owed, he'd left. Had he gotten whatever he'd been promised, or had he changed his mind? Lorenzo couldn't imagine that Drake surrendered a fight easily. It made no sense.

Unless someone else had summoned Drake.

Unless someone else had given Drake what had been promised.

Lorenzo eyed the window blind on the second floor. He shut and locked the door, then raced up the stairs and strode to the apartment in that corner. It was dark in the luxuriously appointed rooms, dark and still. He stood in the shadows of the doorway and listened to the long slow rhythm of his father's sleep.

No, Salvatore was still hibernating. Lorenzo's suspicions melted. His father was only the ghost of what he had been, his vitality having faded abruptly this last century. It was a miracle, truly, that he was still alive. Salvatore couldn't be roused that quickly these days, was often confused, and took a long time to settle back to sleep again.

Salvatore's days of making mischief were over.

Lorenzo was honest enough to admit to himself that he missed them.

He left his father's apartment, still thinking. Drake must have simply given up. It was long odds but not impossible. Even *Pyr* could be less than perfectly predictable.

Lorenzo returned to his plans for the massive spectacle he was planning, vaguely disquieted and distracted.

It hadn't just been Erik's visit. It wasn't just the firestorm burning in the distance. It was the prickle of darkfire. He shook his head, pitying the unfortunate *Pyr* who had been saddled with this particular firestorm and its complications. There couldn't be a woman alive who was worth as much trouble as darkfire could create.

But what Lorenzo didn't realize was the extent to which the darkfire would change the world of the *Pyr*. The fact that he even sensed its blue-green flicker meant that it was changing him, as well.

It would be months before he realized that the third darkfire crystal, the one he had kept secured in his hoard for centuries, had vanished without a trace.

Chapter One

Alexander winced when he smelled the darkfire crystal heating.

As the Dragon's Tooth Warrior with the keenest sense of smell, he always knew the stone was warming, even before the strange light within it began to flicker. Sure enough, his leader Drake lifted the crystal and held it aloft.

That blue-green light flashed within the stone, like lightning trapped in a bottle.

"Yet again," Drake said beneath his breath. If Alexander hadn't been *Pyr*, he would not have heard the softly uttered words. "It's relentless."

Alexander could only agree. He was exhausted, like all of the others, terrified to wander away or risk sleep so long as they kept guard over the unpredictable stone.

Drake gave Alexander, his second in command, a sharp look. "Find the others." His eyes filled with a panic that Alexander shared. "*Now!*"

There was no telling how long it would take the stone to work its strange sorcery. Sometimes it shone for hours before anything changed. Sometimes it lit to brilliance in seconds.

But when it flared its most brilliant light, the one that nearly blinded them all, the Dragon's Tooth Warriors were hurled through space and time.

They would feel the rushing of the wind and feel the sensation of being transported.

And when they opened their eyes, their location would be changed.

It was a strange and unsettling sorcery.

And these warriors had seen their share of sorcery. They'd been beguiled by an ancient viper, enchanted to take the form of dragon's teeth, trapped for millennia until they'd been set free in a future that defied expectation. Their leader, Drake, had changed his name, perhaps to indicate that he was no longer the *Pyr* he once had been. It was so apt that Alexander didn't even think of Drake as Stephanos any more.

In contrast, Alexander felt he continued to survive an ordeal, one that only made him yearn more strongly for the wife and son he'd left behind, one that made him more of what he had always been.

The first time the darkfire had worked its magic had been immediately after Drake closed his hand over the stone, at Lorenzo's home. Since then, it had occurred three more times. Alexander was not even certain where they had been.

The group of *Pyr* had almost immediately realized that only those within some measure of proximity to the crystal were carried along with the company, and this was the cause of their concern. Who knew what had become of the others? Alexander doubted he was the only one haunted by the uncertainty.

With a single shout from Alexander, the other warriors raced closer. Alexander saw his own distrust of the crystal echoed in the wary expressions of his companions.

"Wonder where we're going this time," Peter muttered in his usual grim tone. Peter was the oldest of all of them, a ferocious warrior independent of his age. He tended to expect the worst, a perspective the darkfire crystal was unlikely to change.

His view, however, did little to bolster the confidence of the team and Alexander wished he would be more optimistic.

"It's not as if we have time to look around," Iggy complained.

"Just make sure everyone is here," Alexander commanded tersely.

Drake was regarding the stone with undisguised horror. Alexander knew it was because they'd lost five men already, thanks to the darkfire's unpredictability. It was shocking that there were only twelve of them left, when their original company had numbered in the hundreds. Each curse upon them had taken its toll, but with fewer men, each new loss sickened Alexander. He and Drake had concluded that those men who hadn't been in the immediate vicinity of the crystal when the light flared had been left behind.

Wherever they had been.

Could they ever be retrieved? Would the stone continue to flash until they were all dispersed? The last transition they'd managed to remain together, but Alexander couldn't help wondering how long that would last. They were tired and becoming irritable. It was only a matter of time until one fell asleep, or wandered away to relieve himself at the wrong moment.

Alexander swallowed as the light within the crystal pulsed with greater speed, growing brighter with every beat. He felt his pulse accelerate and sensed the heightened awareness of his fellows. He could hear hearts racing, feel perspiration gathering, feel breathing quicken. They all stared fixedly at the stone.

"Here we go again," Damien muttered. The most handsome of all the soldiers spoke lightly, in his usual manner, but Alexander noted how he licked his lips with trepidation. It was unlike Damien to show any emotion, so Alexander knew he was terrified.

"You just want to find more hearts to break," Iggy said in a teasing tone. Tall, young and lanky, Iggy was often underestimated in battle, but he was of a lean build with fierce power. Alexander always thought of Iggy as a finely honed steel blade. His manner was playful and he would even banter in battle, which also encouraged opponents to miscalculate his abilities.

"Not a lot of time to break hearts with this stone around," Ashe said grimly, folding his arms across his chest. Ashe was stocky and practical, the son of a blacksmith.

"That's why it has to be Damien to do it," Tyrone retorted. "The rest of us don't have a chance." Tyrone was youngest of them all, an orphan who had virtually raised himself. He wasn't one for emotion or undue optimism—and virtually any optimism was undeserved in his thinking.

Teasing Damien about his succession of romantic conquests was a familiar ploy used by them all to defuse a tight situation. Alexander was certain that the joking of more than one of the men—particularly the younger ones—was tinged with both jealousy and respect. Damien was nearly legendary for his successes with women.

"We should challenge him to make a conquest wherever the

stone takes us, without being left behind," Iggy said.

Damien snorted. "No woman could be worth that risk."

They were all trying to make light of their situation, but Alexander could smell their fear and uncertainty.

All twelve of them were present and accounted for. Alexander refused to think of them as survivors. The important thing was that the light was flickering more quickly. He doubted he was the only one afraid to breathe.

"We need a new name," Alexander said, hoping to distract his companions from their situation and the fear it created in them.

"The Survivors," Ty suggested.

"The Last *Pyr* Standing," Iggy replied.

"Careful what ideas you put into the world," Peter advised grimly. "There might only be one of us left at the end."

They collectively stifled a shudder. "The Dragon Legion," Alexander suggested and felt them consider it.

"A Roman legion had more than three thousand warriors," Damien noted.

"We are older than the Roman legions," Drake said tightly. "And we are the best of the best. The last of an elite corps, tested by the challenge of men and of magic."

The men nodded, and Alexander liked how Drake's assertion made them stand straighter.

"The Dragon Legion it shall be," Drake said with authority.

The light flared brighter and pulsed more quickly, silencing them all.

Thaddeus swore softly under his breath, then began to pray. Thad was both the most likely to find a practical solution to a problem and the most likely to invoke divine assistance. Alexander wondered, not for the first time, whether the combination was responsible for his consistent success.

"Any chance we can control it?" Orion asked. Orion preferred to take action, and was inclined to be impulsive and outspoken. "Maybe direct ourselves back to the others?"

Drake shook his head. "Any key lies in understanding what the darkfire is doing."

"And maybe why," Alexander added.

"It's a primal force," Peter complained. "It has no logic or reason."

"Then maybe we should toss it away," Orion suggested. "We could set ourselves free of its power."

"And be trapped wherever it left us," Ashe retorted. "Where are we even now?"

No one knew the answer to that.

"It is our responsibility to bear the darkfire crystal!" Drake said, his tone imperious. "That we do not know the detail of our mission is no reason to abandon it."

"How do we know it *is* a mission?" Peter asked, and Alexander wished the other man would leave it be. Sowing dissent never aided a cause or a company of warriors.

The light flashed with sudden brilliance, and Alexander gritted his teeth as he was momentarily blinded. He felt the shift in the air around him and guessed it was happening again. Thad swore once more, then prayed with greater fervor.

Abruptly Alexander was swept up by a warm wind, one that swirled around him with savage force. As had happened three other times, he was filled with terror at his powerlessness. He reached out and snatched at Thad, who had been beside him, but his hand closed on empty air. He didn't dare to breathe, for he didn't know what surrounded him. It seemed that he was swept in a whirlwind and buffeted by changing winds for an eternity. He couldn't hear or sense the others and the sense of solitude was even more frightening than having no control.

Just when Alexander was certain he couldn't hold his breath any longer, he was flung downward. He felt discarded by some superior force, though he shared Peter's doubt that there was intelligence behind the mystery of the darkfire. He landed with a thud on his hands and knees, then greedily took a gulp of hot, dry air. He knew he'd have bruises on his knees, but the dirt beneath his hands was sandy and arid, with no vegetation. He opened his eyes warily, then quickly counted his companions.

Still twelve. They'd mastered that detail, at least.

Then Alexander glanced around to see where they were. He couldn't believe that he recognized the hills.

"Merciful Zeus," he whispered, easing to his feet to stare.

"Zeus is anything but merciful," Drake muttered, but Alexander ignored him.

It couldn't be.

He knew this village, knew it as surely as he knew the lines on his own palm. He knew the hills of Boeotia, the curve of the road, the fact that that the sea was just beyond the lip of that hill. He knew the village spread at his feet, the names of the occupants of each house, that a potter's wheel stood in the courtyard of the one house that drew his eye.

Home!

Maybe there *was* intelligence guiding the sorcery of the darkfire crystal. Alexander had yearned to return to this place almost since his departure, all those years before, and here it was before his very eyes.

He blinked and rubbed his eyes, but the sight before him didn't change.

"We're home," Alexander said with awe, gesturing to the village. His voice rose higher in jubilation and his heart clenched with unexpected joy. Katina would be here! "We're home!"

The rest of the men turned to look and Alexander saw wonder dawn in their expressions.

"It can't be," Iggy whispered.

"We should find out," Orion declared.

Peter, predictably, was the first to doubt his eyes. "It must be a trick..."

Alexander didn't care. He wasn't waiting for any of them. This was his village. If he was home, there was only one detail of importance.

Katina.

His heart thundered at the prospect of the reunion they would share. Their marriage had always been passionate, even after the spark of the firestorm had been satisfied.

Alexander started down the hill with purpose.

"Halt!" Drake shouted from behind him.

"I must know!" Alexander spun to declare with heat. "I must see her, regardless of the price. She's my destined mate. We had a firestorm!"

"We mustn't break rank!" Drake insisted. "It could be a trick, or a lure. I don't want to lose another man, especially not my second in command."

"Are you even sure she's there?" Peter demanded. "Who knows how long we've been gone. She could have left."

Alexander took a deep breath, focusing his attention on the house he knew so well. He inhaled slowly, dissecting and identifying the scents that were common to any village. When he identified his wife's particular scent, the intoxicating mix of perfume and fired clay and her own body's scent, his heart leapt. "She's here!"

"No. I forbid you to break rank," Drake commanded, his tone making Alexander pause. "All of you! Pledge!"

Drake put out his right hand, his fingers clenched in a fist and his palm down.

"The Dragon Legion stays together," Damien said, placing his hand on top of Drake's. The others followed suit, except for Alexander. He stood a dozen paces away and he felt a muscle tick in his jaw.

Everything he had ever desired was in that village.

He had left once to serve with his own kind.

Wasn't his duty fulfilled?

"Together," Drake repeated with force and Alexander felt his leader's gaze upon him.

"I have served my obligation as a *Pyr*," Alexander said with resolve. He held Drake's gaze. "I left my wife and my destined mate to heed your summons, as I had pledged to do." Alexander swallowed. "Don't ask me to do as much again, I beg of you."

Drake's lips tightened even as his gaze filled with understanding.

"Maybe this is why we're here," Alexander suggested. "Maybe the crystal is letting us repair the wounds of the past. Maybe that's the point."

The others caught their breath and looked at Drake.

"No. You can't know that," Drake argued. "You can't know what you'll find in that village..."

"That's why I have to go."

The two men stared at each other.

Drake was the first to blink. "Go," he commanded quietly. "But hurry back to tell us what you've found."

Alexander laughed. He saluted Drake, then marched down the hill to the village.

"We will wait," Drake called after him, his tone level.

This was a gift Alexander hadn't anticipated. He surveyed the village, taking satisfaction in how similar it was to his memories. He found himself striding closer, anxious to be reunited with Katina again.

He hadn't taken a dozen steps when Alexander smelled the stone heating again. He paused to glance back. He saw the dread in Drake's expression as he opened his hand to display the stone. His commander's features were illuminated by the flashing light of the darkfire crystal.

"Not again!" Peter said.

"Alexander!" Orion cried. "Come here!"

A new fear seized Alexander, a fear that this chance would be stolen from him forever. Maybe that was the trick of the stone. Maybe it would tantalize him with a possibility, then steal it away.

He wouldn't be cheated. He had to see Katina, no matter what the price.

Alexander pivoted and ran down the hill, racing toward the village as quickly as he could. He had to be far enough away from the crystal to escape its pull.

He had to be left behind.

He heard his companions cry out, shouts of protest that had no hold over him. He felt rather than saw the bright light of the stone, as brilliant as an explosion behind him.

Alexander halted at the edge of the village and looked back, his chest heaving. He saw only a fading blue-green flash of light and no soldiers. His companions had disappeared, as surely as if they had never been.

Drake and the others were gone.

Alexander was shaken by his sense of solitude.

He was alone, for the first time in years. Only when it was too late did he realize how much he had come to rely upon the counsel and company of the other Dragon's Tooth Warriors. They had shared the same strange experiences and understood each other. That camaraderie would no longer be part of his life.

Even though he'd achieved his purpose, Alexander was momentarily terrified. What if he was wrong? What if he'd sacrificed everything for nothing? What if he truly was lost from everyone and everything he'd ever known?

No. He checked his wild thoughts. Terror achieved nothing. Alexander exhaled and calmed himself. He'd made his choice, and now he'd make the most of his fate, whatever it was.

Katina held his fate in her hands.

Your future lies in fire and earth;
The world's in the son you birth.

The words of the Pythian oracle had echoed in Katina's thoughts for almost nine years and still the prophecy made no sense to her. She couldn't help feeling that she must have missed the point, because she certainly wasn't happy.

Just as her parents had anticipated.

When she'd been refused as an offering at the Korykian Cave of the Nymphs, the Pythia at Delphi had provided the enigmatic verse as explanation. Katina had believed the greater purpose served when she met Alexander in the temple of Apollo where the Pythia sat. Their passion had been immediate and their marriage quick. Her parents had been relieved. After she bore Alexander's son, he had been the one to suggest she should learn the trade of a potter, to fulfill the rest of the prophecy. She remembered how her life had seemed to be filled with promise.

But Alexander had left soon afterward, never to return, and now her son was gone, too.

And it was an inescapable fact that she was a failure as a potter. After eight years of relentless practice, her pots were still the ugliest to be found. The prophecy had to be a test of her persistence.

Katina both dreaded and yearned for days like this one, when she remembered every detail of her time with Alexander with perfect clarity. She was tormented by her memories of him—her first glimpse of him at Delphi and the magical sparks that had lit the air between them. She'd have noticed him even without the extra illumination, for he was so tall and dark and strong. So handsome. The strange fumes in the oracle's grotto had made their first meeting powerful and memorable, but Katina believed they would have found each other somewhere and sometime. No matter where or when, that first glimpse would have been unforgettable.

Those wonderful memories stood in stark contrast to her present reality.

No wonder he haunted her.

Katina turned the simple gold ring on her finger, the one set with a single cabochon carnelian. She'd never taken it off, not since Alexander had placed it on her finger. She knew Cetos wasn't happy about that—she also wore the much wider golden ring he'd given her, but didn't remove the carnelian. The russet stone gleamed in the gold setting, making her think of the fire and clay of her pottery.

Katina shaped the pot and reminded herself of her good fortune. She had a home. She had food to eat and wood for the fire, blankets for the night and a few ornaments for her hair. Her son was strong and healthy, even if he was gone. There were others less fortunate than herself.

The clay rose between her fingers, coaxed by her touch to take the shape of a bowl as she turned the wheel with her foot. She tried to find the joy in her craft, but it eluded her. The pot looked heavy and graceless, just like all the others she'd made.

Would Alexander have blamed her for letting their son be taken away? She doubted it. He'd been from Sparta, and they were a tough breed of warriors. Alexander had never been afraid to face difficult choices or to fulfill his duties. In fact, he'd probably endured the same separation and training as a boy that Lysander now faced. He probably would have thought it right for Lysander to go.

He certainly would have kept the pledge to his kind. As much as she had admired his sense of honor, there had been times when she felt Alexander dispassionate. He could be so still and impassive that she'd wondered more than once if he was made of stone.

Was that why he hadn't come back? Had their marriage been a duty for him? Had he thought his obligation fulfilled when their son had been born?

Katina wanted to believe otherwise. She wanted to believe that she'd given herself to him with a love that had been returned.

But as the years passed with no word, she had begun to doubt.

She closed her eyes as she formed the rim of the bowl, letting her fingers find the way, and began to daydream. She savored the sense that Alexander was close to her, maybe hovering on the threshold, watching her with that little smile on his lips.

When she opened her eyes and turned, he'd be there, she told herself. He'd be in the doorway, watching her in silence, that familiar heat in his eyes. The sign of his desire had always made her heart leap. In bed, she'd never had any doubt of his passion for her, even if it had been carefully hidden away otherwise.

What she wanted was to be with him again.

That wasn't going to happen. Katina's daydream shattered and she forced her eyes open. She surveyed the bowl before her without satisfaction. It was, at best, functional. Maybe it needed a pair of handles. Maybe she should roll the clay back into a ball while it was soft.

"A customer, my lady," the young slave girl, Zeta, said. "A gentleman."

Zeta's tone showed her surprise, and Katina was surprised as well. She didn't do a bustling trade, not by any means. A sale, even one of compassion, might lift her spirits. She draped the bowl with a damp cloth, before wiping her hands with care.

"How can I be of assistance, sir?" she asked, trying to work a last bit of clay from beneath her fingernail.

He said nothing, although she felt his presence. The skin prickled on the back of her neck, her memory of Alexander coming uncomfortably to the fore. Katina frowned with impatience at her own whimsy. There was no point in dwelling on the past.

She pivoted to face the client, a polite smile curving her lips.

It faded at once.

For Alexander *did* stand on her threshold.

Katina stared. Alexander had changed and not changed. She would have known him anywhere, that was for certain. His hair was still ebony and wavy, so unruly that she longed to push her fingers through its thickness. It was a bit shorter than it had been, but looked tidy and crisp. It suited him. He was tanned to a deeper shade of brown and his clothing was odd, presumably because he had traveled far. She ached at the weariness in his expression and the lines of exhaustion around his mouth. He was still tall and broad and seemingly immovable, a man who might have been a statue—save for his eyes. Her heart clenched with painful force, then began to pound when she saw the heat in his dark eyes.

The passion burned there, the passion she'd never been able to resist. When he looked at her like this, Katina had been certain they were destined to love each other for all time.

"Alexander!" she whispered.

He smiled a little. "You remember."

"Of course!" she said, then voiced her fear. "I thought you had forgotten me."

Alexander shook his head, looking so sad that she wanted to hold him forever. "We were so lost, Katina, but now I am found." His voice was husky with a rare display of emotion, one that brought tears to her own eyes. "My Katina." Alexander lifted his hand toward her and it was all the invitation she needed. Katina threw herself into Alexander's arms and lifted her mouth for his kiss, just as she had done a hundred times before. His arms closed around her, unmistakably real and heartbreakingly familiar.

His mouth locked over hers, his kiss as potent as she recalled. He kissed her as if he couldn't get enough of her, as if he would make up for every lost moment on this very day. Katina tasted her own salt tears in their kiss but didn't care. She wound her fingers into his hair, running her hands over him, arching her back so that she was pressed against his muscled body. She wanted to feel the lean strength of him against her, and she wanted to feel the heat of his skin pressed against hers. As always, Alexander's kiss kindled a passion that Katina couldn't deny and didn't want to. His touch could make her forget everything except the desire between them, and in his embrace, Katina felt warm for the first time in years.

It was a long, slow kiss and one that left her blood simmering.

Alexander finally lifted his head, his regret obvious, but didn't release Katina. He studied her and smiled. Katina knew she wasn't the alluring virgin she'd been when first they met, but Alexander clearly liked what he saw. He wiped her tears from her cheeks with his thumb and arched one brow. His dark eyes twinkled, as if they were filled with stars, and Katina smiled back at him.

"In the courtyard," he teased and she blushed, knowing they'd been so impetuous more than once in the past.

"It wouldn't be the first time," she replied and his smile broadened.

"How you tempt me, my bold Katina."

His tone was so affectionate that she impulsively kissed him again. "Still?"

"Still," he said with conviction, his gaze slipping over her face as he surveyed her closely. She knew he did not miss a single change, and also that he loved her all the same. "Always," he murmured and her heart leapt.

"I would tempt you more," she whispered wickedly. "But the slave girl..."

"Will be glad to have gossip to share," Alexander said with that lazy confidence Katina had so missed. There was something so steady about him, a rocklike conviction that made Katina's world seem secure.

How she'd yearned for his return.

He glanced down at her hand, smiling with real pleasure when he saw his ring still on her finger, and Katina's heart skipped with joy. Alexander brushed his lips across hers, then let his mouth hover over hers as he held her gaze. As always, he gave her the choice, which only made him more irresistible. "Or maybe you didn't miss me in this way?" he murmured, clearly knowing she had. When he teased her, his eyes sparkling and his manner playful, Katina wanted him all the more.

"Of course!" She laughed at him, then caught his head in her hands, pulling him down for another kiss. This time, she was purposeful and passionate, intending to leave no doubt in his mind of his welcome. Alexander caught his breath when her tongue slid between his teeth, then hauled her even closer, kissing her with crushing intensity. His erection strained against his clothing, so large and hard that Katina had no doubt of his desire.

It was intoxicating to know that he wanted her as much as she wanted him. She met him touch for touch, loving the sense of communion she felt in these encounters. Alexander groaned, then swept her into his arms. He strode across the courtyard, never breaking his kiss. Katina wound her arms around his neck, wanting all he had to give.

It had been so long.

His touch felt so right.

In fact, nothing had felt right without him. Katina was on her back on her bed, her belt untied and Alexander's hands beneath her tunic before she opened her eyes. He kissed her again, the intoxicating leisure of his kiss making her forget everything but the magic of his touch. She could think of nothing but this man she loved with all her heart, this man she had feared to never see again.

Alexander's hand closed over her breast, and Katina moaned as he rolled the taut peak between his finger and thumb. He lifted her tunic and bent to take her nipple in his mouth, suckling her so that Katina thought she would be overwhelmed by pleasure. His hands felt large on her body, strong and warm and firm, yet he was so gentle that she couldn't have denied him anything. He was so determined to find pleasure together that Katina knew he had dreamed of this moment, too.

Alexander's fingers slid beneath the hem of her chiton, and she knew what he would do. Her heart skipped a beat, because she had loved this kind of play. She caught her breath at the heat of his hand on her leg, his touch sliding ever upward, and fell back in surrender. She was his for the taking, and she heard from his chuckle that he knew it. His fingers slipped between her thighs, his caress on her wet heat making her gasp with delight.

"Katina," Alexander whispered with awe, then caught her mouth beneath his own once more. He kissed her again, his fingers tormenting her until she writhed on the bed. Her body was filled with a pleasure that surged to greater intensity, like a flame coaxed to burn brighter and brighter. Her hands were on Alexander's shoulders, her fingers gripping his solid strength, his body providing an anchor for her in the storm he roused with his touch.

She was desperate to feel his skin against hers and see him nude again, but his clothing was so strange that she didn't know how to begin to disrobe him. She ran her hands over him repeatedly, then shoved her fingers into his hair.

Alexander lifted his head, his eyes twinkling.

"Don't stop," she whispered and he grinned.

"Not yet." Alexander slid down the length of her, parted her thighs with his hands, and lowered his head to flick his tongue across her arousal. Katina moaned from the depths of her soul. Only Alexander could give her such pleasure. Only Alexander could make her act like a wanton.

And Katina didn't care.

She wanted him, over and over and over again. No matter what price she had to pay, she would have this moment, with no regrets. She felt the heat of Alexander's breath as he paused in his torment of her, then he kissed her in that intimate place and all coherent thought left her mind.

There was only Alexander, only the pleasure he gave and the surety of her love for him.

And in this moment, that was enough.

Alexander's welcome couldn't be mistaken. Katina's body told the truth of her thoughts, as it always did. It had always been easier for them to communicate by touch than with words, and as far as Alexander was concerned, they could talk later. First, they would restore the power of their union. First, they would recover the magic.

Then they could resolve the details.

There was nothing in his universe in this moment except Katina, and his joy to be with her again. For the moment, there was the love shining in her eyes, the dark majesty of her hair, the supple strength of her body and the wet welcome between her thighs. She was as much of a feast as Alexander recalled, so sweet and hot and responsive that he knew there could never be another woman for him. There was no pretense in her and he loved the honesty of her passion. He had never doubted what Katina had wanted of him, and he was profoundly glad to learn that had not changed.

He was more than ready to give her all she desired and wished he could make her dreams come true.

He felt a strange flutter on his skin when his heart swelled with love, but couldn't make sense of the sensation that he'd lost something. He'd found something precious here, against all odds, and he was going to make the most of it.

Alexander urged the tide to rise within Katina, proud beyond all that he could still please his wife so well. He teased her and drove her higher, then withdrew in the right moment, knowing her well enough to extend her torment and her pleasure. She moaned and protested incoherently, but Alexander wanted this union to be perfect.

He wanted to prove that it was worth the wait.

The third time her passion rose, he waited until that ideal moment to graze his teeth across her turgid clitoris. Katina gasped, then gained her release in a shaking torrent. Her legs locked around his head involuntarily and she moaned as if her world was ending. Alexander savored her pleasure. She was flushed when her breathing returned to something like its regular pace, and her eyes were sparkling.

She was so beautiful that his heart ached at the time they'd lost. He did not want to know, not yet, just how months he had been gone. Even if it had been a year, he would make it up to her.

For now, Katina and this reunion was enough.

Alexander rose to his feet, knowing that Katina watched him with a hunger for more. Her thoughts were so easily read when they made love, and he was glad that she'd never had any inclination to play games with desire. She was impetuous and passionate, but utterly true.

Alexander unbuckled his belt and cast it aside, liking how she smiled as he shed his clothes. She sat up on the bed, reaching to touch each exposed increment of skin, as if she were as anxious to caress him as he was to caress her. Alexander shed his clothing and boots with record speed, his boots falling to one side, his shirt and trousers to the other.

"Your clothing is so strange," she said, and a question filled her gaze. "I wouldn't have known where to start."

Alexander didn't want to talk about where he had been. Not yet. The tale would take too long and he wanted this reunion first.

"Is that why you watch me so closely?" he teased. "To have me naked whenever you so choose?"

"Maybe I'll keep you naked for a while. Until you please me enough." Katina laughed, then stopped, confusion lighting her gaze. She stood up and reached a fingertip to touch the tattoo on his upper arm, the one souvenir he still bore from the future. Alexander winced when she touched it, not because it hurt but because he didn't want to explain all of that as yet. "A magical beast upon your skin," she said with wonder, and met his gaze. She clearly was curious.

"It doesn't matter," Alexander said, his voice rougher than he intended. He knew that once her questions began, she would not fall silent until she knew everything of where he had been. Her inquisitiveness was a trait he admired, but he needed her touch first. He put a fingertip on her lips, savoring their softness. "This first," he urged, knowing he would beg if he had to. "I've been without you too long to keep to the thread of any story otherwise."

"So honest." She smiled. "You never could lie."

Alexander shook his head. "Not to you."

Katina was clearly pleased by this. She drew him into her embrace, then granted him a thoughtful glance. "How many other women?" she whispered when he would have kissed her again. Her gaze was searching. "Just tell me that."

"None," Alexander said with finality. "For there can be no other woman for me."

"Only you could have managed that feat," she said with pride, which confused him.

"I don't understand."

"Your word is your bond, Alexander. I knew that long ago. It is something I admire about you." She ran her hands over his head again and her eyes glowed. "Only you could have denied your pleasure so long to keep a pledge to me."

Alexander took that as an invitation. He kissed her and his embrace soon turned hungry, his passion for her contained far too long. Now that he was with Katina, he wasn't certain how long he could last. He'd denied himself for so long, and his passion was a tide that couldn't be stopped. He moved them with purpose to the narrow bed, not wanting to rush her, but compelled by his body's need. Katina smiled and leaned back, opening her thighs to him in invitation.

She'd always understood him so well. Alexander couldn't have refused her to save his life. He slid into her wet heat with a sigh, unable to remember when any sensation had felt so good.

Or so right.

Katina ran her hands over him, delight in her eyes. Alexander rolled on the bed so that he was on his back and she was sitting astride him. She smiled as she pulled her tunic and chiton over her head, then tossed them to the floor. She was even more beautiful than he had recalled. Her nipples were tight and dark, her breasts high and just large enough to fill his palms. Her waist was narrow and her belly not quite flat. He ran his hands over her, remembering how he had loved the look of her when she'd carried his son and wondering if they would have more.

The idea made his chest tighten. It seemed impossibly wonderful that he could have a future again, that he could plan his days and nights with his beloved, that the darkfire had given him such a gift as this.

Then Katina unfastened her hair, letting it fall over her shoulders like a dark veil. It was as glossy and thick as he remembered, as wavy as the curl of the ocean's tide and darker than a river at midnight. It flowed over her shoulders and down her back, cascading all the way to her hips. He'd always loved her hair. At the sight of its loosened splendor, Alexander was lost all over again.

Katina moved atop him, caressing her own breasts as she rode him, her smile making Alexander dizzy. He ran his hands over her slender strength and let the scent of her skin inundate him. How he adored her. How he had missed her. How could she have imagined there could be any other woman who might compare or even suffice? He gripped Katina's hips and urged her to move faster as his need built.

Alexander murmured her name even as his heart pounded with greater intensity. She tormented him as he had teased her, building his passion to a peak then slowing her pace, before building his desire again. Alexander heard himself moan and the bed creak, even as all rational thought left his mind.

There was only Katina with her slick heat, her shining eyes and her sweet smile. He lost track of how many times she teased him, but suddenly knew he could bear it no longer. He whispered her name with greater urgency and she leaned over him, surrounding him in the dark spill of her hair. Alexander closed his eyes and held fast to her, wanting to lose himself in the embrace of the woman he loved. His heart pounded as her breasts fell against his chest, his breath caught when she kissed him. The tide rose within him with sudden vigor and this time, he couldn't hold back.

Alexander caught Katina's nape in one hand and wrapped his other arm around her waist, driving deeper and faster. Her sweet perfume enveloped him, her soft curves were crushed against him, her hair tickled against his skin. Her fervid kisses eliminated his awareness of anything but his lovely lady wife. Alexander came with explosive force, an orgasm that seemed endless and left him shaking with exhaustion.

And then he kissed Katina's temple, feeling more fortunate than he had ever expected to be in this lifetime.

Alexander was finally home.

CHAPTER TWO

The hot spill of Alexander's seed recalled Katina to her senses. How could she have been so foolish?

Alexander dozed in her arms as he always did after his release, looking so handsome and relaxed that Katina wished she could let him sleep. But that was impossible. She'd put everything at risk with her impulsive and passionate greeting. She wanted nothing more than to stay wrapped in his warmth, but she heard the slaves preparing the evening meal. It was becoming darker, which could only mean one thing.

Her husband, Cetos, would return. What would he do to Alexander?

"Wake up," she whispered urgently to Alexander. "Wake up! Alexander, you must leave." She tried to get out of the bed, but he wrapped himself around her, holding her close to his warmth. He kissed her temple sweetly and she knew he'd fall asleep with her trapped against his nude body.

If only she could have enjoyed that pleasure.

"Not yet." Alexander opened his eyes and granted her a sleepy smile that wrenched her heart. "Give me a moment, then we'll greet each other again. The second time is always slower, and better." He slid his fingers into her hair and would have pulled her back down for another kiss, but Katina squirmed out of his grip.

"No!" she commanded in an undertone. "You have to leave before there is talk."

Alexander's smile didn't waver. "There's probably already talk. I didn't sneak into the village." Katina backed away from him, searching for her clothes. "The meal can wait," he murmured, then patted the bed beside himself.

Katina turned away from the temptation he offered, wishing she had been able to resist him before. She tugged on her chiton and knotted the belt swiftly around her waist, noting that her hands were shaking.

Cetos had such a temper. He'd only shouted at her in the past, but she feared that finding her first husband naked in her bedroom might push him too far. She already knew that he resented her choosing Alexander over him before.

The one thing they argued about was her determination to continue to wear Alexander's ring.

"What's wrong, Katina?" Alexander asked softly and she spun to find that he was watching her closely. His eyes glittered and he already sat on the edge of the bed, so taut that he looked poised to leap. She hadn't even heard him move.

"Everything is wrong!" she whispered, not knowing where to begin.

"Everything is finally right," Alexander corrected firmly. He got to his feet with purpose and crossed the room to her side. "I'm home, and we're together again. We'll raise our son and maybe have a few more." He lifted her hair and pressed an enticing kiss to the side of her neck. Oh, how well she remembered that Alexander was never satisfied with one mating.

"There's no time for this! You must go!"

Alexander sobered and his eyes narrowed. He flicked a glance around the bedroom, his gaze lingering on the second bed. His eyes seemed to brighten, and he turned in place, clearly seeking something. "Where's the cradle for Lysander? Is he walking yet?"

Katina was impatient with the question. She picked up one of his garments and flung it at him. "What difference? He has no use of it now."

"What do you mean?" Alexander froze, his expression horrified. "What's happened to him?"

"He's grown up, of course." Katina poked at the garment he hadn't yet put on. "A man named Pelias came last week to collect him."

Alexander didn't move. "Why?"

"For the *agoge*," Katina said, not understanding why Alexander should be so shocked. The mandatory military training for the young boys of Sparta was part of his legacy to their son.

Alexander sat down hard on the bed, as if his legs couldn't support him. "But a boy must be eight years of age for the *agoge*."

"Yes. Please get dressed!"

Alexander gave her a challenging look. "*Eight* years."

Katina stared at him as she understood his surprise. Her fear abandoned her, replaced by a ripple of anger. "Yes, he is eight." She propped a hand on her hip. "Don't you know how long you've been gone?"

If she'd expected him to deny it or make some excuse, she was to be disappointed.

Alexander stared around the room, as if seeing it for the first time. He surveyed every detail, but avoided looking at her.

His confusion tore at her heart, but she couldn't understand how he couldn't know how much time had passed. What game was he playing? "How long did you think you had been gone?"

Alexander's expression turned weary. "It's been as thousands of years for me."

Katina bit her lip. Alexander wasn't a poetic man and she knew it. He could be evasive, and he wasn't one to easily share all the secrets of his heart. Now that their moment of passion had passed, she remembered all the fault lines in their short marriage. There was so much she didn't know about Alexander. He couldn't *literally* mean thousands of years, could he? Where had he been? What had happened to him?

As much as she wanted to know the story, there was no time to hear it. Not now. "You have to leave," she repeated. "Please, dress yourself and go."

"Go?" Alexander frowned at her. "Katina, I've dreamed of returning to you all this time. Why would I leave now?"

"Because you can't stay here."

"Of course, I can stay here." He became indignant. "You're my wife..."

"I *was* your wife, but you left."

Alexander stared at Katina and she knew from the intensity of his gaze that he'd guessed the truth. He took a deep breath, one that made his nostrils flare. His eyes began to glitter with a strange light, one that made Katina take a step backward. "You married again?" he asked as if this were incomprehensible.

"You sent no word," she replied with frustration. "Not a single message in eight years! What would I think except that you'd been killed?"

He ran a hand over his head. "But if it's been eight years, then my service is done," he said, almost to himself, then turned to her with his eyes alight.

Katina refused to be seduced by his hopeful expression. Even so, she knew that if he touched her, she'd lose the battle. She held up a hand between them. "Wait. You *knew* it might be eight years? You knew and you never mentioned as much?"

"I didn't expect it would be..."

"You should have told me!"

He stood up, looking grim. "Would you have married again if I had told you?"

She knew the promise he wanted, but couldn't give it. "Eight years is a long time," she replied. "I had a son. I had no husband. I had to survive. We would have starved in eight years, easily."

"But you had your pottery..."

"And no trade in it."

"Why not?"

"Alexander, I'm not skilled at this craft."

"You should have been able to sell enough."

Katina had to avert her gaze. "And there were stories..."

"What kind of *stories*? What did people say about you?"

"It doesn't matter! No one would come to me to buy, and Lysander had to eat." She spun and paced the width of the room, knowing there was no short version of the story he would accept. "You were gone, and I had no word from you. I made a *choice*, because I had to."

Alexander folded his arms across his chest. His body rigid and there was a curious flicker of blue light surrounding him, although Katina couldn't guess what it was. "Who?" he demanded in a low voice.

Katina simply held his gaze and let him guess.

Alexander swore thoroughly as he turned away from her. He marched the width of the room twice and looked as if he'd put his fist through the wall.

Katina was shocked. She had never known she could provoke him to such a visible display of anger. She supposed it was the sign of his feelings that she'd always wanted, but in this moment, she didn't like the sight.

Alexander returned to face her. He caught her shoulders in his hands so that she couldn't evade his gaze. "Not Cetos?" he demanded, clearly guessing that it was. "You didn't want to marry him before." His voice rose. "I ensured you didn't have to!"

That blue light surrounding his body became more vivid, like a lick of lightning. Katina felt the intensity of his anger, but she was unafraid of him.

Alexander would never hurt her.

Katina held his gaze. "I had no choice," she said, biting off the words. "No other man would have me. I did what had to be done for Lysander. *Our* son needed a future and I was the only one here to give it to him." She decided she might as well tell him all of it. "I asked him to marry me."

Alexander flinched at that, but Katina had no satisfaction from his response.

In fact, she felt sad and empty. He was back but she had to send him away, because of choices she'd made. She knew Alexander's opinion on pledges and promises.

She lifted his hand from her shoulder, kissed his fingertips, then dropped his hand and stepped back. "You must leave now."

Alexander didn't move. "Was he kind to Lysander?"

"He wasn't unkind," Katina acknowledged, sure that Alexander would hear the difference. "He wasn't pleased to raise another man's son, which is why he'll be glad that Pelias came."

"He's not here?"

"He was gone, trading. He'll return tonight." Katina frowned at Alexander's obvious dissatisfaction with her answer. "Cetos never treated Lysander badly. He just ignored him."

That still wasn't enough. Alexander's voice dropped low. "Was he kind to you?"

"I made a vow," Katina said softly. "You, of all people, should respect that."

"No!" Alexander retorted. He was furious, as outraged at injustice as only a man of honor could be. "No, I'm back and I will stay. You don't love him, Katina, and you never did."

"You don't know that..."

"I *do* know that. Your body told me the truth of it." Alexander watched as she caught her breath. "If you loved him, I would never have been in your bed again. We both know that to be true." He put out his hand in invitation and offered her heart's desire to her, as easily as that. "Come away with me. Let's be together. Let's go now."

Katina was tempted. But now she remembered all the moments in her marriage to Alexander when she'd had doubts, when she'd known that Alexander hadn't been telling her all of the truth for whatever reason. When they made love, she felt a powerful connection, but otherwise, he'd often been impassive and beyond her reach. She remembered her own fear that he would discover her secret, and how he might react.

She'd asked Cetos to marry her and he'd kept his vow. Cetos had ensured that she and her son survived. Cetos put no stock in the stories told about her, and even if he saw the truth, she didn't think he'd care. She wasn't nearly as certain what Alexander would think.

Alexander lifted a hand to her in appeal. "Katina, I love you..."

She was swayed more than she knew she should be, for love might not prove to be enough. "Will you ever leave me again?" she demanded.

Katina saw the answer in his eyes. He made no promise and she knew the meaning of that, for Alexander didn't make promises he couldn't keep. She saw the doubt in his eyes, and it was all she needed to know.

Her compromise was better than having nothing at all.

"If ever you cared for me, leave before Cetos finds you here," she whispered. She saw a strange sparkle in Alexander's eyes in the same moment that she heard her husband's step approaching the courtyard.

"Hide!" she muttered, then swept past Alexander to welcome her husband home.

Cetos whistled to himself as he led his burro toward the house he shared with Katina and her son. It had been a long journey, but he was pleased with the results. A weight of extra coin jingled in his purse, the sound making him smile.

His trade had been terrible. The price of olive oil had dropped, due to a large supply after the last harvest, and he hadn't been able to sell his for a price that was worth his trouble. No one wanted Katina's pots, but that wasn't new.

Still she had provided an unexpected asset to him, one that made all the difference.

Talk about an offer Cetos couldn't refuse. He'd sold Katina's son, simultaneously making up the difference in bad prices for olive oil and ridding himself of a nuisance. The boy wasn't much trouble: it was the look of him that caused the problem. The brat so strongly resembled his father—who could have expected there to be no hint of Katina in his features? Alexander might as well have been living in Cetos' house, every glimpse of the boy making Katina sigh for the past again.

Cetos couldn't understand why she didn't appreciate her good luck. He couldn't imagine why she still longed for a man who had abandoned her, and never sent a single word of how he fared. Cetos had done her a favor in marrying her, taking on her son, even letting her stay in the house she'd inherited. But what did she do for him? She was dutiful enough, serving him at table and spreading her legs when he demanded as much.

But she had never yet given Cetos a son.

And worse, she whispered Alexander's name in her dreams.

It was possible that she thwarted him on purpose. They all said there was something strange about Katina, that she'd been touched by the gods and would earn their blessing or punishment. Cetos had been hoping for the former, but it seemed his wife had earned the latter. He was impatient with childlessness and determined see his situation changed.

He needed a son.

He would bed her daily, perhaps twice daily, until she bred.

Then he'd do it again. He'd have half a dozen sons if it were up to him.

Cetos paused before the house, composing his story. Katina wouldn't take well to the news that her son was to leave, but he was ready for that. He'd never tell her that he'd sold the boy: he'd say that he'd found him a paid position, providing companionship to the son of a rich man. He'd say he had to do it, to make up for the low prices of olive oil and the fact that her pots never sold.

He'd say he was ensuring that the boy would eat, that he'd have an education and a future.

She'd be grateful, if he told the story right.

She'd never see the brat again, which suited Cetos well.

It was all arranged. The buyer would arrive at the house after dark, the better to ensure that the neighbors saw nothing. Cetos had planned everything perfectly. Katina would be completely beneath his hand and carrying *his* child before the month was out.

The merchant had been right. Cetos deserved far more from his beautiful wife than she'd given him so far.

Katina had married Cetos.

And he'd been gone eight years.

Alexander didn't know which detail he found more astonishing. Both together were incredible. He hauled on his pants and buckled his belt, then tugged on his boots. If he'd been gone a full eight years, did that mean that his term of service to the *Pyr* was complete? Alexander thought it must be, but he wouldn't make a promise to Katina until he was sure. He put on his shirt but left it open, freezing at the sound of voices in the courtyard.

She'd asked Cetos to marry her. There was another incredible detail.

But then, his Katina was nothing if not practical. If no other man would have her, she would have spoken to the one who would. He had no doubt that she would have done anything possible to ensure Lysander's welfare, regardless of the cost to herself.

But why wouldn't any other man have her? She was beautiful, perfect in his eyes. Alexander couldn't make sense of that. What kind of stories had people told about her?

He also couldn't understand how he'd missed the signs he should have noticed. As soon as he paid attention, he smelled a man's routine presence in this room. Initially, he'd been savoring the scent of Katina and had ignored everything else. Only the joy of seeing Katina could make him forget his years of training and experience.

Alexander stood by the doorway and breathed deeply, familiarizing himself with everything in the house in an attempt to correct his oversight. He smelled now the three slaves in the house, two in the kitchen and one outside. He smelled the olive presses in the storage room, the basis of Cetos' trade. He smelled the burro being led by the slave at the outer door to a lean-to where it would be stabled.

The evidence had been in the house, but Alexander had been too consumed with desire for his wife to notice it.

He had never met Cetos, but had heard his name. He knew him to be a merchant, much older than Katina, and a man who had been content to offer to marry the woman whose family believed she should serve the gods. He remembered also that Katina had disliked Cetos—or at least the differences in their ages—from their first encounter.

Yet she had chosen Cetos in the end.

She had *pursued* Cetos.

He supposed that had to be a measure of her desperation. He had abandoned her with an infant son. The fault was his, both that she had made such a marriage and that speaking of it put such shadows in her eyes. He'd heard the accusation in her tone, and her conviction that she'd had little choice.

The fact was that Katina had been poorly served, and Alexander was to blame. Eight years with no tidings? He couldn't say that his faith would have been stalwart in her place.

Alexander might have chastised himself and regretted his choices—even though he knew he hadn't really had a choice—but he smelled the brimstone of anger.

A man's anger.

The scent teased his nostrils and drew him closer to the door. A heavy footstep sounded on the cobblestones, and a slave murmured to a man who responded in an impatient voice. Alexander stood silently in the shadows of the doorway, knowing who it must be. Outside, Katina stood with her hands folded before herself and her head bowed, a demure pose that made her almost unrecognizable as the opinionated and outspoken woman he loved.

Anger lit within Alexander that Cetos wanted Katina to be anything other than what she was. His prize of a wife was still poorly served, but now by this husband.

A much older man stepped into the courtyard and surveyed it with dissatisfaction. His face was creased in lines of discontent and there was something mean about his mouth. He was a large and swarthy man with small eyes. Katina hastened to remove his cloak, speaking to him in a subservient manner that Alexander despised.

He remembered all too clearly how she had averted her gaze when he'd asked if Cetos had been good to her. One glance at them together told Alexander the truth. The man was like a seething bull, filled with violence and seeking only a target for his wrath.

He wondered whether Katina had felt the weight of this man's hand and his own fury grew.

Alexander knew his valiant Katina would take blows herself to save any other soul in the household, even a slave. She would invite them, to protect another. Had she done as much to save Lysander? The idea that she would be in a situation that might compel her to do as much infuriated Alexander, never mind that he was responsible for it. He clenched his fists at his sides, feeling the shimmer of the change.

He caught a whiff of a deep and rotten smell and his eyes widened in surprise. Was Cetos a *Slayer*? How could that be? There would be no *Slayers* for at least a thousand years, until some of the *Pyr* turned against mankind. All the same, the residue of the scent clung to Cetos, like the scent of a wood fire lingering in one's cloak the next day.

There were no *Slayers* in this time. Alexander chose to distrust his impression. Cetos must have visited some foul place on his travels and that was the scent that clung to him. A horrible one, but not *Slayer*.

Despite his rationalization, the scent put him on edge. He felt himself hovering on the cusp of the shift, ready to fight to defend his mate.

One thing was for certain: Alexander wasn't leaving this house again without ensuring Katina's safety forever. He would see justice served, even if it meant revealing his secret to her abruptly and without explanation. He wished too late that he had told her the truth years before, but Pelias had always counseled secrecy.

He had the power to set her free of this man and he would use it. Whether Katina wanted him as her husband afterward was something he couldn't anticipate.

That didn't affect his resolve.

Katina knew she'd made a mistake in welcoming Alexander with such passion. Her excuse was that she'd been overwhelmed by her love for him, and her relief that he was returned. She'd never been able to hide her emotions well, and with Alexander, she felt so much that she couldn't contain her feelings at all.

She knew though that no explanation could excuse her infidelity.

One look at the expression on Cetos' face filled her with dread. He was a merchant who didn't abide any situation in which he received less than his due. Katina saw the glint in his eyes and knew he suspected her of cheating him of his full measure.

Katina raced to take his cloak from his shoulders, doing her best to appear demure. That usually pleased him, although it wasn't an easy manner for her to adopt.

"Where is your son?" he asked with impatience. "Doesn't he come to greet me?"

"Lysander is gone," she admitted, hoping the news would improve his mood.

It didn't.

"What is this?" he demanded, seizing her arm.

Katina didn't understand his anger, although she didn't doubt it. He'd never grabbed her so roughly before and she didn't like the change. "They came from Sparta..."

"Who?" Cetos shook her. "Who came from Sparta?"

Katina pulled her arm from his grip and took a step backward, unable to explain his attitude. "A man named Pelias. He came to collect Lysander for the *agoge*."

Cetos exhaled mightily, as if mastering his fury. Katina was perplexed. Cetos didn't usually like to have Lysander around. It made no sense that her son's absence was making him angrier than she'd ever seen him.

On one wall of the courtyard were a number of shelves, upon which were displayed Katina's pots and bowls. Cetos went to the display, picking up a pitcher and acting as if he intended to make a purchase. She thought his mood improved. Maybe his journey had been arduous. "And you let the boy go with him? A *stranger*?"

The thrum of anger underscored his words, against all expectation. "He said he'd known Alexander. He told me several stories to prove it. I had no reason to doubt him."

"He might have lied!" Cetos snapped.

"I thought you would be glad Lysander was gone." Katina realized she was still holding Cetos' cloak.

Cetos turned her pitcher with such deliberate care that his move drew Katina's eye. He'd never looked so closely at her work, and she doubted that particular piece deserved such scrutiny. "When was this?"

"Three days ago."

"Three days. And they went to Sparta?"

"I believe so."

Cetos abruptly spun and flung the pitcher across the courtyard. It smashed against the opposite wall, near the doorway to the bedroom. Zeta appeared in the arched opening to the kitchen, her eyes wide, but Katina dismissed her with a curt gesture. The girl fled with obvious relief.

"Worthless bitch!" Cetos roared to Katina's shock. "How dare you send the boy away without consulting me first?"

This was ridiculous. "Lysander isn't your son," Katina retorted. "His fate was mine to decide, and I always believed he should follow in the tradition of his father. It's what Alexander would have wanted for him..."

Cetos seized the shelves and pulled hard, sending the entire structure cascading to the ground. Katina's pots shattered with a deafening noise as she watched in astonishment and dismay.

She took a step toward the shattered ceramics, then halted when she saw the rage in Cetos' eyes. She backed away from him warily, knowing that something critical had changed between them.

She wondered if she would live to tell of it.

"You think yourself so clever, don't you?" he snarled, stalking her across the courtyard with steady steps. "But the only time the boy might have been of use to me, you sent him away."

"I don't understand what you mean." Katina backed away.

"I found him a paid position! I found him employment in the retinue of a man as wealthy as a king, a man with a son the same age as Lysander. I found him a *future*." Cetos dropped his voice. "Now I must go and beg forgiveness of this man of influence, and admit to him that I am not in command of my own household."

Katina couldn't stop herself. "You are *not* in command of my son..."

"You dare to defy me, when I have done so much for you?" Cetos roared, then back-handed Katina across the face. His heavy blow sent her reeling against the wall.

She hit her head. Her hand rose to her cheek and she tasted blood.

He had struck her.

She eyed his angry expression and knew he would kill her, without remorse. She didn't know what had happened to Cetos or why he had changed, but she wouldn't cower before him.

"I thought a wise man never left a visible mark," she whispered.

"Oh, I will leave you black and blue," Cetos snarled. "I will beat you until you learn your place." He spat at her. "And then I will toss what's left of you out into the dirt." Cetos seized Katina, tugging her back into the middle of the courtyard as she struggled. He flung her to the ground, wound one hand into her hair to hold her captive, then raised the other hand.

But instead of him striking a blow, Katina saw a flash of brilliant light and heat. She heard Cetos swear in astonishment. A massive dragon leapt into the courtyard, teeth bared and talons outstretched.

For a heartbeat, she and Cetos stared at the creature in astonishment. Cetos' grip in her hair loosened at his surprise, and Katina pulled herself away from him.

The dragon's scales were the hue of ebony and gleamed as if polished individually by a hundred slaves. The scales on its chest looked to be silver but with proximity, Katina saw they were the color of smoky amethysts. Its teeth were enormous and sharp, and its wings stretched nearly the entire width of the courtyard. It appeared as if conjured out of nowhere, but attacked Cetos with savage force.

The dragon roared and breathed a torrent of fire at Cetos, then struck him down with a fierce blow from its front claw. Cetos fell to his knees and cowered, folding his arms over his head. Katina scurried toward the wall, uncertain of the creature's intent.

She cowered against the wall and watched. The dragon turned its gaze upon her, its expression both hungry and knowing. She caught her breath, wondering if there was any escape from this beast.

She was fiercely glad that Lysander was gone and safe.

In that instant, Cetos seized a shard of pottery and flung it at the dragon, apparently aiming for the creature's face. The dragon roared and thrashed its tail, sending Cetos flying into the opposite wall. The dragon's eyes flashed, then it arched its neck and breathed a stream of fire at Cetos. Katina smelled burning cloth and singed flesh. She heard Cetos scream in agony and turned her face away to avoid seeing his fate.

She supposed a better person wouldn't have been glad that Cetos suffered.

Katina didn't see the dragon approach until she felt the heat of its presence. She glanced up just as it snatched at her. She struggled when its talons locked around her waist in a fearsome grip. She fought against its merciless hold, knowing it was futile to even try to match its strength, then cried out when it took flight.

With her securely in its grasp.

Katina looked down at her home, unable to make sense of what was happening. She'd been captured by a dragon. The dragon was flying through the air. Was it one of the gods, having taken this form? Or was it some strange beast, created by the gods to serve some whim? Where would it take her? And why?

She was still holding the cloak she had taken from Cetos' shoulders. She stared at it as if seeing it for the first time. Then she glanced down at the village that was dropping away beneath her feet.

The courtyard of her home was filled with broken pottery and flames. She saw the slaves run to Cetos and pour a jug of water over him, then she couldn't see him anymore. She saw the neighbors come from their homes to investigate the noise. Several looked up, and their jaws fell slack in surprise.

Then the dragon beat its wings hard, carrying her away from all she had known. Katina looked up at the darkening sky, out over the hills, then back down at the village below.

She was astonished to realize she was glad. She dropped Cetos' cloak and let it flutter toward the earth, a part of her past and not her future. The sight of it falling pleased her so much that she removed Cetos' gold ring and threw it after the cloak.

For the first time in years, Katina felt free.

She owed a debt to a dragon for that. She couldn't help but look up at the impressive creature and wonder what price it would demand as his due.

Alexander could have gnashed his teeth and screamed in frustration.

Because he'd not only possessed Cetos' wife, but he'd attacked the man in his own home. He'd burned Cetos with dragonfire and left him writhing on the ground.

Homes should be sanctuaries and not be filled with violence. There was no doubt that Cetos shouldn't have struck Katina, but still Alexander had been wrong to take vengeance for that in the man's own home.

What price would he be compelled to pay for his transgression? Alexander feared it might be more years of service. He could lose all the promise brought by the darkfire, because of this impulsive choice. All the same, he couldn't have done anything differently. He couldn't have stood back and watched Katina be beaten. He didn't even regret that Cetos might die of his injuries.

But Alexander did regret that he would have to pay for his crime, for he feared it would cost him all that he had been poised to regain.

How could he leave Katina again?

How could he ever win her love and trust, if he couldn't pledge to stay with her?

Why had he been sent back to this time, if not to be united with his mate?

Cetos could smell roasted meat with sickening clarity and only gradually realized that he was the meat. His body was consumed by pain, scorching hot pain that drove all thought from his mind. It was dark and he did not know how much time had passed. There was only pain. The slaves had drenched him in water, and now knelt beside him, but he couldn't answer their questions.

"Step aside," commanded a man, and Cetos nearly fainted at the accented voice.

The rich foreign merchant.

The one he had to disappoint.

Of course, the merchant had arrived as arranged, in order to collect the boy. Even though he couldn't keep the bargain, Cetos didn't want to return those gold coins.

He also didn't want to tell the merchant the truth.

There was something terrifying about this foreigner, something Cetos had found easy to dismiss when the man had offered him so many coins. Now, he recalled the strange cold blue of the man's eyes and the yellow gold of his very short hair. Such coloring was seldom seen in these parts, so seldom that it seemed unreal. The merchant had spoken in an odd way too, impatient and quick, and his choice of words had made him even harder to understand.

And there'd been something else. Something Cetos didn't want to remember.

He kept his eyes closed and pretended to be oblivious to all around him. He heard the slaves move away and felt the attention of the merchant bent upon him. Yes, that was part of it. The stillness. The focus. The intensity—as if the stranger could read Cetos' very thoughts. It wasn't natural. It wasn't right. Men couldn't be so still as this. Cetos could have sworn that the merchant knew he had a son before the question was even asked.

He wondered again if the merchant was a deity in disguise, a god come to walk amongst men for some purpose of his own.

To collect young boys, perhaps.

Why had he wanted to buy Lysander? It was too late to ask.

Cetos' heart pounded as that man walked around him, the soles of his sandals very close, then bent over Cetos.

Cetos heard him sniff.

The sound so startled Cetos that he shuddered involuntarily. His eyelids flickered, too, revealing that he was conscious. He had time to hope that the merchant hadn't noticed, then the visitor chuckled.

It was as terrifying a sound as Cetos recalled. It made him think the merchant enjoyed injuring others and took pleasure in their pain.

"Where is the boy?" the stranger demanded in his strangely accented speech. "Don't tell me you've forgotten our bargain?"

There was something about the merchant's voice that made Cetos want to respond, something that compelled him to try. It was an enchanting voice, so melodious and musical. He looked up and saw once more the flames dancing in the other man's blue eyes.

He'd seen those flames before when he'd talked to this very same merchant, although he hadn't wanted to remember them. They were unnatural and wrong, but as soon as Cetos looked at them, he couldn't even blink, much less look away.

"The boy," reminded the merchant, his voice low and insistent.

"Gone," Cetos managed to whisper.

"Gone?"

Cetos heard the displeasure in the merchant's voice, but the pain of his burns was overwhelming him. The merchant glanced away. Freed from his commanding gaze, Cetos felt his own eyes close.

Then something sharp locked around his neck, like a claw.

He gasped and his eyes flew open. A dragon held him by the throat, those same strange flames dancing in the pupils of its eyes. It wasn't the same dragon as had burned him. This one was enormous and brilliant yellow, the hue of topaz trimmed with gold.

A second dragon. If anything, it was more terrifying than the first one. It seemed cold and merciless, while the other had been passionate.

Where was the merchant? He couldn't look for him, not when the flames in those eyes danced so brightly that they fascinated him.

"Where have they gone?" the dragon demanded.

Its voice was identical to that of the merchant. Cetos was shocked. Was he in the clutch of Zeus? That god dearly loved to change forms, to toy with mortal men, and to inflict punishment for no reason beyond his own amusement.

"Where?" demanded the dragon again, giving Cetos a little squeeze of encouragement.

Cetos realized a little bit late that this exchange was about more than the gold coins he'd coveted.

"Sparta," he confessed, then choked as the talons dug more deeply into his skin.

"Are you sure?" The dragon's voice was low and silky, inescapable.

Cetos started to agree, then had a realization. Katina had left his house. He knew she would pursue the boy to retrieve him. He knew he'd introduced doubt into her mind about her decision to send the boy to Sparta, and he knew what she would do as a result of that doubt.

He shook his head, then tried to draw breath to correct his answer. The dragon loosed its grip slightly and Cetos inhaled shakily. "Maybe Delphi," he managed to say.

"Delphi," the dragon repeated with a low hiss. It took a deep breath, its nostrils almost pinching shut with it and its mailed chest swelling. It turned, his eyes glittering, then abandoned Cetos.

Cetos dared to take a breath in relief. When he opened his eyes, the dragon was holding something in its talons. It looked like the scales that covered the dragon's hide, but it was a purple so dark that it was almost black. Was it from the other dragon?

"You've had a guest," the yellow dragon said, then bared its teeth in a vicious parody of a smile.

Cetos wondered what had pleased him so much, but the dragon returned to his side and he didn't dare to ask. The dragon removed Cetos' purse, spilled its contents into its claw and counted the gold coins. It kept the coins, tossing the empty purse at Cetos.

The gold. It had taken back the gold. Cetos moaned in disappointment.

He had no chance to argue, because the dragon opened its mouth. Cetos saw down the great dark gullet of the beast, then screamed as he was engulfed in flames for the second time. This blaze was hotter and brighter. He was dimly aware of the dragon laughing as it spewed more fire, clearly delighting in burning Cetos to a crisp.

Cetos knew he wouldn't survive this assault.

A boy cried out in dismay, then the dragon set the entire house ablaze. Cetos heard the slaves scream as the dragon hunted them down.

There were more screams, then an eerie silence—punctuated only by the sobbing of a boy. The slaves were dead, Cetos knew it, and he soon would be as well. On every side, there was fire and heat, brilliant light and smoke. He heard the house creak before collapsing around him and becoming an inferno that would never be extinguished.

Cetos rolled to his back in agony and opened his eyes. The last thing he saw was a dragon taking flight into the night sky, something Cetos couldn't identify clutched to its side.

The boy.

The one the dragon claimed was his son.

It was too late for regrets, but Cetos had more than one.

Chapter Three

There was something soothing about the rhythm of the dragon's flight. Katina managed to slow the racing of her heart as the dragon carried her into the hills. Her face still hurt and the backs of her elbows stung where the skin had been scraped away, but she didn't care. She was away from that horrific situation, one she had never expected. Cetos had never been violent before, and it made no sense that he'd been so distressed by not being able to surrender Lysander for some apprenticeship, even if the other man was wealthy.

It was as if a different man had come home from his routine journey.

Was he dead? Katina wasn't sure and she didn't want to think about it. Not yet. She could still smell burning flesh and it made her bile rise.

She was more worried about what had happened to Alexander. Had the dragon attacked him first? Was he still hidden in the bedroom, or had he managed to escape?

Would she ever know? She couldn't help feeling that she was reliving the past in losing Alexander again and being uncertain of his safety or survival.

It wasn't any easier the second time.

Katina spared a glance upward at her captor. She probably should have been more frightened than she was to be in the captivity of a dragon. Its grip upon her wasn't painfully tight, and she had the sense that it had been saving her.

Why? A dragon was unlikely to speak to her, much less confide in her.

She'd never believed they existed, but this dragon was real.

Was it exactly what it appeared to be, or a god in disguise? How could she find out?

Katina could see the deep silvery purple of its chest scales more closely now and also the power of its muscles moving beneath the armor. Its wings beat at almost a leisurely pace, as if it was effortless to both fly and carry her weight. There was a savage beauty about the dragon, and a power that filled her with awe.

"That he was your husband," the dragon said, his voice sounding precisely like Alexander's, "didn't give him the right to strike you." He gave her an intent look, one that reminded her very much of Alexander when he was annoyed. "Ever."

Katina gasped in shock. "You spoke!"

The dragon glanced down at her regally. Its gaze was knowing, as if it would dare her to believe the impossible.

"But you're a dragon," she said, speaking aloud as she considered the possibilities.

"A dragon shape shifter," the dragon corrected and once again, Katina heard her love's voice.

"Alexander?" she whispered and he inclined his head once.

Just as Alexander would have done.

Katina looked away, her thoughts spinning. A dragon shape shifter? Who knew that such creatures existed...never mind that she'd been married to one. But then, the gods were often said to enchant humans, turning them into other creatures or trees. She'd thought the stories whimsical, but they must have a root in truth.

She could easily believe that Alexander would defend her from harm, using any abilities he had.

She just hadn't counted on this one.

Was it possible that she and Alexander had something in common? Katina's heart began to pound with hope, but she tried to stay calm. She had to know more to be sure that this was cause for celebration. "Isn't that impossible?"

"Nothing is impossible, Katina. I've learned that much, at least." He spoke with such conviction that she wondered again where he had been and what he had seen.

"Do you control the change?"

"Yes."

"Is it new for you?"

"No."

Katina was thrilled. "Show me," she said, needing to see the truth with her own eyes.

Alexander didn't answer, but began a spiraling descent. Katina realized that he was targeting the crest of a hill that was well out of sight of the village. He was going to do as she asked. But then, Alexander was always a man whose actions spoke more clearly than his few words.

The dragon landed with easy grace and set her on her feet. Katina held her ground and met his gaze, wanting him to see that she was unafraid of him, whatever he was.

"You should avert your gaze," he advised.

"Why?"

"They say it can make a human insane to witness the change."

Katina wasn't one to put stock in rumors, seeing such a change wouldn't challenge her sanity. She already knew such feats were possible. "Who says that?"

If a dragon could be said to smile, this one did. "Others of my kind insist it's true."

"Have you seen any human go crazy at the sight?"

He considered the matter, then shook his head.

Alexander never lied to her.

"Then I'll keep my eyes open." Katina lifted her chin. "Show me."

The dragon's gaze brightened. The way his eyes glittered was both familiar and alien: it reminded her of Alexander when he was intent, yet seemed reptilian. "My bold Katina," he murmured, the low familiar sound sending a shiver through her.

Then all she saw was the similarity to Alexander.

As she watched, that same strange blue light she'd seen before shimmered around his form. It became radiant, a wondrous yet unusual glow, and then within the halo of illumination, Katina caught a glimpse of the dragon's silhouette changing.

The dragon's wings became smaller and folded along his back, melding into his shoulders. His tail shortened until it, too, disappeared. His claws became hands and feet, his scaled hide faded from view, and Alexander stood before her instead. It all happened in the blink of an eye. That blue light shimmered briefly around his body, before it was extinguished.

He waited in silence for her to respond, watching her with

care, just as Alexander was inclined to do.

Katina wanted to laugh with delight. She had a good look at him, verifying that her eyes hadn't deceived her. Alexander was wearing his strange clothing again, although the front of his upper garment hung open to reveal the tanned expanse of his chest. He was exactly as he should be, and she knew he couldn't possibly have been hiding here or otherwise disguised.

Alexander *was* the dragon.

The dark dragon drawn on his shoulder suddenly made more sense.

It marked him as what he was.

This explained why the dragon had come to her rescue. Katina exhaled, surprised to find her insides quivering with joy. Learning Alexander's secret made Katina feel as if a burden had been lifted from her shoulders. She didn't have to hide her own truth from him any longer. She didn't have to fear his reaction.

They had so much in common.

She walked toward him, cautiously placing one hand on his chest. His heart pounded beneath her hand, beneath the familiar heat of muscle and bone. She hardly dared to believe her good fortune, and had to be sure this was as perfect as she believed it to be. Was there a trick?

"What god gave you this gift and at what price?" she asked.

Alexander studied her, as if deciding what to tell her. He was so still that he might have seen the secrets of her heart. "You aren't afraid," he mused and her heart skipped. "You're not even surprised."

Katina smiled, not ready to explain herself just yet. "You're the man I love, and that doesn't change, even if you have kept a secret from me."

Alexander studied her and she watched admiration dawn in his eyes, as well as pleasure. "My bold bride," he murmured, then closed his hand over hers.

"I knew there was something you weren't telling me."

"How? I was so careful..."

Katina laced her fingers between his. "Not so careful as that. You answered the door before anyone knocked. You lifted a pot from the fire before the food began to burn. You rose from a deep sleep to get Lysander for his feeding before he opened his mouth to cry. I thought you could see the future, but were afraid to admit it to me. I thought you were a kind of oracle."

He looked down at their interlocked hands. His thumb eased across the back of her hand, launching an army of shivers over her flesh. "A gift of prophecy would have been far easier to explain."

"Then how did you know those things?"

"Our senses are sharper. We see farther and hear a greater range of sounds."

That made sense to Katina. She waited but he said no more, so she leaned against him to whisper. "Why didn't you tell me?" She knew the answer to this. It had to be the same answer she would have given in his place, but she wanted to hear it. She wanted him to realize that they had this fear in common before she shared her secret.

"I was afraid to lose you, if you knew the truth." Alexander swallowed and looked down at her hand in his. "Not all women would welcome such news of their husband."

"I think they would if that husband saved them from a beating." Katina retorted. She'd meant to make him smile, but immediately saw that she had said the wrong thing. Alexander frowned, then released her hand and turned away. He looked over the valley now falling into darkness. He propped his hands on his hips and kept his back to her.

Katina felt as if a wide cold rift had opened between them, then guessed why. "What happened to Cetos?"

"What do you mean?" Alexander's voice was carefully neutral.

Katina swallowed. She didn't wish Cetos dead, despite what he had done, but she did want to be with Alexander again. "Am I a widow, free to welcome you again, or not?"

Alexander flicked a hot look her way. "I didn't kill him." He was so sure that Katina knew it was true.

Her heart sank. She was still a married woman. "I won't go back to him," she said with resolve. "I'll stay with you."

Alexander grimaced. "You gave your word to him."

"You invited me to go with you."

"That was before..." He frowned and fell silent.

"He raised his hand against me." Katina felt her lips set even as she folded her arms across her chest. If Alexander was going to be stubborn, she would be more so. "And if I tell him that I welcomed you, he'll cast me out anyway. Do you mean to hold me to that marriage vow, even though he tried to hurt me?"

To her surprise, Alexander said nothing, although his scowl deepened.

"Don't you love me anymore?" Katina demanded, needing to hear the truth.

"I have no right to love you," Alexander said.

It wasn't the answer she wanted, but it wasn't the one she'd feared either. "You'd prefer that I went back to Cetos?" she asked, hearing the hurt in her voice. "You just came to seduce me, not to stay?"

"No," he said with force. "Never that."

"Then what?"

"I won't make a promise to you that I might not be able to keep."

Katina bit her lip and looked over the valley. It was possible that he was bothered by her marriage vow, but she sensed that there was something else, some ethical concern that made him wait. She loved that Alexander was a man of honor, but in this moment, she could wish that he weren't quite so principled.

Of course, then she wouldn't love him quite so much.

Then she remembered his earlier confession. "You don't know if you'll be able to stay," she whispered.

Alexander bowed his head.

"You never could lie," she said softly.

"Not to you." He looked at her then, his heart in his eyes, and Katina realized she'd have to show him that she'd take every moment she could have with him, and savor it. She'd tried to send him away, fearing that Cetos would injure him, but now that they were away from Cetos, she couldn't bear to be parted from Alexander.

And she knew now that he could defend himself against any man.

She recognized that his principles would stand between them, along with her marriage vows. As long as Cetos lived and Alexander was uncertain of his future, he wouldn't touch her. He'd defend her and talk to her, but no more than that.

Katina wanted more. She had to find a way to solve this.

"When will you know about your future?" she asked.

"After I ask the Pythia."

"We have to go to Delphi, then."

He nodded.

"The flames, in the sanctuary," she guessed. "When we first met. I saw them spark between the two of us. I thought it a sign." Alexander nodded agreement. "It wasn't a trick, was it? It didn't have anything to do with the Pythia or the fumes in the temple."

"It was the light of the firestorm," Alexander admitted. "The firestorm burns when one of my kind meets his destined mate."

Katina smiled with new hope. "Then we *were* destined to be together."

Alexander shrugged and Katina sensed that, once again, he would protect her from some painful truth. "It's not such a romantic idea as that. The destined mate is the woman who can bear the *Pyr*'s son. The flame burns until their match is made."

Katina looked away, disappointed that the magic of their first encounter had only been about the conception of Lysander. "Did I have a choice?"

"There's always a choice."

Katina remembered the heat of the firestorm, the power of her desire and the connection she had felt with Alexander in that potent moment. She remembered the consuming attraction she'd felt for him and wasn't sure she could have resisted him then, not for any price.

She stole a glance at him and acknowledged that hadn't changed. She hadn't been able to resist him on this day, even without the spark of this firestorm.

And she didn't want to resist him now.

Suddenly, she realized the implication underlying his words.

"Bear his son," she echoed. "That means Lysander..."

Alexander fixed her with a cool glance that reminded her of the dragon within. "Will be like me," he confirmed with a calmness that seemed undeserved. "Understand, Katina, that if I hadn't pledged to serve, then I would never have answered the summons." His eyes darkened as he watched her, his voice softening. "But if I hadn't pledged, then I wouldn't have been in the sanctuary of the temple at Delphi the night you arrived there. I wouldn't have missed that for all the world."

There was a lump in Katina's throat. "No matter how it ends?"

"No matter how it ends, I can't regret having been with you."

Katina reached out and took his hand in hers again. "I have no regrets, either."

Their gazes locked and held for a long moment. That familiar heat rose between them, reminding her that they had never stopped with one mating. She saw the spark of desire brighten in Alexander's eyes and dared to hope that he might soften in his resolve. She made to take a step closer, to encourage him with a kiss, but Alexander caught his breath sharply.

His entire body stiffened in alarm. His eyes narrowed as he scanned the valley and she saw that faint shimmer of blue around his body.

"What is it?"

"Terror," he said softly. "Danger." The blue shimmer brightened and Katina knew what was going to happen.

She tightened her grip on his hand, not wanting to be left behind. "Take me with you."

His expression turned stubborn. "I won't endanger you..."

"You said there's always a choice," Katina said firmly, interrupting him before he could say more. "I've made mine, Alexander. Take me with you." She stretched up and touched her lips to his, tasting his surprise.

Then he smiled, his eyes glowing. She had a chance to smile back at him before he took a deep breath. She wasn't alarmed to find her fingers locked around a dragon's claw. Wings stretching high overhead, he tipped back his head and roared with savage power.

Then Alexander swept her into his embrace and leapt into the sky, his wings beating hard as the ground fell away. His every move was filled with urgency and she guessed that he feared they would arrive too late. She knew he wouldn't drop her, but she held him tightly all the same. The wind whipped around them and the night air turned cold.

It was when she moved to lean against his chest that she saw the gap in his armor. One scale was missing from the mailed splendor of his chest, leaving a tiny increment of skin exposed.

Katina touched the spot with her fingertip and felt an involuntary shudder roll through Alexander's body. She looked up to find his gaze locked upon her, his expression all the more intense when he was in this form. She smoothed the spot with her fingertips.

"Does it hurt?" she asked, thinking her words would be snatched away by the wind. To her surprise, Alexander heard her—but then, he had admitted to his sharper senses. He shook his head, so dismissive of the idea that she feared he suddenly had the power to hide the truth from her.

What did the missing scale mean?

Alexander had smelled *Slayer*.

Just one tantalizing whiff, as if someone had lifted the lid from a fine hot stew and let one tendril of its scent waft into the room. It was a tease and a temptation.

Again.

It made no sense, but the scent was unmistakable. Alexander knew to trust his nose over his mind—he'd made the mistake of ignoring the information from his senses once already since his return.

Worse, mingled with the scent of *Slayer* was that of human terror.

What had the darkfire crystal done? It was a source of unpredictability, a connection to chaos, but Alexander couldn't guess how much power it truly had. Could it rouse dead *Slayers*? Could it cast all of the *Pyr* into times and places other than their own, or just Drake's company of warriors? Could it change the future as well as the past? He wished he knew more of what opponent he faced before he lunged into battle.

"What do you sense?" Katina asked, and Alexander wasn't surprised that she wanted to know the worst of it. She was clever and might be able to help him to figure out what had happened. He needed to use all the advantages that came his way.

"I smell *Slayer*," he said tersely. "That's one of my kind who has turned against humans." He shook his head, knowing he had to tell her the rest. "I had a whiff of it earlier, when Cetos returned, but ignored it."

"Why would you ignore danger?"

"Because it made no sense. There aren't any *Slayers*...here."

"Yet there is one all the same," Katina said matter-of-factly, much to Alexander's relief. "What do you know of them?"

He considered her question, trying to recall all he knew of them. He'd had precious little contact with *Slayers* in the future, by his own choice. Their scent repulsed him, and he had no interest in being tainted by their evil. "He's revealing his scent at intervals, then disguising it again."

"Like a taunt."

"Exactly like a taunt!" She was right. All *Pyr* taunted each other before battle. He was glad to know what this *Slayer* wanted, if not why. He'd get a fight from Alexander if he was tormenting a human.

"How does he do that?" Katina asked. "I'd think a scent would be constant."

"It should be. Only those *Slayers* who have drunk the Dragon's Blood Elixir have such power," Alexander explained. He knew of two surviving *Slayers* who had consumed that vile potion. Assuming that the darkfire crystal hadn't roused the dead—an assumption he couldn't rely upon—it must be Jorge or Chen cast into the past with him.

Or perhaps one of them had pursued him. Chen had released the darkfire in the first place. Was it under his command? Was that why so much was going wrong?

Katina was watching Alexander closely, waiting for him to tell her more. Alexander wasn't sure how to easily explain the question of passing through time, so stuck with the essentials. "And I smell a human who is terrified."

"You have to save him," Katina said immediately. "Put me down anywhere and fight the *Slayer*. I'll help as much as possible." Her practicality made Alexander remember just how much he loved her.

Perhaps they could work together, as some of the modern *Pyr* worked with their mates. Alexander flew at his quickest speed, following the scent. It was to the south of them, toward Sparta, which wasn't encouraging at all. That it was being unveiled just for him was an unavoidable conclusion—which made it a lure as well as a taunt.

Lysander was en route to Sparta!

He had time to feel a pang of fear before he saw the blaze of dragonfire on the ground.

"There!" Katina said and gripped his arms.

She'd seen the flame, but wouldn't discern the detail as well as he did. Alexander could see the dragon battling a Spartan hoplite in full uniform. He saw the dragonfire reflected in the warrior's greaves and chest plate.

The *Slayer* was brilliant yellow, a dragon the color of topaz tipped in gold. There was something serpentine about this one, for he was large and powerful, but sinuous and sleek, too.

The color of the scales was telling. Somehow, Jorge was here in his own time. That wasn't the best news as Jorge was vicious, but at least he didn't control any old dragon magic.

Chen would have been worse. Alexander had no understanding of magic, be it that of dragons or others, and Chen was a master at dragon magic.

There was no time to be relieved, though. The hoplite slashed at the *Slayer* with his sword, so much smaller than the dragon that the fight could have only one outcome. The hoplite was valiant, but doomed. Alexander saw that the hoplite defended someone smaller than himself.

A boy.

Alexander prayed it wasn't the boy he feared it was. "A hoplite fights the *Slayer*," he told Katina, then breathed deeply. "There's a boy. There might be another. His scent is odd, if so. It's mingled with that of the *Slayer* in a strange way."

"Great Zeus, no," Katina whispered. "Pelias was wearing his hoplite armor when he came for Lysander."

Alexander inhaled again, only recognizing the half-forgotten scent of his mentor when she supplied the name. "All paths lead to the same place," he muttered, hating that she was right.

He flew to the far side of the fight, staying low against the ground. He doubted that he could surprise the *Slayer* if Jorge had invited him, but it was worth a try.

"We'll appear suddenly from the far side of that outcropping," he advised Katina softly. He hoped he wasn't overheard, but there was no other way to communicate with her. "I'll be downwind and he might be surprised. If so, seize the moment. Take Lysander, then run and hide."

"And Pelias?"

"I'll defend him as best I can. You won't convince him to run."

Katina nodded, her gaze locked upon the scene below as they came closer. "I'll hide somewhere too small for a dragon to follow. Somewhere with water." She pointed to the valley filled with large rocks where there might be water. "Down there."

It would be a good start, although Alexander was skeptical that any woman could hide from Jorge. He decided not to frighten Katina and merely nodded. "See yourselves safe. I'll find you wherever you go."

Katina cast him an unexpected smile. "I know."

The look in her eyes warmed Alexander's heart, but there was no time for more discussion. He held her tightly and dove behind the outcropping, like a spear falling out of the night.

The *Slayer* seized the hoplite's sword and flung it aside, then breathed a long stream of dragonfire at his opponent. Pelias held up his shield to defend himself. The red plume in Pelias' helmet caught fire, and he bowed low as if injured. Jorge leapt forward to snatch at him, clearly hoping to triumph.

But Pelias straightened abruptly. The dagger in his hand flashed even as he lunged at the dragon. He covered his eyes, leaping through the dragonfire with incredible valor. Alexander caught a glimpse of the determination in Pelias' expression and the fear in the eyes of the boy who lingered behind him.

A boy who looked much like Alexander. Terror for his son was a cold weight in Alexander's gut. He put Katina down without landing, glad to hear Jorge snarl in pain.

Any weakness would help.

When he rose higher, he saw Jorge's black blood spill and heard it hiss as it hit the ground. Only *Slayers* had black blood. Were the *Slayers* who had drunk the Elixir really immortal? Did they actually heal with unholy speed? Alexander tried to remember all the stories he'd heard about them, none of the details reassuring him in the least. He faltered when he caught the scent of death on Jorge, the scent of Cetos' death, and knew that his mate was reliant upon him again.

Even though he could guarantee her so little. He didn't dare rejoice that she was a widow, not when she could become a widow twice over in one night.

Alexander refused to despair in the face of the unpredictability of darkfire and the malice of a *Slayer*. He focused on the task of defeating Jorge.

Jorge roared with fury and slashed at Pelias with his claws. Pelias leapt backward, snatching up his shield in the nick of time. Jorge's stream of dragonfire was deflected by the shield and turned back on the *Slayer*, who roared in fury. Alexander leapt over the rock and struck the *Slayer* in the back of the head with his tail while he was distracted. Jorge stumbled then turned with a snarl, leaping into the air to fight.

Pelias had fallen to his knees. Alexander caught a glimpse of Katina running toward Lysander, then locked claws with Jorge, intent upon drawing him away from the humans.

He noticed immediately that the *Slayer*'s wings weren't as large or as strong as they should be. He beat his own wings hard and drew Jorge high into the night sky. He wound his tail around Jorge's yellow one and tightened his grip, wanting to squeeze the life out of this evil dragon. He saw the glimmer of malice in the *Slayer*'s eyes, even as he bent forward to bite at his opponent's chest.

The hoplite had managed to wound Jorge, no small feat, his dagger blade having slipped between two scales on the *Slayer*'s chest. Black blood still oozed from the wound, dripping over the golden splendor of his scales.

"Sure you want to take a bite?" Jorge drawled, his modern accent startling Alexander. His eyes gleamed. "I've drunk the Dragon's Blood Elixir. One sip and you're hooked forever."

"I thought you wanted more immortal *Slayers*."

"But there's no more Elixir. I don't need the competition. Find another snack." Jorge lurched sideways, tearing one claw out of Alexander's grip. Alexander slashed at his opponent's chest with his free claw, and the *Slayer* arched his back with the pain. Three long lines were torn in his scales, the black blood running freely from the wounds. Alexander dug his talons in deep, ensuring that he made the blow count. The *Slayer*'s eyes flashed, then he ripped his tail free, striking Alexander hard across the back.

Alexander spun, using the weight of the blow, then seized one of those small wings. It felt fragile and weak, so he ripped it from the *Slayer*'s back.

He knew the other wing wouldn't be robust enough to support the *Slayer*'s weight and Jorge clearly knew it, too. He became vicious in his attack, but Alexander flung him into the sky. The *Slayer* swore eloquently as he fell, flailing as he tried to slow his descent with his one small wing. Alexander flew after him and roasted his back with dragonfire. The second wing began to burn and become smaller, even as Jorge screamed and swore.

He twisted to face Alexander, then exhaled a long plume of dragonsmoke. Alexander knew exactly what the *Slayer* was trying to do. Dragonsmoke could act as a conduit, stealing energy from its target and feeding that strength to the dragon who breathed the smoke. Alexander evaded the tendril of smoke, flying farther and farther from the *Slayer* to do so.

"*An interesting strategy,*" he taunted in old-speak. "*You ensure that I can't save you from a fatal fall.*"

"*I'll ensure that I survive it on my own.*"

"*Your plan doesn't seem to be working.*"

Jorge laughed. "*Only because you mistake my target.*" He turned then and directed his long trail of dragonsmoke toward the earth. The smoke turned and dove downward, as sinuous as a snake. Alexander had never seen dragonsmoke change direction so adroitly.

"Stand up," Jorge roared aloud even as he fell, and a small boy stumbled to his feet. This was the scent that had confused Alexander, the human scent that had been submerged beneath the *Slayer*'s own. Did that mean the boy was in Jorge's thrall?

How? Why?

The boy was pale and thin, as if he had lost weight and health recently. His eyes seemed to be too large for his face and his submissiveness was unnatural. He obediently stood and turned his face upward, then closed his eyes to wait. Alexander was struck that the child moved as if he were in a dream.

The dragonsmoke plummeted toward the boy, aiming directly at his chest. The boy staggered at the impact, but didn't appear to be surprised by it. He straightened and braced his feet against the ground, as if preparing for a familiar ordeal. Alexander watched the line of dragonsmoke and thought of a viper burying its teeth deep and drinking of the boy's essence. Sucking him dry. The line of dragonsmoke became thicker and less ethereal, even as Alexander watched, and he was horrified that he might be right.

He looked back at Jorge to find that *Slayer* grinning. His wing had already grown stronger, because he was able to slow his descent. There was a nub already growing where the other wing had been torn away. Alexander was watching the new wing form.

Jorge's eyes shone as he landed beside the boy. The boy was wilting visibly even as the *Slayer* regained his power. Jorge took one last deep breath, then broke the line of dragonsmoke with obvious regret. His scales shone more brightly, as if they had been polished, and the blood had stopped flowing on his chest. Even those wounds seemed to be closing already.

"A wonderful discovery," Jorge said in his gloating tone. He patted the boy on the head. "I fed him the Elixir, knowing that a rapidly growing boy would make more blood and thus more Elixir for me. He's already repaid me ten times over."

Alexander landed warily, pretending not to see Pelias—or be aware that the warrior was still alive. He could hear Pelias' pulse, slow and steady, and his breathing. The older man was injured but not dead. Alexander wasn't sure he could save either Pelias or this boy, but was glad there was no sign of Katina or Lysander. He assessed the scent of the boy carefully.

"Yes," the *Slayer* agreed. "He is *Pyr*, or he would have been." He smiled down at the boy. "Theo, say hello to one of the Dragon's Tooth Warriors." Theo just blinked slowly. "This is one of the men commanded by your father, Theo, unless I miss my guess."

This was Drake's son! Alexander couldn't completely hide his surprise or dismay, and the *Slayer* chuckled. "What kind of vermin takes advantage of someone weaker than himself?" he demanded before he could stop himself.

"What kind of fools leave their sons undefended?"

"Those who serve for the good of all."

Jorge smiled. "How many boys did you all leave behind?" he hissed, clearly not expecting an answer. "All those young *Pyr*, devoid of fathers and training and protection." He was gleeful at the prospect. "I intend to find them all and put them to work, creating Elixir and energy for me to heal. I'll get all my power back!" His grin broadened. "And if there are mates to sample along the way, I assure you that they won't be overlooked."

Alexander felt sick. "What happened to Cassandra?" he demanded, referring to Drake's wife.

"Tell him, Theo," the *Slayer* invited, his jovial manner no doubt untrustworthy. "What happened to your mother?"

The boy shuddered from head to toe. He lifted agonized eyes to Alexander. "She's dead, sir."

Alexander was glad that Drake wasn't present to see the devastation in his son's eyes.

"I've discovered a taste for mate," Jorge said, his voice so low and silky that Alexander couldn't suppress a shudder. He had no sooner hoped that this fiend was oblivious to Katina's presence than the *Slayer* turned to scan the rocky hilltop, his nostrils working. "Where have the other mate and young *Pyr* gone? Is she yours?" Jorge grinned. "Maybe I'll let you watch."

Katina had urged Lysander into a low and rocky place, one that was dark and wet. She could smell the water there and felt safer in the shadows.

Her son didn't share her view.

"I want to see!" Lysander protested, when Katina would have made him duck low in their hiding place.

"We have to stay safe," she insisted. "I promised your father."

"My father! Is that who the dark dragon is?" At this news, it was even harder to hold her son back. "Pelias said that my father had a gift and that I might have it, too."

"What did Pelias tell you?"

"That my father was Spartan, which I knew, so that I needed to go to the *agoge* and train to be a warrior. But he said that my father was an elite warrior, and that he would watch me to see if I had my father's powers."

"Did he tell you what those powers were?"

"He said that my father was *Pyr*, and that the *Pyr* are charged with the task of defending the four elements and the treasures of the earth, which include mankind. He said that the *Pyr* can change shape, that they are touched by the grace of the gods, and can become ferocious dragons."

It was clear that Lysander aspired to this ability, but Katina was more surprised by how much Pelias knew and had told him. Even so, she was glad to learn more about Alexander's powers. Had he married her because he was supposed to defend the four elements? "He knew all this? He told you all of this already?"

"The very first day," Lysander said. "I was sad to leave home, but he told me I had responsibilities." Her son's eyes lit. "Mama, I have to see! I might learn something."

"You should stay here and be safe," Katina said sternly, even though she was curious herself. Lysander wriggled out of her grip and crept to the lip of the cave she'd chosen.

"Pelias is injured!" he whispered in horror.

"No!" Katina crept to her son's side, holding him back even as the two dragons fought in the air high above.

"And there's a boy." Lysander pointed. "He looks sick."

Katina squinted at the darkness and could barely discern the silhouette of a child's figure. She couldn't have said whether it was a boy or a girl.

"I wonder what that silver thread was."

"What silver thread?" Katina couldn't see a silver thread. The child was wavering on his feet, even as the yellow dragon landed beside him. She could see that Pelias had fallen and that Alexander had positioned himself between the hoplite and the yellow dragon.

"I can't quite hear what they're saying," Lysander murmured in obvious frustration.

Katina cast a glance at the sky because she heard the distant rumble of thunder. The sky was cloudless, though, which confused her.

"That boy's Theo, the son of father's commander," Lysander whispered.

Katina looked at him in wonder. "How do you know this?"

"They said so," he informed her with disdain, as if she hadn't been paying attention. Lysander suddenly ducked back into hiding beside her, his face pale. "The yellow dragon wants to capture all the sons of the elite company." His voice dropped to a whisper and he huddled against Katina. "Like me."

She held her son close, fearful that the *Slayer* would do as he threatened. The yellow dragon lifted his head and surveyed his surroundings, his gaze landing precisely on their hiding spot. Katina had the definite sense that he could see her, even though she was far away and well hidden.

She crouched down and hugged Lysander close. "Would his hearing be sharp enough to hear us?" she demanded, barely giving breath to the words.

Lysander met her gaze in horror. "He already knows where we are," he said, then his features set with resolve. "I need to see." He crept up to the edge of the cave to look again. "More silver thread," he whispered. "But this time, the dark dragon is making it. It's like a noose of starlight."

Katina had to look then, but she still couldn't see any silver thread.

"He's got a scale," Lysander murmured as the yellow *Slayer* displayed something to the dark dragon. Katina looked at her son, awed by his keen vision.

He was *Pyr*.

Before she could say anything, Lysander winced then, burying his face in his knees. "Papa," he murmured when Katina bent over him. "Oh, Papa!"

What was wrong? Katina peeked over the lip of stone to see that Alexander was writhing on the ground. The amount of blood running from the wounds on his chest was frightening, and he seemed powerless to stop himself from changing from dragon to human form and back again.

What had that fiend done to Alexander? She was so horrified that she was barely aware of Lysander peeking over the lip of stone beside her.

"Papa!" Lysander cried. He leapt over the lip of stone and ran toward the fighting dragons.

"Lysander!" Katina gasped, then raced after her son.

Alexander had wanted to keep them safe, but she was sure they'd all be lost.

CHAPTER FOUR

When Jorge glanced over the hillside, seeking Katina and Lysander, Alexander took advantage of the *Slayer*'s moment of inattention to attack. He leapt at the other dragon, using his own trick against him. Alexander breathed a stream of dragonsmoke and latched it on to the *Slayer*'s throat, letting the smoke squeeze even as it stole power. Alexander's dragonsmoke tightened like a noose, surprising Jorge, who stumbled backward. He slashed at Alexander then seized Theo, holding the limp boy before himself. Alexander continued to tighten the noose of dragonsmoke, even as he smelled the *Slayer*'s scales beginning to burn.

The *Slayer* faltered and clearly became weaker. Alexander breathed with greater force, thickening the line of dragonsmoke. He thought about choking the life out of this evil creature, imagined what he must have done to Cassandra, and fueled his breathing with his determination to ensure that Katina never suffered the same fate. The *Slayer* stumbled and began to sway, as if dizzy. The blood flowed from the wounds in his chest with greater force, and Alexander dared to hope he might win.

Then Jorge laughed. He displayed a dark dragon scale to Alexander, turning it so that it caught the light. It was the same color as Alexander's scales. He remembered the sense of something falling when he was making love to Katina and fought the urge to raise one claw to his chest.

She'd asked him about the gap in his armor.

He'd lost the scale when he'd returned home and realized that he loved her even more than he'd believed.

And now he was vulnerable as a result.

"Look what I found when I went to collect the boy I'd

bought," Jorge crowed. "Did you lose something?" The *Slayer* grinned, obviously knowing the source of the scale. He deliberately snapped the scale in half.

Alexander fell to his knees at the violent stab of pain that shot through his body. He couldn't catch his breath, couldn't think of anything beyond the excruciating pain. The line of dragonsmoke broke, because he couldn't control it any longer.

Jorge laughed. He stepped out of the noose of dragonsmoke, then strode to Alexander. He smiled, then snapped the scale again and again, each crack escalating the pain Alexander felt. He writhed on the ground, feeling consciousness slip away.

"That will teach you to challenge me," Jorge said, casting the pieces of scale over Alexander's body with disdain.

Alexander closed his eyes, assessing the damage to his body and knowing the injury would kill him. He tried to close the wounds on his chest, but the blood flowed warm and thick over his hands. He knew he was losing too much blood, just as he knew he couldn't do anything about it.

So, he had returned to his own time just to see Katina, realize they couldn't be together, lose his son and die.

It was far, far less than what he'd hoped to achieve

"Papa!" a young boy shouted in the distance. "No!"

Alexander was consumed by pain, but that cry gave him new strength. Lysander! No, the boy couldn't come close to Jorge!

"Stay back!" Alexander cried.

"By all means, come right to me," the *Slayer* said, then his voice dropped low. He breathed steadily, exhaling a stream of dragonsmoke. Alexander saw a young boy running toward him, a young boy with *Pyr* blood in his veins, and knew his son would be the *Slayer*'s next victim. Behind Lysander was Katina.

Jorge would destroy her next.

Never! Alexander would give his all to see them safe. He knew Jorge's tactic and knew he had little time to make a difference. He breathed dragonsmoke as quickly as he could, choking as he forced himself to loose a long unbroken stream.

Jorge's dragonsmoke swirled high, then shot through the air toward Lysander. The boy froze, his eyes wide in terror. He could see it, proof of his nature.

In that same moment, Alexander drove his dragonsmoke

plume in pursuit of Jorge's. He used every vestige of his power to urge it on. His dragonsmoke locked around Jorge's dragonsmoke, entwining the two streams. He made the tip on his rise up, like a snake preparing to strike, then plunged it into the tip of Jorge's dragonsmoke.

Alexander felt Jorge's shock, but had to make this work. *"Take my strength instead,"* he invited in old-speak, wishing he knew something about beguiling *Slayers. "I have more than the boy."*

Jorge laughed. *"You're trying to be noble."* He said this as if it were a ridiculous trait.

"You're just afraid I'm too strong for you," Alexander taunted. *"You're just afraid a seasoned dragon warrior has too much power for you to tame."*

Jorge snarled. His eyes flashed, then he turned on Alexander, seizing control of the dragonsmoke with lightning speed. Alexander immediately felt the change and was shocked by the *Slayer*'s agility.

The conduit became Jorge's possession, the dragonsmoke drawing energy from Alexander with unexpected hunger. The dragonsmoke felt icy cold, even as it burned his mouth and his tongue. Alexander felt it draw from his mouth, his lungs, his heart, his very soul. He was being sucked dry, while Jorge became larger and more radiant. The *Slayer*'s new wings arched high over his head and flapped with power. His scales gleamed. His wounds healed. His expression was jubilant.

Alexander felt the life leave his body. He felt himself shifting uncontrollably between his human and his dragon form. He knew he would die.

But if Lysander and Katina were safe, it would all be worth it.

He had one more thing to do to ensure that.

"I am recovered!" Jorge roared, when Alexander felt like an empty shell. The *Slayer*'s voice shook the very ground. "I am remade!"

"You should return to the future," Alexander murmured, wishing he had the power to force the *Slayer* to take his advice. *"Defeat Chen while your power is high."*

"What do you mean?"

"Has he drained a Pyr *dry? You said there was no more Elixir. He must be weak, while you are powerful. Triumph could be*

yours."

Jorge grinned. "Your thinking is sound in your last moments of life." His eyes lit and he raged fire at the sky as he laughed and laughed.

Alexander wasn't sure the *Slayer* would take his advice, and he struggled to keep his eyes open. He had to know for sure.

"Take me to Chen!" Jorge bellowed aloud.

Suddenly, there was a glitter of darkfire, like blue-green stars glittering in the distance.

A heartbeat later, Jorge was gone.

Alexander closed his eyes, praying Katina would forgive him for abandoning her again, as all turned to black.

The yellow dragon disappeared so abruptly that Katina feared her eyes were deceiving her. "Is he gone?" she asked Lysander, who took a deep breath.

"I can't smell him anymore. I don't see him either." Her son scampered closer, pausing to bend over a fallen figure. "Poor Theo. Will he get better, Mama?"

The other boy was unconscious on the ground, but Katina was relieved to find that he was breathing. He looked to be exhausted, and there was a burn mark on his chest. "I hope so," she said to Lysander. She picked Theo up in her arms and was shocked by how light he was, like an empty shell of a boy. It was easy to carry him toward Alexander and Pelias.

Alexander, in contrast, didn't move at all, and Katina wasn't even sure he was breathing. "Do you think you can help your father?" she asked. "I don't know if I can, but we have to try. Maybe you can tell me what to do."

Lysander led her toward her fallen husband but stopped abruptly to stare. "There's another silver thread!"

"Where?" Katina asked.

Her son pointed. She saw then that Pelias was breathing slowly and deeply. Lysander traced a path in the air that led from Pelias to the wounds in Alexander's chest.

As she watched, the anguish passed out of Alexander's

expression.

Before her eyes, his bleeding stopped and his wounds began to close.

Katina was incredulous. What was this silver thread and how did it work?

She went to Alexander's side and fell to her knees beside him. The truth was indisputable—he looked much healthier. Pelias, meanwhile, looked worse. She looked between the two warriors, astonished by her realization.

"The silver thread came from Pelias?" she asked her son, who nodded.

Another *Pyr*.

Pelias' eyelids fluttered and he tried to smile at the sight of Lysander. "Your father will train you now."

Lysander sank to his knees beside the warrior. "But what was the silver thread, Pelias?"

"Dragonsmoke." The old warrior licked his lips and swallowed. "We can use it to steal life force from another."

"Or to give it," Katina guessed, understanding what Pelias had done.

"Why didn't you fight him in dragon form?" Lysander asked.

Pelias smiled wanly. "I learned young to hide my powers," he said. "And now, I cannot do shift when distressed." He looked at Lysander. "Shift often so you can do so when you must. Much may ride upon it."

"I will, Pelias."

The older man nodded satisfaction. His breathing became more labored and Katina didn't think he looked well at all. He flicked her a look that was filled with understanding, his gaze lingering on Theo. He nodded slightly as if to reassure her. "I needed to see Alexander return," he whispered. "I knew he would, but I wanted to see it.

"What can I do to help you?" she asked, sinking to her knees beside him and setting Theo down gently. "Water? I have no salve for burns with me..."

"There is nothing to be done for me, Katina. You, with your healer's eyes, know the truth as well as I do."

"I am no healer."

"But you will be. You should be."

Katina averted her gaze. "You know."

"I have seen more than most in my days on this earth," he said quietly. "Tell him. Embrace what you are, and together, you will change the world."

Katina took his hand in hers and squeezed his fingers, wishing she could heal him.

Pelias shook his head, as if he guessed her thoughts. "I will give all I have to Alexander, without regret." Katina's heart clenched at the sight of his burns. "Don't feel sorry for me. I'm an old soldier with a past but no future."

"You'd rather die in battle," Katina guessed.

"And so I shall, but I will make every last breath count." Pelias nodded, the gesture clearly causing him pain. He moved a finger toward Lysander in summons, then indicated something broken on the ground.

"The scale he broke," Lysander said, picking up one piece.

Katina saw that it was the same color as Alexander's scales.

Pelias nodded. "Find all the shards and keep them safe."

"Until when?"

"You will know."

Lysander quickly did as he was bidden. He crouched beside Pelias and assembled the broken pieces, scanning the ground to hunt for every last bit of the scale. When he'd found them all, he looked at the older man.

Pelias watched him with pride. "Good. It is done."

Katina watched as Pelias took a deep breath. He closed his eyes and exhaled slowly and steadily. She could feel the force of his will, even though she couldn't see the dragonsmoke. She took his hand, knowing there was more than one way to share energy.

Pelias breathed steadily and Katina saw Alexander begin to stir in his sleep. Beside her, Lysander watched the older man with wide eyes. There was a faint shimmer of blue around Pelias, a glow that brightened steadily and grew to make an uninterrupted outline of his supine figure. When the glow enclosed him totally, he exhaled with one last great breath.

The blue light faded.

Pelias didn't inhale again.

Katina fought her tears. She reached out and smoothed the strain from the older man's features, then murmured a prayer.

Lysander looked between her and Pelias, his expression stricken.

"It was a noble gift Pelias gave," Katina managed to say. "An honorable sacrifice."

Before she could say more, Alexander cleared his throat. Katina watched in amazement as he opened his eyes. He managed to brace himself on his elbows, seeming disoriented. His gaze danced to Katina and lit with joy. He looked at Theo and appeared to be cautiously relieved. When he saw Lysander, his delight was clear.

Whatever he might have said died on his lips, because his gaze fell upon Pelias. Alexander gave a cry and stumbled to kneel beside the older soldier, checking his breath and his heart.

"It's too late. He gave his last to you," Katina said, tears in her eyes. "With his dragonsmoke."

Katina had never seen Alexander lose his composure, but he lost it in this moment. He gasped in anguish and his tears fell. He bowed over the fallen soldier and touched his forehead to Pelias' chest, weeping silently. Katina held Lysander's hand tightly. She knew that Alexander was overwhelmed, for otherwise he would have remained stoic.

Or maybe the fact that she knew his secret meant he could share all of his emotions with her. If he didn't feel he had to hide behind impassivity to protect his secret, then they could be as one all the time. Their marriage could be potent and passionate.

"He should never have done it," Alexander murmured. "He could have been healed. He could have lived."

"No," Katina corrected gently. "His wounds were too great. He would never have healed." She reached out and touched her husband's hand. "He chose, Alexander, and he didn't regret it."

Alexander's mouth worked in silence as he fought for composure. He bent and kissed the older man's cheeks, his last tears falling as he did so. Then he pushed to his feet and walked a short distance, his hands running over the closed wounds on his chest as if he couldn't believe his own state either.

He turned to look at his fallen mentor again. "I would have talked to him again," he said softly. "I would have told him what I have seen."

"He said he was content to have seen you returned," Lysander said. "He said he knew you would return. How did he know that?"

Alexander looked at his son. "I don't know."

"Because your father gave his word," Katina said, rising to her feet. "And a man of honor always keeps his word. I'm sorry, Alexander, that I doubted you would come back to me."

He looked at her then, his anguish and his love mingled in his gaze, and once again, Katina had the sense that she could see straight to his heart. She might have stood there forever, simply basking in the warmth of his regard, but she knew they couldn't linger.

"I meant to die for both of you," Alexander admitted. "I meant to give my life to see you safe from Jorge. It would have been an honorable deed."

"You nearly did, but Pelias gave his for you instead."

"Is the yellow dragon gone, Papa?"

Alexander frowned. "Did you see blue-green light when he disappeared?

Lysander nodded.

"Then the darkfire has cast him back." Alexander inhaled deeply, narrowing his eyes as if he assessed the scent with care. "I believe he may be gone."

Katina remembered his sense that the *Slayer* could hide and reveal his scent, and knew he wasn't positive. He was being protective, shielding her from his doubts. "Lysander said the yellow dragon had a plan to capture all the sons of the soldiers in your company."

"Yes," Alexander said, recovering himself. He looked hard at their son. "You heard that?"

Lysander nodded proudly. Katina noticed that the pieces of scale had disappeared from the ground and knew that her son had put them safely away. They must be in the small pouch he kept tied to his belt for carrying treasures. "Mama heard only thunder."

"That's old-speak that you heard," Alexander explained. "It's too deep for any other than our own kind to hear, and we can hear it at a great distance. There are those who can whisper old-speak into the thoughts of others, so that it mingles with their thoughts."

"So I am *Pyr*?"

Alexander smiled. "You are the son of a *Pyr*, Lysander. There never was any doubt."

"Pelias said he was going to watch me."

"As he watched me. But now that you have heard old-speak and seen dragonsmoke, our path is clear." He nodded at Katina. "We go to Delphi, for your training will be there."

And to ask the counsel of the Pythia. Katina hoped with all her heart that Alexander would be allowed to stay.

"What training?" Lysander asked. "I thought I was going to the *agoge*."

Alexander smiled. "I'll explain it all to you on the way."

"Will we fly?" Lysander demanded with enthusiasm, but Katina saw the weariness in Alexander's expression.

"Your father has just fought a battle and nearly died defending you," she chided gently. "We can walk while he recovers his strength."

Lysander nodded agreement to this, his excitement at being in his father's presence clear.

"Don't ask too many questions just yet," Katina said. "Let your father catch his breath."

"Yes, Mama."

"You should take Pelias' armor and his cloak," she told Alexander. "Your clothing is too strange, and it would be best if we drew less attention."

Alexander frowned as he considered the older man. "I can't leave him here, not like this."

That hadn't been Katina's intention. "Of course not. How do you honor the dead of your kind?"

Alexander glanced up in surprise. "Pelias was not *Pyr*."

"Then how did he breathe dragonsmoke? And why did he glimmer blue just before he died, exactly as you do before you change shape?"

Alexander stared at his old mentor, clearly shaken by the idea. "He always insisted otherwise," he said. "He always said he simply watched for the signs, but you're right. He couldn't have done that otherwise." His voice dropped in awe, becoming almost a whisper. "I thought I could smell his nature, but he told me I was wrong."

"How could you be wrong about his scent?" Lysander demanded.

Alexander smiled. "I believed my mentor, instead of my nose."

"Didn't you ever see him as a dragon?" Lysander asked and

Alexander shook his head.

"Nor did he ever see me as one. He always encouraged discretion, but I didn't realize how much he showed himself." Alexander frowned, then turned to Lysander. "When the power comes to you, you must learn to manage it. They will teach you how at Delphi, but you must treat it as a secret. You must not show many people or tell them of it. You must trust your instincts, then hone them."

"Because then I will know my fellow *Pyr* by their scent."

Alexander nodded and took the boy's hand. "Come here and draw deeply of this scent. That yellow dragon was a *Slayer*, the most evil of our kind. Learn the smell of them, that you might be warned of their presence."

Lysander did as he was instructed, closing his eyes and breathing deeply. The sight of Alexander teaching his son, something Katina feared she would never see, brought tears to her eyes. She bent to remove Pelias' helmet and his greaves, blinking back her tears.

"You're upset," Alexander said suddenly from beside her. His hand was warm on her elbow and there was a lump in her throat when she met his gaze. Lysander was still breathing and memorizing the *Slayer*'s scent.

"I liked Pelias, though I didn't know him well."

"That's not all of it."

She forced a smile. "You're so good with Lysander. I'm just glad to see you together."

"I'm sure he had no lack in your care."

"I sometimes lose patience with all his questions."

"I shouldn't have left you to raise him alone."

She eyed him, hearing what he didn't say.

Alexander frowned and stepped away, once again putting an invisible barrier between them. "We expose our dead to the four elements, so that their bodies can't be violated," he said to Lysander, his tone practical.

Katina remembered that the *Pyr* were the defenders of the four elements.

"There is air and earth here," Lysander said.

"And there will be fire," Alexander said quietly. "I think you won't want to watch."

The boy's eyes widened in understanding for an instant. "But what about water?"

Alexander winced. He surveyed the arid land that spread in all directions from the rocky hill where they stood. He tipped his head back to consider the sky, which was devoid of clouds.

Katina finally understood why she had been granted the gift she had.

It was time for her to share her secret with Alexander.

"I will give you water," she said with quiet confidence. Alexander turned to her with open surprise but she smiled. "You're not the only one with a secret, husband," she said, then lifted her hands to the sky.

Alexander was incredulous.

He watched as Katina lifted her hands over her head and closed her eyes. She was as graceful and elegant as ever, but to his amazement, her figure began to ripple. He thought his eyes deceived him, but the rippling grew more emphatic. She was murmuring some chant that sounded like the dancing of a brook over stones and with every passing moment, her figure looked more fluid.

More silvery.

More ethereal.

Her hair seemed to flow around her body like a dark river, one that ran far past her hips. As he watched, her form became disguised by a column of water, a pillar that bubbled at its top and stretched toward the sky. Or had she become the water? Alexander couldn't tell, but he saw the water pooling on the ground where Katina's feet had been. It ran over the dry soil. He heard the distant rumble of thunder and watched dark clouds conjure themselves from the clear sky. They rolled closer with remarkable speed, converging from every direction in a way that wasn't natural at all. The storm clouds collided overhead, tumbling into each other where the pillar of water reached into the sky.

There was a crack of lightning and the first drops of rain fell.

Alexander quickly bent to strip Pelias of his armor and set it aside. He lifted Theo gently and nestled him in Pelias' red cloak, the signature garment of the Spartans. He would take care of Drake's son with as much care as his own, and was glad that the boy just seemed weakened. Alexander indicated that Lysander should stay with Theo, then summoned the change.

He was well aware of his son watching him closely, of his wife making it possible for him to do right by his mentor, and his heart filled to bursting with the gifts he had been given. He ached with the loss of Pelias, but already he came to respect that man's choice. He understood it, because he would have made the same one. He was honored by it, because he'd never expected it. He was glad his son had witnessed this powerful lesson. Meanwhile, the change rolled through Alexander's body, firing through every muscle and tendon, making him feel powerful and invincible.

This was the gift of Pelias. Just moments ago, he'd been at death's door, and now he was healed. He tipped back his head and uttered a prayer of gratitude. As he turned the first breath of his dragonfire on the fallen warrior, Alexander admitted that he would be proud to pass from this world in the same way.

Alexander would never forget this legacy.

And he would serve Pelias' memory with honor for all his days.

Lysander was enthralled with his new adventure. It had been exciting enough to leave Cetos' house to go with Pelias for the *agoge*, but even better to learn that he would be like his father. He was fascinated by the *Pyr*'s powers.

He was surprised by his mother's abilities, too, but becoming a pillar of water and attracting rain wasn't nearly as interesting as turning into a dragon at will. Lysander hadn't had the chance to choose, but he would have chosen the very power that he hoped he'd get.

And now, he'd have a new friend, too. Theo looked very ill, but Lysander knew that the other boy would get better and would be his best friend in the world. They'd grow up and be *Pyr* warriors together, fighting back-to-back like their fathers, defending the four elements and the treasure of the earth. Unlike the *Slayers*, they would defend the human race as one of those treasures. He wanted to know everything about being *Pyr*, the sooner the better. He was going to be the best *Pyr* ever. He'd make his father proud and kill evil *Slayers* wherever he went.

Lysander used his keen senses to keep watch while his father honored Pelias. He tried to smell for evil *Slayers*. He stood in the rain and guarded Pelias' armor, watching his father and staying close to Theo.

When his father was done, the rain stopped. His father shifted to human form and knelt with his head bowed. The wind stirred and the ashes of Lysander were blown away, even as his mother stepped past Lysander and put her hand on his father's shoulder.

His father reached up and gripped her hand, as if he were relying upon her. Lysander watched, knowing he'd never seen Cetos and his mother like this. His two parents stood as if they were one. Was that because they both could change shape? Lysander decided that when he had a wife, he and she would stand together like this sometimes. It was like *Pyr* warriors fighting back-to-back, in a way.

"I never knew," his father said softly.

His mother almost smiled. "I think you can imagine why I didn't tell you."

His father glanced up. "And the stories that were told about you?"

His mother nodded, then turned to look north. She had the expression she got when she was deciding what would happen next. "At least four days walk to Delphi from here, I'd say." She picked up Pelias' bag and checked the food and water within it. Then she handed it to Lysander. "Will you carry our supplies?"

Lysander was glad to have a job.

His father smiled at him. He changed his clothing, putting on the hoplite armor as if he did as much every day, then flung Pelias' red cloak over his shoulders. He picked up Theo and held the limp boy against his side. Theo sighed and settled against him, as if glad to be there. Lysander's father nodded at him, then offered one hand to his mother. "Maybe tomorrow, I'll have the strength to give you all a ride."

A dragon flight! Lysander had always wished his real father

had been around, and now he knew that having his father back was just the beginning of the greatest adventure he could imagine. He carried the pack and tried to remember his mother's instruction to not ask too many questions. It might just kill him to keep silent, but he'd try.

He decided to consider it a lesson in discipline.

That's what Pelias would have said.

Katina knew that Lysander's curiosity could barely be contained. She watched their son and knew he was bursting with questions. He might even try Alexander's patience.

They walked down the hill as the sun rose and reached a good road by the dawn. Alexander didn't want to stop, so Katina gave them each some of bread and water from Pelias' pack. Their pace slowed a bit as they walked and ate. Theo stirred and took a little water. He was sleepy, as if he'd survived an ordeal, and Katina suspected he had.

"They'll help him at Delphi," Alexander insisted, and she believed him.

Katina offered more bread to Alexander. He might have declined but she urged it upon him. "You're the one healing from a battle. Don't fight me."

"She's like that when she decides," Lysander informed him solemnly. "You should just take it."

Alexander smothered a smile, his eyes twinkling as he glanced at Katina. "And do you always just do as you're told?"

"Mostly," Lysander admitted with a flush.

Alexander laughed, then sobered. "When you train, you'll have to do better than that. You must always obey, for the safety of your fellows can rely upon it."

Lysander nodded solemnly.

Katina found herself watching Alexander. He walked with an easy grace, eating slowly and surveying the surrounding hills. She had no doubt he was using his keen senses to ensure their safety and she doubted he'd sleep before they reached Delphi.

She wanted him more than ever before. She wanted to kiss

him, to run her hands over his chest to ensure that he was truly healed. She wanted to make love with him over and over again, to reassure herself that they had survived that encounter. She was aware of the heat in his gaze when he glanced at her, and it made her thoughts turn in a very earthy direction.

She couldn't remember when they had ever done it just once.

On the other hand, she felt shy after revealing her secret to him. She'd never shown anyone what she could do without experiencing unpleasant repercussions. She both wanted to know what Alexander thought and was afraid to hear it.

"Why Delphi, Papa?" Lysander asked when his curiosity overwhelmed him. Katina was impressed that he'd contained himself as long as he had.

"Can't you guess?"

Lysander shook his head, and Katina couldn't help but notice the sidelong glance he cast at his father. She saw the adoration in their son's eyes and was gladdened by it.

"Then let's figure it out," Alexander said. He didn't speak down to Lysander but addressed him as he spoke to all adults. "Whose shrine is at Delphi?"

"Apollo's."

"Do you know the story of Apollo's link to Delphi?" Alexander spoke as if it were a story not known by many. Lysander shook his head. "Then let me tell you."

Katina was surprised. She had never known Alexander to be talkative, and she certainly had never heard him tell a story. He was trying to be a good father and the realization warmed her heart.

They walked for a few moments while Alexander chose his words. "In the beginning, there was only Chaos, and not a soul in the universe. First to form in this realm was Gaia, or mother earth. She is the root and origin of all we know and most sacred of all divine beings. Next born was Eros, the god of love and desire, and when he touched Gaia, she felt the yearning for a husband." Katina couldn't look at Alexander when he said that, because she was feeling a similar yearning. "She created Uranos who lies over her as the sky envelopes the earth. His cloak is of black velvet and adorned with stars. Gaia also created the mountains and the seas. From her union with Uranos were born the twelve Titans."

Katina was thinking about having twelve sons—and how much lovemaking it would take to conceive them all. She tingled at the possibilities.

"The grandson of Gaia was Zeus. He was the youngest son of her son Cronos and the only one who survived his father's wrath."

"And father of all the gods on Mount Olympus."

"Yes. It's said that Zeus wanted to find the center of the earth, to identify the most sacred place to worship Gaia. He loosed two eagles, commanding them to fly around the earth in opposite directions. Where their paths crossed would be that sacred place. Where do you think they crossed?"

Lysander shook his head.

"It was at Delphi. And so the main shrine to Gaia was established there and guarded by a fierce dragon called Pytho."

"Was he *Pyr*?"

"No, because he couldn't change shape."

"Is he still there?"

"No. That's what brought Apollo to Delphi. You see, there was a beautiful woman named Leto. She was a Titan, the granddaughter of Gaia, and renowned for her beauty and gentle manners. As you might expect, the gaze of Zeus fell upon her and he desired her. He seduced Leto and she conceived twins by him."

"Apollo and Artemis," Lysander said, interrupting his father in his enthusiasm. "I remember this story!"

"Do you remember what happened when it came time for the twins to be born?" At the boy's frown, Alexander continued. "Hera, the wife of Zeus, punished Leto by rousing Pytho. At Hera's command, Pytho chased Leto so that she couldn't find anywhere to rest and bear her children. Eventually she found refuge on the island of Delos, for Pytho couldn't swim. She delivered Apollo and Artemis there."

"There's a shrine to Apollo at the island of Delos," Lysander said.

"There is," Alexander acknowledged with a smile. "Apollo, as you might imagine, wasn't inclined to forget his mother's ordeal. While still a boy, he hunted down Pytho and found him guarding the sanctuary of Gaia at Delphi. Apollo killed Pytho with the first arrow he ever shot. The dragon fell into a crack of the earth, as if gathered to his mistress's bosom, and died."

"Good for Apollo!" Lysander declared with enthusiasm.

"Not so good as that," Alexander corrected, his tone so stern that it caught Katina's attention.

"But he was avenging a crime."

"But he did it in the wrong way." Alexander flicked a look at Katina that seemed portentous. "Apollo violated the sanctuary and home of Pytho, so he had to be punished for his transgression."

Katina understood then the root of Alexander's fear. He saw his attack upon Cetos as a violation and wasn't sure how he would be punished. Her mouth went dry.

"How was he punished?"

"He was doomed to travel for eight years, doing service to mankind."

Eight years. Alexander had been gone eight years. His first duty had been served. Did he fear he'd be assigned another similar term for his transgression?

Katina had to focus on putting one foot in front of the other. Alexander had only just returned. She couldn't imagine losing him for another eight years so soon. She knew he would do his duty. She straightened, knowing that this time, she would wait for him, confident of his return.

She gave him an intent look and caught a glimpse of his surprise. Then he continued his story. "When Apollo returned to Delphi at the end of his service, he established the Oracle called the Pythia."

"Why?"

"In his travels, Apollo persuaded Pan to reveal the art of prophecy to him. Upon his return, Apollo recognized that the fumes rising from the cracks in the earth at Delphi could induce visions in a person of purity. It was said that these fumes rose through the fissures in the earth that abound in that area and that they came from the decaying corpse of Pytho."

Lysander shuddered and made a face. "I wouldn't want to smell that."

"It smells mostly of herbs and fire to visitors."

"Barley and laurel leaves," Katina contributed. "That's what they burn on the sacred hearth."

Alexander nodded. "Remember that Apollo saw the fumes as a gift of Gaia to mankind. Only the Pythia herself is engulfed in the fumes."

"Who's the Pythia?"

Alexander indicated Katina and she replied.

"The Pythia is the oracle of Apollo. A woman gives her life in service to the shrine, keeping herself pure so that she can hear the prophecies clearly."

"The Pythia sits on a tripod perched over the crack in the sanctuary of the temple and speaks of her visions," Alexander added.

Lysander looked between his parents with awe. "You've been there."

"Of course." Alexander cast Katina a quick smile that warmed her to her toes. "I met your mother in that same sanctuary in Delphi."

Their son's confusion was clear.

"I was taken as an offering to the Korykian Cave of the Nymphs by my parents," Katina explained.

"Why would they do that?"

"Probably because of what we just saw," Alexander said, his gaze lingering upon Katina. He seemed to be admiring, which made her feel more confident of his reaction.

She continued speaking to Lysander. "They didn't know what to make of my gift, except surrender me to the gods. There are stories in our family of others like me, although we are said to be born only every seventh generation. My grandfather called me a Waterdaughter and said our family had been touched once by the divine. There was a naiad who fell in love with one of our ancestors and chose to become mortal to remain with him."

"What else can you do?" Lysander asked.

"I can call the rain, or summon fresh water from a well gone dry. It is said that we can heal and give prophecies, too, which is what I'd hoped to learn."

"Did you?"

Katina shook her head. "No, because they wouldn't accept me as an offering. My parents were confused as to what to do, so they took me to Delphi to ask the Pythia about my fate. They paid for a prophecy."

"*Your future lies in fire and earth; the world's in the son you birth*," Alexander said quietly.

"Is that the prophecy?" At Katina's nod, Lysander frowned. "What does it mean?"

"Well, it meant your mother couldn't serve in a shrine, because to fulfill the prophecy she had to have a son." Once again, Alexander gave Katina a simmering glance. Were their thoughts as one? "Women who serve must remain untouched by men, all their lives."

"So, what did you do?"

"I met your father when the Pythia gave her prophecy, for he was serving in the sanctuary. And, in that moment, it seemed my destiny was clear." Katina caught her breath in recollection of the first spark of the firestorm, the flame that had seemed to ignite her very soul.

That was when she knew she had to feel Alexander's heat within her again, at least one more time.

Lysander, fortunately, didn't seem to notice the way his parents were looking at each other. "Is that prophecy about me?"

Katina smiled. "I don't have another son."

His delight was clear, then he turned to his father. "But why were you there?"

"Pelias saw that I was *Pyr* and took me to Delphi," Alexander said. "We *Pyr* are said to be the spark cast by Apollo's killing of Pytho, so we serve at his shrine."

Katina watched their son consider this. "Is that why you're taking me to Delphi?"

Alexander smiled and put his hand on his son's head. "Yes. You will serve in the sanctuary, just as I did, and you will be taught how to manage your abilities as they develop." He flicked the quickest glance at Katina before he continued. "One day, you may be summoned to serve mankind for eight years. If that occurs, you will go."

"Why?"

"Because you will swear to it when you pledge yourself to Apollo and Gaia." Alexander paused for a moment, as if debating the merit of saying more. Katina was glad when he did. "There are three pieces of wisdom engraved on the walls at Delphi, Lysander, and they are words that will stand you in good stead if you remember them."

"I will remember them."

"The first is 'Know Thyself.' At Delphi, you will be trained to know your abilities." Katina considered how much she had to learn about her own abilities. Would that quest take her away from Alexander? She hoped not.

Lysander nodded.

"The second is 'Nothing in Excess,' a maxim I learned well myself long before I came to Delphi. Doing that will ensure that you use your powers well." He fell silent then, despite the boy's inquisitive looks.

"And the third?" Katina prompted.

Alexander met her gaze steadily. "'Make a pledge and mischief is nigh.'"

Katina frowned, thinking of all the pledges each of them had made. She eased closer to Alexander and dropped her voice. "You don't want to be called to serve, because of your transgression."

Alexander nodded and took her hand, his thumb sliding across her skin in a smooth caress. "Cetos is dead," he said softly. "Jorge killed him."

Katina bit her lip, glad that Cetos was out of pain, and out of her life. She felt that strange sense of freedom and optimism again. "It's been said that any man who covets a naiad will die childless of a broken heart."

"Is that why your parents didn't support our marriage?"

Katina winced. "I think they liked you. They feared for your future."

Alexander's gaze trailed after Lysander, who was marching ahead of them. Theo had gone back to sleep again. "They didn't know that I wasn't a man."

Katina met Alexander's gaze, her heart pounding. "No. But I don't think you were to blame for Cetos' death."

Alexander didn't appear to be convinced. "It depends. It could have been my fault that Jorge came to your home. I certainly had no right to possess Cetos' wife." Katina might have argued but Alexander raised a finger. "I have to ask the Pythia. I won't make another pledge to you until I'm sure I can keep it." Alexander caught her hand in his and kissed her fingertips.

But Katina would have more than that salute from him before they reached Delphi, if only to have a night to remember.

CHAPTER FIVE

They stopped in the evening in a village, where they rented a room from an older woman who was glad of the coin. She fed them a hot meal, even managing to coax Theo to eat a little. The story that they were going to Delphi to seek counsel made perfect sense to the woman, who fussed a bit over Theo in his obvious weakness. The long day of walking and the hot meal made Lysander sleepy with comical speed. Alexander left Katina with the boys as she settled them into bed, then returned to the empty courtyard of the house to look at the stars and think.

Did he dare to hope for a future in this world, with the woman he'd missed so much? Was Jorge truly gone? Could he believe his family was safe? Alexander wasn't one to pray, but he did so that night in the darkness.

"Where were you?" Katina asked quietly.

He turned to find her in the doorway of the room they'd rented, her hair loose over her shoulders and her eyes tired. She was wearing Pelias' cloak, the red hue favoring her coloring.

Alexander had known it was only a matter of time before Katina asked him for the truth—and that he'd share it with her. He moved along the bench and she came to sit beside him, nestling against his shoulder.

"Would you mind if Theo stayed with us?" he asked and Katina shook her head.

"You don't think his father is coming back, do you?"

Alexander took her hand in his and sighed. "I would hope that one of my comrades would do the same for Lysander in my place."

"Of course," Katina said. "I'll take care of him, even if you can't."

She spoke with the generosity of spirit that he admired in her, and Alexander felt some of his tension ease away. They could be good partners, if the Pythia gave them the chance. He didn't want to promise her too much, but he dared to take her hand and smiled when she curled her fingers around his.

They sat together in silence for a while, the stars glinting high above them. He was aware of the enticing scent of her skin, the rhythm of his son's breathing a dozen steps away, the sounds of the rest of the household in slumber. He could feel the beat of Katina's heart, the bright spark of her curiosity and recalled his old conviction that there was something special about her.

More than he'd guessed. Now, he could see the silvery glimmer to her skin, the hint of her powers that never completely faded from his view.

Now that he knew how to look.

He understood why her eyes were as dark as a fathomless pool, why her hair flowed down her back like a turbulent river, why she had such empathy for all of those around her, how she could accommodate any change or challenge—much as a river will find its way around any obstacle.

"What started the rumors about you?" he asked.

"I can never forget what I can do," Katina admitted softly. "There's so much good that can be done with such a gift. There was a drought in the village and children were thirsty. I couldn't bear the sight of their suffering."

"So you made it rain." Alexander could guess the rest. "And someone saw you."

She shrugged one shoulder. "I can only assume so. No one would talk to me directly about it, but the whispers began. They whispered about the gods and their influence. I was never certain whether more people feared the favor of the gods—because they are so capricious—or their wrath. No woman would let her husband or son come near us. Lysander was told stories about naiads and their insatiable desires for men. He repeated them to me without any understanding of why he was being told them." She met Alexander's gaze. "I had to do something so that he wouldn't be damaged by what I am. I had to protect him. No man would have me, so I sent word to Cetos, asking if he still wished to marry me. He did."

"I'm sorry I was gone," Alexander said.

"I have no regrets in my choices. It was always said that my kind would be unhappy in marriage, and I'd been lucky for a year, at least."

"It's not enough."

"It had to be enough." She looked at him with all the light of the stars in her eyes and he ached that he couldn't make her the promise they both wanted to hear.

"I wish we had been honest with each other sooner," he said and meant it.

Katina smiled and curled her fingers around his. "What's important is that we're honest with each other now."

"You only know part of the truth, Katina, and the rest isn't good."

His bold wife didn't flinch or avert her gaze. "Tell me," she urged.

Alexander stared at the ground, uncertain where to start, but once he did start, the words flowed more easily. He wondered, even as he spoke, whether that, too, was part of her gift. He told her of marching away with Drake and the company of *Pyr*, of their sworn task to hunt those of their kind who had turned against mankind and silence them forever.

"We called them vipers."

"But what do vipers do?"

"They bury themselves deep in the earth and whisper a spell of evil. Their songs aren't discerned by men on a conscious level, but they enchant the men within their range. They fill the hearts of those men with wickedness and incite them to violence."

Katina shivered. "Like old-speak. We can't hear it clearly, but it can influence us."

Alexander nodded. "And like beguiling." At her questioning glance, he continued. "A *Pyr* can enthrall a mortal, by lighting flames in his eyes. The mortal stares and is entranced, at which point he can be told what to believe or what to think."

Katina frowned, as Alexander had known she would. "Have you done this?"

"I don't have the skill and don't wish to learn it."

She looked away from him. "Maybe that's what happened to Cetos." At Alexander's frown, she held up a finger. "He was never violent before or so filled with rage. And it makes no sense to me that he would agree to send Lysander away. He wasn't happy that I had a son, but there was never such a desire to be rid of him, much less entrust his welfare to a stranger. He was like a different man. What if he was enchanted? What if the merchant who wanted to buy Lysander was Jorge?"

Alexander was startled by the idea, but the more he considered it, the more sense it made. Trust Katina to see what he'd overlooked. He squeezed her hand. "You're right. Jorge could have smelled *Pyr* on Cetos and pursued him. I smelled *Slayer* when Cetos came home."

"I've interrupted your story," Katina said, smiling at him. "Tell me."

He told her of their company hunting a viper to its lair and their attack upon that fiend. He cast a glance at her, knowing that few other women would believe this part of the story. "We thought we had defeated him, but that was part of his spell. In fact, we were enchanted ourselves and captured by the viper."

"How?"

"Each warrior snared by a viper becomes another of his teeth, a weapon that can be used against mankind against his own will."

"You became teeth?"

"All of us. In time, the viper aged and grew soft, more like a worm. His teeth fell out, although we were still enchanted. The teeth were discovered, collected, even coveted by men who sensed there was something potent about them. We were trapped in that form until we were sown in the earth and given release." He ran his thumb across Katina's hand. "And when that finally occurred, more than two thousand years had passed.

She stared at him in astonishment.

"I thought to never see you again. I thought all of this was as dust and lost to me forever, but then something strange happened."

Katina bit back a smile. "Only the first strange thing?" she teased.

Alexander couldn't smile because the next part of the story troubled him deeply. "My kind know of a special flame, called darkfire. I don't know its origins, but it burns with a blue-green light. Some wizard had locked this force into three quartz crystals, but a *Slayer* broke one of them in those future times, releasing it."

Alexander sighed. "Its talent is in introducing unpredictability. Strange things become possible when the darkfire burns, and assumptions are challenged if not overturned."

"That's how you got back," Katina guessed. "That's what the light was that glittered when Jorge disappeared."

"Drake, our leader, believed we had to take custody of one of the remaining darkfire crystals, and so we did."

"Why?"

"He heard a summons and took it as a command. I don't know if the crystal commanded him or another *Pyr*, but with Drake, there was no question but to obey."

"Drake is the commander you knew here as Stephanos? The father of Theo?"

Alexander nodded. "He believed his past was lost beyond retrieval, we all did, so he chose to take a new name. The enchantment changed us, all of us."

"Yes," Katina said quietly, then reached to kiss his cheek. "How could it not?"

Alexander looked at her, needing to know if she preferred him now or before.

Katina smiled a little, affection in her eyes. "Your emotions are easier to read. Maybe I've changed, too, but I feel closer to you now, not just when we're making love."

A lump rose in Alexander's throat. Could the darkfire give him a gift? He knew it could, just as he knew it could snatch away any delight for some caprice of its own.

He cleared his throat, knowing that Katina waited for the rest of the tale. "As soon as Drake had the crystal in his hand, the light of the darkfire within it began to brighten and pulse. It would flare to brilliance and when its light faded, we would find ourselves transported, through space and perhaps through time. We weren't sure what was happening, but we lost many men along the way. The fourth time, it deposited us near the village and I knew where we were." He frowned, staring at her hand, and his voice dropped low. "Drake said they would wait, but the crystal lit once again." He glanced up at Katina. "I ran away from them, to ensure that I was left behind. I had to see you."

He saw immediately that she understood. "You think it will collect you again. You think you will be taken back with your company again. It's not just the Pythia's judgment that concerns you."

Alexander took a breath and said his fear aloud. "I fear the price of my transgression will be losing you all over again." He tightened his grip on her hand. "I don't know how to endure it."

To Alexander's surprise, Katina framed his face in her hands and smiled at him. Her eyes shone brightly, as if she might cry, but still she smiled. "Then let's make every moment count, Alexander. I've waited eight years to feel your body against mine again, and once was never enough for either of us." She brushed her lips across his and her voice turned husky. "Love me, Alexander," she urged. "Love me as if we could be parted at any time. Love me with a vigor that will give both of us something to remember."

Alexander couldn't argue with that.

They came to Delphi three days later, Katina's love for her husband bolstered by three nights of thorough loving. Katina walked beside Alexander, her hand clasped in his. She felt closer to him than ever and more in love than she could have imagined. They whispered to each other at night, exchanging secrets and confessions, learning more about each other and their powers. He'd told her stories of all he'd seen and she'd told him of all the gossip from the village. They explored ideas of what they might achieve, as well as exploring the pleasure they could give each other. Katina didn't want this interval to end.

But all the same, she wanted to know Alexander's fate.

She could feel his strength returning and his body healing, but worried about the spot on his chest that was missing a scale. Even in human form, it was red and angry-looking. Worse, it didn't seem to heal. She didn't like the possibility that he was uncertain about the yellow dragon, either.

And she wasn't looking forward to the Pythia's pronouncement. That one woman could hold their entire future in her hands seemed unfair, but Katina knew Alexander would do whatever the Pythia demanded of him.

She dreaded the reappearance of the darkfire, too.

Theo had awakened on the second day and walked a bit more each day. He was still weak, but made steady improvement.

They reached Delphi late in the evening and should have waited until the next morning to visit the shrine. Katina couldn't imagine how she would sleep, knowing that judgment was so close.

"Let's go now," Alexander said. "In case we aren't too late."

As soon as he made the suggestion, Katina was in full agreement. They immediately began the ascent to the shrine, Lysander walking ahead of them and Alexander carrying Theo.

Katina glanced up the hill at the white columns on the sanctuary of Apollo's shrine and felt Alexander's grip tighten on her hand.

They climbed to the shrine of Athena Pronaia at Marmaria first, giving honor to the goddess even as they marveled at the beauty and ancient power of the place. High above them towered the twin peaks of Mount Parnassus. The land spilled below them, dropping steeply to the Gulf of Corinth. It felt, on this journey just as on the last one, to be a place outside of time, a place where gods might walk alongside one.

Or maybe where two beings with unusual powers might find a way to make a future. Katina stood with Alexander in the round Tholos temple, with its three circles of columns and looked over the site with awe. She felt serenity well within her, a confidence that all would come right and that the gods would hold her and Alexander in the palms of their hands. There must be a reason for them to have their abilities and to be together. There must be a way they could aid the future.

She remembered the Pythia's prophecy and wondered how Lysander might save the earth.

"My pottery," she said, stopping for a second in her surprise that they'd missed the obvious.

Of course, she hadn't known his secret then.

"Your fire and earth, like the prophecy," Alexander said.

"But what if that's not it?" Katina said, her excitement rising. "What if there's a reason I was never any good at it?" She tightened her grip on his hand. "What if you're the fire I need?"

Alexander looked at her for a long moment. "In the future, the *Pyr* are each said to have an affinity with two elements. Each mate has an affinity to the two elements her *Pyr* lacks."

"So, together, they create a united whole!" Katina said with delight. "I'm water. You're fire."

"One of us must have earth and the other, air." He squeezed her fingers as they walked more quickly. "The future *Pyr* associate air with ideas and dreams and prophecies. That's you."

"And what about earth?"

"They associate it with practicality and reliability."

Katina laughed. "That would be you."

They continued in thoughtful silence to the Kastalian spring and Katina wondered if she were the only one feeling a tentative hope for the future. "We wash ourselves here," she told the boys. "To purify our bodies before we enter the temple."

"Isn't Kastalia a naiad?" Alexander asked quietly and Katina nodded. "Maybe she's the forebear of your kind."

Katina didn't know. It was difficult to learn much about her powers, since revealing her nature usually meant being ostracized by others and she'd been rejected at the shrine.

But when she reached for the water of the spring, it surged toward her like a tide. The water splashed high, sprinkling her, as if greeting her home.

"Did you do that?" Lysander asked, but Katina could only shake her head.

"The water recognized you," Alexander murmured and Katina thought he was probably right, even though nothing like that had ever happened to her before.

She reached into the water as if to embrace it and was startled to see a dozen women's faces in the water. They smiled at her, their hair streaming back over their shoulders and their voices as light as a rippling stream. "Welcome, sister," they said, and Katina realized that her companions hadn't heard them.

Welcome, sister.

When she raised handfuls of water to her face, the water caressed her skin like a thousand kisses.

Could her home be at Delphi?

They passed through the gate to the Sacred Way and climbed the steep road past the treasuries. Alexander pointed out the monuments from Sparta to the boys. The sun was setting, painting the entire scene in orange and gold when they climbed the last increment to the temple itself.

A sacrifice had been made on behalf of all supplicants earlier that day, so they only had to pay the *pelanos*. "The Pythia should have stopped already," complained the attendant. "But today, she insisted upon remaining. She said she's waiting. I'm not sure for whom."

Alexander and Katina exchanged a look that was filled with hope.

They all held hands as they proceeded into the temple's interior, which was filled with shadows. The boys walked between Katina and Alexander. Katina could see the silhouette of the laurel tree that grew in the central sanctuary, its branches stretching as high as the tallest columns. She smelled the fumes that rose from the cleft in the earth and heard the Pythia murmuring to herself. She saw the glow of the sacred fire on the hearth of the temple, the fire that was used to light the hearth fires throughout Greece. She smelled the laurel leaves that had been burned on the altar, along with barley.

It was hazy and dark within the temple, a place beyond time and as distant from her own world as Katina could imagine. She remembered so clearly the first time she had entered this place, how she had walked through this same entry with her parents, how she had seen the young men pledged to Apollo's service standing at the perimeter, how the sparks had danced between her and Alexander. It had seemed then to have leapt from the altar of the temple.

Alexander held tightly to her hand as they proceeded, and she saw a line of other young men standing silently in the shadows around the perimeter of the space.

Were they all *Pyr*, as well?

One attendant gestured that they should continue to the small space where supplicants waited, out of sight of the Pythia, for her pronouncement, but the old woman cried out.

"Fire and water, come to me! This is a union I must see."

Alexander and Katina stepped toward the oracle, leaving the boys to wait. The air in the core of the temple was even more hazy and the smell of the fumes was strong. It seemed dangerous and unpredictable, on the verge of chaos beyond their understanding. Katina saw that blue light begin to glow around Alexander, the glow that indicated he was on the cusp of change. He was watchful and intent, prepared to defend her against any threat.

They fell to their knees together before the enthroned Pythia and bowed their heads, Katina's gaze drawn to the long cleft in the earth that divided the temple, the one that emitted the strange vapors. That crevasse worried her, although she couldn't say why. It hadn't troubled her when she'd been here before.

Then the Pythia spoke and she listened with care.

> *"Evil must face its just defeat,*
> *By* Pyr *trained to soldiers elite.*
> *Apollo makes this task your price,*
> *A life of service will suffice.*
> *You, naiad-spawn, lost and found,*
> *Have gifts beyond any count.*
> *Here you will learn skills still unknown;*
> *Here you will bear sons more of your own;*
> *Here you and* Pyr *will live as one;*
> *Here you will lay future's cornerstone."*

Katina gasped with delight. Alexander would be staying in Delphi, and she would remain with him. She knew he would love training the young *Pyr* as his service, and that he would excel at it. They exchanged a glance and his hand tightened over hers.

The Pythia descended from her tripod then, and came toward Alexander and Katina. She was old, her face lined and her cheeks sunken. She stood straight, though, and walked to them without assistance. Her chiton was made of yellow silk, as was her tunic, and both were embellished with rich purple embroidery. Her feet were bare, and when she paused before them, she put out her hand, palm up.

Alexander and Katina looked at her in confusion.

"I will heal you, *Pyr*," she said quietly. "But you must assist me."

"The scale!" Katina said and the Pythia smiled. Lysander had been listening because he hurried forward. He pulled all the broken pieces of Alexander's lost scale from his pouch, then fell to his knees and offered them to the Pythia in both hands.

"Become what you are," the Pythia commanded Alexander.

The blue shimmer became brighter and he changed shape in a flash of light. Katina thrilled to find the deep purple dragon beside her, his head bowed before the Pythia and his claw beneath her hand.

The Pythia smiled and turned to survey the eight young men who stood as attendants in the shrine. The youngest was a few years older than Lysander, the oldest no more than seventeen. There was a brilliant shimmer of blue light, as they all changed to their dragon form. They reared up tall in the temple, moving with that same slow majesty as Alexander did. Lysander stared between them all in obvious amazement.

The Pythia beckoned to Theo, then kissed his cheeks in turn. "Be healed, young one," she murmured as she reached to brush her fingertips across his chest.

"He's mine!" came a shout loud enough to shake the temple.

Katina scanned the sanctuary for the source of the cry. She realized that all of the young *Pyr* seemed to have been struck to stone, and the Pythia was frozen, with one hand upraised. What was happening?

Alexander was scanning the sanctuary, a sign that he knew what to expect. "*Slayers* can move through space and time," he murmured quietly, and she searched for some hint of the yellow dragon.

A flicker of movement drew her gaze to a yellow salamander on the lip of the crevasse. It leapt toward Theo with remarkable power for its size. Alexander roared and breathed dragonfire at the small lizard.

"The *Slayer!*" Lysander cried in the same moment, and Katina guessed he had identified the creature's scent. "Stop him, Papa!"

Alexander's dragonfire was vivid orange, hot and fierce, but the salamander jumped through it unscathed. Katina was frightened to see that this *Slayer* could also survive dragonfire. The yellow salamander landed on Theo's shoulder and bared his teeth to bite the boy's neck.

"No!" cried Katina and Lysander together.

Alexander slashed at the salamander and a spark of blue-green light leapt from his talon to the salamander. Alexander looked as astonished as the *Slayer*, and Katina recalled his statement that darkfire was an unpredictable force.

The *Slayer* cried out as he was struck by the spark, then

illuminated as if he'd been hit by lightning. Katina saw the creature silhouetted in the blue-green light of the darkfire, his legs splayed, then the light flashed brighter and he vanished completely.

"How did you command the darkfire?" she demanded, but Alexander only shook his head.

"I did not. It came to our aid." Alexander continued to survey sanctuary for some new threat and Lysander was sniffing diligently. Katina had a strange certainty that the *Slayer* was gone.

Forever.

"Is he here, Papa?"

"I don't think so."

No sooner had the light of the darkfire faded than a single spark leapt from the fire on the altar. It divided in the air as Katina watched, then struck both her and Alexander simultaneously in the chest. She saw the light of the firestorm leap between them once more, then felt its heat slip through her body. It had a blue-green shimmer for a moment, then faded to the familiar orange glow of their first meeting.

"Darkfire rekindles the firestorm," Alexander whispered. "Against all odds."

Darkfire was giving them the gift of a second chance. That was when Katina knew that the *Slayer* was truly gone.

It was also when she realized the darkfire was on their side.

The young *Pyr* along the walls shook themselves, as if waking from dreams, and looked around in confusion. Katina had the sense that the *Slayer*'s attack had been a moment stolen out of time.

Theo shuddered beside her and might have collapsed to the ground, but Katina caught him in her arms. The Pythia stepped forward and touched the burn mark on Theo's chest, as if her gesture had never been halted. "Be healed, young one," she said again and his color improved with her touch. When Katina helped Theo to his feet, he stood straighter and his gaze was clearer.

That was when Katina saw the black dragon mark on his upper arm, exactly the same as the one Alexander had gotten in his travels. At her gasp, Lysander pushed back his tunic and grinned at the similar mark on his own arm. There was a little shimmer of blue-green that shot around the perimeter of the mark, but when

Katina blinked it was gone as surely as if she'd imagined it.

"Know thyself," the Pythia murmured with satisfaction.

The Pythia then took the pieces of the scale from Lysander. "Your kind are vulnerable only to love," she told him. "And the loss of a scale indicates a heart is lost. Your father loves a woman more than life itself, and there should be no weakness in that."

Katina felt her cheeks heat with pleasure.

The Pythia cast the pieces of scale into the fire on the altar and the boys gasped in unison. The flame on the sacred hearth burned high with sudden vigor, the orange light reflecting off the scales of the dragons who watched.

When the flames died down again, the Pythia reached into the fire and removed the scale with her bare fingers. "The *Pyr* protect mankind," she told Lysander. "And so this scale will not burn my mortal fingers." She reached out, placing her other hand on the gap in Alexander's armor. "All four elements must be present to heal a scale." She looked at Katina. "Water, sister."

Katina summoned the power of the element within her. She was aware of Alexander's admiring gaze as she let her body change into a rippling cascade of water. The Pythia passed Alexander's scale through the stream and it hissed slightly as it cooled.

She offered it to Alexander even as Katina took her human form again. "Fire," she said, and he breathed fire on the scale, controlling the plume of flame so that it didn't touch the Pythia's fingers. She smiled at this, then held the scale toward Katina again. "Air," she commanded, and Katina blew on the scale.

"And earth," the Pythia concluded, scattering a handful of dust from the floor of the temple over the scale. She then pressed the scale firmly to the gap on Alexander's chest where it belonged. He bared his teeth and tipped back his head, and Katina knew it hurt.

"A gift from you," the Pythia demanded, extending a hand to Katina. "A gem to make the scale adhere."

Katina impulsively pulled off the gold ring Alexander had given her years before, the one she'd never removed, and pressed it against the scale. The carnelian set in the gold shimmered for a second, winking like a small dragon eye. Katina felt the scale soften and the ring melted into it with a shimmer. Then it was just a stone, just a ring, just a circle of gold embedded in the deep amethyst scale on Alexander's chest.

The Pythia stepped back and flung out her hands. "All hail, your new commander!" she cried and Katina heard a rumble like thunder.

"Old-speak!" Lysander said with wonder, turning to look at the young *Pyr* around him. Katina realized they were hailing Alexander, as commanded.

Alexander stretched his wings wide, displaying the perfection of his repaired chest, then shifted shape quickly. The other *Pyr* in the temple changed shape in the same moment, becoming strong young men who stood at attention once more. The temple looked as it had when they'd entered, except for the golden light of the firestorm.

Alexander caught Katina's hand in his and the light flared between them. She felt the heat of the firestorm slide through her body, making her keenly aware of Alexander standing strong and tall beside her. It was more subdued than it had been before, but the radiant glow between them couldn't be disguised in the comparative darkness of the temple. Her future was with Alexander, here in Delphi, ensuring that the *Pyr* were prepared for the challenge of their future.

The Pythia smiled secretly. "I told you before that your future was with fire and earth."

"Alexander," Katina breathed.

"No more pots," Alexander agreed, a twinkle in his eye.

The Pythia glanced down at their interlocked hands and the sparks dancing between them. "A gift, to one of Apollo's faithful," she said. "Use it wisely." She smiled, then returned to her tripod, even as Katina planned the conception of their second son.

She turned to face the man she loved, knowing that she would seduce him so completely on this night that even the darkfire wouldn't be able to steal him away again.

Alexander smiled, as if he'd read her thoughts and agreed, then kissed her soundly right in the sanctuary of the temple.

Kiss of Darkness

They will sacrifice anything to regain the loves they've lost...

Damien, the heartbreaker of the dragon shape shifter warriors called the *Pyr,* can't forget Petra, the only woman who could both captivate him and destroy him. He's haunted by their firestorm, the prophecy that compelled him to leave her—and her subsequent death. When the darkfire crystal takes the Dragon Legion to the underworld, Damien seizes the chance to save his son. To his surprise he finds Petra just as enticing as ever...and still pregnant. When his kiss makes their baby stir to life again, they both hope for a different future. Can they learn from the past and trust each other? Even if they solve the riddle of the prophecy, will they be able to escape the underworld, claim the promise of the firestorm and save their son?

CHAPTER ONE

When the light of the darkfire crystal faded and its wind had stilled, Drake and his men found themselves in a sunny but empty plaza. It was early in the morning, dew fresh on the flowers in the heavy planters that were scattered across the space. One man watered the flowers, starting when he turned to find eight men had silently arrived in the space. A large fountain was in the middle of the square, water splashing from it and sparkling in the sunshine. There were buildings around the square, their windows shuttered or dark.

They had manifested in the shadows near what was clearly a restaurant. It was closed now, but the tables and chairs were still set up under awnings on its patio. The company of warriors pulled together a pair of tables and sat down together, flicking anxious glances around themselves.

Damien knew he wasn't the only one who was hungry and exhausted. He guessed they were in southern Europe, maybe back in the twenty-first century again. He'd know better when the women appeared, by the style of their clothes.

Drake, their leader, had immediately counted their dwindling company. Damien had noticed that Aeson was gone. They were down to eight survivors: Drake and Damien, Thad and Ty, Peter and Ashe, Orion and Ignatio.

Drake scanned the plaza with unfounded optimism, then his lips tightened. He looked down at the large quartz crystal in his hand, and Damien was relieved that the light within it had dimmed.

For the moment. The darkfire crystal seemed intent on flinging them across the universe. Repeatedly and without warning.

"Aeson," Ty said, defeat in his tone.

"One more lost," Peter said with a grim satisfaction. He was always looking for the dark clouds on the horizon. "Besides Alexander, that is." He glared at Drake. "You shouldn't have let him go."

"I have no wish to deny a man his greatest desire," Drake said, his tone as tired as Damien felt. He held up the dark crystal, then closed his hand over it. "I wish it hadn't lit so soon. I wish we could have waited for him." He passed a hand over his forehead, and Damien saw how much this ordeal was costing their usually stalwart leader.

"He chose to look for Katina," Ashe said to Peter, his tone defensive. "It's our responsibility to defend our mates after we've had a firestorm. Alexander did what was right."

"He ran to her," Ty added. "Making sure the crystal left him behind."

"Well, I hope she was there," Ashe said, practical as ever. Drake cleared his throat but the younger man glanced up. "Well, I do! It would be terrible if he'd taken that chance only to find her gone."

"Married," Iggy added.

"Ancient," added Peter. "There was no telling how much time had passed for her."

"Or dead," Damien felt obliged to add. "Alexander might have ended up alone."

A shudder rolled through the group of men, as their worst fear was expressed aloud.

"That would suit you," Iggy said to Damien, obviously trying to lighten the mood of his fellows. "Love them and leave them, that's our Damien. Mr. Heartbreaker."

Damien smiled at their teasing.

"Do you even have a heart?" Ty joked. He and Iggy as the youngest of the group were most envious of Damien's sexual success. They wouldn't have been envious of Damien's experience, that was for sure, but he was never going to confide that story in them. "I remember that one in Paris." Ty whistled through his teeth and Iggy grinned. "She could have had my heart and soul just for the asking, but not Damien."

"He takes what they offer and leaves them behind," Iggy concluded.

"And we'll refrain from commentary on how that serves the good of mankind," Peter muttered.

"They're happy for a little bit," Damien said, refusing to be defensive. "It's not like I trick them. They know what they're getting." He spread his hands, as if he himself were enough of a gift.

Ashe rolled his eyes and Drake pretended not to have heard. Ty and Iggy laughed. Peter snorted with a disgust that had more to do with his lack of success with women than Damien's luck.

A pair of older women came into the square at the opposite end, unlocking a door and moving inside. Mid to late twentieth-century, Damien guessed, by the cut of their clothing.

Then he smelled the coffee they had started to make. His stomach growled audibly.

"It's a bakery," Ashe whispered. "Get ready for temptation when they get that oven going."

There was an almost-silent groan from the men. "If we're still here, we'll go see if we can buy something," Drake said.

"Or make a deal." Iggy nudged Damien. "If our money's no good, maybe Mr. Charm can get us some breakfast." Damien smiled as Iggy and Ty began to needle him, speculating on how he could obtain breakfast for eight hungry warriors for free.

"By Zeus, maybe that's the point," Thad said suddenly, interrupting the conversation. The others turned to look at him. "What if the darkfire crystal isn't as unpredictable as we think? What if it's got a plan to fulfill?"

"Such as?" Peter demanded. "What possible reason could be behind this insanity? Every time it flashes, we get picked up and flung down somewhere else. We don't know where we are..."

"We don't know *when* we are," Ashe interjected.

"I'd say Italy, roughly 1972," Damien murmured.

Drake peered at a church tower and shrugged. "Rome," he said flatly.

Peter flicked a look at the pair of them that spoke volumes, then shoved a hand through his silvered hair. "We can't eat, we can't sleep, we don't dare wander away from Drake and the stupid crystal in case it lights when we're too far away and we get left behind. What kind of plan could there possibly be?"

Thad looked untroubled by the older man's scathing tone. "Maybe it's not an accident. Maybe the crystal is returning each of us to the place we belong. Scattering us like salt through the ages."

"But how would it know?" Peter demanded.

"The firestorm," Drake murmured, and the other men looked at him.

Orion frowned. "You mean that the darkfire crystal took us to Alexander's village, precisely so he could be reunited with Katina?"

Thad nodded with enthusiasm. "It makes sense! Darkfire doesn't have to be irrational. It's disruptive and it's unpredictable, if you don't understand what it's doing or why, but mostly, I think it makes unlikely things happen." He nodded at the others. "And it's linked to us. It's a force associated with the *Pyr*. Why wouldn't it enable the firestorm?"

"So, it sent Alexander back in time more than two thousand years to be with his wife and son," Ashe said thoughtfully.

"So he could keep his duty to defend his mate and son," Iggy agreed. "Makes sense to me."

"If they're there," Peter said. "If she still wants him."

Another beat of silence passed. "That's all well and good," Orion said, pacing around the group with his usual impatience. "But what can we do? How can we guide it? How can we guess where we are and why, or control where we go next?"

"Who else has had a firestorm?" Ty asked. "If Thad is right, the crystal will take us back to the mate."

Excitement now passed through the small company, along with a sense of possibility that Damien didn't share. He knew that Petra was dead. If Thad was right, he was going to end up alone with the crystal, which wasn't an enticing possibility.

The more implausible possibility was even less enticing. Damien shivered.

"I left a wife and son," Drake admitted, his words soft. "Theo was a little older than Alexander's son and Cassandra..." His voice faded and he stared into the distance.

"I don't think you should tease yourselves," Damien interjected, knowing he had to say something.

"Why not?" Iggy demanded.

"It's better than doing nothing," Orion said.

"Because now one of you is thinking that your destined mate must be here," Damien said, his tone harder than usual. "And each of you who hasn't had a firestorm is going to want to break rank, no matter where we end up. You don't know what the darkfire crystal is planning, if it's planning anything. You could end up doing something stupid."

Peter gave him a hard look. "Did you have a firestorm?"

"Yes," Damien admitted, noting their surprise. "And no power is ever going to take us to where she is."

Ty nudged Iggy. "We're right. He doesn't have a heart because he already gave it away."

"You don't know anything about it!" Damien snapped, and the rare glimpse of his temper silenced the two of them.

Orion caught his breath suddenly, drawing the attention of his fellows. He lifted his hand and his eyes widened as fire began to glow around his fingertips. The flames grew, becoming a dancing halo of flame.

"Great Wyvern," Orion whispered in awe. "So this is what it feels like."

Damien got to his feet, knowing what he was witnessing. Sure enough, a woman had come into the square and was knocking on the door that the older women had unlocked. Her hair was dark and long, and he guessed she was in her mid-twenties. Her shoes were flat and her skirt short, her legs perfect.

A spark exploded from Orion's fingertip and arched through the air toward her. An answering spark rose from the woman, and the two sparks collided in a brilliant burst of yellow light over top of the fountain.

She turned to look, her eyes wide with astonishment.

"She's the one," Orion said and began to march across the square. Damien watched with mixed feelings: he was glad that his friend was experiencing his firestorm, but hoped Orion's ended better than his own firestorm had.

Even given his experience, though, Damien wouldn't have missed his firestorm—and knowing Petra—for the world.

"You were right," Iggy whispered to Thad, whose mouth was open in surprise.

"Not again," Drake muttered.

Damien turned to see the blue-green light beginning to pulse in the center of the darkfire crystal.

"Run!" Ty shouted and Orion did, bolting across the square, drawn to the woman who could bear his son by the heat of the firestorm. Damien saw her smile at Orion, then the darkfire became a blindingly brilliant flash.

Once again, they were tossed through the air and lashed by a vicious wind. Finally, Damien was cast to the ground and grunted at the force of the impact.

The darkfire faded to nothing, leaving the air as dark as pitch. It was still, wherever he had landed, and it was cold.

As cold as the grave.

Damien got to his feet, sure that his guess had to be wrong. His heart was pounding, even as he saw the deadened trees, the starless sky, the inky black river that separated them from a land filled with shadows. His heart felt heavy in this place, burdened by sorrow as it seldom was, even though his fellow warriors still surrounded him.

Petra had to be here.

Damien knew he'd made the right choice in leaving her, knew there was no point in dwelling on the past, knew there certainly was no chance of changing what he'd done. There had been the prophecy. It had all been so clear.

Why had the darkfire brought him here? He and Petra had no future... Damien had no sooner wondered than the answer became clear to him. The darkfire was giving him a chance to save his son.

It made perfect sense. It wasn't their son's fault that he and Petra hadn't remained together. His son was *Pyr*, like Damien, and deserved a dragon's education. The *Pyr* could use another dragon warrior in their corps. The firestorm, Damien was certain, had brought him to the underworld to retrieve his son.

Which meant it must be possible.

As Damien watched, a flat boat left the far shore. The hooded ferryman pushed his pole into the river, guiding his boat toward them. There was only darkness within the shadows of his hood and his fingers gleamed because they were bare bones.

"Charon," he whispered, without intending to do so. Despite himself, Damien scanned the distant bank, seeking a glimpse of Petra. She'd been the most beautiful woman he'd ever seen—when she was alive. What did she look like now? How would he feel when he saw her? Just the possibility made him want to know for sure.

He doubted she'd surrender their son easily. Petra had always been stubborn.

But she was a mother. Surely she would sacrifice her own desires for her son's welfare?

Damien didn't know what to expect from her. He eyed the cold dead land on the other side of the river and remembered Petra's passionate nature. He could doubt, but he guessed the darkfire would continue to bring him to this place until he accepted the opportunity it offered.

With that, Damien's decision was made.

A dog began to bark then and was joined by the barking of two others. Damien narrowed his eyes to see the three-headed dog Cerberus on the far shore, its teeth white and sharp as it barked before a pair of gates.

"We're in the realm of Hades," Peter whispered in horror from behind him.

"All seven of us," Drake said.

"That'll be six, now," Damien said, taking a step toward the shore. "This would be my stop." He reached into his pocket, glad to find that he had two coins for the ferryman, and looked across the river. As he stepped closer to the shore, the dead who lacked the fare for the ferryman milled around him. They were no more substantial than a dark mist, but he shivered at the press of them on every side.

He still had a few moments to figure out how to get past Cerberus.

Never mind how to leave Hades alive.

Petra would be another challenge altogether. His son would certainly be with her, a babe in arms who wouldn't be easily surrendered. Petra was loyal to those she loved, and a part of Damien regretted losing that distinction.

To his surprise, he felt a flicker of anticipation and a quickening of his pulse as the ferry drew closer. It made no sense. He knew what Petra was. He knew she'd been only an interlude in his life, a connection that couldn't be sustained. The firestorm had brought them together to ensure his son's conception, no more than that. He couldn't be looking forward to seeing Petra again.

He was thrilled by the chance to save his son, no more than that.

As soon as Damien had stepped onto Charon's vessel, he felt the flash of the darkfire. He glanced back at its brilliant light, then it faded to nothing.

The other Dragon Legion Warriors were gone.

He swallowed and paid the ferryman, knowing the way forward was the only possible way out. He still had a few moments to figure out how to get past Cerberus.

Never mind how to leave Hades alive.

Boredom was the worst part of being dead, as far as Petra was concerned. The underworld was locked in twilight, perpetually on the cusp of evening. It always felt like the middle of winter, although there were no seasons. The trees were stark and barren, the air was damp and chilly. The shadows stayed the same depth and darkness and hue. The underworld was colorless and devoid of sensation. Every single moment was identical to its follower and its predecessor. She and all the dead were frozen in time—yet Petra was trapped in the most awkward state of her life.

She was at the full term of her pregnancy.

On the one hand, it was a consolation that her son hadn't been abandoned in the world of the living as an infant. With Damien gone and her family far away, there would have been no one to care for him in her absence. On the other hand, it was devastating to her that he had never taken his first breath. She'd never seen the son that she and Damien had conceived, never held him, never named him. She carried a reminder of everything she had lost and couldn't forget whose fault it was.

She cursed Damien regularly—for his charm, his good looks, his heart of ice.

If his heart had been made of stone, their partnership might have had a chance.

Petra's state might have been uncomfortable, if she'd still felt her body. In this realm, she was numb, or even less aware of sensation than that. The dead had no appetites, no occasions, no celebrations, no work, no craft. They had no purpose, no pain, no sorrow and no joy. She alone was restless and impatient among the dead. She alone yearned for novelty, for a quest, and yes, for vengeance.

But then, Petra had always been different. She was used to the sense that she didn't fit in. The difference was that she'd once had hope that she'd find a partner, that the old saying of her kind would be fulfilled and she'd have a companion forever.

She'd been so sure that partner was Damien.

She'd been so wrong about him.

A strange blue-green spark lit at her feet with sudden brilliance, then disappeared as if it had never been. She wondered whether she'd imagined it, because it was both unlike anything she'd seen before and unlike everything else in the underworld.

Was this a delusion?

Would it be better or worse to be insane as well as dead?

Petra refused to think about that. She searched for the spark and was delighted when it glimmered at her feet again.

This time, it reminded her of a similar spark, one of brilliant yellow that had set her heart afire and changed her life forever.

The spark of the firestorm had launched all of her woes.

When the blue-green spark appeared a third time, Petra pushed the firestorm from her thoughts. It wasn't relevant anymore. Damien had abandoned her and was never coming back. She was trapped in the underworld forevermore. The novelty of the spark was just a welcome distraction.

The spark disappeared, then lit again a dozen steps away.

The pattern repeated, a fifth light appearing briefly beyond the fourth.

Petra decided it was an invitation and followed it.

She waited where the last light had shone, impatient in her anticipation. When the next blue-green spark appeared, Petra followed the trail. She was intrigued by the way the spark seemed to wait for her, the next illumination occurring once she'd reached the last indicated point.

This was the most interesting thing that had happened since her arrival here.

It was the *only* interesting thing that had happened since then.

She couldn't help remembering the hot spark of the firestorm. She could see again the glow of it in that tavern, the way light had danced between her and the most handsome man in the place. A stranger. She remembered how she had blushed and how he had smiled. She remembered how he hadn't looked away, how he hadn't been afraid of her, and her strange conviction that he was the one. She remembered how well she'd sung that night, how sinuously she'd danced, because she'd been performing for him alone. She could recall the heat of desire that had filled her when the firestorm had flared, her sense of the inevitability of their partnership. She would have done anything for Damien—and in fact, she had done a great deal.

Not that he'd appreciated any of it. Petra's hand fell protectively to the ripe curve of her belly.

She wouldn't think about his rejection.

She would think about passion. She would think about that first sweet hot kiss, and how his glorious seduction might just have been worth paying any price. She'd remember how the firestorm had flared and burned between them, how magical and powerful it had been, how lovemaking had been beyond anything she'd ever experienced. She wouldn't think about the way her adoration of Damien had eclipsed everything else in her life.

Because it made her feel stupid.

Bitterness filled Petra's heart and she found herself walking more quickly after the blue-green sparks.

The lights stopped abruptly at the gates of the underworld. The dark pillars of stone rose high then made an arch overhead, casting a cold shadow over the ground. A dead vine with blackened leaves twined around the stone. There should have been a breeze here from the river that flowed beyond the gates, but the air was still and stagnant.

Petra shuddered and tried not to look at the dark surface.

On the far shore were thousands of ghostly forms, milling aimlessly along the side of the River Acheron. They were the ones without a coin for the ferry, the ones Charon refused to take to the realm of the dead because they could not pay. They waited endlessly for a transition that would never come. Petra remembered their sense of despair and how it had engulfed her as she'd passed through their ranks.

She shuddered again.

Cerberus was barking furiously, as if he'd happily devour whatever or whoever arrived in the underworld. The three-headed dog that guarded the gates against trespassers—and kept the dead securely inside—was large and fierce. He didn't usually bark so much, though. Petra peered around the pillar of the gates with curiosity and sure enough, Charon was guiding his barge to this shore.

But he wasn't just bringing the dead. The man who stood at their fore, scanning the shore, was very much alive.

If Petra's heart had still been beating, it would have stopped. It was the very man who had been filling her thoughts.

Damien.

She immediately felt flustered, as she seldom was. Why would he come here, when he was still alive? There was no doubt of his state, given the vibrant color of his skin and the flash of his eyes. He was no corpse.

Could he have come for her? Petra knew she shouldn't hope for a different ending to their story, but she had sung too many love songs not to be a romantic in her heart. She chided herself silently for not having learned her lesson when she had the chance. Would he be repulsed by her? She knew she didn't look as she had when they'd been together.

One thing was certain: Damien couldn't intend to die in this realm. No, he must have some heroic feat planned and despite herself, Petra was curious as to what it might be. She watched from the shadows, halfway hoping he'd fail. It would serve that cocky dragon right.

Damien didn't look as if he considered any possibility other than success. He was so trim and handsome that Petra felt a traitorous yearning. She'd forgotten just how attractive he was, and the way he could look so resolute. He'd looked like that when he'd first met her and the firestorm had burned—but she'd been the target of his attention.

She felt a strange warming within her, but it must have been an illusion or a memory. The dead felt nothing.

Even if she could have sworn her heart was fluttering.

Would Cerberus rip her faithless lover to shreds?

Petra couldn't decide if she wanted that to happen or not.

She'd been angry with Damien for so long, but one sight of him was making her remember other sweeter emotions. Did that mean she'd learned nothing by having her heart broken?

Damien leapt from the ferry, as fearless and strong as ever. Petra watched openly. He turned a cool glance upon the hellhound of Hades just as Cerberus lunged toward him, jaws snapping. Damien glared at the dog, something cold in his eyes.

Petra knew that expression and was thrilled that she would see him again in his dragon form. Damien could shift shape to a dragon of dark green, so strong and beautiful and virile that the sight of him made her mouth go dry. His scales were so deep a green as to be almost black, and each one was tipped in gold, as if it had been dipped in the molten metal. His eyes became more golden when he changed shape, and he was altogether magnificent. His dragon form was a perfect expression of the best part of his nature, his power and commitment to a cause, his ability to fight for justice.

And a hint of what they had in common.

Petra narrowed her eyes, waiting for the pale blue glow that would surround his figure just before he changed shape. He'd taught her to never watch him change and to close her eyes at the first glimmer of blue.

She was ready and waiting for that light to appear.

Except it didn't.

Damien was astonished.

He couldn't shift shape.

That couldn't be right! He'd summoned the change from deep within himself, just as he was leaping from the ferry to the shore, but nothing happened. There was no pale blue light. There was no surge of heat through his body, no tumult of the change.

He landed on the dark mud of the shore in human form, shocked.

And fearful of the hellhound's bite. What had happened to him? He pulled his dagger and kicked the dog in the chest, darting backward as he tried to shift shape again.

No luck.

Damien looked back to see the dead sliding from the barge to the shore. They were a dark shadow of indistinguishable faces, a crowd in which he could discern no features. They jostled him slightly, like a cold bank of fog, and he heard the clatter of their belts and swords. Charon waited, his pole driven into the mud of the shore, Damien's promise of extra payment having stayed his departure.

For the moment.

All Damien had to do was get past the dog, enter the underworld, find his son and get back to the river. He heard the dead on the far shore of the river wailing for the ferryman and saw the strange glimmer of blue-green darkfire dance over the dark surface of the water.

Had the darkfire set him up?

Cerberus stood with all four feet braced against the ground, barking and snarling. The dog's eyes burned bright red as it awaited his next move. The dog let the dead pass untroubled. The gates to the underworld arched high and dark, a shadow against the night, twenty paces away.

The hellhound was the largest dog Damien had ever seen, as tall as his chest, and all lean strength. It was black, darker than midnight, its eyes lit with an infernal flame and its teeth numerous. That it had three sets of teeth was less than ideal.

Damien tried to shift shape again, still without success.

The hellhound lost patience. It leapt toward him, teeth bared. Damien stabbed with his dagger but missed the dog's chest. Cerberus bit him with ferocious power, its teeth sinking deep into Damien's thigh.

Damien shouted in pain, but the dog clenched its jaws more tightly. The pain was excruciating as it tore flesh, and Damien feared the dog would eat him alive.

He punched that head between the eyes, glad to see the light dim slightly in its strange eyes. The dog loosened his bite enough for Damien to kick the beast away. He backed up, his dagger held high, as the warm rush of his own blood streamed down his leg and soaked his pants.

The dog snarled.

The blood was slipping into Damien's boot when he realized

the scene before his eyes had changed—or that he could see it more clearly. The dead surrounding him had faces now, and he could distinguish them from each other. The hellhound was more detailed to his view. He saw the silver in its fur, the blood on its jowls, the mane of snakes on each of its three heads. The snakes were black and glistening, thousands of them rooted to each head. They reared up and hissed at him like cobras, their eyes glinting and their fangs bared.

Damien felt a trickle of sweat run down his back.

He hated snakes more than anything in the world.

The hellhound leapt for him again and Damien lunged with the dagger. He missed the dog's head, but sliced off a hundred snakes from one head. Their bodies wriggled on the ground even after they were cut free, a sight that made Damien's blood run cold. He focused on the dog just as it went for him again. He swung the dagger and missed once more, then kicked the hellhound between one set of eyes. The beast attacked, its claws digging deeply into Damien's chest and knocking him backward.

He fell and the hellhound leapt atop him. It was heavy, so heavy that he couldn't budge it. One set of jaws locked around each arm, holding Damien captive.

Damien was incredulous. He couldn't die here, not before he even entered the underworld. He couldn't fail at his quest before it began.

But he couldn't shift shape, and a man was no match for a hellhound.

Damien didn't surrender easily. He thrashed and fought, even though his efforts made no difference. The dog's teeth dug deeply into his flesh, making his blood course freely. The snakes bit him, too, tormenting him with a thousand needle bites. The eyes of that middle head shone brilliant red, then the dog bared its teeth and bent to rip out Damien's heart.

He was powerless to do anything but watch.

Why had the darkfire betrayed him?

Damien roared in frustration, still struggling to shift. He moaned as he felt the hellhound's hot breath on his flesh.

And then the sound of a woman's voice floated to his ears.

She sang in the same voice that haunted his dreams.

Petra!

He glanced up and the sight of her was like a knife to his gut. Petra was just as lovely as she had been before. Her hair flowed in dark waves over her shoulders and she was deliciously feminine. But Damien was startled to see how pale she was, more like a ghost than the vivacious woman he'd known.

Dead. Of course. But no less alluring for all of that.

And she was singing to save him. Maybe that was a sign that his mission could succeed.

Damien felt the teeth of Cerberus graze his skin and decided he'd take hope where he could find it.

As furious as she was with him, Petra couldn't let Damien be torn to pieces by the gatekeeper of the underworld.

She didn't think about the tune, just sang the first familiar melody that came into her mind. It was after the second line that she realized the choice she'd unwittingly made.

She was singing the love song she'd first sung to Damien on the night the firestorm had sparked.

But she couldn't stop now.

The blue-green light sparked from her fingertips and leapt through the air toward Damien and the hellhound. It illuminated the shadows, showed the confusion on the faces of the arriving dead, and cast a strange light over the deadened world. Petra was surprised, for this was no magic of her own. Charon watched from inside the deep shadows of his hood, his pose utterly still.

To her relief, Cerberus paused before ripping open Damien's chest. The head that had been bent over Damien lifted and turned to Petra, the red glow of its eyes dying to pale gold. The snarl on the dog's lips disappeared and its ears flicked.

The second head of Cerberus released Damien's arm. It also turned toward Petra. The tangle of vipers in its mane slowed, swaying like grass in the wind. The animosity faded from its eyes, as well.

Petra sang even more loudly, putting all her heart into her song.

The strange blue-green light of the darkfire swirled around her, sparkling and glowing with increasing intensity as it danced between her and Damien. It was like the firestorm, but the wrong color. Petra felt the same heat of desire as she had that first time — but it seemed even stronger.

Unpredictable and exciting.

She felt dizzy with the promise of a thousand possibilities and excited as she hadn't since Damien had left her. The feeling couldn't last, but she couldn't resist the opportunity to enjoy it.

Meanwhile, the third head of Cerberus sniffed at the air. The dog jumped from Damien's chest, abandoning him before it sauntered back to the gates. Its movements became more sleepy with every step. Damien sat up, wariness in his expression, but Petra continued to sing to the hellhound.

It sat down before Petra, its eyes now pale gold. To her relief, one head yawned elaborately. The other heads quickly began to yawn as well, then the dog circled and laid down before the gates. It sighed as it put its heads down.

Its manes of vipers stilled, as if they too fell asleep.

Then Cerberus began to snore.

Petra wanted to shout with joy.

Except that Damien was striding toward her, purpose in his every step, and that dagger in his grasp. He wore strange clothing, but that didn't disguise his muscular build, his vitality or the blood on his leg. He paused to peel off his upper garment, then tore a length of fabric from the hem while Petra stared at the perfection of his body. He bound his wounded leg tightly, but the blood continued to seep through it. She saw his bare chest, his muscles, a mark on his arm, and remembered the hard press of his body against her.

It was too easy to recall his arms wrapped around her and his heat inside her, his lips against her ear.

Even knowing what she did of him, Petra yearned. He'd promised her a night, but he'd stayed three months. Had their partnership really been that ill-fated?

Damien shoved the dagger into his belt and threw away the torn remains of his garment. He resumed his march toward her, limping slightly, his burning gaze locking on her face. Petra's heart seemed to skip in anticipation.

They'd either fight or make love. It had always been that way between the two of them. She was taken aback to realize just how much she'd missed her fiery dragon. Ever since he'd left her, life had seemed flat and monotonous—although the underworld was even worse.

Petra eased behind the pillar, guessing his plan and not liking it. There was only one more thing he could want her to surrender to him.

"You could have enchanted the hellhound sooner," Damien said, his low voice sending a familiar thrill through her even as his words surprised her. He arched a brow. "Or was that your way of getting even?"

Petra hoped she looked more indifferent to his presence than she felt. "I assumed you had a plan. You always do." She shrugged as she dared to provoke him. "I guess it wasn't a good one this time."

Damien's eyes flashed, although Petra wasn't sure if his reaction was anger or desire. She was less sure it mattered. That blue-green light swirled around them, intoxicating her with its circling patterns. It leapt between them and touched her skin intermittently. It should have distracted her but instead, it made her world smaller, tightening her focus on Damien.

They could have been alone in the underworld.

"You knew Cerberus would attack me," he said, then gestured to his leg. "Was this what you wanted?"

"I knew I wouldn't be able to speak to you unless you shed blood."

Damien blinked, then shoved a hand through his hair. "I didn't know that." His eyes narrowed and Petra knew he was thinking about what he had seen, weighing his experience and observations against her words. She'd never met a more analytical or observant man and a part of her wanted his attention turned upon the riddle of her again.

"Because you don't pay attention to stories," she chided. "You never have."

"They're not real." He was dismissive, just as he'd always been. "I'm interested in truth."

Petra folded her arms across her chest. "So, you've given up on prophecies?"

Damien inhaled sharply and she saw that he wanted to take a

step back. His trepidation made her angry with him again. "Stories are as real as you and me," she informed him. "Or do you prefer to think of every kind other than the *Pyr* as just stories?"

Damien grimaced, which she could have anticipated, then avoided the question, which was even less of a surprise. He bent to press the flat of his hand against his wound, as if he'd close it by sheer willpower. "I always hated snakes," he muttered.

Petra refused to feel sorry for him.

At least, she refused to give any sign that she felt sorry for him.

"Then you should leave. This place is thick with them."

He glanced up. "Why are there so many?"

"Darkness, the underworld, lost secrets and hidden desires. It's all the business of snakes."

He almost smiled and Petra was shocked by how alluring she found him. "And I'd know that from listening to stories." His words were low, teasing, in the same tone he'd always used in bed. He looked up, a glint in his eyes, and if Petra could have blushed, she was sure she would have.

"Just because they're stories doesn't mean they don't contain facts," she said as she'd said a hundred times to him before. She was startled when Damien said the same words simultaneously. She loved the sound of his voice mixing with hers and was impatient with herself for being so easily seduced.

Maybe he had learned something.

But he'd left her once he'd discovered what she was.

"That's how I know it," she said, her voice harder than she'd intended. "But there are thousands of them here. Run now, while you can."

Damien straightened, leaning closer to her. She could almost feel his gaze boring into her mind. "Is that what you think I did before? Run away?"

Petra held his gaze unflinchingly, letting him see that she did think that.

Damien raised a finger. "This time, I'm not leaving without my son." He cast a glance back at Charon, who still waited. "Where is he? The ferryman won't wait forever."

His determination was familiar, as was the resolve in his eyes. Damien always achieved his goals and never expected any woman to deny him.

But his words were unwelcome. Just as Petra had feared, she'd only been useful to him. He only cared about his son. Anger burned hot in her chest and she enjoyed the fact that she could shock him in turn.

"Sadly for you, he and I are eternally together." Petra stepped away from the pillar, revealing her figure to Damien.

His gaze fell to her round belly. "But you're pregnant!"

Petra gave him a skeptical look. "You did have a part in that."

"But..." He was at a complete loss for words, and Petra realized she'd never seen him so confused.

She wouldn't feel compassion for him.

She'd savor the sight of his plan failing to come together.

"I was pregnant when you left," she reminded him more gently than she knew he deserved. "Not quite this far along, but still visibly pregnant."

He swallowed and frowned, his agitation clear. His reaction undermined her determination to despise him. "But you shouldn't have been on the ferry while you were pregnant. You were going to go home *after* our son was born."

"I changed my mind." Petra waited, hoping for some sweet confession and knowing she shouldn't believe it if it came.

"I thought..." His voice faded. Damien looked at her, then back at Charon. When he turned to face her, his expression was set. Petra knew he'd decided something, but wasn't prepared for him to snatch her off her feet.

"What are you doing?" she cried. She struggled, as much against his grip as her own unwelcome reaction.

"I'm saving my son!" Damien lifted her in his arms with both care and firmness, then began to march back toward the waiting ferry. Charon watched, silent and still.

"Idiot!" Petra said as she twisted in his arms. "That's impossible."

"Doesn't seem to be impossible. We're doing it."

"Your son's as dead as I am. Neither one of us can leave."

"Are you going to tell me to listen to stories?" Damien taunted. "How about Eurydice and Orpheus?"

"He looked back at her at the gates and lost her forever," Petra snapped. "Although why you should feel any common ground with a man with no control over his desires, I can't begin to guess."

"You liked it once when I had no control over my desires."

"That was before I was dead."

Damien grunted as she squirmed, but still easily kept his hold on her. "What about Persephone?"

"She's stuck here for a third of each year. That's not an escape." Petra knew he was hampered by his determination not to hurt her, but she had no such constraint.

"Hercules."

"Please. Don't compare yourself to epic heroes. They weren't doomed to failure."

Damien chuckled, surprising her. He looked like a daring renegade, the same one who had stolen her heart away. "The only way to know for sure is to try."

"Not all the rules change just because you want them to."

"You're coming with me. We'll argue about it later."

"Because your son is in my womb, and you can't take him without me?" Petra demanded. "Is that the only reason you're taking me along? You thought you'd just come and get him, but leave me here, didn't you?"

There was a beat of silence, which told Petra all she needed to know.

She was just as foolish as she'd been the first time she'd met Damien.

But that had just changed.

CHAPTER TWO

Petra fought harder. Knowing the truth of his intentions meant she had no intention of going with Damien at all. "And what happens if we do get out of here?" she demanded. "What happens after our son is born? You'll just abandon me again? I don't think so!"

"He's my son!" Damien protested.

"And mine!"

"But..."

Petra was so angry that she kicked Damien hard, right in the wound the hellhound had just given him. He roared in pain, stumbled, and his grip loosened enough for her to get her feet on the ground again.

Miserable, self-centered dragon!

Petra regained her balance quickly and kicked Damien harder, in exactly the same spot. He paled in pain as he fell to one knee, then she decked him. Damien swore as he fell back, even though Petra knew she hadn't hurt him that much.

"You want your son? Then come and get him!" Petra spun and ran into the shadowy depths of the underworld. She was livid, but ran as fast as she could, wanting only to leave as much distance as possible between herself and the infuriating, sexy father of her child.

Oh, she hadn't called Damien nearly enough names when he'd left her before. He was selfish, he was conceited, he was insensitive and indifferent to the desires of others, he was...

"Petra!" Damien roared from the gates.

She didn't waste time looking back but kept running. Damien was taller, faster and he wasn't nine months pregnant. He was also a dragon shape shifter. It was inevitable that he'd catch her, possibly also inevitable that he'd win his way, but she wanted to make him work as hard as possible for his victory.

Maybe she was getting even.

Or maybe she was the one who didn't believe, now.

"No!" Damien bellowed suddenly. The dismay in his voice convinced Petra to look back. She laughed to see that Damien's plan was falling apart before his eyes. Charon was calmly plying his pole to guide his ferry back across the river. He was already too far from the shore for Damien to jump and the River Acheron ran darkly between them. Damien stood on the bank and shook his fist at the departing boat.

"I paid you to wait!" he bellowed, but the ferryman continued on his way, deaf to Damien's cries. Petra felt a twinge of sympathy when Damien's shoulders sagged.

She knew her dragon would never accept defeat easily. He always mustered his resolve for another foray.

Which was why it had been so devastating when he'd left her forever.

Again, she expected the pale blue glow that announced his intention to shift, and again, she didn't see it. Petra felt a whisper of concern.

Was something wrong?

Damien pivoted to glare into the underworld, his eyes blazing with fury. "This is your fault," he said, flinging out his hands in frustration. "You could have just come along. You could have just cooperated, but every single thing has to be an argument."

"You mean I could have trusted you. Again." Petra spoke quietly, knowing Damien's keen senses would allow him to hear her, even at such a distance. "Too bad your firestorm wasn't with a stupid woman."

Damien's eyes flashed. He strode toward the gates, resolve giving him new power. Petra felt a thrill of anticipation. When they'd argued like this while alive, they'd made up with equal passion. She wondered whether he intended to win her agreement with a kiss and couldn't wait for him to try. She stood her ground, telling herself that Damien's kiss wouldn't be half as marvelous as she remembered.

But she was going to find out.

As Damien approached the gates, Cerberus stirred, one head rousing to yawn.

Petra saw the dog sniff the air.

She heard it growl at Damien.

Damien growled back.

Petra turned to run, telling herself she didn't want to see whatever happened next. She heard Damien swear, then the dog yelp. When she looked back, Damien had plunged under the gates of the underworld to pursue her and was closing fast. Cerberus stood on the other side, barking after Damien with all teeth bared.

The hellhound wouldn't let anyone pass through the gates to return to the River Acheron and the world above. That was forbidden and the injunction even applied to Damien.

It was possible he didn't realize as much, or that he was just focused on the moment, because Damien seemed untroubled. Petra knew he had no shortage of confidence. It took a brave man to walk into the underworld when he wasn't dead, and a braver one to imagine he might be able to leave alive whenever he wished to do so.

Damien looked furious. His eyes were blazing and his muscles were pumping. He was all male and so gorgeous that Petra almost wished to be caught and kissed into submission.

Instead, she ran. Would she spend eternity trying to outrun Damien? The realm of the underworld was nearly endless. She could lead him across its vast wastelands for untold ages.

Except, of course, that Damien was mortal. Even he would fade without food and water. And if he consumed anything in this realm, he'd be trapped here as surely as if he were dead.

That bothered Petra more than she knew it should.

A glimmer of blue-green light crackled along the deadened ground, drawing up alongside her then racing ahead. Petra couldn't make sense of it, but she didn't have time to think about it. She spared a backward glance to find Damien closing fast, his expression murderous. She stumbled over something and looked forward again just as blue-green brilliance flared. It lit into an orb of light so bright that she had to close her eyes against it. It appeared so abruptly that she couldn't keep from running straight into its glow.

Then her footsteps faltered to a halt as she stared in wonder.

Because Petra was abruptly surrounded by the past and filled with the ache of all they'd lost.

Trust Petra to be unpredictable and uncooperative.

Trust Petra to start an argument instead of helping them both to escape.

This quest should have been easy. Damien should have been able to fetch his son, return to the ferry and have Charon take him back to the side of the river that touched the land of the living. It should have been quick and relatively painless. He should have been heading back into the world he knew, his son safely with him, but nothing with Petra ever went as planned.

She'd always defied expectation—in fact, that had been one of the things Damien had once admired about her. She challenged him and surprised him, as no one else had ever done. She was fearless and defiant, and completely captivating. Their relationship had been fiery from the start, filled with arguments and passion, filled with battles of words that ended in ferocious lovemaking. He'd felt so alive with her, so embroiled in a constant battle of wits and challenges.

Challenge was the right word for Petra.

Look at their firestorm. He'd planned to fulfill it, conceive their son, and leave again. She'd been agreeable, even wanting to experience it. Instead, he'd stayed one day, then another, until he'd been with her for three months. It was only because he finally had left, to make a quick trip to Delphi, that he'd learned the truth about her and been able to leave for good.

The strange thing was that he knew he should be furious with her, but Damien felt invigorated. He was startled to realize how glad he'd been to feel that old flame leap to life between them. He'd missed Petra, even knowing how dangerous she was. Maybe that was part of the reason she intrigued him. Either way, he wasn't nearly ready to step away from her again.

That should have worried him more than it did.

Damien had to wonder if she was the one who had ensured he couldn't shift shape to fight Cerberus. It would have been like her to want him in her debt for something.

Maybe that was why she'd enchanted the hellhound, so Damien would owe her.

What did she want in exchange? It was a question that only Petra would be able to answer.

Except that she was running away from him.

Damien couldn't believe that his son hadn't been born before Petra had drowned, but the evidence was unmistakable. That made his mission more complicated, and he wondered if she'd planned it that way in advance. It seemed a bad time to acknowledge that he had no clear idea of her powers. Had she seen the future? Guessed where and how they'd meet again? He had a thousand questions, but Petra was clearly disinclined to explain herself. Why hadn't she waited for their son to be born? It had been irresponsible for her to undertake such a journey so close to her time, and he felt angry with her for her choice.

An unwelcome voice in his thoughts reminded him of his own lack of responsibility, but that had been different. He couldn't have stayed with Petra, not once he'd learned the truth about her.

Not once he'd known that she could kill him at any time.

He would have gone back for his son sooner, if he and his fellows hadn't been cast across the centuries.

And now Charon had forgotten his bargain and had headed back to the far shore. Damien doubted there would be a refund or a credit on the extra fare he'd paid. Petra was running like the wind, running faster than he could have imagined a woman in her state would be able to run. It would have been simple to catch her if he'd been able to shift shape, but no amount of effort seemed able to rouse the dragon within. Damien pursued her, realizing as they moved deeper into this strange territory that the underworld wasn't a place he wanted to explore alone—much less a place he wanted to remain.

But Petra had been trapped here. He felt a pang of sympathy for her.

In fact, the first sight of her, round with his son, had shaken him. She'd always been lovely and had always had lush curves. But pregnancy had ripened her in a way that made Damien remember very well all the pleasure they'd had creating that son. The strange blue-green light of the darkfire had flattered her in a way he hadn't expected, drawing him closer, making him want to caress and seduce her all over again.

He saw the darkfire crackle along the ground ahead of him, illuminating this dark and dreary realm. It flared up suddenly in front of Petra, almost like an explosion. He shouted a warning but she didn't stop. Damien tried to run faster even as she stepped right into the brilliance and disappeared.

Damien cried her name in horror. He feared the worst, although when he thought about it, he couldn't think of what would be worse for her than being dead. He passed into the light of the darkfire, feeling a shiver pass over his flesh at its cold touch.

And then, he was surrounded by the past.

Damien had just stepped into a tavern, taking shelter from the night along with Orion. The cool of a winter evening was at his back. Inside the tavern was a crowd of people, laughter and food.

And music.

The music had drawn them, turning their steps in this direction like a spell of enchantment. Now, surrounded by the glow of candlelight, Damien stood in silence and stared.

A gorgeous woman played the lyre in the middle of the tavern, to the obvious delight of the people listening. She evidently played a familiar song, for they all knew the words and sang along. A plump man who had to be the proprietor stood by the door to the kitchen, smiling with satisfaction.

Orion heaved a sigh of satisfaction. "Finally, a decent meal and some good company."

"I'm not such bad company as that," Damien retorted and Orion grinned.

"You could be the most beautiful woman in the world, and after a month in your company alone, I'd still be ready for a change."

Damien laughed, unable to be insulted. "That's the most beautiful woman in the world," he said, gesturing to the musician. "It would take more than a month for me to tire of her companionship."

Orion might have replied in kind, but as Damien gestured, a spark lit at the end of his finger. The brilliant orange light flared, arching across the room to land on the musician's parted lips.

She gasped in wonder.

She considered him.

Then her eyes lit and she smiled.

"The firestorm," Orion said, a tinge of jealousy in his tone. "You'll satisfy it in a night, won't you?" he teased. "Never linger."

"Lingering only builds expectations," Damien replied softly, his gaze fixed on the woman who could bear his son. His blood fired in anticipation of the night they'd share. "And the firestorm is extinguished as soon as it's satisfied. One night is all it will take."

She ended the tune, stilling the strings of the lute with one hand as her audience applauded. There were calls for drinks and food that sent the proprietor scurrying, but the woman immediately began to play another song.

It was a love song, low and seductive, the words sending a pulse of heat through Damien.

Or maybe it was the way she sang the song to him that fired his blood. Damien stood utterly still, his gaze locked with hers, as her song filled the tavern. Her voice was so rich and pure that she might have been born of the gods. He heard the rapturous sigh of one of the patrons. Damien was barely aware of Orion clapping him on the shoulder, then pushing him forward. He took one step and then another, moving closer to the beguiling beauty who sang just for him.

With every step, the heat of the firestorm burned brighter. With every step, he heard her song more clearly and was more smitten. Her eyes were darker than dark, filled with a thousand lights. They tipped up slightly at the outer corners, giving her an exotic appearance, and her ripe red lips seemed to caress each syllable of the song as the words spilled forth. Her hair was long and dark and wavy, hanging past her hips in flowing ebony. Her skin was so fair that it might have been carved of ivory, and the contrast made her even more strikingly attractive.

She wore a chiton of fine white cloth that was cut full, then tied at her narrow waist with a gold cord. She was curvaceous, her breasts enough to fill his hands, her waist narrow, her hips sweetly curved. *She danced barefoot, the glimpses of her feminine feet beneath the hem of her tunic making Damien's pulse pound in his ears. Her tunic was hemmed in golden embroidery and the light played with the thread, making her look like a precious gem.*

His gem. His mate. The firestorm told no lie. This was the woman who could bear Damien's son, and he wasn't going to bypass the opportunity.

He was going to make the most of it.

And he'd be gone in the morning.

The way she sang for him, her eyes dancing and her smile drawing him closer, told him that she liked what she saw, as well. It wasn't just the light that burned brighter between them with every step he took closer—it was the desire that surged through his body with greater demand. By the time he halted before her, he was burning for her, determined to woo her in bed, to make this night a night that neither would ever forget.

He was captivated by her dark eyes, her knowing smile, her grace and her lovely voice. The song could have lasted a lifetime or the duration of a single heartbeat. Damien didn't know or care. There was only the musician and her song.

And when she held the last note, drawing it out into a tone of impossible richness, her smile was only for him. The others applauded but Damien took the last step between them. "Pure magic," *he said, then caught her face in his hands. She gasped at the spark of heat that fired between them, then smiled at him in the illumination of the firestorm. She held her ground though, undaunted by the strange light.*

She was as remarkable and bold as he'd hoped.

"Thank you for the song," *Damien whispered, then bent his head and kissed her.*

She was as sweet as the finest honey, her lips both soft and firm, the scent of her perfume enticing. To Damien's surprise, she slipped one hand around his neck and pulled him closer, deepening the kiss when he might have stepped back. Her tongue touched his, her welcome enflaming him.

He knew he should break their kiss but didn't have the willpower to do so. She opened her mouth and rose to her toes, inviting him to partake of all she had to offer, and Damien couldn't have resisted her—or the firestorm—at any price.

Petra was back in the tavern, on that fateful night. She felt the firestorm even before she saw Damien, although she hadn't known what it was at first. She turned in surprise at the unexpected heat just as he walked into the small tavern.

And her world stopped.

At first glimpse, she was snared. Damien paused at the back of the tavern, looking unpredictable, confident and alluring. He watched her, a smile on his lips and a seductive glint is his eyes. It was more than the fact that he was handsome, more than his muscled build, that drew her eye.

He was surrounded with golden light, and she felt as if she was looking straight into the sun. His eyes even seemed to be lit with gold, although later she would see that they simply had hazel glints in them. In that moment, she thought he could have been a god come to walk among them. Petra guessed there was something different about him. He had a raw power that she could sense even at a distance, see even with a glimpse, and her heart soared with hope.

Could it be that there was a man worthy of her love?

Could it be that there was one man who would love her for what she was?

After just one song, he was striding forward to claim her with a kiss, as if he, too, knew that there was strange magic between them. That golden light burned and flared, becoming brighter the closer he came to her. His touch seared her soul and his kiss melted her bones.

She was his for the taking. Their meeting was destiny at work; their happiness together assured. She couldn't bear to share his company with anyone and led him outside the back of the tavern, where the night sky was thick with stars.

He kissed her again, slowly and thoroughly, leaving her flushed and filled with desire. The golden light burned even brighter between them, sparking off her fingertips in a way that made her laugh. She played with it as he watched her, touching his shoulder to make the flame flash brighter, then drawing her hand away, over and over again.

Each touch made her desire stronger.

Each touch made his gaze burn with greater intensity.

There weren't any other people outside and Petra was thrilled that they were alone, that this intriguing man was bent on winning her favor. She toyed with the light that sparked between them, and its growing power took her breath away. She was dizzy with her awareness of him and her desire for him. At the same time, she didn't know what to say to him. Did he have this effect upon all women? Her thoughts were filled with questions, but she loved the sensation of standing with him in the velvety darkness of the night, caught in a golden glow that tantalized and teased them both.

"Surely such a beautiful woman has a name," he prompted finally and Petra smiled.

"Petra. And you?"

"Damien."

Petra nodded approval. "A good strong name. A warrior's name."

He smiled, watching her play with the sparks. "You're not afraid of it."

"Should I be?"

"Many people would be, particularly if they knew what it meant."

Petra smiled at him. "Does that make me bold?"

The heat in his eyes made her heart pound. "Maybe."

"Is that a problem?"

He shook his head. "I like bold women, strong women, and women who know what they want."

"Sounds as if you like a lot of women."

Damien laughed. "I have, but none such as you."

She surveyed him, summoned a spark from one of his shoulders with her fingertip and passed it to his other shoulder. She had to narrow her eyes against its bright flare. "Does this happen often to you?"

He shook his head. "Never before, but I know what it is all the same."

"How so? Have you seen it before?"

He shook his head, his eyes dancing as he watched her try to figure it out.

"*You've heard of it, then.*"

"*Many times. It's called the firestorm.*"

"*I've never heard of it.*"

"*Of course not. You're not one of us.*"

Petra's heart skipped a beat at the inference that he was different from other men. Maybe he was just as different from men as she was from women. "*Us?*" *she echoed lightly.*

He smiled, nodding back toward the tavern. "*My friend and I belong to a company of warriors called the* Pyr." *He watched her then, waiting to see if she recognized the name.*

Petra did. "*Dragons,*" *she breathed, her fingertips rising to her lips in awe. She could believe that Damien had the ability to change into a fire-breathing dragon. She could believe that he had been chosen by some divinity to be more than just a man.*

Maybe to be her partner.

"*Not many have even heard of us.*"

"*I collect stories and songs. It's my trade. I've heard of the* Pyr *and hoped they were real.*"

"*As real as can be.*" *He spread his hands, inviting her admiration. Petra didn't trouble to hide it. In fact, his confidence made her want to laugh out loud. She'd known so many men with doubts and had had plenty of her own. It was infinitely appealing that he appeared to have none.*

"*So sure of yourself,*" *she teased.* "*Exactly as one would expect a dragon to be.*"

"*I've got to live up to your expectations.*" *He must have seen her confusion because he leaned closer, dropping his voice to a seductive whisper.* "*It's the demand of the firestorm.*"

"*That you fulfill my expectations?*" *Petra demanded. She played with the sparks again.* "*It must mean more than that.*"

"*Yes and no. It means that you're the woman who can bear my son.*"

Petra blinked, but he held her gaze unflinchingly. "*And this happens to you* Pyr *all the time?*"

"*It happens only once for each* Pyr, *so is an opportunity not to be missed.*" *He caught her hand in his, seeming bemused by the array of sparks that lit at the point of contact. Their golden light made him look vital and powerful, a man who might be more than he seemed to be.* "*I couldn't have asked for a more alluring lady to light the flame." He bent over her hand and kissed her fingertips gently, sweetly. "But I won't lie to you about what it means."*

Petra's mouth went dry as she watched his firm lips touch her skin, that dizzying glow burning so bright that it seemed he'd mark her forever with his kiss.

"And afterward?"

"We are warriors. We fight."

"You'll leave," she whispered and he nodded once. He might return, though, and this sensation was one Petra wanted to explore.

Damien glanced up, his gaze knowing. "What other expectations do you have of the Pyr?" he murmured, his breath fanning her skin.

"So you can fulfill them?"

"Of course!"

"Loyalty." Petra bit her lip when he nodded. "Power. Protection." He nodded after each and she studied him, wondering. "Immortality?"

"Longevity," he corrected, which was a relief to her. "We're said to age more quickly once the firestorm is satisfied."

"The ability to solve riddles," Petra added.

He grinned. "I hope to solve yours."

"It'll take more than one night."

He chuckled at that, not so worried about his independence as she'd expected.

"A passionate nature," Petra whispered.

Damien traced one finger down her cheek, leaving a sizzling path in its wake. "You can verify that yourself." He cupped her chin in his hand, then bent to kiss her. It was a sweet seductive kiss, one that heated with every passing moment. Petra found herself opening her mouth to him, her need growing in the golden heat of this firestorm. When Damien's strong fingers slid into her hair, drawing her closer, she caught her breath and stepped back, not quite ready to surrender to him.

"Keen senses?" she asked, her voice husky. She liked that he let her go, but then he had that confidence. He knew she'd surrender to him, and the patience of a dragon meant he'd wait.

A little while. Petra had a hard time catching her breath as he studied her. Could he read her thoughts? Had he already guessed her truth?

"Keener than those of men." he admitted.

"Prove it."

He straightened, listening and looking. "The men in the tavern are talking about your beauty and your songs."

"Of course they are!" Petra scoffed, showing some confidence of her own. "They all talk about me, all the time."

"Someone named Dmitri is insisting that you'll be his wife, but another man, one with a deeper voice, is laughing at him, saying you've declined him three times." He arched a brow and Petra couldn't argue with what he'd heard.

"How long have you been here?"

"We just arrived moments ago." Damien smiled at her. "Do you think you really could have overlooked me, and this?" He touched her mouth with one fingertip, making the light flare brilliantly between them.

It was a point she couldn't argue. She turned and kissed his fingertip, then grazed his skin with her teeth. His gaze brightened. "I can't be persuaded to have a child as easily as that, whether you're Pyr or not," she said, folding her arms across her chest to face him down. "You'll have to seduce me."

He laughed. "But that's exactly what I intend to do."

Petra could believe it. This was a man who had seduced a hundred women, even without those disorienting sparks on his side, and left not a one of them with regrets. "First, show me what you are," she challenged.

Damien didn't try to deny her request or pretend he didn't understand. He smiled and stepped away from her, casting one glance toward the noisy tavern before he looked back at her. "You shouldn't watch," he cautioned. "There are stories of people losing their sanity."

"I have a good hold on mine," Petra replied and arched a brow. "I think you're stalling." She didn't think that, not at all, but she liked how he grinned when she challenged him, as if he wasn't used to anyone provoking him.

"Protect yourself," he said, suddenly serious. "I need to know that you will."

Petra nodded, chastened by his concern.

As she watched, a pale blue glow appeared around Damien's

body, its radiance increasing with every passing moment. She saw Damien throw out his arms, then she felt a surge of power that was achingly familiar to her. She closed her eyes, following his advice, and she felt the force of a transformation wash over her.

When she looked again, Damien had become a dark green dragon with gleaming scales. Each scale looked to be dipped in gold and his dark wings stretched high overhead. His talons shone gold and his teeth were numerous and sharp. He was both beautiful and terrifying, but there was something in his golden eyes that reminded her of the confident warrior. He breathed a plume of fire toward the stars, as if overjoyed at his own abilities, then turned a glittering look upon her.

He was so beautiful that he should be overjoyed.

And she was just as thrilled to be in his company. Damien didn't know it yet, but they were two of a kind.

When he offered one claw to her, Petra saw the firestorm's spark leap from the end of his talon, arc through the air toward her. She closed her eyes as it struck her right in the heart, as burning a wound as one from Cupid's own arrow. She took the step between them and put her hand in his claw before she dared him again.

"Take me for a ride," she urged, then turned and pointed. "I want to be seduced on the top of that peak."

She wanted to be surrounded by earth and stone when this union was made.

Damien smiled, showing every one of his sharp dragon teeth. He inclined his head slightly even as his wings rose higher behind him. "Your wish is my command," he said in that same wondrously low voice. Then he caught her close, holding her with all the care due a precious gem, beat his wings and carried her into the night.

It was perfect, every dream come true. As the wind rippled her hair and the distant peak drew nearer, Petra knew she'd finally met her match. This was the man who could win her heart forever. This was the man who would remain by her side. This was the man who would be unafraid of what she was.

He believed their union would be fleeting but Petra knew better. The child would forge a bond between them, one that would encourage his return.

She would be his, forever.
Starting on this night.

Damien opened his eyes to find Petra in his arms, and the darkfire fading around them. She tasted like wine and sunlight again, a combination so seductive that he remembered every spark of their firestorm. He didn't want to stop what they'd started, but wanted to explore the passion between them once again.

He was startled to realize that they stood in the shadows of the underworld, not on the peak of a mountain with the stars shining above. He was re-living the satisfaction of the firestorm and wanted to do it all again. The ripe curve of her belly was between them, a telling reminder that the firestorm had been consummated. Damien wondered whether she'd experienced the same vivid recollection that he had, but then noticed an amazing thing.

Petra was changing color. She'd been pale when he'd seen her at the gates, as pale and ethereal as a ghost. But now, he watched a flush of color suffuse her cheeks, spreading from her reddened lips to make her look as rosy as she had when she was alive. Her eyes became the rich dark brown he remembered, her hair looked thick and dark and lustrous. Her lips were red and her skin was warm. She caught her breath in obvious surprise, shook off his embrace, then backed away.

"What have you done?" she demanded, her fingertips rising to her lips.

"Proved you wrong, I think. You look alive again."

Petra's hands touched her cheeks, then ran over her body. It was clear she didn't believe what she saw or felt. "You can't do this. It's not possible."

"I have done it." Damien winked at her. "Maybe you'll have to write a new song about it." He reached for her hand. "Let's go."

"It's a trick," Petra said, snatching her hand away from him. "Terrible things happen to the dead who try to leave the underworld. You're trying to convince me to make a mistake."

"I'm trying to save you."

"It's too late for that!"

"Then let me save my son!"

"You can't," Petra began and then she fell silent. Her face paled as if she'd had a shock. She turned away from him so abruptly that Damien knew she was trying to hide something.

"What's going on? What happened?"

"Nothing."

She was lying and he knew it. "Something happened," Damien began to argue, and Petra spun to confront him.

"Why did you leave me?"

"You know why."

"I can guess why." She folded her arms across her chest and challenge lit her eyes. "I want you to tell me."

"Because of what you are, what you can do."

"You're afraid of me," Petra asserted.

Damien took a deep breath, knowing that he had to be completely honest with her to win her agreement. Petra had always been perceptive. "Yes. But I think it's smart to be afraid of someone who can kill you."

"I'm not afraid of you and you can kill me," she countered immediately. "Does that make me stupid?"

"It's not the same thing..."

"It's exactly the same thing," Petra corrected. She leaned closer, tapping her finger on his chest. The darkfire sparked at the point of contact, sending a burst of heat through his veins that made him want to silence her with a kiss. "The difference is that I trust you and you don't trust me."

Damien didn't know what to say to that, because it was true.

"Wait a minute," he said, snapping his fingers. "You saved me from Cerberus. You didn't have to do that."

Petra arched a brow. "No, but I've just wanted to tell you what I think of you for a long, long time."

"I'm thinking it won't be complimentary."

"Are other women complimentary when you abandon them, pregnant with your child?"

"You're the only one. There's only one firestorm. And it wasn't like that."

Petra's lips tightened. "I beg your pardon, but it was exactly like that. I was there. You left too quickly for me to explain exactly how I felt about your choice."

"What about your choice?" he demanded in exasperation.

"I did what I had to do."

"So did I!"

Petra snorted her skepticism.

Damien swore under his breath, then pointed back toward the world they'd left behind. "You turned everyone in that village to stone while I was gone!"

Petra was unrepentant. "And you never asked me why."

"Could there possibly be a reason to justify that?"

"Obviously, I thought there was." Her eyes were shining in brilliant and alluring challenge. If anything, her reaction told Damien that he'd been right to leave her.

Even if she was right that he'd never asked why. The darkfire skipped between them, almost daring him to ask a question.

To take a chance.

He heard his voice rise in his own defense. "Well, you're wrong." He jabbed his thumb into his chest. "My kind are charged with defending humans, as one of the treasures of the earth. Turning people to pillars of stone is a violation of that sacred duty."

"Even if it's only for a day?"

Damien blinked. "One day?"

Petra nodded, obviously enjoying his discomfiture.

Only one day. That meant it was temporary, not permanent. Damien surveyed her, wondering what else he didn't know. "You never told me that."

"You never asked," she replied archly.

"I was surprised. Who wouldn't be?" he demanded. "You never told me what you were!"

"I thought you knew. I thought you'd guessed." She leaned closer, challenging him again. "Aren't dragons supposed to see more clearly than normal men?"

"But I'd never heard of an Earthdaughter."

"So, your lack of education was my fault?"

"You don't understand..."

"I do understand, and that's the problem. I could have imagined you might be surprised." She scoffed at him. "I never expected you to be afraid. You're a *dragon*, for the love of Zeus!"

Damien had to avert his gaze to hide his reaction, but he

wasn't surprised that Petra noticed. Her fingertips landed on his arm, and her gaze brightened.

"Aren't you?" she asked, her voice so low that he knew she suspected the truth.

Damien turned away, having no intention of confessing his weakness to her.

"A dragon could have easily finished off even a three-headed dog," Petra said, as clever and determined as Damien remembered. "Why didn't you shift shape?" She smiled. "Was it a ploy? Did you want me to rescue you?"

"No." Damien glared at her. "I don't want to owe you anything. I take care of myself."

"Really? It didn't seem to be going very well."

He exhaled in irritation. "I didn't shift because I couldn't."

Petra's smile was cool. "Don't feel badly, Damien." He was shocked at how his heart skipped when she said his name. It sounded like music on her lips, but then, he'd once thought everything did. Her next words surprised him again. "Everyone has to sacrifice something to come to this place."

He sobered as he studied her. "Even you?"

"What do you think?"

What if both of them had lost their powers?

That would change everything. Damien could have stayed with Petra if she hadn't had powers of her own, if he'd been the one to defend them and their roles had been clear.

He realized there was a question he should have asked on the day they parted. "Why did you do it? Why did you turn the villagers to stone?"

"Why are you asking now?"

"Because I really want to know. Because I was wrong not to ask you before."

Petra lifted a brow, the pleasure in her eyes making Damien catch his breath. "They were saying that you were unnatural. They were saying that you had been touched by the gods and that you would bring ruin upon them. They blamed your arrival for the crops failing and the storms that had come that year." She leaned closer, her gaze hot. "They were going to trap you and burn you alive."

Damien was shocked. "I could have defended myself..."

Petra was dismissive of the idea. "You would have been vastly outnumbered, and even if you'd gotten away that time, they would just have attacked again. They would have waited until your guard was down or you were asleep or otherwise vulnerable." She straightened, her eyes shining with determination. "I learned young that the way to stop this kind of nonsense is to instill fear. So I did." She looked him up and down. "I did it for you."

"But only for a day?"

"A day and a night. They wouldn't have forgotten. They never did, actually."

"You protected me." Damien was humbled—until he remembered what had happened after he left. "Was that avalanche for me?"

Petra's lips quirked. "What avalanche?" she asked with completely unconvincing innocence. She looked so mischievous that Damien almost forgot how terrified he'd been.

"The one that came out of the mountains unexpectedly, right when I was approaching Delphi after leaving you. The one that nearly killed me."

"Oh, *that* avalanche." She failed to keep control of the smile she'd been hiding, which only annoyed Damien.

"You could have killed me."

"Could being the operative word."

"You have the ability to control rocks and earth..."

"I am an Earthdaughter. I told you that before."

"So, you *did* start an avalanche to kill me when I left you? All that shows is that I was right about you. The prophecy was about you..." He took a step back, but Petra pursued him with purpose.

Her voice dropped to a whisper as she jabbed a finger into his chest. "If I'd intended to kill you, you'd be the one trapped in this place, not me."

Damien didn't know what to say to that. He had perfect control of his own powers and could kill or not depending on his own choice.

At least, he'd had control before his powers had disappeared.

He'd been so shocked by that sudden avalanche—and so hard-pressed to get out of the way—that he hadn't realized Petra had been similarly in control.

"I thought you just started it," he said cautiously. "Then nature took its course."

Her lips tightened. "I finished it, too. To do any less would be irresponsible."

Damien was so shaken by the way she challenged his assumptions that he couldn't hold her gaze. "I don't even know what you can do."

"So, you ran away, abandoning me and your son, rather than finding out." Petra's tone was scornful. "Some dragon you are." She pivoted and began to march deeper into the underworld, leaving Damien searching for a good answer to that. "But then, you aren't one anymore, are you?"

Annoyance shot through Damien at the reminder and he shouted after her. "Why did you take the ferry early?"

Petra spun to face him, an answering anger making her eyes flash. "I didn't! Your son was too stubborn to be born."

"He came by that honestly," Damien muttered.

"He did!" Petra replied. "Like father, like son." She turned to walk onward as Damien struggled against his guilt.

"It wasn't my fault!" he roared, not entirely certain that was true.

Petra just gave him a pitying glance before she continued on her way.

Damien set his teeth and strode after his mate.

This argument wasn't half done.

CHAPTER THREE

Petra felt alive again.

It was a strange, intoxicating feeling, and one that was more than welcome. She tingled. She felt warm. She could feel her heart beating and the blood coursing through her veins. She was keenly aware of Damien, not just because of his kiss, and recalled all the pleasures they'd shared.

She wanted to experience them again.

It was because Damien had kissed her. She'd forgotten the little glimmer of hazel in his eyes, the way his eyes looked so seductive after he'd kissed her, the little smile that quirked the corner of his mouth. She'd forgotten how strong and sure he felt, how safe she felt in his embrace.

She'd forgotten just how good it had been between them. Just as before, his kiss confused her thinking, made her forget everything except the power that drew them together. One taste of him only left her hungry for more.

What if she'd been right the first time and destiny was on their side?

They couldn't have long to make amends. Petra guessed the influence of Damien's touch upon her in this realm was temporary, just as the shedding of his blood would only allow him to communicate with the dead for a short period of time. She knew this newfound vitality would fade, but she wanted to make the most of it while it lasted.

The most incredible thing was that she'd felt the baby move.

Petra had chosen to take the ferry because of her dawning

conviction that something was wrong with her son. He'd become still in the womb and as the days passed and her labor didn't begin, she'd been afraid. She had no experience of childbirth and no one to talk to—after the turned-to-stone incident, the villagers had kept their distance. She'd decided that she had to be with the Mothers and on the third day that the baby had been still in her belly, she'd left. He'd been still ever since.

Until Damien had kissed her.

Petra already doubted her recent impression. It couldn't be possible. The baby was dead, just as she was.

And yet, and yet, Petra didn't feel dead anymore. Her skin didn't look as if she were dead. What if her son could be saved? The prospect was enticing. What if Damien could take him back to the world of the living? She couldn't deny her son that chance, yet she had to somehow ensure that Damien could be relied upon not to abandon his infant son just as he'd once abandoned her.

She heard Damien following her, that familiar purpose in his step. The measured sound of his footfalls made her smile. He was relentless in pursuit of a goal. He had an agenda and he would stick to it. She liked his kind of determination, even if he did sometimes infuriate her enough that she called him stubborn.

In bed, she'd called him persistent. She bit back her widening smile before Damien saw it. He had been an amazing lover, but the last thing this dragon needed was encouragement or anything that would feed his confidence.

"Petra, we have to talk about this..."

He was right.

Maybe for the wrong reason, but he was still right.

Petra spun to face Damien, seeing his expression turn wary at her unexpected move. She lifted a hand and that blue-green spark flickered at the end of her fingertip, just as the brilliant orange light of the firestorm had once lit between them. She reached toward him, and the spark jumped, illuminating a brilliant arc of light before it exploded against his chest. He blinked and took a half-step back, as if startled by the impact, then kept walking toward her.

"What's the light?" Petra asked.

He tried to dismiss the question. "What difference does it make? We need to talk about getting out of here..."

Petra was sure the spark was part of that. "This light is drawing us together. It led me to the gates and it's awakening memories. I feel like it's trying to remind us how good it was."

"Before you tried to kill me," Damien noted. He paused before her and smiled slightly as he looked down at the glow of blue-green becoming brighter between them. "Except you didn't, really."

Petra smiled at him and their gazes clung for a long hot moment.

"Is it part of your plan to win my compliance?"

"As if it could be so easy," Damien murmured, his tone rueful, then smiled at her. He winked at her, clearly not disliking that they argued so much, and Petra's pulse skipped. "Darkfire is beyond my control," he said then and she believed him. "It seems to be mimicking the firestorm."

"Does it usually?"

"No."

"It's a different color." Petra had to admit that its effect upon her was similar. She felt edgy, excited, filled with a desire and even more aware of Damien than she had been before. She was watching the curve of his mouth, the glint in his eye, the way he moved and spoke. She ran her tongue over her lips without meaning to do so and tasted the sweetness of his kiss again, felt herself burn with wanting.

Damien's gaze met hers and Petra couldn't look away. She couldn't swallow and she couldn't breathe. Her heart was pounding and her skin was heating.

It was a wonderful feeling that left her yearning for more.

"What is darkfire?" she asked.

"It's a force associated with the *Pyr*, but an unpredictable one." Damien's brows drew together as he tried to explain it. Yet again, Petra appreciated that he had never disguised the truth about himself or his kind from her, and had never compromised an explanation. "It's said to create possibility where there was none and turn assumptions upside down."

"Magic," Petra whispered, watching the light grow, and feeling the answering desire within her multiply.

"Chaos," Damien said.

"Second chances?" Petra guessed.

"Some think so."

"And you?"

"I think it opens doors that were closed." He shrugged. "For better or for worse."

"Like the gates of the underworld."

Damien nodded. Petra's hand fell to her ripe belly as the baby moved.

When Damien watched her gesture, Petra surveyed him. He was changing somehow. The blood in the cloth he'd tied around his leg was darker. Where she'd struck him, the skin had bruised, but now looked oddly dark. Maybe it was that the rest of his complexion looked so pale. Maybe he was dying because he was in the underworld or maybe he'd given some of his life force to her. Either way, he didn't look as vital anymore and she didn't want him to be trapped here like her. She feared they were running out of time and didn't want his quest to fail.

Not now that her son was moving again.

"If we have a second chance, that means we made a mistake," she said. "That means we have an opportunity to choose differently."

Damien folded his arms across his chest. "I believed I was right to leave you."

He looked so self-assured that Petra could have decked him again. "I just explained to you why I did what I did, that I did it for you."

"It wasn't up to you to try to save me," he replied, as stubborn as ever.

"We conceived a son together. We were partners."

"No," he insisted. "It was my task to protect you..."

"Would you say that to another *Pyr* who saved you from danger?"

Damien was visibly startled. "Of course not, but they're not women..."

"And they're not Earthdaughters," Petra replied, interrupting an argument that wouldn't do anything to improve her mood. "We had an opportunity to work together, Damien, to create something wonderful, but you were too afraid to take a chance."

"It's not the same. A *Pyr* must defend his mate, as the most precious jewel in his hoard..."

As much as Petra liked his choice of language, she had to get to the bottom of this. "And if she has the ability to defend him, she should let him die?"

He was apparently so startled by this idea that he didn't know what to say.

"Your powers have abandoned you in this realm," Petra reminded him. "Your ability to influence me will fade. When your blood dries, we will lose the ability to communicate, and you may lose your chance to leave this place. If you let any substance cross your lips, you will be trapped here forever."

"Stories," Damien said, glancing about himself with obvious concern.

"They carry the grain of truth. Your skin is changing color. You are fading."

Damien scanned himself in alarm.

"Damien, we have a chance to change the future. We always did have that chance, but your darkfire is making it possible again. The key lies in trust."

Damien nodded and she loved how he listened to her. "You believed in the firestorm's promise, right from the beginning."

"I was waiting for a man like you." Petra smiled. "The *Pyr* aren't the only ones with prophecies, you know."

"The firestorm is just about creating more *Pyr*..."

"Then why did you stay three months?"

Damien exhaled. "I didn't intend to," he admitted, his eyes lighting. "But you were unlike any woman I'd ever known."

"And now you know why." He parted his lips to ask for more but Petra held up a finger in warning. It was time for him to choose. "We need to find our way out of here, but I need to know that you will try again."

"How?"

"What I want is partnership with you, otherwise my son stays here with me. Decide now."

Damien considered Petra and weighed his options. What she was suggesting was much like the relationships the *Pyr* in the future formed with their mates. He thought of their conviction that the whole was greater than the sum of the parts. He remembered their certainty that a *Pyr* couldn't really be complete without his mate by his side.

He thought of how they healed their scales—and why they lost a scale in the first place.

Being with Petra reminded him how powerful their time together had been—and made Damien realize he'd missed her.

Maybe his relentless pursuit of women ever since had been an attempt to regain what he'd lost.

No wonder that was so dissatisfying. There was no one else like Petra.

Could he trust her, without knowing all of her abilities?

When he didn't answer her immediately, she began to turn away, her disappointment clear. He didn't blame her, but he didn't want her to go either.

"Is it too late to ask what you can do?" he asked, halfway expecting her to ignore him.

But Petra never was vengeful, no matter how angry she was. She paused and glanced back at him, a tantalizing smile curving her lips. "It's never too late to ask," she whispered. The look in her eyes pierced Damien's heart like an arrow, and he took a step closer without even realizing what he'd done. "It's never too late to forgive, and it's never too late to try again."

Damien smiled. "That sounds like part of a story."

Petra smiled and the sight of her pleasure made him realize everything he'd risked and lost.

"Then, show me," he said, knowing he'd beg if he had to. "Please."

"You mean it," she said, with undisguised delight.

Damien nodded and Petra immediately tipped her head back.

She was beautiful, so strong and feminine. It made sense for her to use her powers to defend him, just as he used his to defend her. It was different from his expectations, but was logical when he considered it.

Did they have more in common than he'd imagined? Was that why she captivated him so thoroughly?

It was an enticing possibility. Damien knew that no woman had ever challenged him as much as Petra—and none had ever satisfied him so well either.

As he watched, a rosy glow rolled over Petra's body, like the sunrise touching the lip of the earth, and his heart skipped. Her body looked firmer and more solid, and her movements became impossibly slow. She breathed only once for each dozen breaths he took and he could almost have believed that she'd turned to stone. Her eyes opened slowly, their brown color replaced by the simmering orange of a volcano's heat, and the glow around her body brightened. She looked so fearsome and powerful that Damien fought the urge to take a step back.

It was when the snakes began to erupt from beneath her feet that he remembered he'd lost his ability to become a dragon.

He was powerless in a strange realm and he knew it.

But Damien was resolute. There could be no greater test of his trust in Petra, and he was determined not to sacrifice the firestorm's promise again.

Petra dared to hope.

She'd known all her life that she wouldn't find happiness with a mortal man. That was the curse of her kind. But she'd always hoped that she would be one Earthdaughter who found a man with his own powers. When she'd met Damien, she'd imagined that future with him, one filled with love and trust. It had been devastating to learn that he was afraid of her.

She'd made a mistake by reacting in anger.

They had a second chance and he was willing to see the truth.

Even given that, Petra had concerns about showing him the fullness of her powers, lest she frighten him again. There would be no third chance.

Yet the truth offered the only way forward. Damien had to see it all, trust her, and still love her, or she'd never be able to put her hand in his again.

At least he was willing to try.

She had to meet him in the middle. That was the essence of partnership.

Petra closed her eyes and slowed her breathing, turning her

thoughts inward. Deep in the core of her mind was a place of stone and rock, a center that couldn't be moved. It was her anchor and her sanctuary, her source of confidence that the world would be as it always had been.

Because there always would be Earthdaughters, and they would keep custody of Gaia and her legacy. Petra had thought that she and Damien had common ground in this, so to speak, since the *Pyr* were the guardians of the earth and the custodians of the elements. She'd expected them to understand each other.

Maybe this was their chance to do so.

The key might lie in the prophecy, the one she'd heard only once and didn't recall. As the power built within her, Petra realized that her dragon warrior would remember every word of the prophecy given to him.

Dragons had long memories, after all.

First things first.

The kernel within Petra grew as she bent her attention upon it. There was a connection established between the relatively quick rhythm of her human body and the unhurried cycle of the earth. She felt her heart slow and her breathing become shallow. Her muscles became more rigid and her movements were imperceptible. She stood outside of time as she knew it, answerable to the wind and the rain, and the years.

And then she hummed.

The hum began deep in her chest, growing gradually in volume until her sternum vibrated in time. She felt the resonance slip through her body and coaxed it to build. She felt the ground beneath her feet start to vibrate as well, felt the fissures in the stone open into gaps, felt the ground crack and shake. She felt the creatures of darkness come to her, the snakes rising in the earth, the moles and voles and bats that took shelter in Gaia's embrace, the spiders that lurked in the dark chinks between stones.

The power rolled through her, as ancient and powerful as that of Gaia herself, and Petra was glad to have no secrets from Damien any longer. He would see, he would know, and he would still love her. She believed because she had to. It was their shared destiny and she would make it come true. Petra roared, the sound of an earthquake bursting from her mouth, and the earth jumped in sympathy with her triumph.

Suddenly she felt her son go still.

Too still.

The baby was like a rock in her belly again, a leaden weight that felt wrong and horrible. It was just as he had been before she'd taken the ferry. Not again!

Petra gasped, even as her hands fell protectively to her stomach. She couldn't have to pay this price. She spun in place, turning her back on Damien for fear that he would see her reaction. He was perceptive, thanks to his inner dragon, and she only wanted to hide this fear from him. It was kinder if he never realized his presence in this realm had awakened his son, better if he believed the child lost all along.

But Petra was distraught. She folded herself around her belly, whispering to her unborn son, even as she forced her power to retreat.

The underworld came into focus again, but Petra didn't know where she was. A deadened plain stretched in every direction.

She had time to fear, then her son kicked hard. In fact, Petra was winded by his powerful kick. It was as if he wanted her to have no doubt that he was alive.

Alive. Petra felt tears on her cheeks. She glanced over her shoulder at Damien, intending to tell him the truth this time.

But her dragon warrior was gone.

Petra was alone in the underworld, no sign of a living being in any direction.

Damien was determined to face Petra's truth.

Even with snakes.

He swallowed when Petra's eyes burned with brilliant light and refused to think that she could smite a man with a glance. She looked powerful and immovable and he felt the ground vibrate beneath his feet in response to her summons. He knew she could create an earthquake and an avalanche, and he told himself to believe in her. He knew he should trust her, just as she'd trusted him, and he believed her claim that she could control her powers.

Even so, he felt sweat on his brow when the snakes erupted

from the ground and slithered around her feet. They were black and glossy vipers, long and thick and sinuous. Damien swallowed as they began to wind over her body, as if they couldn't get close enough to her. His heart pounded when the fissures opened in the earth, radiating from her body in response to her low cry.

When the darkfire sparked all around Petra, he was concerned but resolute.

He gripped his dagger and waited, ignoring the way the darkfire shone off the scales of the snakes. He refused to think of how numerous they were. He refused to think of his own safety, or the fact that he couldn't shift shape to defend himself. His fate was in Petra's hands, and the earth was crumbling on all sides.

Her gaze blazed into his own, daring him to trust her, and Damien did.

Then she gave a cry of horror and stepped back. He reached for her as she spun away, but his fingers only brushed the cloth of her tunic. The ground crumbled on all sides of him, dissolving beneath his feet with terrifying speed.

Damien screamed as he fell.

He fell into an abyss, one filled with darkness, the glint of darkfire, and a thousand hissing snakes. There was nothing to grab but the snakes that fell with him, no way to save himself, and he had no ability to shift shape.

He tried.

Over and over and over again.

Damien landed on a rocky patch of dirt, the impact hard enough to steal the breath from his lungs. He closed his eyes in horror at the sound of snakes landing on the ground all around him. When he looked, some of them were still wriggling, while others had slithered away. It was still twilight, although there were no stars.

There was no sign of Petra.

Damien sat up with caution. Where had the darkfire cast him now?

He was in a deadened forest, silence on every side. The trees were barren of leaves, their branches stretched upward, as if straining toward a sun that never lit this realm. Even though their boughs were empty, it was darker within the ghostly forest and more still. It was colder even than the rest of the underworld and

Damien shivered. The bark of the trees was grey, more like stone than wood.

Fear slid down Damien's spine.

There was fog near the ground, a fog that became denser with every passing moment. It sent a chill through him and he noticed that there was no spark of darkfire in the pale haze.

He didn't trust its absence.

Damien heard a rustling and spun to defend himself, his dagger at the ready.

There was no one behind him, just a tree.

He might have turned away but he saw a contorted face in the trunk of the tree. A person was trapped inside, silently screaming for a release that would never come.

Damien backed away, not trusting his own eyes. His back collided with another tree, and he spun to find another anguished face just behind his shoulder. He ran from tree to tree, realizing there were people trapped in every one.

Frozen forever.

And Damien was engulfed in a memory he'd have preferred to forget.

Damien was returning to Petra after a quick trip to Delphi, the teasing of his fellow warriors echoing in his thoughts. What if he was falling in love? Damien couldn't think of a woman more likely to fascinate him forever than his Petra.

He hurried, shifting shape and flying over the mountains to save time. Even though he didn't bring the best news, he wanted to be with Petra sooner. His journey had gone as planned and he was striding out of the hills, in human form, by twilight.

Damien was tired and dusty, hungry but ready to see his lady again. Three days away had been too long. He was anticipating an evening before the hearth, savoring Petra's kisses and her laughter. He didn't care if there was only dry bread to eat. Her company would be enough. He imagined a long night in bed, of sharing kisses and confessions. He loved how their son was making her figure more full and her features more soft.

They had stopped in a village when Petra became ill with her pregnancy and had lived there several weeks. It was small but not too small—they could be overlooked in its confines, but also recognized. He and Petra kept to themselves, always paid promptly and in full, and were courteous. Although Damien didn't like to remain in one place for long, he'd reconciled himself to remaining here until his son was born.

But it looked different on this night. To Damien's astonishment, there was a forest where the village should be. He stopped and stared, doubting the evidence of his eyes. No, the forest had filled the village, for the houses were still there. Damien couldn't make sense of it. He walked closer, cautious as he tried to determine a reason for the change.

It was quiet, too quiet. He strained his ears but could only hear the crackle of a single fire on a hearth. He knew it was in the courtyard of the house he shared with Petra. There was only stillness, other than the breath of the wind, and the motion he could hear from their home. Petra was there, bustling around as usual, as if in anticipation of his return.

But where had these trees come from? What had happened to the village? There was usually some activity, even until dark.

Damien realized the trees had no branches. They were more like pillars, or trees that had been sawn off at about his height. He had a very bad feeling as he stepped into this strange forest, although he couldn't have named the reason why.

Then he saw the first face and realized the truth.

They weren't trees: they were people.

He reached out and touched one, shocked to find the man as cold and hard as stone. It was the farmer who lived beside them. There was his wife next to him, similarly immobilized. Though they couldn't move, their eyes were filled with accusation. Damien touched another and another, then realized they'd been enchanted and turned to stone.

He thought of the prophecy that had just been given to him and feared for Petra.

He ran to their home, flinging open the door and bursting into the central courtyard.

Petra turned to smile at him in welcome. She was fine, much to his relief, humming as she stirred a pot of stew that was set over the fire. He stood shaking in the doorway but she smiled, as if nothing was wrong at all.

"I thought you would return tonight," she said easily. "I kept the stew warm for you." He realized that she was completely different from his mother. There was no demand in her expectation, no need. On another night, he might have been relieved, for his mother had nearly destroyed his father.

On this night, he was cautious.

How could she not know what was outside these walls?

Petra came to him and kissed his cheek, catching his hand in hers and giving it a slight tug. "You must be tired. Come and sit and tell me what you've seen."

"Have you been out?" Damien demanded, for that could be the only explanation for her calm manner.

"Yes. Why?"

He stopped and stared at her. "Didn't you see?

She glanced at him quickly, something in her eyes made him believe she knew exactly what he meant. "See what?"

"All of the village is turned to stone!"

Petra wrinkled her nose. "Oh. Yes." She stirred the stew. "Are you hungry?"

"Wait!" Damien seized her arm, compelling her to face him. "How can you be so indifferent? Do you know something about this? Are you responsible for this in some way?"

Petra's eyes narrowed slightly. "What makes you think that?"

"You're the only one who isn't enchanted."

"I'm the only one who's pregnant," she said lightly, her gaze locking with his. "But you're right. I'm also the only one who is an Earthdaughter." She said this as if it were perfectly routine, but Damien didn't know what she meant.

He felt a terrible dread. He remembered his father's warning that being bound to a single woman could only lead to sorrow and a loss of powers. He thought of the prophecy he'd just been given, the one that said much the same thing. Was Drake's summons to serve offering him an escape just in time?

"What's an Earthdaughter?" he asked, trying to keep his voice level. If she'd turned the villagers to stone, there was no reason she couldn't do the same to him.

Making the prophecy come true. What of the rest of it? Would it all come true? Damien had tried to dismiss the dire prediction, but now he couldn't.

"You're not the only one with powers in this household, Damien." Petra spoke in a practical tone, as if they discussed the weather. She smiled at him slightly. "I wish I could have found another way to tell you, but in the end, there was no choice." She shrugged and began to ladle out some stew for him. "It was really only a matter of time before you knew and now you do."

Damien wanted her to say it aloud. "You did this to them?"

"Yes." She was unrepentant, which angered Damien as little else could have done.

"How could you do such a thing? And why? There is nothing they could have done to you to merit such treatment..."

"Nothing?" she asked, lifting her chin with a familiar defiance.

"Nothing!" Damien replied. "Don't you think I deserved to know about your powers before we conceived my son?"

She folded her arms across her chest and glared at him. "I didn't know about all of your powers before that happy deed was done."

"It's not the same!"

"It's exactly the same. You're more than human and so am I. Frankly, I thought that we'd understand each other as a result."

"No!" Damien paced the central courtyard of the house. "This is all wrong." He paced the courtyard, then pivoted to face her. "You might as well know. I have to leave and I might not be back."

Petra looked shaken. "I beg your pardon?"

"I've been called to duty." Damien didn't feel as much regret as he had just moments ago. He knew that Petra saw the truth in his eyes. "I have to go."

Her lips set. "When will you be back?"

"I don't know." He swallowed then said it. "Maybe never."

She held his gaze for a long potent moment. "You're just fabricating an excuse, because you're afraid of what I can do."

Damien didn't know what to say to that, but Petra didn't give him much time to think.

"Did you get your prophecy, at least?" she asked.

Damien took a deep breath and recited the oracle's pronouncement:

A lost child mourned for many years
A mother who will shed no tears
A dragon warrior turned to stone
A woman abandoned, all alone.
Firestorm's promise will fade to naught
Until stone and fire pay death's cost.
After a *Pyr* sacrifice is made
Destiny's promise can be claimed.

"Cheerful," Petra said tightly. Her displeasure was a palpable force. "So, you're leaving, because I obviously am the person who can turn you to stone and your son isn't going to survive anyway."

"I don't want it to be true, Petra."

She gave him a hot look. "Then you could ask some questions. You could try to find the hidden truth of the prophecy. They often have double meanings, as I'm sure you know."

"No," Damien said, shaking his head. "No. This time, the prophecy is as clear as can be. I'm sorry, Petra. I wanted to believe in the firestorm."

"Not enough to fight for it," she replied, her tone hard.

He knew she was right. He also knew that given his upbringing and his father's end, the prophecy and his call to duty, that there was no other answer. He'd been honest with her, but felt she'd deceived him. Repairing the damage would take time, time they didn't have, and a sacrifice he was unwilling to make.

Their gazes locked and held for a charged moment, and Damien noted the slight rounding of Petra's belly. He couldn't believe she would lose their son, not when she looked so healthy in her pregnancy, but he couldn't accept what she had done. If he remained with her, even for one night, it would be an endorsement of her deed.

"What will you do?" he asked.

She shrugged, pretending to be indifferent when he knew she wasn't. "I can't imagine you care." Her tone was hurt and he felt guilt at his role in that.

"I do."

She turned away then took the pot off the tripod over the fire. He'd never seen her cry and that convinced him that she was the mother of the prophecy.

"I'll go to the Mothers if I need to," she said, surprising him. He'd never heard her refer to a home or a family.

"But the prophecy..."

She turned on him, her eyes blazing, and he took a step back at the sign of her anger. She seemed to be more than a woman in this moment, and he was sure he felt the ground quaking beneath his feet.

What was an Earthdaughter?

"I don't believe your prophecy," Petra declared. "I refuse to believe that my son is as good as dead just because some woman in a grotto uttered a verse." She jabbed her finger at her own chest. "I will believe in his safe arrival. I will believe in his good health. And I will do everything in my power to give him exactly what he needs."

Damien might have been chastened, but those people turned to stone just steps away couldn't be forgotten. Petra's stern tone and his uncertainty about her powers made him fear the mother of his child. "I don't think I want to know what 'everything in your power' might mean."

She smiled coolly. "No, you're just a dragon. Run away, Pyr warrior, if that's so much easier than trusting in me."

Damien was offended. "It's not easy to trust someone with hidden powers..."

"And it's not easy to believe in love. I thought you were more than a man, not less than one, but you're afraid." Petra straightened and glared at him, her expression filled with challenge.

"I'm not afraid."

"Then stay and see what I am." Her eyes were bright with challenge and there was a rosy glow surrounding her body. Damien wanted to stay and see her truth, just to prove her expectation wrong.

But when the ground rumbled beneath his feet, he shifted shape instinctively, taking flight in his dragon form. He hovered in the courtyard, but Petra stopped her humming and shook her head. She spat on the ground beneath him, her disgust clear. "Run away, dragon. I'll wait for a man bold enough to love me."

Damien knew he could have melted Petra's resistance with a

touch, but he didn't want to reconcile. The idea that he could be mated with the woman who would destroy him was too real a possibility for him to try to stay. He'd watched his father's powers ebb away to nothing, leaving him a shell of a dragon. And there hadn't been a prophecy. He'd never be able to sleep again in Petra's presence.

He gave her one last look, yearning for what he had believed to be true of her, then flew high in the sky. He flew over the strange frozen company of villagers before beating his wings hard to ascend over the hills.

He'd always said he'd never fall in love. He'd always said he'd never surrender his future to one woman. He'd fulfilled his firestorm and very nearly succumbed, but had escaped the consequences in time. Damien told himself he had done the right thing, that his son couldn't be saved, that the oracle was right.

But Petra's disgust echoed in his ears and his heart.

Little did he know then that it always would.

Damien came to a breathless halt in the endless forest. He was panting and winded, feeling an exhaustion that wasn't characteristic of him. He looked down to see his leg was turning black. His toes were numb. The rest of his skin was becoming pale.

Petra was right. Time was running out.

He spun to examine the grey trees. They were just trees now, trees without human faces or captives, and he wondered if his eyes had deceived him.

He swallowed, knowing the prophecy had deceived him. There had never been a woman who had made him feel as powerful and alive as Petra, never a woman who surprised him and captivated as she had done.

He realized that even though he'd left her, against every inclination of his heart, he'd still been turned to stone.

Damien had gone on that mission with Drake and the others, the quest to oust one of their own kind. They'd followed a dark trail into the depths of the earth, the evil spell of the viper wafting into their ears. Many had their hearts turned against their true intention. Others fell back, unable to continue. The trail had led those who could endure the viper's chant to one of their own.

Cadmus.

And in the battle to defeat him, those who fought at Drake's back had been enchanted.

Turned to stone.

And trapped for centuries.

The prophecy had come true, but not due to Petra's powers. Damien was ashamed that he had assumed the worst of her on that day, that he hadn't asked for an explanation or given her a chance. He'd acted foolishly and couldn't blame Petra for her anger.

But according to that same prophecy, once each obstacle was confronted, their firestorm would have a chance of a future.

He had to find Petra and change her mind.

At the very least, he owed her an apology.

To his relief, he saw a woman's silhouette ahead. She was standing on the periphery of the strange forest, her back to him. He shouted Petra's name, but she didn't seem to hear him. She didn't turn around, even when he ran toward her. He called her name repeatedly as he ran closer, then touched her shoulder.

When the woman turned, Damien realized he'd made a mistake.

It wasn't Petra.

This woman was hideously ugly and ancient, as well. Her face was lined and cracked, like an exposed rock. Her long dark hair was actually hundreds of small black snakes, their eyes bright and their tongues flicking. Bat wings stretched high behind her back and she bared her teeth, showing her fangs. Worse, blood ran from her eyes in a stream of red tears, sliding into the crevasses in her skin.

He tried to shift, again without success.

The monster lunged for Damien, her nails like yellowed talons. She screamed, and made a cry like a bird being strangled. Damien saw her forked tongue and smelled her foul breath as she fell against him. She was heavy and strong, intent upon attacking him.

Damien pulled his dagger and buried it in her chest without hesitation. She fell back with a cry, blood flowing from the wound, then attacked again. Was she immortal? Or dead already? Damien feared the odds were in her favor, especially as he felt his own strength fading. He knew he was fighting for his life, and he was determined to win.

Being trapped in the underworld forever wasn't the future he envisioned with Petra and his son.

The fight was vicious and seemed to last a lifetime.

Finally, the monster was motionless on the ground, lying in a pool of her own blood. Damien stood over her, watching for her to make another move, his heart racing. He was bleeding from a dozen wounds, exhausted and hungry. He stared down at the fallen creature until he felt someone's presence behind him.

He spun, his dagger at the ready, only to find Petra behind him.

"For the love of Zeus," she whispered, her horror clear as she looked at the corpse. "What have you done?"

CHAPTER FOUR

Petra couldn't believe her eyes.

The creature at Damien's feet was clearly dead.

He couldn't possibly have made a worse choice. Petra rubbed her forehead, knowing that the chances of either of them escaping the underworld had just diminished to less than nothing.

Damien read her reaction well. "What was she?"

"One of the Erinyes," Petra admitted, then gave Damien a look.

He had paled. "The Kindly Ones?"

The sight of him frightened her, for he looked more dead than she was. "They aren't kindly and you know it. That's just flattery, to keep them from doing their worst."

Damien eyed the fallen creature and shuddered.

"You couldn't have just scared her off, could you?" Petra asked, worry sharpening her tone. "You couldn't have just injured her a little, instead of killing her outright?"

"She attacked me! I didn't have time to think or consider. It was her or me."

He was probably right about that.

Damien fixed Petra with a look. "But everyone in the underworld is dead already, except me. How could I kill anyone here?"

"The Erinyes are half-divine."

"So, anything is possible." Damien winced before she could say more. He passed a hand over his forehead, swore, then sank to his knees beside the fallen monster. "Of course, the Erinyes have a connection with Hades."

"They work for him, doing his will by tormenting the dead who don't deserve to rest." Petra glanced about them. "This must be Tartarus."

"It doesn't look any different from the rest."

"No, but the Erinyes are said to guard its gates and punish its occupants for Hades."

"Then where are the occupants?"

Petra heaved a sigh. "I think we should be glad to be unable to see them. Maybe we're only half-dead now."

"I feel half-dead," he muttered, then surveyed the corpse again. Damien's disgust with himself was clear—and a perfect echo of Petra's own. "I had no idea what she was."

"Stories," Petra reminded him, unable to resist.

"I never had much opportunity to listen to stories, even when I was a boy."

"Why not?"

His frown deepened. "My father was consumed with serving my mother's will. She kept him drunk, hungry, and a slave to the pleasures of her bedchamber. She liked having a pet dragon." He shook his head. "There were no stories in our home."

"I'm sorry."

He continued, his tone so matter-of-fact that she knew he was still pained by the memory. "My father said I should be sent to train as soon as my powers were noted. I was eleven years of age when I was sent to Delphi."

Delphi. He'd gone to Delphi for that prophecy.

"My mother didn't want me to go. She would have kept me back, just to have another dragon at the ready. My father defied her for the first time ever. He said the Spartans sent their sons to the agape to train at eight years of age. By his reckoning, she'd had three extra years by then."

"Your father must have won that battle," Petra said.

He met her gaze steadily. "She'd been giving him a potion for years. It was from the east and intended to weaken him. He was a slave to pleasure with no thoughts of his own. His defiance over my fate surprised her and angered her. He roused himself, what was left, and commanded me to run. It was the only order he'd ever given me and I didn't dare to disobey."

"Did she kill him?" Petra asked.

Damien nodded. "I prefer to think that he let her win."

Petra stared at the ground, realizing why Damien had been afraid to trust her with his survival. She considered him now and feared that he too would be destroyed by a determination to save his son.

"Could you tell me the prophecy again?"

"You don't remember?"

"I don't have a dragon's memory." Their gazes locked and held for a hot moment, then Damien spoke softly, reciting the verse.

"A lost child mourned for many years
A mother who will shed no tears
A dragon warrior turned to stone
A woman abandoned, all alone.
Firestorm's promise will fade to naught
Until stone and fire pay death's cost.
After a Pyr *sacrifice is made*
Destiny's promise can be claimed.

He looked at her hard. "There's a promise in it, a chance if its conditions are fulfilled. At the time, I heard only the warning."

"And you were sure that I'd be the one who turned you to stone."

Damien looked embarrassed. "I didn't even know that such a thing was possible. I was surprised, Petra, and reacted badly." He stood up and came to her, taking her hand in his. She didn't dare meet his gaze, not when he ran his thumb across her hand and bent his attention on her as he did now. He was trying to convince her of something and Petra knew his task was half won. "I didn't tell you what happened to my company of warriors, or where I've been."

His words surprised her into looking up, and then she was snared by the intensity of his gaze.

"We went to hunt a viper, which is what we call one of our kind turned bad. This one was enchanting men in his vicinity, turning their thoughts to wickedness. He was inciting war and hardship. He turned his spell on us."

Petra caught her breath. "He turned you to stone."

"To teeth, actually. Warriors defeated by him were turned to dragon teeth, used by him in attacking others. But when he died and his remains became part of the earth, the teeth turned to stone."

"That would have taken a long time."

"Centuries." Damien's lips tightened and his thumb stilled against her skin. "We were enchanted for almost two thousand years, Petra, until another *Pyr* guessed how to break the spell."

"By planting the teeth, sowing them like seeds," Petra guessed.

Damien looked up in surprise.

"It's in a story," she explained with a smile and he shook his head. "But two thousand years?"

He nodded. "I have seen the future. I thought this world lost to us." He sighed. "We all thought ourselves adrift, until the darkfire was released."

"Released from what?"

"It was trapped in a stone by some sorcery. Actually, there are said to be three darkfire crystals, according to the *Pyr* of future times, and one of them was broken, setting the force of darkfire loose in the world." He frowned. "Everything can change when the darkfire burns."

Was everything changing for her and Damien? Petra wanted that to be true so badly that she didn't want to say it aloud.

"The darkfire brought you here, then."

Damien nodded. "Our commander, Drake, took possession of one of the crystals. He thought it ordered him to do so. Once he had it, it began to flare intermittently. Whenever it did that, we were flung through space and time, cast down in a strange place until the crystal lit again. We lost men along the way. It was before we came here that Thaddeus suggested the crystal was taking us to our firestorms. One of us, Alexander, was taken back to the village where he left Katina and his son."

"What happened to him?"

"I don't know. The crystal lit again, and Alexander ran from us, determined to be left behind." He met her gaze steadily. "Then it took us to a place where Orion's firestorm sparked. He pursued her and the crystal brought us here. As soon as I saw the River Acheron, I knew the darkfire was giving me the chance to save our son." He squeezed her hand slightly. "What if the darkfire is giving *us* a second chance?"

The baby kicked just as his father spoke. Petra would have turned away, but Damien was too observant to miss her reaction. He was leaning over her in a heartbeat, her elbow in his hand. "What is it?"

She had trusted him from that first night, and even though he had disappointed her, Petra realized she still did trust Damien. He wasn't the only one who had made a mistake, after all.

She took his hand and placed it over her ripe belly. He was momentarily confused, then the baby kicked hard.

"He's alive!" Damien said with such delight that tears rose to Petra's eyes. "Has he been doing this all along?"

"No." Petra shook her head. "No. The labor didn't start, Damien, and he went still. He'd been kicking and kicking, but suddenly stopped." Her breath caught. "I felt that he had turned to stone and I was afraid."

Damien drew her into his arms and held her tightly against his chest. Petra was alarmed to realize that he wasn't as warm as he had been. "That's why you took the ferry, even when the sea was rough."

"I had to go back to the Mothers."

"Where?"

"The closest place to home for me."

Damien pressed a kiss into her hair and Petra felt her tears begin to fall. "I was so wrong, Petra. Please forgive me for not trusting you as I should have done." He framed her face in his hands and kissed her tears away.

"You're not the only one who made a mistake," Petra admitted quietly.

"I don't understand. You've done nothing wrong..."

"I did. I invoked the Erinyes."

Damien looked down at the corpse again. "Just now?" He leaned down, nearly touching his nose to hers, his determined gaze boring into her own. "Why did you do it?"

"You're not condemning me?"

"Not until I give you a chance to explain." His grin made her heart skip a beat. "Second chances only work if you learn from your mistakes."

"It was after you left," she admitted. "When I was on the ferry."

"When you knew it was going to sink."

"I was still angry. I thought everything was your fault." She flicked a glance at Damien, surprised to find his expression thoughtful. "How could I know that carrying a child would make me want more?"

Damien caught a tendril of her hair between his finger and thumb, then wound it around his finger. His smile was crooked. "You remember that I wasn't exactly gone the next morning."

"No, you stayed three months. I thought that was your plan."

"No. One night was the plan, but you were a temptation that I couldn't easily leave."

Petra once again hoped their thoughts were as one. "But you would still have followed Drake, even if we hadn't argued, and you still would have been enchanted. You still wouldn't have returned."

"Don't believe that. The darkfire still would have been loosed, and I might have found you faster." Damien was winding her hair more tightly around his finger, his body pressed against her own. He leaned down and touched a feather light kiss to her earlobe, one that weakened her knees and made her heart pound.

"You don't know that."

"I believe in stories, especially the ones that end well."

Petra stole a glance at him and the resolve in his expression made her mouth go dry.

"What if we start again?" he murmured, his breath a seductive caress. "What if I apologize for leaving you and you apologize for invoking the Erinyes?"

"Then what?" Petra asked, her voice husky.

Damien brushed a kiss across her lips, a fleeting touch that filled her with yearning. "Then we just have to figure out how to get out of here."

"Partners," Petra breathed and Damien grinned.

"If you'll have me."

"If you'll trust me," she said quietly and his smile broadened.

"I've learned from my mistake." He kissed her then, sending a wonderful heat through her body and filling her with a new conviction. When he lifted his head, she was simmering and optimistic.

Until her gaze fell on the dead monster.

"We have to go to Hades and appeal to him for release."

Damien winced. "Even I know that never goes well in stories."

Petra shook her head and took Damien's hand, trying to encourage him. "But no one in the stories ever had darkfire on their side."

Damien nodded, his expression thoughtful as he scanned the bleak terrain of Tartarus.

"What is it?"

"There's no more darkfire." He lifted their linked hands and Petra saw that there was no glimmer of blue-green light between their hands. She looked but couldn't see a single spark, even though it had haunted her since Damien's arrival.

Had the darkfire abandoned them here?

"It's leaving us to our own resources," she guessed.

Damien nodded and squeezed her hand. "Fortunately, we have plenty."

His optimism was undeserved, though, at least in Petra's opinion. She could see that her dragon warrior was fading and feared that he might be the sacrifice that was required.

Not if she had anything to say about it.

"He is supposed to hold court on the other side of Tartarus," Petra said, refusing to believe that everything could be lost. Damien nodded and tightened his grip on her hand, setting a quick pace in the direction she indicated.

"You have to be joking." Damien folded his arms across his chest and glared at the dark ribbon of water. Its surface was moving in a way that he distrusted. They had walked for ages, even though there was no good measurement of time in this place. He was tired and his stomach was so empty, it felt hollow. He was having a hard time keeping his thoughts focused and now this. "We have to cross the river without a ferry?"

"I don't see a ferry," Petra said mildly. "I've never heard of there being one on the River Leche. If you want to appeal to

Hades, we have to cross it."

"We have to go deeper into the underworld."

"Until we reach its heart."

Petra moved toward the water with a confidence Damien couldn't echo. He watched the water and realized its surface was covered with dark creatures. "Snakes," he muttered under his breath.

"Well, I told you. They make sense here," Petra continued calmly. "We're in the underworld, deep in the earth, which is where snakes are supposed to live. In stories, they symbolize lost secrets and forbidden desires." She gave him a smile that reminded him of all his desires for her.

"I hate snakes."

"Maybe you'll conquer your fear."

"It's not fear..."

"They're said to only attack in self-defense. Don't hurt them and they won't hurt you."

"That's only a rumor."

She didn't answer him, just smiled then walked to the bank.

Damien shifted his weight from foot to foot, the sight of those black snakes making him sweat. There had to be thousands of them, maybe millions of them, writhing over each other in a kind of frenzy. The idea of being surrounded by them, of having them touch his skin, was enough to make him feel sick. "It's fine for you to take such a chance. You're dead already."

She cast him an amused glance. "Such a bold dragon," she said under her breath, her gaze taunting him.

Damien was on the cusp of arguing that he wasn't a dragon any more, or at least not in this place, but she wasn't really talking about his shifting powers. "Can't you cause an earthquake and make the seas part?"

"It wouldn't necessarily get rid of the snakes."

"I say it's worth a try."

"I'm saving my strength," she said, and he heard that she was tired. He saw her hand cup her ripe belly again and wondered if she felt the baby's time was coming. "They're just snakes, Damien."

He marched down to the river to stand beside Petra, deeply uneasy about the whole exercise. "It would be a lot easier if I could still shift shape," he noted. "We could just fly over the river."

"Which might be the point. This might be a test of your determination."

He gave her a sizzling glance. "I'm determined enough."

"We'll soon find out. This river isn't supposed to be very deep."

Even the possibility of snakes up to his waist made Damien shudder. "Does anybody know for sure?"

"No one who's telling."

He exhaled and tried to find his courage. It also would have been much easier without the sight of all those sinuous bodies entwining and tangling, glistening wet, and much easier if he'd been feeling his usual self. "Doesn't this river have some kind of power?"

"You're stalling," Petra teased with a laugh.

"I'm gathering information to make the best choice," Damien retorted and she laughed again. He couldn't help but smile that she knew him so well.

"The Leche is called the river of oblivion, which is a tempting prospect in a way."

Damien was surprised. "What could you want to forget?"

"You broke my heart, Damien," she said softly. "And forgetting that ache would make any situation easier to bear."

He caught her hand in his, wanting to make this right while he could. He had absolutely no confidence that he could pass through this river unscathed, and this one thing, he had to set straight with Petra while he could. He turned her hand in his, trying to find a way to explain. "I thought I was supposed to take care of you."

"I thought you were the one man who could accept me for what I was."

Damien nodded, knowing he should have done better. "I've been with others of my kind while I've been gone," he said. "These other *Pyr* have an idea that their mates are more than the mothers of their sons."

"I like them already."

"They think of their mates as their partners, and in fact, they believe that making a permanent bond with their mate makes them stronger."

"The whole is greater than the sum of its individual parts?"

"Exactly." Damien nodded. "I know I disappointed you, Petra, and I know I was wrong, but I'll take that chance you offered."

She considered him. "I thought you came just for your son."

He smiled at her. "I thought so, too, but seeing you again has made me realize how empty my life has been without you. Come with me, Petra. Be partners with me."

She averted her gaze, her throat working. "It's not up to me. We have to appeal to Hades, but you have to know that he never lets anyone leave."

"I won't believe it. The darkfire has to be making the impossible possible. I have to believe that if you decide to be with me, then we will be able to leave."

She considered him for a long moment. "You won't abandon me again?"

"Never."

Petra studied him for a long moment. She squeezed his hand and kissed his cheek, then turned and walked into the dark water. The water stained the hem of her tunic first, making the fabric look dark. She walked steadily into the water, showing a bravery Damien wished he felt, especially when the first of the snakes wound around her legs. He shuddered and couldn't bear to watch, but couldn't turn away either.

As Petra continued to wade deeper, the snakes merely slipped around her body. They seemed to create a path for her and carry on with their own business, untroubled by her presence. It looked as if the water was only as deep as her hips.

"I wish I were an Earthdaughter," Damien muttered.

Petra laughed. "You aren't. Hurry up."

He clenched his fists and tried to control his breathing. He eyed the distance to the far shore and tried to estimate the number of steps. He wished he hadn't lost his shifting powers. He wished the river wasn't full of snakes. He wished he didn't have to cross it to ask Hades to make an exception. He wished he wasn't so terrified.

But Damien had to follow Petra. He forced himself to take a step closer to the water, and then another. He took a trio of deep breaths, told himself he could do it, and took a step into the dark water. The first snake wound over the top of his boot, sinuous and revolting.

But it continued on its way. Damien felt cold sweat slide down his back as he took another step. The water was over the top of his boots in three steps, cold and slimy enough to make him shudder as it ran over his feet. He wouldn't think about snakes slithering in there with it, wouldn't think of how many of them there were, wouldn't think about the way it was hard to push his legs through the barricade of their bodies. He shivered, feeling chilled to the bone.

He kept his thoughts on his goal. He lifted his gaze to Petra and the far shore.

He looked up just in time to see her slip.

She cried out as she fell and he guessed that she had lost her balance because of the baby.

Then she disappeared under the water.

"No!" Damien shouted Petra's name in dismay. She didn't answer, and she didn't surface. He tried again to shift shape, but it still didn't work.

All the while, he was striding further into the river, wanting only to reach her. She couldn't drown, not in this place. He couldn't lose her again.

He flung aside snakes, clearing his path with his hands and fighting his disgust. The only thing that mattered was Petra. Damien targeted the spot where he was sure he'd seen her go under. It was taking too long to reach her, he feared, and he would find her when it was too late.

He barely noticed the slight pain on his chest, and he certainly didn't see the dark green dragon scale slip from beneath the hem of his shirt, slide over the bodies of the snakes, then disappear as it was submerged in the River Leche.

Forgotten.

He didn't know if Petra could die again, but he did now that if he lost her in this river, he'd lose her for all time.

Nothing could keep him from giving his all to prevent that, even millions of snakes.

Petra was drowning all over again. She felt that first dismay

like a sharp pang, reliving the moment when they'd realized the vessel was in danger. She saw the dark water gathering on the bottom of the boat, and knew it was coming in too fast. She looked, as she had that fateful day, and noted how far it was to shore. In a heartbeat, she knew they could never reach safety before the boat sank.

She fell to her knees, helping to bail the bottom of the boat, shaking with the certainty that all efforts were futile. The wind whipped at the sails, spinning the boat like a toy. The women on board wept. Petra could only feel the weight of her unborn child, and the burden of her failure.

The water was up to her knees in no time, dark and so cold that she soon couldn't feel her feet. She wished her gift had been associated with water or with air, but this was one place her link with the earth could do no good.

She felt powerless for the first time in her life, and despair washed over her.

She cried out to the Erinyes to avenge her on the father of her child.

Then the boat sank with startling speed. Petra was terrified when the water touched her belly and she heard herself scream when the boat dropped from beneath her feet. She was plunged into the cold sea, struggling to reach the surface. She wasn't a swimmer and never had been, but her instinct to survive was strong.

She reached the surface and took a single breath before an angry wave crashed over her. She was driven down into the depths again, as if Poseidon himself was determined to claim her forever. Petra fought her way upward again, losing her direction as the sea churned around her. She was alone and wondered what had become of the other people on the boat.

This time, she had a chance to look when she broke the surface. All she could see was churning water in every direction. She shouted, but the wind snatched away her voice. She thought she could hear cries for help, but couldn't guess the direction.

She couldn't even see land anymore. The sea rose and fell, swirling around her and tugging her down. Petra panicked, then saw a piece of the boat not far away. The wood was smashed but floating. She fought to approach it, then the sea lifted it on a wave.

She had a moment to think that providence was on her side, that the water was bringing her the piece of wood and she'd be able to survive. Then the wave crashed over her and the wood slammed into her temple.

Then there was only darkness on all sides.

Darkness and oblivion.

Petra sank, knowing there'd be no reprieve for her now.

Damien's knees weakened when he reached into the snakes and felt the curve of Petra's hip. He plunged his hands in so that he was up to his shoulders in cold water and slithering snakes.

Petra was there. He grabbed her and hauled her to the surface, clearing the muck of the river and a few smaller snakes from her face. He couldn't tell if she was breathing or not and didn't intend to linger in the river to find out.

Her expression was peaceful, her features so tranquil that he feared the worst.

He strode to the shore that had been their destination, relieved to find the ground rise up quickly beneath his boots. He laid Petra on the dry bank, even as rivulets of water ran from her clothes. Her lashes fluttered slightly, but he saw that the color that had bloomed in her cheeks after his kiss had faded again. Her pallor and the chill of her hands terrified him.

He found himself whispering her name, as if his voice alone could rouse her or repeating her name could reassure him. He ran one fingertip across her cool lips before he realized the same strategy might work again. He bent and touched his lips to hers, hoping against hope that she would revive beneath his touch.

To his relief, darkfire burned and shimmered between them, touching Petra's features with its ethereal glow, filling Damien's body with heat. He could only hope that his kiss passed it to Petra. He kissed her again and again, hoping the spark would light to a flame, that the power of his kind could save the woman he loved.

He loved Petra, and he'd never told her so.

Damien only hoped he hadn't realized the truth too late.

When Petra lifted one hand to his shoulder and parted her lips beneath his own, Damien's hope surged. He caught her close and deepened his kiss, pouring all he felt for her into his touch, telling her with his embrace what he'd never told her in words. Petra clung to him, her arms wrapping around him to hold him close, her kiss meeting him measure for measure. He saw the darkfire brighten between then and heat to a brilliant white glow, a hot white light that wouldn't soon be extinguished. When he lifted his head and reluctantly broke his kiss, she was flushed and rosy again.

Even more importantly, she smiled at him. Her gaze was so warm that he could have basked in it forever.

"Well," she said. "Thank you."

"I owed you for Cerberus."

"Does that make us even then?" Petra teased. "So we now go our separate ways?"

"No! Though we are even," Damien said gruffly, pleased and confused. Feeling both at the same time was disconcerting, but not all bad. He'd survived the electricity of living with Petra before, after all, and had missed the spark she put in his day.

She was waiting for him to say something, so he tried to indicate his changed feelings. "It's important in a partnership to keep everything balanced."

"Is that so? Suddenly you know so much about balanced relationships?" She was teasing him, her tone light and playful.

"No, but I'm trying to learn."

"Oh, I want to meet these other *Pyr*," Petra said with purpose, reaching for his hand to get to her feet. Damien caught both her hands in his and lifted her up. "I want to meet the dragons who managed to change your thinking."

"It wasn't them," he admitted. Damien saw the tentative hope in her eyes and reached to draw her closer again. "It was you." He tipped up her chin with one fingertip. "I love you, Petra. Let's be partners."

She smiled and her eyes lit with the promise of their future. "Oh, Damien, I've loved you all along."

Damien bent his head to kiss Petra again, to secure the agreement with a scorching kiss, but his lips never touched hers.

There was a scream overhead, and he looked up to see two enormous birds descending toward them. He tried to shelter Petra beneath him and struggled again to shift shape without success.

"The Erinyes!" Petra whispered, and Damien saw that she was right. Just like the creature he'd killed, they were women, not birds, women with wings like bats and blood running from their eyes. They had fangs and long yellowed nails, just like their sister.

And writhing snakes for their hair.

Of course.

"Is this when we pay death's price?" Petra whispered, but Damien pulled his dagger. He was aware of Petra humming, but concentrated on the Erinyes. They swooped low, snatching and screaming. The stench of them was foul. When they dove at him, Damien managed to nick the wing of one of them.

They screamed even louder, even as the blood spurted.

"You broke your word!" she cried at Damien.

"You betrayed her trust," screamed the second.

He expected Petra to do something, because she'd been humming as she did when she invoked her power. He spared a glance her way and she shook her head.

So, neither of them had their powers.

This was not good.

The Erinyes swooped low again and Damien leapt up to stab at the second one. There had to be a way out of the underworld and a lesser price they could pay than death. What sacrifice would work? He'd already killed one of these creatures.

A snake launched itself from the leg of the second sister, falling on Damien as it hissed and spat. He decapitated it and flung its body aside.

"Oath-breaker, oath-breaker," chanted the Erinyes overhead.

"He didn't break his word," Petra shouted. "He never promised me anything."

It was true, but didn't sound like much of an endorsement to Damien's ears.

"I invoked you in anger," Petra said, her tone firm. "It was a mistake."

The Erinyes screamed as if being tortured, but they didn't fly away. They dropped lower, wings flapping, eyes bleeding, snakes hissing. Damien wasn't sure what to watch or where to strike.

Petra distracted him then by crying out in dismay. He looked back to see that her water had broken, and that dark liquid was spreading across the ground. "Our son," she whispered, the light of hope in her eyes. "He's coming."

Damien had to get Petra and their son out of this realm.

"He still murdered our sister, Tisiphone," the two Erinyes whispered in unison, then lunged at him, claws bared as they screamed for vengeance.

Damien roared and dove after the Erinyes, his dagger held high. They leapt out of his path, in the same moment that a flash of lightning blinded Petra.

She opened her eyes to find Hades himself standing before them. The god was dressed in long dark robes. His beard and brow were silvered and his expression was grim. They weren't in the same place anymore, because the River Leche was gone. To Damien's dismay, they were back in the forest of stone trees.

And the corpse of the Erinye he'd killed was at the god's feet.

"Who dares to slaughter one of my own?" he demanded in a voice like thunder.

The two surviving Erinyes landed on either side of Damien. Before he could evade them, they seized his arms and shoved him forward, so that he fell on his knees before the ruler of the underworld.

He looked up and doubted he had anything to offer that Hades might want.

But Damien was determined to try.

Damien loved her.

It was everything Petra had ever wanted and more. He hadn't just said the words she'd wanted to hear: he'd proved his feelings with actions, as a dragon ought to do. He'd saved her, he'd committed to being partners with her, and now she had to use her powers to get them free of the Erinyes and the underworld.

She would have tried but her water had broken, and the sensation had been enough to take her to her knees. Her womb contracted and she felt her son moving downward.

Petra had feared the worst when the Erinyes attacked, for they could devise the most vicious torments. Damien was determined to defend her, but she knew he was weary. They couldn't both be confined here forever, not now!

Petra couldn't argue her case, not with her whole body tightening in preparation for another contraction. It seemed that her son wasn't just as stubborn as Damien but as resolute, too. Now that he'd decided to be born, he wasn't going to waste any time about it.

"Did you do this deed?" Hades demanded of Damien, gesturing to the lifeless Erinye at his feet.

"She attacked me," Damien said. "I had no choice."

"No choice but to die," Hades said. "And you were already in the realm of the dead." He bent down and touched the cheek of the ancient hag. Even the snakes of her hair had stilled. "She was always a loyal servant."

The other two Erinyes began to wail, and the blood flowed more quickly from their eyes. Hades spared them a glance, then granted Damien a stern look. "You will pay a price for this."

"I apologize for killing one of your own," Damien said tightly.

Hades smiled. "The price will be higher than that." He straightened then reached out one hand in obvious expectation. A servant leapt forward and put a chalice into his outstretched hand. Petra assumed it was wine or another refreshment, but Hades only sniffed the contents. He then poured the dark liquid over the body of Tisiphone. "Tisiphone, the face of retaliation and the avenger of murder, take life again and exact your own vengeance upon your murderer and his kind. Pursue them through all eternity, until your thirst for revenge is sated."

As Petra watched, the body of Tisiphone began to change. She shifted shape from a winged harridan to a cobra then to a lithe woman with red hair. In the blink of an eye, she was a harridan again, the rotation between forms becoming faster and faster until her form blurred.

And then she disappeared.

"Where did she go?" one of her sisters asked.

"You all three have walked in whichever realm you chose. Tisiphone will live only in the realm of the living until her vengeance is served." He gave Damien a hard look. "She will strike among the living, even as she abides in secret. His kind will never know of her vendetta until her vengeance is served."

Petra was appalled. She could see Damien's consternation and knew of his loyalty to the *Pyr*. "But they have to be warned!" she said, even as her womb tightened for a contraction.

"I see no reason for it," Hades said.

"Let her go," Damien begged the god. "Let her go so our son can live."

"It could be argued that he's dead already," Hades replied mildly.

"Take me instead," Damien said with a vigor that shocked Petra. "Take me instead."

"You just want her to warn the *Pyr*."

"Forbid her to do that, but let her go!" Damien appealed, and Petra was amazed that he was more concerned for her than his fellows. "Let her have our child in the world. I'll stay here instead."

"Forever?" Hades asked.

"Forever," Damien said with resolve.

"Snakes and all?" Petra whispered.

Damien swallowed, then looked her in the eye. "Even with the snakes."

"There's no guarantee she'll survive childbirth, even if I do agree," Hades observed. "Your son might not even survive. You could be sacrificing yourself for nothing."

"I don't care. I want to give her the chance." Damien was resolute. "She gave me a chance and I didn't deserve it."

Hades considered them for a long moment and Petra found herself breathing quickly as the pain rose within her.

"No," he said flatly. "It would set a precedent. It's far simpler for both of you to stay."

"You can't keep Damien here," Petra argued. "He's not dead."

"It's only a matter of time before that's resolved," Hades said. "And we have nothing but time in this realm."

Petra felt her womb tighten even as her fury rose. She called to the earth, to the stones, to the rocks and roots of the world. She felt the tumult build even as her own contraction grew. She summoned it and gathered it and drew it unto herself to wield it.

"Petra," Damien whispered in awe.

"What is this?" Hades demanded, even as the ground underfoot trembled. "Stop this immediately!" he cried.

"No! We will not stay!" Petra opened her mouth and roared, commanding the earth to move just as her womb contracted. "We have sacrificed! We have paid! And we are alive!" She felt her son move and channeled the pain with her powers, compelling the element of earth to respond to her command.

The ground underfoot shook hard. It buckled and rolled, then suddenly cracked wide. A large dark fissure opened between them and the ruler of the realm, and snakes spewed from it to scatter in every direction. Damien muttered an oath, but held fast to Petra's hand. There was a rumble of moving rock.

Petra summoned her strength and pushed harder, directing her efforts upward. The entire realm shook, like a straw house in the wind. There was a deafening boom and the darkness overhead split wide open.

A ray of sunlight stabbed into the underworld. The dead shouted in mingled dismay and delight, but Petra wasn't done. Their escape path was clear, but they weren't through it yet. She called to the earth, she drew upon her powers and the land beneath their feet rippled.

It convulsed.

Another contraction began deep in her body and she used it, clenching her fists to drive the power as she wished. The ground folded and shifted, and shoved them high into the sky. Damien caught her close so she wouldn't lose her footing, and she held on to him tightly.

"No one leaves this realm!" Hades cried in dismay.

"Try to stop us," Damien muttered, resolve making his eyes shine. "Come on, Petra. One more good shove."

"Yes," she agreed, and mustered her strength again. She was tired, but she had to save Damien and their son. She pushed hard, closing her eyes as she gave her all.

Suddenly, there was a thunderclap. The crack began to close overhead, sealing the underworld once again.

"No!" Damien cried and leapt upward.

He might have called to the shaft of sunlight. It pierced the darkness as if targeting him and struck him like a bolt of lightning. Petra saw the shimmer of blue-green darkfire roll over Damien's body and feared Hades had claimed his life, after all.

Then Damien shouted with joy and her relief made her

tremble.

"Yes!" he bellowed and Petra knew what would happen. She laughed when she saw the pale blue shimmer of light surround his body and squeezed her eyes shut. Damien shifted shape with glorious speed, and she thrilled as always at the beauty of his dragon form. She opened her eyes to find herself securely in his grasp, his scales cool and hard beneath her hands. She could feel his muscled strength and she delighted in the power of his wings and tail.

Without a moment's hesitation, he soared toward the sky, holding her safely against his chest as his powerful wings beat hard. Petra felt a waft of fresh wind on her face, smelled the green of the hills and dared to hope that they would succeed.

The crack was closing steadily, as if it would cheat them of freedom right at the last. Petra knew that if they were trapped in the underworld, Hades would make them pay for their transgression for all eternity. She could hear him shouting far below and willed the earth to shake violently in the hope of silencing him.

"Faster," she whispered to her dragon, even though she knew Damien was already testing his limits.

The crack began to close even more quickly. Petra was afraid it was already too narrow for Damien's width. He surged forward, his wings beating furiously. He leapt through the crack with a final burst of speed, twisting as he flew to work himself through the narrowing gap.

The fissure snapped shut behind them and he shouted as it claimed the tip of his tail.

Against all expectation, they were free.

"Are you all right?" Petra demanded and Damien laughed.

"Never better." He soared high in the midday sky, clearly reveling in the return of his powers. The sunlight glinted on his scales, making him sparkle like a gem.

"Your scales," she said with wonder.

Damien looked over himself, then grinned with pride. "Like it?"

The color of his scales had changed, from deep green dipped in gold to gold dipped in green. He was magnificent in the sunlight, like a piece of jewelry designed to dazzle.

"It must be because you survived the realm of the dead." Petra couldn't help thinking that one day they would both return there.

"I sacrificed the tip of my tail, Petra," Damien said, his eyes dancing. "And we will spend the rest of our days paying homage to Hades in gratitude for our release."

"You think that will appease him?"

"I plan to spend a lot of years working at it." He smiled at her, and his confidence was infectious. "I think we have a very good chance of fulfilling the prophecy, Petra."

Her heart clenched tightly. Claiming the firestorm's promise sounded wonderful to her, but her son had a more immediate plan. She held tightly to Damien as another contraction rolled through her body. He watched in concern, keeping them airborne.

"A mountaintop?" he asked her. "The soft soil of a clearing? Tell me where you want to be, Petra, and I'll get you there."

"With the Mothers," she said softly. Petra opened her eyes and saw immediately that Damien was missing a scale on his chest. She'd never noticed that before, but there was no time to ask him for details.

Petra surveyed their surroundings and was thrilled to recognize the land. "There," she said, pointing to a peak crested with stones.

"You're sure?"

"Very sure. We're near the Mothers, Damien, which is exactly where I had hoped to be."

He didn't bother with questions, although she could see his curiosity. He flew toward the peak she'd indicated, moving more quickly and surely than she'd imagined possible. Petra's chest tightened as she saw the familiar circle of stones cresting the peak, the clearing in the middle thick with green plants.

She directed Damien to the spot and he circled with caution before he landed, checking their safety. As he deposited Petra with care on the thick greenery, the ground shifted slightly to one side, startling him.

Petra smiled, having anticipated that the Mothers would take care of her. A spring bubbled from the crack in the ground, trickling beside her.

"But where are the Mothers?" he asked, glancing around himself in confusion.

"All around you," Petra said, indicating the standing stones that encircled them. "You'll see."

CHAPTER FIVE

Damien shifted back to his human form in time to watch Petra endure another contraction. It was hard to watch her in such pain, yet he felt lucky to be in her presence. He was amazed that his son might be saved, after all, and terrified that the infant might not survive. It seemed that Petra always prompted a mix of emotions in him, all powerful, all impressive. He watched as Petra clenched her teeth at the pain and he hoped their son would arrive quickly. She was panting when this one was completed, her fingers dug into the moss and sweat on her brow.

Damien tried to distract her with a comment.

"You knew that spring would spout," he said as he knelt beside her.

"It's the gift of the Mothers," Petra said, gesturing again to the circle of stones around them.

Damien barely spared the stones a glance. If she wanted to call stones by a particular name, that was fine by him. He was more concerned that he knew nothing about the arrival of children and they were on an isolated mountaintop.

Surely he couldn't make another mistake that would cost him Petra?

"This is where you intended to come?" he asked as she caught her breath.

"I thought it superstition that Earthdaughters should give birth in the presence of the Mothers. I thought the rules didn't apply, not if I'd found a man who was more than a man."

"But when the baby stilled..."

Petra nodded. "I feared that I'd broken the rules. I tried to come here then."

Damien took her hand, because he didn't know what else to do. He tried to hide his concern and speak calmly. "But Petra, we're on the top of a mountain and I know nothing about the birth of children. Should I find someone to help?"

"The Mothers are here," Petra said through her teeth. He could tell from her expression that another contraction was coming.

"But..."

Petra cast him a smile. "Look, Damien. *Look* at the forebears of my kind."

And Damien looked. To his astonishment, he saw faces in the standing stones that surrounded them. Women. Old women. Wise women. Kindly women. As the next contraction ripped through her, Petra gripped his hand hard. Damien saw that the Mothers had moved closer, as if they bent over one of their own. He could see concern in those frozen faces, a concern that hadn't been there a moment before.

He looked at Petra in amazement.

She laughed a little at him. "You think you have all the marvels?" she teased and he was embarrassed that he had thought as much. "They come out of their stones for a birth," she said, bracing herself for another contraction. "They ensure that all is well. I can see them and those of my kind can see them." She spared him a look, then asked a quick question. "Can you see them?"

Damien smiled. "It's like the stones are melting," he whispered. "They're breaking free of the rock."

"The Mothers are eternal," Petra winced.

"But what are they? Why are they like this?" He had to wonder if this would be Petra's fate, and as much as she held the Mothers in esteem, he hoped not.

"They are Earthdaughters who never met a man who was more than a man."

Damien's gaze locked with hers. "And what of those who do?"

Petra smiled tightly. "Who would sacrifice a partnership like ours to become a standing stone?" Damien had only a heartbeat to smile at that, then Petra screamed as the next contraction ripped through her body.

Damien saw the stones move even closer, one bending over on either side of Petra. When he narrowed his eyes, he could see the forms of elderly women, their hair grey and their faces lined, their eyes filled with the wisdom of the ages. When he strained his ears, he could hear them murmuring, like pebbles falling into a crevasse.

He knew they were advising Petra, because she nodded and smiled at them, following their instructions. He sat back and simply witnessed the birth of his son, within the circle of the Mothers, so wise and kind and giving.

As Petra finished her contraction, there was a whisper in Damien's ear.

"Harder," he said. "Push harder the next time."

Petra flicked a skeptical glance his way. "I thought you knew nothing about the birth of children."

He flashed her a confident smile. "The Mothers are teaching me. By the time we have our next son, I'll be able to help you alone, wherever we are." He laughed at the shushing of the Mothers, their soft disapproval on all sides. "But I'll bring you here, even so." He felt the ripple of their satisfaction, then Petra's next contraction came.

She pushed and she panted, she screamed when she had to and she held fast to Damien's hand. The sun had sunk a little lower by the time Damien saw the baby's head appear and was dipping low when his son's lusty cry reverberated from the stony peak.

He was a beautiful hale boy, with hair as blond as honey.

Damien smiled at the sight of him, a survivor of the underworld. Both of them had been touched by their time there. Damien had realized the value of what he had left behind, and knew better than to make that mistake again. His son had been given the opportunity to live. Darkfire had given Damien the most precious gift possible, in the second chance of his firestorm.

He washed his son while Petra dozed, and the Mothers slowly returned to their previous positions. He wrapped the baby in Petra's chiton, beneath the gazes of a circle of roughly hewn grey stones.

Petra opened her eyes then and Damien helped her to clean up. Finally, he tucked their son into her arms, made a fire and wrapped himself around her back for warmth.

"Our *next* son," Petra repeated. "What makes you think I'll let you seduce me again?"

Damien laughed. "What makes you think you'll be able to resist me?" He kissed her soundly then, loving that she met him touch for touch. His breath was coming quickly when he lifted his head, and he grinned down at her even as she frowned.

"Your hair," she said, reaching up to touch him.

"What about it?"

"It's pale now, like flax."

"Like our son's, you mean."

Petra looked startled, then checked their son's head. She met Damien's gaze in amazement.

"Good thing you had a fair son, or people would think he wasn't mine." He pretended to be horrified by the thought and Petra laughed.

"It's because you escaped the realm of the dead," she guessed. "It had to leave some mark on you and him."

"And what about you?"

"I was dead. I belonged there."

"Until the darkfire gave us a second chance." Damien held her closer as she traced the tattoo on his upper arm with one fingertip.

"Where did you get this mark? You didn't have it before."

"We all got them. It's called a tattoo and is made with needles and dye."

Petra peered more closely at the tattoo. "But it's what you are. A dragon."

Damien nodded. "The entire legion got them at once. Our nature was the one constant in our world and it seemed like the right thing to do at the time."

"You don't know where they are," Petra said softly.

"If the darkfire has taken them to their firestorms, I know they're happy," Damien said with resolve. Petra smiled at him as the baby stirred. His lips pursed as he rooted against Petra's breast, seeking a nipple.

"Impatient, just like his father," Petra murmured.

"He needs a name," Damien said. "I don't think Impatient or Stubborn will work."

"You had a friend," Petra said. "That night the firestorm sparked."

"Orion."

She watched him with a smile. "A good friend?"

"A very good friend." Damien smiled. "Last I saw him, he was having a firestorm several hundred miles west of here and several thousand years in the future."

"You won't see him again, then."

"You never know, not when the darkfire's burning." He pressed a kiss to her temple. "But I like the idea of naming our son after him, either way."

Petra caught her breath as their son found her nipple and closed his mouth around it. "Hello, Orion," she whispered. "I suppose all of you *Pyr* warriors know what you want and aren't afraid to go after it."

Damien didn't laugh at her joke. Between two of the Mothers, the vegetation was moving in a distinctive way.

"Snakes," Damien hissed.

He jumped up and drew his dagger. Petra turned to look, then smiled.

"They bite," Damien insisted.

"Not this one." Petra put her hand on his arm. "Put the weapon away and take the baby."

"How do you know?"

"Where do snakes live?"

"In the earth."

Petra gave him a hard look and Damien ceded the point. She must be able to hear or understand them. He didn't like it, but he sheathed his dagger, then lifted his son from Petra's arms. He nestled the boy close, then offered her his hand. Petra smiled at him as she accepted his help.

"Partnership," she murmured, coaxing his smile again.

Then she knelt down to part the grass. Her move revealed a snake of the same blue-green hue as the darkfire. Its tongue flicked, then it turned and disappeared into the vegetation.

Something gleamed on the ground where it had been. Petra gasped in surprise when she reached for it, and Damien tried to see over her shoulder. There was a large green scale on the ground, one tipped with gold.

A dragon scale.

"It brought your missing scale!" she said with delight, bending to pick it up.

"My scale?"

"You have one that's missing," Petra said, placing a fingertip on one side of his chest. "I noticed when we flew out of the underworld." She looked up at him. "Can it be repaired?"

"Yes," Damien said with authority, then he smiled because their path had become clear to him. "And now I know exactly where we have to go."

"Where?"

"Delphi."

"For a new prophecy?"

"For a future. The *Pyr* have always had a strong link with Delphi. I have a feeling it's gotten stronger." He tapped the scale, certain that he'd find Alexander or word of him at Delphi. He was sure that Alexander would have created a plan for the future and that he could have a part in it, just for the asking.

Petra studied him, clearly mystified by his mood. "You know something I don't know."

"I hope more than one thing," Damien teased and Petra laughed.

"Tell me!"

"These *Pyr* I met, each one loses a scale when he falls in love with his mate." Damien grinned at her, inviting her to make the connection. He could see in her eyes that she understood and was pleased, but she teased him all the same.

"What if the mate doesn't love her dragon back?"

He pretended to be downcast. "Then I guess she wouldn't help him repair his armor. He'd be vulnerable when he fought, if he didn't die first of a broken heart."

Petra's lips parted to argue, then Damien began to smile. He heard the distant beat of dragon wings and knew they wouldn't have to go all the way to Delphi for his scales to be repaired. Petra studied him for a moment, trying to guess what was giving him such pleasure, then turned to scan the evening sky. The stars were just coming out, but Damien pointed out the silhouettes of a phalanx of approaching dragons.

"Alexander!" Damien shouted.

"How can you tell?" Petra demanded, for the dragons were still far away.

Damien tapped the side of his nose. "We recognize each other by scent." He narrowed his eyes, using his keen senses to inspect the new arrivals. "There's a woman with him, probably his mate, Katina. Six *Pyr* I don't know and two young boys with them." Damien took a long deep breath, liking that he could show off for her. "Also *Pyr*, but too young to shift shape." He cast her a look. "If Alexander has two sons, we're going to have to catch up."

"I suppose I should have expected dragons to be competitive," Petra mused and Damien laughed. Then he shifted shape to greet his fellows, carrying his son to meet his old friend.

Petra was entranced.

She'd never seen any of the other *Pyr* before, and the sight of so many of them at once took her breath away. The splendid sight of Damien in dragon form make her heart leap, and the change in the hue of his scales would remind them both always of how close they'd come to sacrificing everything.

The company of dragons landed in the clearing, their eyes flashing and their scales gleaming. Petra heard a rumble like thunder, even though the sky was clear, then there was a familiar glow of pale blue light. She closed her eyes and opened them again to find Damien leading a man with dark hair and dark eyes toward her. He held the hand of a pretty woman who smiled at Petra in understanding.

This must be his mate. Petra smiled in return, feeling that she looked less than her best but guessing the other woman must understand.

"Petra, this is Alexander. He was Drake's second-in-command, and we served together. His wife, Katina, his son, Lysander, and Drake's son, Theo."

Petra spoke to each of them, then was introduced to the others in the company. They admired her fine strong son and made her feel welcome. She noticed Damien and Alexander standing together, as if in conference, just as there was another rumble of thunder. The two *Pyr* warriors looked serious. Petra glanced at the sky in confusion.

"Old-speak," Katina said, appearing at her side with a smile.

"It's how they communicate with each other when they don't want us to overhear."

"It's not always that," Alexander protested. "Sometimes, it's just habit."

The women shared a smile, then Katina dropped her voice. "I'll guess that Alexander is asking for tidings of Drake."

"He's still with the darkfire crystal, as far as I know," Petra murmured and the other woman nodded. "How did you know where to find us?"

Katina smiled. "I don't mean to alarm you, but I'm a naiad. Some call us Waterdaughters. I have very strong intuition and I had a compelling sense that we should come to this place right now." She glanced around, her gaze assessing. "It seems a powerful place," she mused, then looked at Petra.

"For a woman to choose to give birth, you mean?"

Katina nodded.

"I don't mean to alarm you, but I'm an Earthdaughter," Petra echoed with a smile. "You are standing on sacred ground for my kind." She gestured to the stones. "These are the Mothers, those of my kind who have gone before and provide sanctuary to us in times of need."

Katina surveyed the stones, assessment in her eyes. "Does it violate the sanctity for us to be here?"

"Not if it is in aid of me and my son."

She glanced down at the scale Petra held in her hand and seemed to know immediately what it was. Relief crossed her features, then concern. "We would ask your permission, and that of the Mothers, to repair Damien's armor here, within the circle of their protection."

Petra felt a lump in her throat. "I believe they would be honored to witness it."

"We will leave an offering, of whatever is fitting."

"The request is enough," Petra said, because she knew it was true.

"There must be a gift from the mate," Katina said quietly, her gaze searching. "It ensures that the repair holds and that his armor is complete."

"A gift?"

"Something of one of the elements associated with you in this partnership would be best. You must decide and you must give it freely."

"I am earth and Damien is fire," Petra mused.

"But one of you also represents air and one, water, as well," Katina said. "Having all four elements in concert gives the firestorm its power."

Petra had Damien's scale already. What she most wanted to do was share the protective powers of the Mothers with her dragon. She looked around the clearing, wondering how that could be done. One of the Mothers wavered, just outside her field of vision, and when Petra turned to look, a small stone broke free of the large standing stone. She hurried to pick it up, liking how powerful it felt when her hand closed over it.

She glanced up to find Damien's gaze upon her, and his smile warmed her to her toes. Of course, he and Alexander had heard every word, with their keen hearing, and she wasn't surprised to see Alexander summon the others to the fire as soon as she had chosen the stone.

"We will take our dragon forms, each in turn," he said and the younger *Pyr* nodded. They were all attractive men and clearly a disciplined company. Each one had a mark on his body, like the dragon mark on Damien's arm, even though they couldn't be of his company of Dragon Legion Warriors lost in time. She wondered how these *Pyr* had obtained their tattoos.

There was no time to ask, though, for the dragon warriors were moving with purpose. Damien stood on Alexander's left, with Petra and their son beside him. Katina stood on Alexander's right, with Lysander and then Theo beside her. The others took their places around the fire, forming a circle.

The fire in the middle burned higher when the circle was complete, and Petra realized that these *Pyr* warriors had their own link to an element. She remembered the prophecy and smiled.

Fire and stone must pay the price.

That was Damien and herself, and they'd paid it in full.

Now the firestorm's promise would be theirs.

Alexander shifted shape first, becoming a dark dragon in the same moment that the flames leapt skyward. Damien shifted next, and Petra loved how the fire again stretched for the sky, its light reflecting off his newly golden scales. The other *Pyr* shifted shape in unison and she saw that they were all darker and smaller than the two fully fledged warriors. She saw glimpses of color in the scales of each, but guessed that their hues had yet to develop.

When all had shifted shape, Alexander extended his claw to her, obviously requesting the fallen scale. Petra surrendered it to him and he held it between the tips of his talons, then pushed it into the flames of the fire. The bonfire burned higher, as if fueled by the scale and Petra couldn't see it in the brilliant blaze of orange.

"Fire," Alexander intoned and the *Pyr* echoed him. He extended his hand to her again, and Petra gave him the stone. Alexander removed the scale from the flames and it was the same bright golden color of the rest of Damien's scales. He pushed the stone against it and Petra saw that the scale was so hot that it was molten. Alexander drove the stone into it, as if forcing a gem into a setting.

"Earth," he said and the other *Pyr* repeated his word.

Alexander pushed the scale back into the fire and the flames licked it hungrily. When he removed it again, both it and the stone from the Mothers had fused into one and were so hot that they were pale yellow and smoking.

He extended the scale and Damien blew on it.

"Air," Alexander said, along with the other *Pyr*.

Alexander lifted the scale and pressed it against the bare spot on Damien's chest. Petra heard the hiss as it seared his flesh and she stepped forward in concern. Damien tipped back his head and roared at the pain.

To Petra's surprise, Alexander touched her cheek with his claw. "Water," he murmured, transferring her tear to the hot scale. The water sizzled against it, sending up a stream of vapor as it disappeared. To her relief, the scale darkened immediately and Damien shuddered in relief.

Alexander then lifted her son from her arms and held him high. "Welcome, Orion! Welcome to the new *Pyr* among us!" The *Pyr* roared approval, each one tipping back his head to send a blaze of dragonfire into the sky.

There was a crack like lightning and a blue-green bolt of

darkfire appeared out of nowhere. Petra gasped when it touched her son, but then it was gone and he was gurgling happily. The flames of the bonfire leapt toward the sky, casting a joyous spray of sparks in every direction as if in celebration, and Damien caught both her and her son close to his chest.

Petra checked the baby, only to discover that there was a small mark on his arm, just like his father's.

"He's one of us," Damien murmured to her and Petra nodded, glancing at the Mothers. He was of her kind as well, and she couldn't wait to see what that combination brought in the future.

Damien flew a triumphant circle around the peak of the mountain, making Petra laugh with his obvious happiness. The *Pyr* cheered as he landed and shifted shape quickly, holding Petra fast against his chest.

When he kissed her thoroughly, Petra could only return his embrace in kind. Her heart was alight with happiness and she had the urge to sing that love song to him again. Against all expectation, they'd been given the second chance they needed to make their partnership work.

Nothing would ever drive them apart again.

Kiss of Destiny

He will sacrifice anything to win his destined love...

When the darkfire crystal takes the dragon shape shifters Thad and Drake to an unknown location, only fulfilling his firestorm matters to Thad. Little does he know that in following its light to his destined mate, he's stepping into the realm of the gods, a place so forbidden to mortals that any who enter it must die. Aura has always been skeptical of long-term promises—but Thad is irresistible. No sooner does Aura surrender than the gods demand their due of her dragon shifter. Can she save Thad and make the dream of the firestorm come true?

PROLOGUE

Drake had never been more exhausted in his life. He could barely keep his eyes open, but he didn't dare to close them. He didn't trust the darkfire crystal to sleep while he did. He didn't know how long they'd been suffering through this ordeal with the unpredictable stone, but he didn't think he could survive much more of it.

There was just himself and Thad left, the younger Dragon Legion Warrior filled with an enthusiasm that Drake couldn't match.

They were together in a nameless park, sitting on the lip of a concrete fountain. Night was falling and the stars were coming out. The park, which had been busy earlier in the day, was becoming more and more quiet, as people returned home with their children and dogs. Unless Drake missed his guess, this park was in an American city in the twenty-first century. Their clothing blended in well enough here for them to avoid scrutiny.

Drake wondered if that would be the case if they stretched out and slept on the benches.

"I wonder why it brought us here," Thad mused. He was like a curious child, thrilled with every place the darkfire crystal deposited them and intent upon figuring out the stone's logic.

"It could be whim," Drake said.

Thad shook his head. "No, there has to be a reason. There has to be a point."

Drake said nothing. He'd learned long ago that many events in life didn't have a point. All the same, he remembered having

Thad's optimism once, many, many years ago.

"There's no firestorm's spark," Drake couldn't help but observe. "Maybe your theory is wrong."

"No, it makes perfect sense for the darkfire crystal to take us to our firestorms. That way, we find our destined mates and make more *Pyr*."

"Perhaps the darkfire thinks there are enough dragon shape shifters in the world. It was released by the *Slayer* Chen, and he has no fondness for our kind."

"It's older than he is, I think, and strong enough to use him for its purposes."

"You don't know."

Thad grinned. "No, but I like that answer better."

"Even if it isn't the truth?"

Thad leaned closer and bumped shoulders with Drake, a gesture of such familiarity that Drake was shocked. "Come on," Thad said. "Don't you want to go back to Cassandra?"

Drake didn't answer that. He stared into the depths of the stone and admitted his secret fear. Although he'd been happy enough with the results of his firestorm at the time, the centuries had changed him. He wanted more than sex and sons. He knew Cassandra was self-reliant and didn't doubt that she'd provided well enough for herself in his absence. She was practical and not afraid to be tough. She would have raised their son well. He knew, though, that if he returned to her after all his adventures, he would do so as a changed man. The man he had become might not be so content with Cassandra.

And, to be fair, Cassandra might not be very content with him. He turned the large quartz crystal in his hands thoughtfully.

When Drake thought of women, he remembered the military widow he'd helped in the modern world. Although their acquaintance had been short and businesslike, Ronnie had made an impression upon him. She was both vulnerable and strong, a woman who was used to having a partner's support to rely upon, but one who had only begun to understand her own strength. He'd found her extremely attractive, even though he knew his feelings were inappropriate. He'd been shocked that he could find a woman alluring who was so different from his Cassandra.

Her full name, Veronica, meant 'little truth,' and Drake had since concluded that it had been their brief association that had shown him the truth about himself. He wasn't the man he had once been. He didn't want what he'd wanted before, or even what he'd had. As much as he wanted to see his son and as much as he understood his responsibilities, Drake had very mixed feelings about being cast back in time to finish what he had begun.

He couldn't tell Thaddeus that, of course. The other *Pyr* wouldn't have understood. Thad was so filled with wonder and enthusiasm and optimism that Drake couldn't introduce the idea to him that the firestorm might not be right every time, or that it might not be right forever.

He might have hoped the crystal would stay dark, but that would have been cowardly.

When the blue-green spark trapped deep inside the stone began to glow more brightly, it was all Drake could do to keep from groaning aloud.

Thad noticed immediately. "This is it!" the younger warrior declared. "Do you think it will be you or me this time?"

"If you're right that the darkfire is taking each of us to our firestorm, then I hope it's you." Drake knew he sounded as weary as he felt.

Thad shot a bright glance his way. "That makes no sense. You're just thinking of the men under your command before you think of yourself." Thad paused but Drake didn't want to shatter his illusions. "I know you want to return to Cassandra and your son. It would only be right."

Drake kept silent and watched the darkfire brighten. Where would it take them this time? Was this the time that they'd be separated once and for all? Or would his Dragon Legion be reunited, after the stone completed its quest?

"That's what Alexander did," Thad said with confidence. "He returned to his Katina..."

"You don't know that for certain," Drake said sternly. "You know only that the darkfire took us to the village where he had lived with her."

"Well, why else would it do that?"

"I can't begin to guess." Actually, Drake had many ideas of what might have happened. He and his men had been enchanted for centuries. There was no telling what had occurred at their homes in their absence. There hadn't been any way to tell *when* Alexander had arrived at that village. It could have been before he'd even met Katina or long after she'd died, missing him. She could have married again or been glad to be without him, or they might not have gotten along after his return.

"You sound dire, like Peter always did." Thad laughed. "I couldn't believe the look on his face when his firestorm sparked."

"There's nothing saying he succeeded in satisfying it."

Thad laughed and the stone brightened even more. It seemed to pulse with that inner energy and Drake could feel it heating his skin. A wind swept through the park, shaking the trees and tugging at their clothes. Drake got to his feet and Thad stood beside him.

Drake supposed that one of them should have stayed in this place, and that the stone would bring them back until the dragon in question did stay. He wasn't ready to step away from his last fellow warrior, though.

Neither, evidently was Thad. The younger *Pyr* grasped his commander's shoulder so he wouldn't be left behind.

And just in time. The darkfire cracked like lightning and the park disappeared in a swirl of dust and fallen leaves. They were picked up from the ground and flung hard through the air, as if a tornado had seized them. Drake couldn't see anything but he reached out and grabbed Thad's arm, not wanting to lose the younger man.

They were cast down hard upon a stony surface and the wind stilled. The spark in the stone died to a mere pinprick of light as Drake sat up cautiously. The stone even felt cold in his hand.

They were surrounded by fog, but he had the definite sense that they were at some elevated altitude. The air seemed thin and the silence resonant. He felt there was nothing but wind and sky.

He realized belatedly that Thad was unusually silent and turned to the younger man in concern. Thad was fine, but sitting on the ground cross-legged. He was staring at the tip of the fingers on his left hand, probably because golden sparks had lit on them. His mouth had fallen open in awe but he grinned when he looked up at Drake.

"I've never felt like this," he whispered and the light wind seemed to steal his words away. "She's here. She's here somewhere and the darkfire has brought me to her!" He leapt to his feet and spun around, holding up his hand in search of a direction. Predictably, the flames flared when he stretched his hand out to one side. The rocks seemed to climb higher there, as if the peak of the mountain was that way.

Drake had time to dread Thad's reaction before the other man strode to him and shook his hand heartily. "I don't know when we'll meet again, Drake, but thank you. Thank you for all you've taught me, and all the times you've defended me, and everything." His eyes were alight with anticipation.

"Maybe we should follow the flame together," Drake managed to say before the light in the crystal shimmered again.

"Your turn is next!" Thad insisted, then shocked his commander by pulling him into a tight embrace. "Thank you, Drake. May the Great Wyvern always be with you."

And then he was gone, leaping over the rocks in pursuit of the firestorm's flame. His figure was swallowed by the fog in no time, leaving Drake looking down at the blinking stone in trepidation.

He closed his eyes when the wind raged around him. He kept them closed when he was swept off his feet. He grimaced as the maelstrom spun around him, casting him this way and that, tearing at him like he was made of straw. He both wanted it to end and feared what he'd find when it did. He winced when he fell hard against a smooth surface.

Like concrete.

The wind stilled and snowflakes landed on his face. It was cold and there was a stiff wind, one that smelled of water. It could have been blowing off a lake. He could hear the distant sound of traffic and he sensed the presence of a dragonsmoke barrier, breathed thick and deep. He caught a whiff of gunpowder and sulfur, of the chemicals used in pyrotechnics, mingled with the scents of *Pyr* he had known.

He sensed one particular dragon shape shifter, the leader of the *Pyr* himself.

Drake opened one eye warily, already having guessed where he was. He was in Chicago on the roof of the building that contained Erik Sorensson's loft, and despite himself, he was relieved. He looked down at the crystal in his hand, only to find that its heart was completely dark. Even when he peered closely at it and strained his vision, he could see no glimmer of darkfire within it.

Its quest was done. Drake was cast into the future to stay.

The darkfire crystal had brought him here as its last act, because its rightful place was in the hoard of the leader of the *Pyr*. Drake pushed to his feet wearily, only having the strength to rise because he knew he would be able to sleep as long as necessary within the protective barrier of Erik's dragonsmoke boundary.

And that was a greater gift than he'd ever expected the darkfire to give him.

CHAPTER ONE

His firestorm!

Thad barely managed to contain his excitement. He was surrounded by a dense white mist, a fog that obscured everything beyond an arm's reach. Even so, the fog was lit with a radiant orange light, the light of his firestorm, and he spun in place, trying to discern which direction was brightest.

She would be there.

He could see the rocky path beneath his feet and feel the chill of the air, but not much more than that. In three steps, he'd lost Drake completely.

Suddenly, a blue-green flash of the darkfire illuminated the fog behind him. It grew to blinding brilliance then disappeared completely. Thad swallowed, knowing that Drake was gone.

He was alone.

But the firestorm's light meant he wasn't really alone. Its golden glow shimmered on his fingertips. He lifted his hand and turned in place and, just as earlier, the firestorm sparked to flames that leapt from his fingertips to guide him to his destined mate. He felt a heat in his body and a tingling of desire, one that reminded him of the earthly aspect of the firestorm. The sparks leapt from his fingertips, as if to urge him to hurry. He took a step, saw the flames build a little higher and felt the heat increase in his body.

What did she look like? What was she feeling? Would he fall in love with her immediately, or would it take time? Thad was desperate to know. He summoned the change in his body with impatience, wanting to have the fullness of his dragon powers for this moment of moments.

Even the change seemed to be fueled by the firestorm. It swept through his body with a vehemence he'd never experienced before, making him feel so powerful that he might have been invincible. In his dragon form, Thad breathed fire at the sky in triumph. He was delighted that even his plume of flames bent in the direction of his mate. Could she feel the firestorm? Was she waiting for him? He took flight, using his keener dragon senses to try to discern more.

The fog was impenetrable, but his heart skipped at the faint scent of perfume. It came from the same direction as the firestorm's sparks led and was wonderfully feminine. It smelled of flowers and made him think of soft warm skin. Thad closed his eyes and took a deep beguiling breath of it, then flew on at reckless speed.

His dream was coming true.

Before he and his fellow Dragon's Tooth warriors had been enchanted, he'd had few expectations about the once-in-a-lifetime mating experienced by his fellow *Pyr*. The sparks flew to identify the woman who could bear the child of the dragon shape shifter in question. For most of the *Pyr* Thad had known then, a firestorm was the chance to create a son and not much more. His own mother had been loving and kind, but as a child, Thad had always felt the household was incomplete. He hadn't been able to name the omission until he came of age.

Thad had met his own father when he'd been collected from his mother's household and taken to Delphi. Theirs had been a short acquaintance and not a talkative one. His father had believed in leaving the training of young dragons to those who did it best. His obligation to his kind had been fulfilled by satisfying the firestorm, creating a son, then bringing the son to be trained when he came of age. Even though Thad had felt a yearning to know more about his father and to build a connection, his father hadn't shared his dream. After their arrival at Delphi, Thad had never seen his father again.

Drake had been different, even when Thad had first met him. Not only was Drake an experienced and respected commander, but he had married his mate and lived with her and his son. He was the first *Pyr* Thad had ever met who had made that choice. The notion of having Drake as a father and knowing him, of having the ongoing opportunity to learn from him was incredible to Thad.

But so enticing.

He supposed he shouldn't have been surprised that the *Pyr* like Drake were drawn to his command. Alexander was another who had made a commitment to his mate. After the enchantment had been broken, Thad and his fellows had found themselves in a future. There, the *Pyr* who followed Erik Sorensson made permanent relationships with their mates. They were partners, not just biological parents, and worked together to fulfill the mission of the *Pyr* to defend the earth and its treasures. Some of those dragons had multiple sons, which was remarkable to Thad. The *Pyr* almost invariably had male children, since there was only one female of their kind at any given time, but for a dragon shifter to remain with one woman and create a family was a modern notion. The contentment of those *Pyr* was clear to even a new arrival like Thad.

He had yearned to feel the spark of his firestorm in that world.

Yet mingled with the promise of such a partnership was a fear that the Great Wyvern had forgotten the old firestorms or the more ancient *Pyr*. In being enchanted, Alexander and Drake had been separated from their mates. Thad had worried about this. Was it a sign that the firestorm wasn't forever? Did it mean that the Dragon's Tooth warriors were different? Did it mean that the firestorm's promise could be fleeting?

When the darkfire crystal had cast them through space and time, it had been Thad who discerned the truth and Thad who had been most relieved. Now, his own firestorm sparked at the end of his talon. He would do anything to see it satisfied and pledge whatever was necessary to the woman who would bear his son.

His chance to do all that and more was only moments away.

Thad couldn't wait.

Aura considered the sparks that danced in the wind with suspicion. They erupted nearby in a sudden flurry, then swirled around her like tiny brilliant orange lights. When they were extinguished, as sparks loosed from a fire are, even more replaced them—yet there was no fire to create the sparks. While she observed them, she felt a strange heat fill her body.

How could sparks create lust? Aura didn't know but these ones did. She felt her skin warm and tingle, then a flush spread over her body. She thought of pleasure and sensation, hot kisses and ardent nights. She imagined a man, a handsome young man, with dark hair and dark eyes, watching her with a smile and an answering heat in his eyes. His chest was bare and his body muscled to perfection, his skin tanned, his intent clear. Aura swallowed, even as her body responded to this vision.

Who was he?

Even though she only saw him in her mind's eye, Aura knew she'd never seen him before. His clothing was strange, but she was more interested in the man himself. She'd remember a man that handsome, no matter how long it had been. And why was she seeing him? As a nymph, Aura had the power to see through the guises taken by deities and shifters, to see all of their realities at once.

He had something to do with the sparks. Were the sparks one of his guises?

Aura decided to disperse the sparks. She built herself into a gust of wind, one so violent that it shoved back mist and cloud. The blue sky was clear overhead after that one breath, and the rocky mountaintop bared below.

The sparks, to her surprise, didn't fade.

In fact, they followed her.

Aura blew down toward the mountain. She shifted shape in a glitter of silver and took human form, the hem of her white tunic rippling around her bare feet. The fog still dissipated around her, visible on all sides but at a distance. She could see a golden glow of light in one direction, and sparks spilled from it. One fell toward her, then flamed more brightly as it touched her. Aura caught her breath as lust shot through her, and she felt her nipples tighten. The spark extinguished itself but not before the man in her mind's eye came closer. She saw the handsome stranger bend to kiss her, saw his hand rise to cup her breast, felt his breath against her cheek.

She wanted him with a vehemence that surprised her, even though she was a nymph with healthy appetites.

Aura stepped back and eyed the sparks. They weren't borne by any breeze she knew, and Aura had thought she knew them all. A hot wind could have been her uncle Notus, but it wasn't him. He was much older than the man in her thoughts and not nearly so alluring. Aura took a deep breath, and the sparks moved in response, changing their direction as if they would have her swallow them.

She hoped by Hades that the sparks—and the man—weren't divine. She'd seen enough nymphs possessed by a deity in disguise then left to raise a half-divine child—or worse, cursed to take the form of a tree or animal. Aura didn't want any part of that, but the gods could make themselves so irresistible that a nymph had little choice. The gods understood the desires that existed in every nymph, the love of pleasure, the affection for adoration. It was so much easier to never be noticed, but she'd succeeded at that long enough that she knew she was due for a challenge.

The sparks smelled of earth and fire, of a magic not common on Mount Olympus.

Aura felt her own body turning against her better judgment. She was tingling in anticipation of his appearance, already yearning for a kiss, even before he stood before her.

Who was he? Aura concentrated and a dragon replaced him in her mind, a dragon touched by a fire similar to the sparks that surrounded her.

He was a shape shifter?

Like her?

Aura had never met another shape shifter, other than the nymphs who were her relations. They were all women. A handsome man who could become a dragon, who created sparks from his presence and filled her with lust? This was a dangerous possibility, all the more so because it fascinated Aura. She should run, she knew it, but she wanted to see this marvel.

The sparks brightened suddenly, burning hotter and more yellow than orange. To her dismay, an answering heat filled her body, making her yearn for a man's touch.

Not any man, though. Only the one in her thoughts. He was more clear to her, almost as if he stood before her, and she knew he was drawing closer. This was her last chance to flee.

Curiosity might be her undoing, and even knowing that, she didn't run.

She heard him then, a creature flying through the mist without the least bit of caution. What drove him? A quest? A message? Or simple lust? With every beat of his wings, the passion within Aura grew and the sparks multiplied in number. She was overwhelmed with thoughts of pleasure. The air filled with a radiant and golden glow, one that seemed to Aura to be filled with anticipation.

A dragon of deepest black popped out of the mist in that moment. The golden light surrounded him and caressed the edges of his scales, making him look gilded. He hesitated in his flight, evidently startled to be out of the fog, and surveyed his surroundings.

He was magnificent, so graceful and noble a creature that one sight of him could never be enough. His wings were large and black, spread high and wide above him. His scales were deepest black but gleamed with golden lights. His eyes were like burnished gold, nearly glowing with intent. A strange flame illuminated his body, the orange color of the fire making him look even more primal and powerful than he would otherwise.

He was the handsome stranger in other guise. Aura could see his two forms overlapping each other when she eyed him, the one he had chosen more dominant but the other still there. Aura yearned to caress him, a desire that frightened her with its intensity. It wasn't natural, even for a nymph, to burn with such lust from only one glance. She wanted to know how his scales felt. She wanted to feel the strength of his body. She wanted to touch him in both guises. The sparks were filled with a kind of magic. Already she knew the desire would only be sated by this stranger.

She peered into the mist, seeking a sign that she could indulge herself without repercussions. To Aura's enormous relief, she saw no child.

She could have him.

With that conviction, there was no question of fleeing.

Aura felt his gaze as surely as a touch. His glance swept over her and he flew closer, seeming to savor his first look at her. His eyes glowed and he breathed fire, as if in anticipation. The glow heated to brilliant white, making Aura burn in a most primal way.

She stood with her head thrown back as the black dragon flew around her in a tight circle. His obvious awe made her want to preen.

It certainly made her smile.

The sparks were getting hotter.

Aura was getting hotter. She felt a lust building in herself that was beyond anything she'd experienced before. She was a nymph, not a vestal virgin, but this desire was sizzling.

It was a spell. It had to be.

Aura hoped it would last for more than just one taste of him.

The dragon flew closer, and Aura couldn't help but admire his grace. He changed his posture to land right in front of her, and the light crackled as it became brilliant yellow. They were caught in an orb of sizzling heat when she saw a flicker of cool blue. It was almost like a lick of lightning, gone so quickly that her eyes could have been deceived.

But Aura recognized that shimmer. He *was* a shape shifter, just like her. She resolutely kept her gaze fixed upon him, wanting to witness the change. Just before his feet touched the ground, he became a handsome and athletic young man.

The same one she'd envisioned, of course.

The change was seamless and quick, accomplished in the blink of an eye and with the same elegance he showed in flight. Aura smiled at his prowess. The way he smiled back at her gave Aura ideas.

The flames that burned between them gave her more ideas.

They simultaneously took a step to close the distance between them, then smiled at each other that their thoughts were as one. The light between them lit to palest yellow. Aura could feel perspiration on the back of her neck and feel her desire for him redoubling with every heartbeat. She wanted to run her hands over him and rub herself against him, she wanted to kiss him and taste him and feel this heat build to a crescendo...

He lifted his hand to her chin. Aura gasped at the brilliance of the spark that lit from the point of contact. Its heat surged through her body, melting her reservations and weakening her knees.

"I am your servant," he murmured, his voice low and deep. His gaze searched hers and she smiled a welcome. She looked at his mouth in time to see the corner lift, then he bent forward and kissed her.

He kissed with surety, firmly but gently, a man who knew what he wanted and wasn't afraid to ask for it, a man who could be turned aside with a fingertip. He wanted her to want him, too, and that realization dissolved the last of Aura's resistance.

She was lost in his kiss and didn't want to be found.

She was perfect.

The firestorm was perfect.

Thad didn't even know his mate's name and he didn't care. The firestorm was right. The Great Wyvern had found the perfect woman for him, and he was going to satisfy the firestorm. Even his first glimpse of her had been enticing. She'd stood on the hilltop waiting for him, her white tunic blowing slightly. He'd been able see her slim curves through the sheer fabric. Her hair was a rich brown and cascaded in loose curls to her hips. It blew behind her, as well. Her lips were rosy and her eyes dark, her lashes thick. She was smooth and feminine and luscious.

Thad wanted her as he'd never wanted a woman before.

He saw her look at him and realized she wasn't surprised when he shifted shape. He thrilled that there would be no secrets between them, then touched her chin and felt the heat of desire race through his body. When he touched his lips to hers, it seemed to Thad that the firestorm exploded. He saw white light and was aware only of the feel of her soft lips beneath his own. He smelled that sweet perfume and knew he'd be able to find her anywhere.

She gave a little gasp of surprise and he swallowed the sound, gathering her in his arms as he deepened his kiss. In one way, he wanted to make the satisfaction of the firestorm last as long as possible; in another, he couldn't stand it. He wanted her and he wanted her now. He felt her hand on his shoulder, and her fingers slide up his neck to tangle in his hair. Her kiss was sweet and intoxicating, and he loved how she opened her mouth to him, inviting him closer. The touch of her tongue made him catch his breath. He liked that she was honest about her desire.

Their thoughts were as one, as they would be from this day forward. He had one arm around her waist and let the other hand slide over her cheek, to her nape, then down her back. He cupped her breast, convinced it was the most perfect size and shape, then broke their kiss. He bent to take her taut nipple in his mouth, and she moaned.

"I don't even know your name," she whispered, her fingers winding into his hair.

"It doesn't matter," Thad said, lifting the front of her tunic to bare her breast to his gaze. He flicked a glance at her and smiled. "We have to satisfy the firestorm, first."

"The firestorm," she echoed, then caught her breath when he flicked his tongue over her nipple. He caressed her breast even as he closed his mouth over the tight peak, suckling and licking as she arched back in his embrace. He felt her fingers lock into his hair and felt her heart racing.

His own heart matched its pace to hers, a sensation that made Thad dizzy. He was snared in a glowing orb of light, a slave to sensation and pleasure, wanting only to savor his mate and please her completely.

She tugged his hair. "What's the firestorm?"

"This!" Thad straightened and caught her shoulders in his grasp. He watched the flames grow and spread from his hands, their golden light burnishing her skin. Of course, she would be the finest treasure in his hoard. His mate. His love. His partner. "This heat, this fire, this blaze! It's all the firestorm."

"And it goes away?" She pursed her lips, pouting a little, even as her eyes sparkled.

Thad smiled. "When we create a son, the sparks will die."

"A son?"

"That's what the firestorm's about."

Her eyes flashed then, but Thad didn't think it was with passion. She stepped out of his embrace, putting distance between them.

"No," she said with such force that he wondered who she was trying to convince. "There can't be a son."

"When we satisfy the firestorm, there will be." Thad had no opportunity to present his plan, because she simply disappeared. He saw a shimmer of silver and felt a breath of wind, and then he was alone on a high mountain peak. The land fell away before him, and the clouds below had cleared enough that he could see fields and a coastline far below.

But there were no caves or trees. There was no place his mate could hide.

Thad turned in place, confused. Where had she gone? How had she vanished into thin air? Why had she gone?

He held up his hand, but the firestorm had died to a faint glimmer emanating from the tip of one finger. He held his hand before himself, turning, but the light didn't brighten no matter which way he was facing. Thad felt a ripple of panic. How would he find her again? How would he fulfill their destiny together?

Why had she left?

Then he took a deep breath and smelled her perfume. A triumphant sense of his own power rolled through him and Thad used it to shift his shape. In dragon form, he took flight and soared over the mountain, seeking the trail of perfume.

When he found it, he found the spark of the firestorm, too. The light brightened as the scent grew stronger. Encouraged, Thad flew in pursuit of his mate, knowing it was fate that she would bear his son.

All he had to do was convince her of that.

There was a spring in a glade, high on Mount Olympus, shielded from the view of the gods by a hovering mist. The glade was protected from the curiosity of mortals by location: it nestled within a circle of jagged peaks filled with dangerous precipices and was prone to bursts of wind. The mist was perpetual between the peaks and an abundance of alpine flowers grew on the slopes. The spring flowed constantly from a crack in the rocks and flowed into a pool with a surface as smooth as a mirror.

The nymphs gathered here, lingering as their responsibilities and whims demanded. The glade was subjected to fleeting breezes, periods of light rain, fog and rainbows, as the nymphs came and went in their alternate forms. It wasn't the Garden of the Hesperides, but it was much closer. Aura, in the form of a breeze, blew toward the glade with purpose.

She wanted to be with her own kind.

She wanted to know if anyone else had ever experienced a firestorm. Could she make love to this dragon shifter without conceiving his son? Aura was desperate to know. His kiss had done nothing to minimize her desire—in fact, she felt that she was filled with an even more consuming lust. If she hadn't left him, she would have been entangled with him already.

To Aura's relief, Nephele was in the glade. Nephele was as fair in coloring as the clouds she could become and knew so much more of the world than Aura. Nephele trailed her hand in the water as she listened to the gossip of the other nymphs, characteristically quiet and attentive.

One of the Anthousai was there, easily identified by the strong scent of hyacinth flowers. Aura didn't know this one's name but she was dark-haired and pretty like all her sisters. The flower nymphs looked more or less the same to Aura, and she found none of them to be very clever. They were sweet, though, and forgave much.

Arethusa was standing before the spring, her words sparkling as they fell. She was a naiad, a nymph of the fresh waters, and the fact that she hovered on the cusp of change was a sign of her excitement.

Aura blew near to their circle and changed shape, even as Arethusa exclaimed. "She was one of us, but not immortal." Droplets fell from the nymph in her agitation. "She called herself an Earthdaughter." The other nymphs tried the word, then Nephele nodded to Aura. "She could make the earth heave and start an earthquake."

The nymphs exchanged glances. "Like a goddess!"

Nephele snapped her fingers. "I've heard of women like this. They're similar to us, but are mortal. They tend to stay in human form and live in human society. There was one I blew past a while ago on a mountaintop. She called herself a Waterdaughter and could change into a shimmering pillar of water."

"But that's what you can do," the flower nymph declared. "Change into water."

Arethusa shook her head. "We're bound to a specific source. I can only come to you because the water flows from here to my well. It's not the same as being able to wander around like a mortal and change shape whenever you want."

"As a Waterdaughter, you could pursue a man, instead of waiting for him to come back," the flower nymph said with a sigh.

"Or anything else,' Arethusa said. She sat down, her expression revealing that she had more to tell. "Here's the remarkable thing." She looked between the nymphs, verifying that she had their attention, then dropped her voice to a whisper. "A man came after *her*."

"Did she entrance him and seduce him?" the flower nymph asked.

"She was already pregnant with his son."

"Impossible," Aura said with resolve. "They never come back once we're pregnant."

"This one did!" Arethusa was triumphant. "He didn't just come back: he sought her out." The nymphs exchanged glances. Aura knew she wasn't the only one who had never heard of such a thing.

"But you said you saw her in the Underworld," Nephele protested quietly. "You mean he was dead, too?"

"No, he was mortal and alive, but he came after her." Arethusa nodded. "He fought Cerberus and pursued her into the Underworld."

"He willingly entered the realm of the dead," Aura murmured, amazed. She wasn't sure whether to believe Arethusa or not. Men, in her experience, weren't self-sacrificing at all.

But if one was, he'd be exactly the kind of man she wanted. Aura admired those who didn't always consider themselves first.

"Then he really did want to be with her," the flower nymph said. "How romantic!"

"How could you know this?" Nephele asked.

"Orphne told me that she saw it all."

"Because she was in the River Acheron," Aura contributed.

Arethusa nodded again. "She said he fought Cerberus and was losing, but this Earthdaughter sang the hellhound to sleep, to save him. They argued at the gates and she went into the Underworld, but he *followed* her."

This story showed unusual dedication on the part of the man. Aura had problems believing it was true. After all, he had had his pleasure of the Earthdaughter, and Aura knew better than to expect a man to linger after that.

"Did he come out again?" the flower nymph asked. "Or was he lured to his death?" She seemed to take a salacious glee in the possibility.

"They came out together. That's what I saw."

"Your waters flow far and deep, Arethusa," Nephele said with a smile.

"Not far enough that I could hide from Alpheus," the nymph said bitterly. "If justice had been served, I would still be paying homage to my lady Artemis, but my choice to remain chaste was irrelevant to him."

"Chastity is over-rated," the flower nymph said slyly. "We keep our youth and vigor by claiming men." She smiled. "As many as possible."

"You said it was romantic that he came back," Nephele pointed out.

"Because it would make a repeat conquest easier," the flower nymph declared with a toss of her hair. "Much easier than enchanting him and keeping him captive." She pouted a little. "Don't they say that absence makes the heart grow fonder? Something about seeing a captive all the time makes me want him less."

"Because you remember your conquests so clearly," Nephele said with false sweetness. Nymphs were of two varieties: those who adored sex and couldn't get enough of it, and those who chose to remain chaste. Of the first variety, the flower nymphs were notorious for being insatiable.

Nephele was one of the few nymphs who tried to keep her desires in balance without being chaste. Aura had always admired her for that and tried to strike a similar balance. She enjoyed sex enough that she wanted it to remain a special act.

She shivered in recollection of the dragon shifter's kiss. What would it be like to be with him?

"Actually, I don't," admitted the flower nymph.

"If one came back, would you even know you'd seduced him before?" Nephele asked.

"Would it matter?" countered the flower nymph and Nephele shook her head.

She then returned to Arethusa's story, pointedly turning her back on the flower nymph. "When the Earthdaughter and her mortal lover escaped from the Underworld, was Hades angry?"

Arethusa nodded. "Very! Because one of the things this man

did was kill an Erinye."

The nymphs all sat back in horror. "Which one?" Aura whispered, even though any one of them would be bad enough.

"Tisiphone!"

The nymphs gasped. This was the worst possible situation.

"And Hades pronounced his judgment. He poured the contents of his cup over Tisiphone's body—"

"Not that vile potion," the flower nymph said with a shudder.

"The very one," Arethusa said before continuing. "And then he said *'Tisiphone, the face of retaliation and the avenger of murder, take life again and exact your own vengeance upon your murderer and his kind. Pursue them through all eternity, until your thirst for revenge is sated.'*"

"As if that would ever happen," Nephele murmured and Aura nodded.

Arethusa spread her hands to finish her story. "And she changed!"

"To what?"

"To a woman with hair the color of fire."

Nephele rolled her eyes. "You *are* telling a story. No one has hair of that color."

"She did!" Arethusa protested.

"And then?" prompted the flower nymph.

"And then she disappeared." Arethusa lifted a finger. "One of her sisters asked where she could be found and Hades said *'You all three have walked in whichever realm you chose. Tisiphone will live only in the realm of the living until her vengeance is served.'* He looked at the man before this last bit. *'She will strike among the living, even as she abides in secret. His kind will never know of her vendetta until her vengeance is served.'*"

Nephele shuddered. "You have to feel sorry for him. Imagine being responsible for bringing a curse like that down on all mortal men."

"But he wasn't a mortal man, not really!" Arethusa crowed. Her audience regarded her in bewilderment. "He changed into a dragon and they flew out of the Underworld, right through the crack in the world that the Earthdaughter made."

Aura gasped, even as Nephele shook her head in skepticism.

The flower nymph made a little purr in her throat. "A man who could become a dragon. I'd like to seduce one of them."

"Surprise," Nephele muttered.

"Wait," Aura said. "Did either of them talk about a firestorm?"
It was Arethusa's turn to stare. "If they did, I didn't
understand. What's a firestorm?"

"And how do you know anything about it?" the flower nymph
demanded, her eyes bright.

Aura might have explained, but she felt a delicious sensation
of heat slide through her body in that moment. Sure enough, she
glanced down at her hand to find a glow emanating from the tips of
her fingers. She turned to face the source of the heat, just in time to
see a black dragon fly through the low hanging fog over the glade.
His eyes were brilliant gold and he breathed a stream of fire when
his gaze locked upon her.

"Mother of Zeus," the flower nymph whispered, fanning
herself as she stared in awe.

"How could anyone follow us here?" Nephele said, sparkling
silver as she changed to a cloud before Aura's very eyes. The
cloud that was Nephele rose high, but didn't go through the mist.

No, Nephele would want to watch.

"I know that look," Arethusa muttered. "He might be a dragon,
but he's after the same thing they all are." Without waiting for
agreement, she dove into the pool of water created by the glade.
The surface of the water rippled, then shimmered as Arethusa
changed shape. Aura had a glimpse of her face, then the nymph
disappeared into the depths of the spring.

The dragon roared and Aura turned to face him. Once his gaze
locked with hers, she could only stand and stare.

And want. The force of the firestorm had redoubled since she
had fled from the dragon earlier, burning hotter and brighter and
more insistently. She was trapped in an orb of heat, one that grew
with every beat of the dragon's wings and drained her of any
desire to flee.

The only desire she had was for him.

She knew how Arethusa had been pursued by a river god. She
knew how Coronis had been raped by Butes of Thrace. She knew
that dozens of nymphs had been coveted, seduced and left
pregnant—if not cruelly transformed—by their lovers, both mortal
and divine. In a way, the desire of many nymphs to beguile men

and use them sexually made sense, for it was a kind of retaliation for eons of abuse.

Aura knew all of that, but when the firestorm flooded her body and the dragon flew closer, when she could see the dragon he was and the man he could become, she could only think of his potent kiss.

This was not good. She had to find out about this son. Aura didn't want to be abandoned by her lover to have his child alone. No matter how wonderful the firestorm was, it couldn't be worth that life.

It was clear that she could run but she couldn't hide.

Which meant she had to convince him to stop this firestorm. Sooner would be better. Aura licked her lips in trepidation, held her ground, and waited for her dragon.

He'd found her!

Thad flew directly toward his mate. She stood straight and tall by the side of a pool with a surface as smooth as glass. She held his gaze, as fearless as any dragon, even as the firestorm burned brighter and brighter. By the time he landed in front of her, shifting shape just before he touched the earth, there were sparks flying between them as brilliantly as fireworks.

Thad watched the orange and yellow light with wonder. He could feel the firestorm heating his body, sending a surge of desire through his veins. It was like the change slipping over him but intensified a thousand times.

It was all focused on his mate. He took a step closer to her and smiled, seeing the flush in her cheek and the sweet fullness of her lips. He wanted another kiss, if not a hundred of them, and wanted to make love to her forever.

For a moment, she looked soft and willing, then she shook her head. She took a step back, her move dimming the firestorm's intensity a bit, and folded her arms across her chest. "What do you want from me?"

"To satisfy the firestorm."

"What does it mean?"

"I told you. The firestorm means that you're the woman who can bear my son."

"And he'll be like you?"

Thad nodded.

"And what are you?"

"A *Pyr*. We are dragon shape shifters, charged with defending the treasures of the earth and the four elements." Thad cleared his throat and recited the foundation story of his kind, placing his hand over his heart as he did so. "In the beginning, there was the fire, and the fire burned hot because it was cradled by the earth. The fire burned bright because it was nurtured by the air. The fire burned lower only when it was quenched by the water. And these were the four elements of divine design, of which all would be built and with which all would be destroyed. And the elements were placed at the cornerstones of the material world and it was good."

"But the elements were alone and undefended, incapable of communicating with each other, snared within the matter that was theirs to control. And so, out of the endless void were created a race of guardians whose appointed task was to protect and defend the integrity of the four sacred elements. They were given powers, the better to fulfill their responsibilities; they were given strength and cunning and longevity to safeguard the treasures surrendered to their stewardship. To them alone would the elements respond. These guardians were—and are—the *Pyr*." He finished with a flourish, because the passage was his favorite.

"To them alone?" she echoed, her skepticism clear.

"That's the story." Her question made Thad wonder whether she knew something he didn't.

She surveyed him, nibbling on her bottom lip. "It doesn't mention anything about a firestorm," she noted and he was disappointed that she wasn't more impressed.

"Yet here it is!" Thad lifted a hand toward her and a spark shot from his fingertip. It landed on her chest, right above her heart, and there was an explosion of light on contact. She gasped even as Thad felt a stab of hot pleasure in his chest. He heard her heart skip a beat again, then felt that dizzying sensation of his own heart matching the pace of hers. They could have been one being, drawn together by destiny and fated to remain together forever. He reached for her, but she backed away again.

She had doubts.

That wasn't unreasonable. Thad wanted her to choose to be with him, not to just be overwhelmed by the firestorm. He didn't want her to have regrets.

"I can imagine that this is a surprise to you," he said, keeping his voice low. "My kind say there is nothing like the firestorm. I knew of it and it's still shaking my universe."

"You expected it?" Her skepticism was clear. "It happens all the time?"

Thad held up a finger. "Once in the life of each *Pyr*, he will experience a firestorm. He has one chance to create a son and a future." He knew she didn't think much of his answer.

"A future for your kind, you mean."

"A future for himself."

"What about the mate?" she demanded, and her tone was a bit sharp.

Thad swallowed and tried to make a coherent argument, even as his body raged with desire. "*Pyr* and mate are brought together by destiny. Once it was believed that satisfying the firestorm was the end of it. But I have met those of my kind who create a permanent relationship with their mates, who become partners for the future."

She eyed him warily. "Why?"

"Because they complement each other. The firestorm finds the mate best suited to the *Pyr* in question. It seems incredible, but that's how it works. They make a team and raise their sons together. It's what I want."

Something in her eyes softened. "How long of a partnership?"

Thad smiled, sure that he was making his case. "Forever." He took a step closer, the sudden increase in the heat of the firestorm making him close his eyes against it. When he opened them, she'd retreated again.

"You're immortal, like a god?"

"No, but we are long-lived. So, for a long lifetime together, maybe even beyond that."

"No guarantees?"

"Only because I don't know what happens then." He offered one hand to her, but she simply stared at his outstretched fingers.

"Spending all my days and nights with my destined mate is fine by me."

"What if your destined mate doesn't want to have a son?"

"She doesn't have a choice." Thad smiled and reached toward her. "I'll try to make it worth your while."

She looked indecisive. He could see the desire in her eyes but also that she was resistant to the idea. He knew she wanted him. She kept looking at his mouth, at his hands, then catching her breath. He eased closer, lifting a strand of her long hair. As he wound the curl around his fingertip, the firestorm blazed golden. The light touched her features, making her look like a gilded treasure, and Thad's chest clenched. He watched as she parted her lips, then bent quickly to steal a kiss.

The way her lips clung to his told him that she wasn't that resistant.

"My name is Thaddeus," he whispered against her mouth. "My friends call me Thad."

"Aura," she whispered, her eyes were dark and wide. She studied him as he repeated her name softly, and Thad dared to steal another kiss. This one lasted longer and was more potent, making his heart pound and filling his body with a need for more. He felt her fingers in his hair, lightly first, and then when he slanted his mouth across hers and deepened his kiss, her grip tightened.

Pulling him closer. Thad caught her close and lifted her against himself, liking how she framed his head in her hands. Their kiss turned hungry and demanding, kindling to an inferno that demanded satisfaction. He wanted to feel his skin against hers and he slid his hand under the hem of her chiton.

As soon as his skin touched hers, she spun out of his embrace. She backed away, her lips swollen and her cheeks flushed, and eyed him warily. Thad could see the tight beads of her nipples making peaks in the soft fabric and the smell of her desire made his dragon roar. He took a deep breath in a bid for control, determined to let her set the pace.

Then he realized one good thing.

"You're not disappearing this time," he said. "How did you disappear like that, anyway?"

Her smile flashed, as if he'd given her an idea. "You think you're the only one who isn't human?" she asked, but Thad was confused.

She laughed, then lifted her arms and disappeared in a sparkle of falling light.

He spun in place, but she was gone again.

He had to find her!

Thad suddenly felt a wind ruffle his hair, like a woman's fingers sliding through it, except the spark of the firestorm crackled there, too. The caress slid down the back of his neck, both a breath of wind and a flurry of sparks, swirled around to cross his chest, then danced down his arm. He stretched out his hand and felt as if fingers of wind interlaced with his own, or maybe a breeze slipped through his fingers. Sparks cascaded from his fingertips as the wind faded to nothing, and he turned in place, wondering where she was.

"You're a nymph," he exclaimed, remembering the stories he'd been told as a child.

A whirlwind spiraled to the ground right in front of them and he smiled as the firestorm touched it with gold. In a heartbeat, his mate stood before him again, her hair blowing as it settled over her shoulders. She was smiling at him, and her eyes shone with intent. "This is what I am, *Pyr*. Does the truth change your mind?"

Thad shook his head and saw her eyes sparkle. "It gives us more in common," he said with resolve. He dropped to his knee before her. They caught their breath simultaneously as he took her hand in his and kissed its back, a potent stab of heat racing through Thad's body at the contact. "Be with me, Aura," he murmured, holding her gaze.

She inhaled sharply and her eyes were wide. "Catch me first," she whispered, her eyes dancing with challenge. That shimmer returned as she disappeared into the whirlwind. It spun up toward the clouds, churning as it rose, the glint of the firestorm fading with distance.

Thad roared and shifted shape, leaping into the air in dragon form to pursue his mate. He knew he didn't imagine that she laughed before the whirlwind disappeared into the clouds overhead. They swirled, sparks falling from them like strange rain. Thad plunged into the cloud to pursue her, following both her scent and the heat of the firestorm.

Chapter Two

It would have been too easy for Aura to surrender.

She hadn't just been tempted: she'd been on the cusp of giving her all to Thad. But as willing as her body was, and as persuasive as his argument seemed to be, she couldn't help thinking that he was saying what he needed to say, in order to seduce her.

She couldn't help worrying that as soon as the firestorm was satisfied, he'd be gone, and she'd be left with the son of a dragon to bear and raise. She'd seen the same thing happen to nymphs over and over again. It had happened to her mother. Aura had been determined that it would never happen to her.

Even if Thad was nearly irresistible.

She resisted by changing form. It was the only thing she could do to save herself from making what had to be a mistake. She couldn't figure out how he could be so sure that there would be a son, yet she couldn't see a child in her future.

Aura had to think—and when Thad kissed her, she couldn't think responsibly. She could only think of seducing him completely and worrying about the consequences later.

Was that part of a dragon's spell?

Aura did her best thinking when she was a breeze. Her thoughts flew then and associations were quickly made. Her intuition was stronger and she was more creative. When she shifted to a breeze, a part of her loved that Thad was not surprised.

Even more than not being surprised, he was seeking her. She saw his eyes narrow and heard him take a deep breath. It was exciting not to be certain she could disappear completely from his perception, to imagine that they had a kind of understanding because they were both different from others.

Aura soared out of the glade and through the protective fog that sheltered its secrets. She heard Thad roar behind her and knew he must have shifted shape: she could feel the sparks of the firestorm blaze hotter as she swept over the summit of the peaks. It was wonderful to race across the sky, and even more exciting to be pursued by a dragon nearly as fast as she was.

"I like him," Nephele whispered, her admiration feeding Aura's confidence in her impulse to trust Thad. *"And I believe him."* Aura looked back. She saw that one of the clouds had trailed behind her but that a black dragon had flown past it and was closing fast.

It wasn't Nephele who Thad was determined to seduce.

Aura tumbled down the side of the mountain slope, a zephyr of fresh air or a sigh from the mountain top. The trees swayed with her passing, and their leaves rustled. Thad was so close behind her that she could feel the beat of his wings through the air. She turned hard when she reached the green pastures and raced through the flowers, making them wave with her passing like the surface of the ocean.

"Give him to me," whispered the flower nymph.

Aura didn't think so. She might not be certain she would take the risk to be with Thad, but she wasn't going to give him up just yet either. He probably would have insisted that the firestorm marked their partnership as a destined one.

Was he right? Did he mean it?

She liked that Thad didn't give up the chase. That was a good sign. She thought of all he'd said, and all he'd promised, and felt an answering yearning within herself. She wasn't young and she wasn't old, but Aura had been alone long enough to find the idea of a partner appealing. Like the *Pyr*, nymphs lived long but weren't immortal. She was pleased that they had that longevity in common.

That was when she knew. The golden apples of the Hesperides. If he would follow her to Hera's garden, one bite of a golden apple would compel him to speak the truth to her. Then Aura would know, without doubt, the truth in his heart.

Perfect.

She soared over a river that was splashing down from the peaks of Mount Olympus and followed it, racing just above its surface. She spun and spiraled, knowing her dragon was right behind her. She made the water froth and the spray splash high, even as the sparks of the firestorm glowed in her wake.

Thad roared, and she looked back to see his eyes glowing as he pursued her.

"Remember she-who-should-not-be-named," whispered Arethusa. *"It might not be his choice to abandon you."*

Tisiphone. Arethusa had been confident to say the name of the Erinye while they were on Mount Olympus, in the domain of the gods, but here in the land of mortals, she showed more care. That made sense, since Tisiphone was supposed to occupy this realm until she avenged herself upon the *Pyr*.

Could Tisiphone kill Thad?

She could, without doubt. The Erinyes were merciless and horrible, and never forgot a grudge. *Would* she kill Thad? Aura couldn't bear the possibility, no matter what future was between her and Thad. She stilled, a wind falling idle, and he swept around and through her, like a bird soaring through the leaves of a tree. Aura felt a wonderful shiver of heat in the instant that he was closest to her.

The firestorm's glow faded to a pale light and Thad halted. The change in its light alerted him that he had missed something. He turned with grace and headed back toward her, his eyes bright with resolve.

"You can protect him," Nephele whispered, her voice distant but clear.

And Aura yearned to do so.

So long as his intentions were true.

Her decision was made.

Aura swirled in the sky before Thad, waiting for him to fly closer. When he drew near her again, she rose beneath his wings, bearing him higher in the sky with the current she could create. He was startled, then eyed the radiance beneath his wings and laughed.

"Aura! It's you!" he cried. "Let's fly together." He beat his wings hard and Aura became a faster wind, pushing him out over the Mediterranean. They swept high in the sky together, higher

than Aura had ever flown alone. It was easy to be bold in the
company of a dragon, and easy to believe anything was possible in
the face of Thad's optimism and conviction. He made her feel
buoyant—and she could buoy him up. Thad's wings moved so
slowly that his flight looked effortless. Even if there was never any
more than this, Aura knew she'd never forget this shared moment.

"I've never flown so high or so far from shore," he murmured,
his low voice sending a shiver through her. She could have
shivered again that his thoughts were such a close echo of her own.
"I've always wanted to be sure I could land."

"It's like you said," Aura whispered, hoping he could hear her.
Most mortals couldn't hear the speech of the nymphs when they
were in their alternate form, but she saw Thad's head tilt, as if he
listened to a faint sound.

"How so?"

"We're a team. We're doing more together than apart."

He laughed then, a joyous sound that made Aura's heart skip.
"Is that how you and your kind speak to each other?" he asked.

"Yes, and you can hear me. Most mortals can't."

"Most of them can't hear us, either, at least not well enough to
distinguish the words."

"Show me how you speak to your kind."

"It's old-speak, very low and slow." Thad took a deep breath.
"Like this." The two words hung in the air for what seemed like
forever. If Aura hadn't been listening to him closely, she might
have dismissed the sound as a rumble in the earth or the crash of a
wave on a distant shore. Because she was listening, she heard the
words, as steady as the beat of his heart.

"Tell me a secret," she urged in her nymph whisper.

"The Pyr *I most admire fall in love with their mates and honor
them for every day and night of their lives,"* Thad said in old-
speak. He scanned the air around himself as he flew and eyed the
dancing sparks of the firestorm. *"Let me fall in love with you,
Aura."*

It was an enticing offer.

If she hadn't been her mother's child, she would have
surrendered right then and there. As it was, Aura kissed his cheek
with a breath of wind, ran over his muscled body in a breeze that
only made her want to touch him with her hands. She caressed the

length of his tail and he laughed at the sensation, then she spiraled before him. Each time she slid past his body, the firestorm heated another increment, filling her thoughts with the prospect of pleasure. In her mind's eye, she saw him in human form and wanted to feel his hands upon her, his flesh against her own.

"*Far out there,*" she said, blowing him so that he faced the west.

"*I see only the sea, stretching endlessly.*"

"*Not so endless. At its far reaches are the Pillars of Hercules. Beyond that is the Garden of the Hesperides, a refuge of my kind in the mortal world.*" She swirled around him again. "*And maybe a haven for us.*"

"*A long flight,*" Thad said, his wings beating with greater power. His determination to live up to her expectations fed her own confidence that she was making the right choice. "*I will do my best, Aura.*"

"*And I will help you,*" she vowed, urging his flight forward, as if he were no more than a seed in the wind.

Thad had never experienced anything like this before. He felt a sense of camaraderie with his fellow *Pyr* overall, plus the Dragon Legion fought well together, anticipating each other's moves. This sense of union he felt with Aura was similar, but amplified. Flying with Aura, feeling her slide beneath his wings while the firestorm crackled and burned all around them, was exciting in every possible way. He hadn't been joking about never flying so far or so high: given their dimensions, dragons were better suited to shorter flights. He knew that some of the other *Pyr* flew far, even across the Atlantic Ocean, but he had never been so bold.

Maybe because he couldn't swim.

In Aura's company, though, he was filled with optimism and sure that they could achieve anything together. The sun was sinking in the west when he first saw the two large stones, standing like gate posts on either side of the turquoise water of the Mediterranean. He soared past them, with Aura's help, then turned as the wind she had become changed direction.

Immediately, he saw the green gem of the garden she had mentioned. It was nestled far below, between the peaks, so vivid a green that it could have been an emerald. The ocean was dark blue beneath him, crested with white waves, and stretched seemingly endlessly to the west. The western sky was smeared with orange light and in the east, far behind them, the first stars were emerging.

Thad had never flown so far in his life. He never would have attempted it alone. He was tired in one way, but in another, his body hummed with excitement. The firestorm's heat couldn't be forgotten, and its sparks tingled against his scales, promising a reward for his feat. On this night, they would consummate the firestorm. Thad had spent the entire flight trying to think of ways to prolong the flame, but doubted he would be able to. All day long, his desire for Aura had increased. All day long, the heat of the firestorm had filled his thoughts with the promise of pleasure.

With no small anticipation, he descended toward the garden. Aura's wind was still beneath his wings, guiding him to the spot. He knew it was a good sign that she was taking him to a refuge of her kind. Hers was a choice that spoke of trust, and hinted at the shared future he wanted more than anything. The air rising from the garden was sweet, something in it heated by the sun of the afternoon, and he could smell apples.

Of course. The golden apples of the Hesperides. That was another story he'd been told, but Thad had never believed they were real. That made him smile, for more legends and myths were proving themselves true than he had expected.

Were their powers real? He had heard stories that eating just one bite from such an apple granted immortality, or universal knowledge, or made every dream come true.

Aura undoubtedly knew their real properties. That made him think of all the tales and truth they could share, and how much better they would be equipped to face the challenges of the world together.

To his surprise, she took a turn just before they entered the garden. The wind that was Aura guided him to the sloping path beneath the garden. It was a barren slope, and the path was hard and dry. There was a single tree, though, its leaves silvery green. Aura led him to it, for some reason, and he saw the breeze that was her rustle the leaves. He turned over the tree and headed back up to the garden, certain she was showing off.

Then there was the garden itself. The shadows were already drawing long in the shelter of the garden and the space was filled with velvety green darkness. He could discern that there was a well-tended orchard below them, and that the boughs of the trees were heavy with golden fruit. He heard the sleepy hum of bees and the trickle of water, he smelled rich soil and herbs like lavender, and knew that this garden must be an earthly paradise.

Aura hastened ahead of him, because the firestorm's heat dimmed to a glow and the wind that had driven him so far faded to a breeze. There was a sparkle on the ground between the trees, then Aura in her human form appeared. She turned and opened her arms to him in welcome, her smile and her gesture making his heart pound.

Thad flew toward her, the firestorm feeding his desire to a higher pitch with every beat of his wings. He heard her heart and felt his own match its pace, a sensation that nearly overwhelmed him with the conviction that their partnership was right. He was over the trees, preparing to land, when another dragon erupted from the shadows of the orchard below.

The dragon was of deepest green, and he had nine heads, each of which was breathing fire at Thad. His eyes could have been burning coals and his talons were as sharp as knives. There was something of a snake in his agility and form, and Thad knew instinctively that he was ancient.

The other dragon had surprise on his side. He had latched a talon on to Thad's tail before the *Pyr* could respond.

Ladon, Thad realized. This must be Ladon, the guardian of the golden apples, and another myth come to life. Even as they locked claws to grapple for supremacy, Thad knew he couldn't injure his opponent. Thad managed to shake his tail free, but Ladon's teeth left bleeding holes in his flesh. He tried to hold his slithering opponent at bay, but Ladon showed no such restraint. The fire he breathed was burning Thad's scales, and he bit again, sinking his teeth into Thad's shoulder.

"Ladon!" Aura cried. "He is a friend!"

"Only nymphs can enter the garden!" Ladon cried with one head. At least that one stopped breathing fire for a moment. "I let no others pass, by order of Hera herself."

"But I brought him here!" Aura argued. "He is my guest!"

"Never trust a nymph!" Ladon twisted and bit, biting deeply into Thad's wing with another head. The blood flowed from Thad's wounds, and he knew that this dragon would willingly kill him.

It was one thing to fight to the death. It was another to let an opponent win a battle for the sake of honor. It was still a third to let a dragon of any kind interfere with the firestorm.

Thad roared with fury and began to fight in earnest.

Aura had never seen dragons fight, and she wasn't sure she ever wanted to again.

She had feared that Thad would be easily beaten. Ladon had taken him by surprise and seemed likely to overwhelm her dragon. The smell of burning scales was terrible and it was worse to see Thad's blood flowing. She worried that Thad was tired from their flight and that even a robust dragon could be defeated.

Had she put him in danger? She felt foolish for wanting to test him and responsible for his injuries. At the same time, she knew she could never fight Ladon and win. Ladon had to be tricked for a nymph to survive an encounter with him.

Just when Aura feared the worst, Thad's manner changed. He spun and turned on Ladon with a roar of fury that put the ancient dragon to shame. To her delight, Aura realized that Thad had been holding back. He breathed a torrent of fire at the other dragon that was fearsome in both volume and intensity.

Oh, there was much to be admired about a man—or dragon—who used his power with discretion. Aura thought twice about her scheme, but stealthily stole a single golden apple anyway. The tree made a cry of pain, just as she had anticipated it would—they were terrible snitches, these trees—but Ladon didn't hear the sound.

He was too busy crying out in pain himself. Ladon fell back from Thad's plume of fire, but Thad flew right after him. He seized the green dragon and spun him around, striking one head then locking claws with him again. They spun through the air, their tales locked and their teeth flashing as they bit at each other. Aura hid the apple in her tunic just as Thad flung Ladon at the ground. The other dragon crashed through one of Hera's trees, breaking a number of branches, then hit the ground so hard that it trembled. Thad pursued him in furious flight, teeth bared and talons outstretched.

"Don't kill him!" Aura cried. "Hera will curse you!"

Thad hovered in the air above Ladon, seething. Aura was glad he'd listened to her, but uncertain as to what he would do.

Ladon seized the moment and took advantage of Thad's momentary hesitation. The other dragon twisted around, then leapt into the air once more. He breathed fire as he launched himself at Thad. Aura lost track of them both in the blazes of fire.

To her dismay, Ladon seemed determined to kill Thad. If Thad was defeated now, it would be her fault! She couldn't just stand by and watch, and she couldn't let Thad be burned when he couldn't fully defend himself. She changed to a breeze and blew into one of Ladon's mouths in a gust of wind, extinguishing the fire he breathed before it reached Thad.

She heard Thad laugh in triumph and Ladon snarl in frustration. She watched Ladon closely and targeted each of his mouths in turn, stopping the fire he would have breathed. Her efforts gave Thad enough relief from the fire that he could fight back harder. The air glowed between herself and Thad, and sparks danced wherever she touched his scales.

It soon became clear to Aura that Ladon was older or less used to fighting his own kind, while Thad was a warrior accustomed to battle. Ladon had started out fighting hard, but he was fading quickly. Thad was consistent, pacing himself so that he could sustain a longer battle. There were a flurry of punches exchanged, then Thad's claws tore through Ladon's wing.

Ladon lost altitude, but bit into Thad's wing with one set of teeth. He tore the leather and Thad cried out in pain. Ladon breathed fire with another head, moving so quickly that Aura didn't manage to put out the first spurt of fire. It burned Thad's wing so that it smoked. Aura extinguished the blaze with a gust of wind, then blew beneath Thad's wings to keep him airborne.

Ladon bellowed with fury. "Interfering nymph!" He lashed at the air with his tail, as if he would injure her, and his tail cut through the glow of light generated by the firestorm.

Thad's eyes blazed. "The fight is between you and me!" he cried.

"Then keep her from interfering!" Ladon shouted back.

"Stop, please, Aura," Thad said, just before he flew directly at Ladon and sank his claws into the other dragon's chest. Ladon's blood flowed over his scales from the wounds, and he breathed fire with new desperation. He struggled and bit, even as Thad's scales smoked, and Aura hated that she couldn't help.

Would Thad's sense of honor be his undoing? Ladon took a deep breath and breathed fire with all nine mouths, creating a blaze so bright that Aura couldn't look at it.

"No!" she cried, but Thad slammed the other dragon into a tree. He held him there, and punched each head until it sagged on its neck. He left one, then cast Ladon high into the air.

"You're no better than a viper," Thad declared, sending the other dragon flying through the air with a thump of his tail. "No other dragon would dare to interfere with a firestorm. No other dragon would think to injure a mate!"

Ladon fell heavily and the ground shook with the impact. Thad dived after him, but the other dragon held up a claw.

He coughed and considered Thad. "A firestorm?" he echoed, looking between Aura and Thad. For the first time, he seemed to notice the radiant orb of light between them. His eyes widened as he considered Thad. "You are *Pyr*."

"Aren't you?" Thad demanded. He was still agitated, still ready to fight. He flew in restless circles around the other dragon, and his eyes were narrowed to watchful slits. Aura noted the blood that stained his scales and winced that they were so singed.

"I am a dragon through and through," Ladon said with audible regret. "I have no power to change shape."

Aura could see that, for there was no alternate guise visible when she looked at Ladon. Thad, though, was clearly surprised.

"I've never known a dragon," he admitted.

"I've never known a *Pyr*," Ladon countered and Aura would have laughed out loud at their mutual astonishment if she'd had a better idea what to expect from the guardian of the garden.

To her relief, Ladon held out a claw in concession. "Help me up and show me this firestorm of legend."

Thad lifted Ladon bodily from the ground and eased him into

one of the more sturdy of the apple trees. The dragon sighed contentment to be there and coiled his tail immediately around the trunk. His wings fluttered to his back and his chins settled on various boughs.

Aura shifted shape and stood at the edge of the forest, close to Ladon. She saw the eyes close on six of his battered heads, but one of his gazes remained locked upon her. A second head watched Thad, while a third surveyed the garden at large, seeking intruders. Thad flew overhead, circling the garden as he peered in every direction. Aura frowned at the delay, but Ladon chuckled.

"They are said to be more protective than the rest of us," he said softly. "But the treasure held most dear by a *Pyr* is not a golden hoard or even an orchard of golden apples."

"What then?" Aura asked, curious.

Ladon smiled, revealing many sharp teeth. "His mate." Aura's heart skipped a beat and she couldn't hold Ladon's knowing gaze. She turned to watch Thad circle back toward her. "You are fortunate, Aura. It is said that there is no woman better loved than the mate of a *Pyr*."

Aura smiled, remembering Thad's words. *Let me love you.*

The glow around her heart made her think it might not take very long for her to love him back.

But a son.

Thad landed with that athletic grace, shifting shape just before his feet touched the ground, and Aura realized to her dismay that his injuries followed him between forms. He strode toward her, blood staining his strange clothing, and Aura ran to him in her concern. The firestorm's light brightened as she approached him but he smiled, obviously noticing her fears and appreciating them. "It's not so bad as it looks. I just need to wash out the wounds."

"A fierce glow," Ladon murmured. "Does it hurt?"

"Hardly," Thad said.

"But it burns," the other dragon said. "I can see that it must."

Thad smiled. "But not in a painful way."

Ladon looked between them, then smiled in understanding. His gaze seemed to linger on the flush in Aura's cheeks and she assumed he could sense that her heart was fluttering in Thad's presence.

"I have one favor to ask you before we satisfy the firestorm,"

Aura murmured and saw how her words pleased Thad. She might be a nymph but she didn't want an audience for their intimacy. She took Thad's hand to lead him to a stream. It was clear how much it pleased him that she touched him first, and she liked the way his fingers curled around hers. They shared a smile that heated her to her toes, and one she thought might have done so even without the firestorm's help. They had taken a dozen steps when the other dragon hailed them.

"A viper," Ladon called from the tree, like an old man determined to gossip at the worst possible moment. Aura looked at the ground and tried to summon her patience. "What do you know of vipers, young *Pyr*?"

"Only that they have to be killed," Thad said. His tone was hard and Aura glanced up to find his jaw set.

"Because you've done it?" Ladon was taunting, which Aura didn't understand.

Thad nodded only once. "I belonged to a force charged with that task."

"What are vipers?" Aura whispered.

"*Pyr* or dragons who turn against mankind," he replied quietly. "They sing a spell, low and deep, one that turns men's minds to hatred and bloodshed."

Aura nodded. She could already see his sense of honor and duty. Was he a dragon of his word? Aura liked to think so, and she knew what promise she wanted him to keep.

"Then you know what happened to Cadmus." Ladon's tone turned sharp. "Maybe you were responsible for the attack on Cadmus."

"I was there," Thad said tightly. "We fulfilled our mission." He looked back at the old dragon slithering in the tree, pride in his stance and confidence in his gaze.

"You failed," Ladon sneered.

"Only the first time."

"So you say. Maybe we old dragons can teach you *Pyr* a few things."

"Maybe not." They stared at each other, antagonism in Thad's stance.

What did Ladon know that Aura didn't? Ladon might be the guardian of the orchard but Aura had never really liked or trusted him. He was owed respect for his role as guardian, but he did seem to like making trouble.

"If he's dead, who struck the killing blow?" Ladon hissed. "If he's dead, who's singing his spell?"

"It doesn't matter," Thad replied. "What had to be done was done. You can believe me or not."

He dismissed the old dragon then, turning his attention to Aura. He smiled down at her and tightened his grip on her hand. "Lead on," he murmured, his gaze warm. The light of the firestorm burnished his features, making a wonderful glow between the two of them. He bent and stole a sweet hot kiss, one that made Aura more than ready to see him naked. "Will you bathe me, Aura?" he murmured.

Aura would have led him to the stream to do just that, but Ladon called out again. "They said the ones who attacked Cadmus were enchanted for their audacity and lost forever to the sands of time."

Thad froze and Aura felt the tension in him.

Was it true?

Thad turned with care and faced Ladon again. "They were wrong. I'm back."

"But Cadmus still sings."

"He won't do so forever," Thad said, his voice hard.

Ladon laughed. "Why should I believe you?"

"Because I don't lie."

"Is he lying?" Aura murmured.

Thad shook his head and gave Aura an intent look.

Would he confide in her? She hoped so.

She led him away from Ladon and the serpent's questions, although now she had a number of questions of her own.

Ladon had made her realize there was a lot she didn't know about Thad, his alliances and any missions he might have. She knew he must be honorable and knew he would fulfill any promises or duties. She could see already that that was his nature. But what about fighting these vipers? Could he be compelled to leave her and any son they had, no matter what she did and what he chose?

That wasn't a very encouraging possibility. Aura had to know more.

Ladon's words were like a toxin. Thad felt their effect upon Aura and saw the new hesitation in her manner. His anger flared at that. How dare that dragon meddle in a firestorm? How dare he undermine everything of importance?

"Were you enchanted?" Aura asked softly, so softly that even Ladon wouldn't be able to hear her.

"Yes, but I'm not anymore."

"Are you cursed?"

"Not unless you consider my nature to be a curse. I don't." He smiled at her, hoping to reassure her, but Aura seemed to still be troubled.

"What about she-who-should-not-be-named?"

He eyed her in confusion. "Who?"

"Hades gave her the right to seek vengeance on your kind in the mortal realm."

Thad frowned. "I don't know anything about that."

"But the viper?"

He turned to face her, knowing he had to reassure her. "It's true. We hunted a viper and we thought we killed him." Her eyes widened but he carried on. "It was Cadmus, who had turned against mankind."

"And thus was violating your mission." She squeezed his hands. "I like that you ensure the integrity of your own kind."

"We have to. It's part of our responsibility."

"I still like it," she admitted with a smile that encouraged Thad.

"He triumphed over us that first time, and we became dragon's teeth. Each warrior was enchanted to be a tooth in his maw." To Thad's relief, this didn't seem incredible to Aura, but then she was a nymph who heard regularly about enchantments.

"You each became a weapon to be used against others. That's very unpleasant, if clever. What saved you?"

"He was ancient then and withered, and soon he became no more than a pale worm in the shadows. Over the centuries, his teeth fell out and were buried in the earth. We slumbered in that form, trapped."

Her eyes were round. "Beguiled by his song?"

"Probably to some extent," Thad admitted. "One day we were found. The collection of teeth sold and traded hands, until it came into the possession of a *Pyr* who knew what we were and how to break the spell."

"How did he do it?"

"He sowed the teeth in the earth, like seeds, and we sprang forth from the soil, warriors once again."

"Was Cadmus dead?"

"Faded but not dead. He still sang his poisonous song to beguile men, even without his teeth, even with his faded strength. Under the direction of our old commander, we gathered and hunted him anew, and the second time, we triumphed."

Aura's smile faded as quickly as it had appeared. "But you said centuries had passed."

Thad nodded. He wasn't sure how she would accept or believe what he told her, but he wouldn't have any lies between them. "This happened almost twenty-five hundred years in the future."

"Yet you are here now. Can you journey through time? Is this a magical power of your own, or of your kind?"

Thad shook his head. He was glad that she was asking questions, and even more glad to be able to answer them honestly. The firestorm lit the night to a golden glow around them, and they spoke quietly together even as they walked. It was intimate and romantic and honest, everything Thad had always wanted to experience with his mate.

The answering light in Aura's eyes convinced him that the firestorm had chosen the perfect mate for him. He loved how she helped him in battle, and how they were already learning to use their powers together. He liked that they were both shifters, too.

They didn't have to have any secrets from each other.

"There is a force known to the *Pyr* called darkfire," he explained. "It's a strange and unpredictable power, and centuries ago, it was trapped within three quartz crystals to keep it contained. One crystal was broken in that distant future and the darkfire was set free. The light in another crystal was awakened and it called to our leader. When he had it in his hand, it carried our company through time and space, gradually separating us from each other."

"Which is why you are alone," she said, her sympathy clear.

Thad smiled. "I'm not alone. The darkfire brought me to my firestorm." He gripped her hands more tightly and the flames emanated from their linked hands. "It brought me to you, Aura."

"You don't miss your fellow warriors?"

He held her gaze with resolve. "I do, but I have faith that all will be as it should be. The darkfire brought me here for a reason, and I will see this firestorm a success if it is the last thing I do."

Aura studied him, so serious that he waited for whatever she was building up the courage to say.

"Will you do something for me?" she asked finally, her tone hinting that it was a request Thad might prefer to decline.

He nodded immediately.

She smiled at that. "Without even knowing what it is?"

"Of course. I trust you and I want you to trust me."

Aura reached beneath her flowing tunic and produced a golden apple. It was more than yellow in tone; it looked to be made of gold. It was perfectly formed, like a sculpture of an apple. "Take a bite, and tell me that everything you've said to me is true."

Thad smiled then, his confidence unshaken. "So, one of the stories is true," he murmured. He didn't wait for her answer, but took the apple from her.

Their fingers brushed during the transaction and a flurry of sparks erupted from the point of contact. The brilliant orange light was reflected in the gleaming surface of the fruit and in the darkness of Aura's eyes.

Thad bit into the apple, uncertain what to expect. It tasted as sweet as honey, and the flesh was firm. "It's pretty good," he said, surprised at the discovery, and Aura smiled. She might have laughed, but she was waiting. He sobered and looked into her eyes. "Every single thing I have told you, Aura, is the absolute truth." He reached for her hand and laced their fingers together, savoring the heat that built between their palms. "Let me love you."

"You don't want me to take a bite, too?"

"I trust you."

"And I trust you," Aura replied with a smile. She leaned closer and bit into the apple, her gaze locked with his. Her smile broadened, then turned mischievous. "Let's satisfy the firestorm," she murmured and Thad's heart leapt.

"I don't see any reason to rush," he whispered, then bent to kiss her cheek. Her skin was so soft and her perfume tempted him as none other could. He heard her catch her breath and yet again, his heart matched its pace to hers. The firestorm flared with a predictability that warmed his heart as well as everything else. He closed his eyes and kissed her earlobe, loving how her heart skipped in response. "How long do you think we can endure the firestorm's burn?" he whispered.

"I don't know," she murmured in reply and Thad melted at the brush of her lips across his own cheek. "But I'm willing to find out."

They were in perfect agreement about that.

The *Slayer* Jorge despised darkfire.

He had never been the kind of dragon who allowed others to control his choices, and having this incomprehensible force fling him through time and space did not suit Jorge's agenda at all. He had tried to make the most of being cast into the ancient world, after being dragged into the depths of the earth by Pele during Brandon's firestorm. That journey had ended badly for him at Delphi, with another sojourn in fathomless darkness before the darkfire had appeared again. He would have liked to have ignored the blue-green spark that beckoned him onward, but darkfire had gotten him into trouble and Jorge reasoned only darkfire could get him out of it.

He didn't trust the garden. He didn't trust it one increment more than he trusted the darkfire. There were no humans in the vicinity of the garden, which seemed to be hidden in a mountain pass, so he had no idea why he was there. There was no one to victimize or use for his own purposes, which made the garden a wasteland in Jorge's view. He took the form of a salamander and sulked over the injustice of his situation in the shade of rock.

He wasn't sure how long he'd been there when he felt the spark of a firestorm. He brightened at that, because a firestorm meant there'd be at least one human within proximity. Since he blamed the *Pyr* for many of his woes, Jorge liked the idea of taking out his frustrations on an enamored dragon shifter. Assassinating the mate of a *Pyr* would be a perfect way to improve his mood.

He smiled when he smelled the *Pyr*. It was one of the Dragon's Tooth Warriors, unless Jorge missed his guess. They had a distinctive scent about them, one that was evocative of the past yet not dusty or rotten. They were less readily distinguished from each other than their modern counterparts, but had firestorms all the same.

He couldn't smell the mate, even when he saw the shadow of the *Pyr* in question descending into the garden in dragon form, the heat of the firestorm illuminating him brilliantly.

Jorge crept out from the shade of his rock, cautious but curious.

If a salamander's eyes could widen in shock, those of the golden yellow salamander that was Jorge would have done so.

Because he suddenly caught a whiff of Viv Jason, the so-called ally of the *Slayer* Chen. She was here, and he could smell the heat of her fury.

Had the darkfire snared her, as well?

Surely, she couldn't be this *Pyr*'s destined mate?

Jorge had to know for sure.

Chapter Three

The apple had shown Aura the truth. Thad believed there would be a son, that the firestorm must result in the conception of a son.

But the apple revealed to Aura that there was no son in her future.

Thad was wrong.

It wasn't a crime to believe in the tales of his kind, and Aura actually counted his faith in his favor. He liked the story. He wanted it to be true.

She knew it wasn't, so she could be with him.

And Thad had immediately rewarded her decision with his plan to take their time. Aura had been seduced by more than one man, but they all had a single thing in common: they were in a hurry to satisfy their pleasure. Thad's intent to prolong the firestorm was wonderful and enticing to Aura.

It was a perfect evening in a perfect garden. The moon was rising and was full, its silver light almost as bright as sunlight in the garden. Aura led Thad to a sparkling fountain that was wide and deep. Stars were reflected in its surface and even better, there were no nymphs who claimed this water.

She would have her dragon all to herself.

Her blood was humming when she turned to face him. She removed her tunic, liking how he caught his breath at the sight of her nudity. She removed her sandals, feeling beautiful and provocative, simply as a result of the heat of his gaze. When she straightened, Thad has shed his strange clothing and was nude beside her. She flicked a glance over him and smiled.

He was everything she could hope a man—dragon shifter or not—could be.

"You undress quickly," she teased. "Is that anticipation?"

"Training put to good use," he replied. Aura didn't understand his words and she guessed that it showed. "We have to undress quickly to hide our clothes when we shift shape."

She reached to touch his injuries, dipping her free hand into the fountain and stroking away the blood. His wounds were already healing, a sign that dragon shifters were as vigorous as she would have expected them to be. "Can you shift back without them?"

"The story is no." He grinned, that crazy crooked confident smile that made her heart gallop. "The reality is not something I want to explore."

"Don't tell me a dragon is afraid."

"A wise dragon compensates for his weakness," he said with a lift of one brow, offering his hand to her in silent invitation.

She put her hand in his and the light of the firestorm flared brilliant yellow between them. "And how will you compensate for that one?"

"By having a partner who can be trusted completely." He kissed her fingertips, his gallant gesture prompting her smile. The heat in his eyes filled her with anticipation, and the touch of his lips on her fingers made her knees melt. He turned her hand and kissed her palm, folding her fingers over the burning imprint of his lips.

Aura sighed with delight. Thad spared her a mischievous glance, his hair falling over his eyes, then kissed the inside of her wrist. He trailed kisses up the inside of her arm, blazing a trail to her shoulder that dissolved every last shred of her inhibitions. Aura let her head tip back when he kissed her shoulder, her throat, her ear, then gasped as he bent to kiss her breasts.

She had never felt anything so good in her life.

She ran her hands over the muscled breadth of his shoulders, then up his neck, spearing her fingers into his hair. She laughed at the sight of the firestorm's sparks in his dark wavy hair, like fireflies in a thicket at twilight. She ran her fingertip over the dark blue mark on his skin, the image of a dragon, and the firestorm's light made it look touched with fire. He straightened and captured her lips beneath his own, claiming her with a kiss.

Thad swept Aura into his arms in one easy gesture. He carried her into the fountain, and Aura felt the water surround her as he sank into its depths. The fountain was deep enough that the water came to his shoulders, and the cascading spray fell all around them like a spring shower. The water, too, turned golden in the firestorm's light, as golden as Hera's apples and gleaming just as richly. She felt his hands slide over her beneath the surface and liked that his touch was both firm and gentle.

Thad pulled her astride him and Aura felt the size of his erection. As much as she wanted to feel his heat inside her, she twisted in his embrace. Thad broke his kiss and regarded her with concern, his expression making Aura feel playful. "You didn't change your mind," he whispered and she laughed, because it wasn't possible.

Not now.

"No, but the firestorm won't burn long this way," she teased, and his grin flashed. Then she pushed him back so suddenly that he lost his balance. He disappeared beneath the surface and Aura pursued him, seeing how he was holding his breath. She ran her hands over the hard lines of his body with unrestrained delight. She had wanted to touch him before and had caressed him as a breeze, but now she wanted to feel him with her hands. She felt his calves, his thighs, his buttocks, then closed her hands around his erection.

Thad caught his breath and locked his arm around her waist. He lunged out of the water, carrying Aura with him, and caught a deep breath at the surface. "I can't swim," he confessed.

"But I can," she said with a smile. She dipped below the surface and cupped her hands around him, then replaced them with her lips. She felt him moan as much as she heard it. As a nymph linked to the element of air, she was at ease in the water as a naiad. She breathed a stream of tiny bubbles, which frothed against Thad's skin even as she took his strength in her mouth. She closed her eyes against the brilliant glow of the firestorm and bent her attention to giving him pleasure. She felt his hands close around her head. She heard him catch his breath. When she wrapped her arms around him, she felt the pounding of his heart against her palm. The firestorm glowed with greater intensity, even as she gave him all the pleasure she could give.

She sensed that he was on the cusp of release when Thad seized her by the waist and drew her to the surface. He kissed her deeply and possessively, then lifted her to sit on the lip that surrounded the central pillar. He parted her thighs and kissed the insides of her knees, his playful glance making her blood simmer as much as his artful kisses. When his mouth closed over her, Aura leaned back and moaned from the depths of her being. The water was cascading all around her, the golden glow of the firestorm lit the night and her dragon was determined to make her roar.

Three times Aura found her pleasure that night, each peak higher than the last, before Thad lifted her out of the water, spread her on the lush grasses of Hera's garden and claimed her, body and soul, forever.

Chicago—June 1, 2012

Erik, leader of the *Pyr*, sat vigil.

He had been watching Drake sleep for three days and three nights. The other warrior had been utterly still in his slumber. Only a *Pyr* could detect the slight motion of Drake's chest as he breathed, and Erik had leaned close several times, just to be sure. Drake didn't move or roll around, just remained supine with his hands folded on his chest.

Three days and three nights.

Erik had to wonder if Drake would sleep for months. Forever? He leaned back in his chair and let his own breathing slow. Erik had been sure that Drake would have stories to tell him. He wanted to know what had happened to the other Dragon's Tooth warriors.

He wanted to ask if Drake knew why Erik's mind was afire.

Where had they been? Where had they gone? What had befallen them?

The darkfire crystal no longer held a spark. It was dead and empty, the crystal too faceted to even make a good scrying stone. Erik had stored it in his hoard, but he wasn't certain it had value anymore.

He let his eyes narrow to slits and listened to Drake's slow breathing. Eileen was maintaining the normal rhythm of their lives, sleeping at night and rising with the alarm clock. She looked in on him and reminded him to eat, even as she hurried to work and took Zoë to daycare. Erik waited with Drake, wanting to be the first one to hear of his experiences.

Wanting to ensure that Drake didn't slip away without telling him more.

As he sat in the darkened room, Erik did as he always did. He reviewed the locations of the *Pyr*. He felt a connection with each of his fellow dragon shape shifters, which was how he had inherited the task of leader. He was always aware of them, but when he sat in the dark, the links felt more tangible. There could have been a fine copper wire stretched between him and every individual *Pyr* who drew breath. Or maybe they were lines made of fire, for they shone in the darkness of his mind like long, thin conduits of flame. At the terminus of each was a larger flame, one that burned in a color or a way that reminded him of the *Pyr* in question.

There was Quinn, the Smith of the *Pyr*, charged with the power to heal their dragon scales. Sapphire and steel in his own dragon form, Quinn was staring into the glowing coals on the hearth, in his house outside Traverse City. He was listening, even while his partner Sara and sons Garrett and Ewen slept, and he was turning his challenge coin in one hand as if he sensed danger approaching.

There was Donovan, the Warrior of the *Pyr*, restless in the middle of the night at his home in Minneapolis St-Paul. Lapis lazuli and gold in his dragon form, Donovan was always learning new fighting skills. On this night, though, he was listening, standing still in his garage by his Ducati while his partner Alex slept. His sons Nick and Darcy slept while their father began to pace.

There was Delaney, Donovan's younger brother, standing at the front window of the house he shared with Ginger in Ohio. Erik heard Delaney's awareness that the dairy cows they raised were serene in the barn, and his surprise at that. Delaney was copper and emerald in his dragon form and more wiry than his older brother.

He inhaled deeply of the night air, as if expecting to catch a whiff of something in the wind, and listened to the world outside the house while Ginger and their sons Liam and Sean slept.

Niall Talbot, the Dreamwalker of the *Pyr*, was changing a diaper, his keen sense of smell so affronted by the odor that Erik smiled. Niall and Rox had twin boys, Kyle and Nolan. Erik was aware that Rox was beside Niall, changing the other boy's diaper, and that Niall was also listening for a sound that had not yet come.

He was not alone in his sense of foreboding.

Erik found that reassuring.

He followed a brilliant and sturdy line of fire to his old friend Rafferty, secure within the line of dragonsmoke that defended his townhouse in London. Rafferty was gold and opal in his dragon form and was humming softly, reinforcing the dragonsmoke even though it was already deep and thick. It was early morning there, and the *Pyr* abandoned his creation of dragonsmoke when his partner Melissa embraced him. Erik turned his attention away on purpose, not wanting to intrude, but noted that Rafferty also was preparing for a sensed threat.

Stretching beyond Rafferty's thread of gold was the glittering line that led Erik to Lorenzo, stage magician and chameleon of the *Pyr*. Lorenzo was staring out of his home at the waters of the Grand Canal in Venice, looking so intently into the water that it seemed he expected something or someone to suddenly appear. Erik felt Lorenzo jump when his partner Cassie spoke to him, a remarkable thing given how observant Lorenzo was.

On a shoal west of the Hawai'ian islands, Brandon scanned the horizon, as if expecting a storm. He stayed close beside his pregnant partner, Liz, and Erik felt the younger *Pyr*'s readiness to leap into a fight. Brandon's father, Brandt, even farther away in Australia stood on a beach and listened to the sound of the wind with care.

Erik spared only the barest glance at Thorolf, because he was so disappointed in that *Pyr* and his choices. Given his lineage, Thorolf should have been not just a large dragon with fearsome appetites but a force for change and good in the world. Instead, he fought, drank and seduced women. Erik knew he shouldn't be surprised that Thorolf alone was oblivious to any threat, engaged in a bout of lovemaking with some woman in Bangkok. Erik didn't want to know if that *Pyr* was also drunk so he turned his attention away quickly.

In California, Sloane, the Apothecary of the *Pyr*, was stirring some concoction as it cooled. He stood in bare feet in his kitchen, the glass doors slid back and the evening breeze sweeping through his house, which perched on a hilltop, his attention distracted from his task by something he sensed drawing nearer.

They all—with the exception of Thorolf—sensed the same portent that Erik felt. He wondered if their minds were aflame like his, too. Because that was the sum of the *Pyr* remaining. Their numbers had dwindled over the centuries. Though Erik had hopes for the next generation of dragon shifters, they wouldn't come into their powers until puberty. In a sense, they were slumbering like Drake. He was used to an array of glimmering lines of gold in his mind, enough that he could count them readily, enough that he could feel comforted that he wasn't alone, enough to cast a glow in the darkness of his dreams.

The problem was that lately, there had been a fireball in his mind. He could see and follow the same lines that he knew well, but hovering on the edge of his vision was a brilliant halo of light. Erik could make no sense of it.

But it drew steadily closer. It had first lit when Drake took the darkfire crystal from Lorenzo, and it had become almost blinding in its intensity when Drake appeared at his door three days before. It was clear to Erik that his fellow *Pyr* sensed a change as well, though none of them knew what it might be. There were others of their kind, *Slayers* who had turned to the shadows, but the *Slayers* who survived had drunk the Dragon's Blood Elixir. That extinguished them completely from Erik's network of lights and made their doings mysterious. It wasn't the first time he'd worried about Chen and his doings.

The light was brighter on this night, and it seemed to Erik that a thousand points of light converged on him. He shook his head and sighed, frowning at Drake. He didn't know whether to dread or celebrate the fact that one of these days, the source of this new light would become clear.

There would be a partial eclipse in three days. Would there be a firestorm sparked by the eclipse? If so, whose? Sloane? Thorolf?

And what did this sense of foreboding mean?

Erik debated the merit of awakening Drake immediately, but the older warrior seemed worn thin. He sat back in his chair, impatient but determined to give Drake the time he needed.

For the moment.

The pilgrim paused in his journey to cough.

He didn't have much choice, really. The urge came from deep inside him, and he feared that once he began to cough, he wouldn't be able to stop. Each spasm was longer than the last, more exhausting, more painful, and seemed more likely to be his last.

He coughed. He choked. He felt his chest clench and his body shake. He saw blood in his spittle, more than the last time, and was profoundly grateful when his coughing stopped.

He was also exhausted. His knees were trembling and he felt too close to the end.

Unfortunately, his journey wasn't complete. He looked up the ascending road to the pass that he believed led to the fabled Garden of the Hesperides. He'd hoped to reach that place before he died. He'd hoped to throw himself at the mercy of Hera, and maybe, just maybe, to be given a bite from one of her golden apples. That fruit was said to have the power to heal anything, and he had pursued every other cure, without success.

Now he feared he would die before he reached the garden at all.

He sighed, more weary than should be possible, and noticed a tree at one side of the road. This path was mostly barren of vegetation. He'd thought it a feat of the goddess herself, in order to increase the impression of the garden's lush greenery by contrast. If so, he doubted he'd ever see that contrast.

He stumbled to the tree and almost collapsed beneath it, leaning back against its sturdy trunk. The sun hadn't risen yet, but the air beneath the tree was still cooler and fresher, almost rejuvenating in itself. He looked up and smiled at the way the leaves blew, stirred by a breeze he could not feel. He could see the stars through the tree's boughs and he felt safe, as if sheltered from harm.

He shook his head at his own whimsy and reached into his pack for his skin of water. There was nowhere safe in all the world, he'd learned that the hard way, and a tree's branches were no refuge. He supposed his illness had progressed to the point that he was losing his wits.

He tried to be accepting of that and failed.

He opened the skin with a savage gesture, resenting that he should be the one to fall so ill, that his body should fail him when he was still comparatively young, and that was when he saw her.

A woman was hunkered down and watching him, not ten steps away. She wore a dark cloak of roughly woven cloth, one that she'd pulled over her head so that he'd mistaken her for a rock in the shadows. Her eyes shone from within the darkness of her hood though, her gaze so bright that he shivered.

On impulse, he offered the skin of water. "Thirsty?" he asked. "It is yours, if you want it." He gestured to himself. "There are those who want nothing from a sick man like myself, and I wouldn't blame you if you chose to die of thirst instead."

To his surprise, she scuttled forward, moving more like an insect than a woman. She paused an arm's length from him, considering him warily, then snatched the skin away. She drank of it so gratefully that he felt sympathy for her.

"It was hot yesterday," he said. "Did you drink all the water you'd brought?"

She nodded, then halted to offer the skin back to him.

He smiled, knowing she must still be parched. "Drink some more. It won't help me as much as it will help you."

Again she studied him, little discernible of her features except those glinting eyes. She drank again, gratefully and greedily, and the pilgrim was glad that something good had come of his journey.

"You're going to the garden," she said, when the skin was nearly empty. She offered it to him again and he drained it.

Then he nodded. "Well, I was, but I won't make it there now."

"Why not?"

"Because I am sick, so sick that no one can help me." He shrugged. "I had an idea that Hera herself might show mercy upon me, if I asked her politely."

The old woman cackled. "Can you ask nicely enough?"

He grinned. "I could try." She gave him such a skeptical look that the pilgrim had to consider himself, so gaunt that his bones showed, running sores on his flesh and his hair almost gone. His teeth had fallen out months before and his nails had turned black. The idea of him courting the favor of a great goddess, even as he looked as he did, made him laugh at the absurdity of it all.

That launched another coughing spasm, one that left him shaking beneath the tree long moments later. The blood in his spittle was bright red. He could taste it and knew there was more of it than ever before.

So, he would pass under this tree. It was no so bad a place to die.

To his surprise, the old woman hadn't left. "You are sick," she said, helping him to sit up. She had an unexpected strength and her hands, when he glimpsed them, were as unlined as those of a maiden. She hid them away so quickly that he wondered if his vision was fading, as well.

"I am dying," he said, having no need for pretense. "It will not be long now. You should go. Take the rest of my provisions, and may your journey go well."

But she didn't go. She moved closer and took his hand in hers. He would have looked but the pain rose within him, and he closed his eyes against it, taking comfort from her touch.

"I will stay with you," she said, her voice gentle. "If you like."

The pilgrim gritted his teeth against the rise of another spasm, trusting himself only to nod.

"I will tell you a story," the old woman said, settling herself beside him with his hand firmly locked in hers.

Thad awakened hours later, relaxed and content. The sky was turning rosy in the east and the plants in the garden were heavy with dew. He could still see stars in the western sky, but his attention was captured by the beauty nestled in his embrace. Aura had been everything he'd hoped and more. The firestorm had lived up to its reputation. And now, Aura would have his son and they would create a life together.

He bent and kissed her forehead. A spark crackled between her soft skin and his lips, making Thad withdraw in shock.

Had he imagined it?

Aura turned and nestled against him, her hand trailing down the length of his chest. To Thad's astonishment, a glow lit in the wake of her caress, as if the embers of the firestorm were being stirred to life again.

But how could that be? The firestorm was always satisfied the first time a *Pyr* and his destined mate made love. He and Aura had made love more than once the night before. How could the firestorm still burn?

There could be no doubt, though. The light caress of her fingertips summoned the heat within him again, and radiance began to grow between them. The light was deep orange but becoming brighter and whiter by the moment.

She wasn't pregnant.

She wasn't carrying his son.

He was being punished. But why? Why was he unworthy? He had served with his fellows. He had hunted vipers. He had been enchanted and survived, then returned to finish the viper Cadmus. He had obeyed Drake without question.

Had Cadmus cursed the Dragon's Tooth Warriors forever? Had he somehow been cheated of his birthright?

Thad rolled away from Aura, unable to think of another reason the firestorm could continue to burn. Worse, he couldn't think of a way to set things to rights.

He was so filled with restless energy that he might have gotten to his feet and paced, but he felt Aura's hand on his shoulder. As well as the brush of her fingertips, there was the warming glow of the firestorm on his skin, heating him from within, making him think that another romantic interval might solve the issue.

But it wouldn't. Thad knew it.

"Awake already?" Aura murmured. "Come back to me. I like mornings."

Thad turned around, captured her hand and kissed it. "I can't," he said, and saw her confusion. He stood up then and shoved a hand through his hair, uncertain what to do.

"What's wrong?" Aura was braced on one elbow, her hair tumbling over her shoulders, her lips so soft and ripe that Thad yearned for another taste. He turned his back on her, wanting to solve the problem.

"The firestorm is still burning."

"So, it is."

Thad heard her get to her feet. She made a little incoherent sound as she stretched and he couldn't resist the temptation to look. She was as luscious and alluring as when he'd first glimpsed her. The firestorm heated to a simmer, driving practical issues from his thoughts.

Aura caught his gaze and smiled, extending one hand to him. "We wanted to prolong it and it looks like we succeeded. Let's put that spark to good use." It took everything within Thad not to take her up on that offer.

He had to make his case while he still could. "Don't you see? The firestorm is still burning!" He gestured and sparks flared from his fingertips when his hand neared her.

Aura folded her arms across her chest and watched him warily. "This was a good thing last night, but it's a bad thing this morning?"

"It shouldn't have happened."

"It did happen. We can enjoy it."

"But you should be pregnant!" Thad flung out his hands. "The firestorm should be satisfied the first time a *Pyr* and his destined mate are intimate."

"Because she always conceives the first time?" Aura asked, her tone skeptical. Thad nodded and she smiled. "*Every* time?"

"Every time! That's how it works."

"Well, I don't think we did it wrong," Aura teased, coming to his side. She ran her fingertips over his shoulder and down his arm, her gaze following her touch. Thad swallowed, feeling his entire being focus on her and the heat she generated. She bent and touched her lips to his shoulder, sending a surge of desire through him that weakened his knees. "We could try again, just to be sure," she whispered against his flesh, then closed her hand around his erection.

Thad shut his eyes, not having the strength to step away from her caress. "Aura, you don't understand. This is important. I must have failed the *Pyr* somehow..."

Aura froze. "You? Never! There has to be another reason."

"What could it be? The firestorm sparked, I followed its heat to you, and it should be satisfied." He glanced down to find consideration in her gaze. "You should be carrying my son."

Aura regarded him with new wariness. "And without the son, you don't want me?"

"I want both!"

She leaned closer, her gaze intent. "Which do you want more?"

Thad stared at her. He knew his answer was important to her, and he could guess why, but the situation made no sense. "I shouldn't have to choose," he said. "The firestorm should be satisfied, and we should be planning a life together, you, me and our son."

Aura shook her head. "What if I told you that I was never going to have your son?"

"What?" Thad took a step back, moving away from the distraction of her enticing touch. "Why not? Don't you want to have a child?"

Aura held his gaze, her own resolve clear. "I don't want to *only* have a child, Thad, and I don't want to have a child alone."

"But I promised you..."

"I know." Aura frowned. "But you were wrong and I knew it." She met his gaze and smiled slightly. "I couldn't resist you."

Thad took a step back. "I don't understand. You knew the firestorm wouldn't be satisfied, and you didn't tell me?"

"I didn't know that, not exactly." Aura sighed. "I see the future, Thad. It's my gift. When you came to me, I looked into the possibilities of the future. There was no child in our joined future."

Thad shook his head. "That's impossible. That's how the firestorm works."

"I know you believe that. I was uncertain, because you were sure there would be a son, yet my vision was so clear that there wouldn't be one."

"That's why we came here," Thad said in sudden understanding. "That's why you wanted me to eat a golden apple."

"I needed to know whether you were telling me the truth." Aura shrugged. "You were, at least as much of it as you knew." She smiled slightly, her expression apologetic. "But you were wrong, Thad. There is never going to be a son from our union." She lifted her hand and the firestorm's flames danced between them. "Looks like you're the only one who expects otherwise. Is that so bad? We could have a lifetime of nights like this together." Aura reached for him. "We can share so much pleasure, without worrying about consequences. Think of a hundred nights like last night, a hundred flights across the seas, a hundred secret refuges that only you and I can reach together. We could have so much together."

Thad was tempted, but he caught her hands in his. "Not if I'm a failure to my kind."

"You don't know that's true."

"There has to be some reason! The firestorm is always satisfied."

"We could have each other," Aura urged.

Thad spun away from her and paced. Was it a curse from Cadmus or his own failure at root? The problem was that he couldn't think of how he had failed his kind. He felt Aura watching him and was aware that the firestorm's heat faded with distance. He turned back to study her and couldn't help but notice that she wasn't as agitated as he was.

In fact, she seemed disappointed. He couldn't bear the sight of her resignation. Just then, Thad remembered Rafferty's firestorm. Rafferty's mate hadn't been able to conceive a child at all, but the firestorm had brought them together and subsequently brought a daughter to them. Was there something wrong with Aura? He couldn't believe it. Was there a kind of sorcery in this garden that obstructed the firestorm? No matter what was going on, he had to follow Rafferty's lead and be true to his mate.

He marched back to Aura's side, feeling the heat build between them with every step. He saw the sheen of tears in her gaze, although she tried to hide it. "Tell me," he invited in a murmur.

"I had hoped that I might be enough."

Her words cut deep, because Thad had never meant to imply that she was less than his every dream come true. "You are enough," he insisted. "I will stay with you. The Great Wyvern chose you as my destined mate because our futures are entwined, and because there is more that we can do together."

She eyed him. "But a son was part of your expectation."

Thad had to nod agreement to that. "But you accepted me,

only because there *wasn't* going to be a child," he said, no accusation in his tone. She dropped her gaze in acknowledgement and his heart clenched. "Why don't you want my son, Aura?"

"It's not your son, Thad. It's any son. Any child, really."

Had Aura been able to interfere with the firestorm's promise?

Aura turned her back on Thad, and he knew this was important to her. He followed her and caught her shoulders in his hands, bending to touch his lips to her neck. He felt her shiver in response to the same shimmer of heat that erupted from the point of contact and rolled through his body. He could have tried to change her mind with passion, especially with the firestorm on his side, but Thad sensed that he had to listen. "I won't abandon you, Aura. I promise. Son or no son, our futures are bound together."

Her hand rose so that her fingers entangled with his, and he felt her trembling. "I believe you," she admitted quietly, and he was relieved. "But I still don't see a son in our future."

"You think you know why," he dared to guess and she nodded once. "Aura, tell me."

She glanced up at him, both enticing and vulnerable. "Remember that tree?"

Thad was startled by the change of topic. He spared a glance at the orchard of golden apples, but Aura shook her head. "Not those trees."

"The one outside the garden?" he asked, unable to think of another she'd singled out for his attention. Aura nodded. The tree had something to do with the firestorm?

"Let's go there, now, and I'll tell you a story."

Thad was ready to do anything to fulfill the firestorm and to win Aura's trust, even if he couldn't understand her reasoning as yet. He summoned the change from deep within himself and savored the surge of power that rolled through him with his transformation. He took flight over the lush garden, then hovered over Aura.

She had picked up the golden apple, the one they had shared. It had two distinct bites out of it but was otherwise intact. She tucked it into her tunic, hiding it from view, then smiled at him and lifted her arms toward him. "Show me what it's like to fly with a dragon," she demanded, and Thad was only too glad to comply.

She was his mate. She was his future. He would spend every

moment of his life believing in the firestorm and proving as much to her.

And if the firestorm burned for all of that time, he would savor every spark.

Thad swept down and gathered Aura up, chuckling at her shout of delight. He soared high over the garden, even as her hair swirled around him and tickled his scales. She was unafraid, her eyes shining. He showed off a little, wanting to prompt her laughter, but only until she pointed to the road outside the garden.

"The tree," she commanded, so fearless that he knew she was his match in every way.

"The tree," Thad agreed, fixing her with an intent look. "And the story."

Aura nodded and settled against him, leaning her cheek against his chest. Thad raced out of the garden and over the lip of the mountaintop, spiraling through the air in a way he knew Aura would appreciate. He was so busy trying to show her the similarities between their powers that he didn't notice the scale from his chest fall free and into her hand.

The dark scale lifted from Thad's hide so easily that it might not have really been attached. Aura caught it in her hand and glanced up at him, realizing immediately that he hadn't noticed it fall. He was intent upon flying, and while she admired his skill, the scale mystified her.

Did the *Pyr* lose their scales like this all the time?

It couldn't have hurt him to lose it, or he would have noticed. Maybe the *Pyr* routinely shed scales and grew new ones. But when Aura looked over Thad's muscled dragon form, she couldn't see another missing scale anywhere. The dark scales were locked over each over in perfect rows, as if providing complete protection.

Except for the spot this one had left bare. Aura could see a bit of uncovered skin, and it worried her to think that her dragon had any vulnerabilities. She'd ask him more about the scale after she told him the story she'd promised him.

The sky was brighter in the east and the sun had crested the horizon. When Thad flew high, they were above the lingering shadows of the night, and a crisp wind lifted Aura's hair. She wondered if it was anyone she knew, a notion that made her smile.

"I'm waiting," Thad murmured in old-speak and Aura smiled.

It was so easy to confide in Thad. Aura knew that was because she trusted him to keep his word.

"Once upon a time," she said. "There was a beautiful nymph."

"I know a beautiful nymph," Thad interjected and she poked him.

"A different nymph."

"Then she must have been less beautiful than my nymph."

Aura smiled at his possessive tone then continued. "She loved to make music in the world around her. She would make water spray so that it splashed on broad water lily leaves, or cast it tinkling into a pool of still water. She would blow through the rushes so they whistled and race through icicles so they made a sparkling tune. She was happy with these amusements and would have stayed so."

"But..." Thad prompted.

"One day, Zeus himself spied her and was filled with lust. She refused his advances but he was determined to have her. He tricked her by becoming a tree with silvery leaves that made music when they were stirred by the wind. She discovered this and couldn't resist the tree, for the music it made was sweeter than sweet. The third time she blew through the tree's leaves, Zeus surprised her. He changed shape, captured her and claimed her by force. Once he had had his fill of the beautiful nymph, he abandoned her on a remote hilltop and went in search of another beauty to claim."

Thad stilled at this and fixed her with a look that commanded the truth. "Are you certain I don't know this nymph?" He looked dangerous and ready to avenge her, even against the king of the gods.

"Positive," Aura said, liking how Thad closed one claw more protectively around her. He flew higher, taking a turn over the mountain that sheltered the garden and narrowed his gaze as he stared toward the horizons. Was he checking the area for amorous gods? Aura could believe not only that, but that he wouldn't flinch from defending her.

The warm glow of the firestorm surrounded them, like an orb

of golden light, its caress making her imagine many earthy ways to reward her loyal dragon.

But first, the story.

"Hera knew of her husband's infidelity, but she blamed the nymph for tempting Zeus. She came to the nymph, determined to punish her. Once Hera saw the result of what her husband had done, though, she felt only pity for the nymph who had been so ill-used. She also knew at a glance that the nymph would bear Zeus's daughter. The nymph had no desire to play or change shape any more. She was weary of the world and begged Hera to help her somehow. She vowed to accept any price to avoid the lust of gods and men.

"This suited Hera very well, for she didn't want Zeus returning to the nymph—not for the sake of any of them. So, Hera made the nymph an offer: she would change the nymph into a tree, a tree with lovely silver leaves that made music in the wind, and the nymph would be safe forever from the desires of men and gods in that guise. The nymph loved this idea and would have accepted immediately, but Hera told her that she was going to have a daughter by Zeus. The nymph felt snared by this news and appealed to Hera for help.

"Hera had been trapped by the children of Zeus and his lovers before, so she resolved to make an ally of this unborn daughter. She offered to raise the nymph's daughter as her own, letting the girl grow up in the Garden of the Hesperides, which was tended by other nymphs. The nymph gratefully agreed, asking only that her daughter knew the truth of her conception. Hera said she would do better than that and give the daughter the gift of foresight, so that she would know the result of any union before it occurred. She took the nymph to the Garden of the Hesperides and after her daughter was born, Hera kept her promise and raised the child there. She ensured that the daughter not only knew her mother's story but visited her mother often on the hill below, stirring the silver leaves to make music."

Thad turned high in the sky then and dove toward the tree, his choice telling Aura that he understood her meaning. It was as thrilling to soar down toward the mountain in his grasp as it was to do it herself and Aura held fast to his mailed chest as he descended. He flew around the tree with a flourish, and Aura saw that there were two pilgrims beneath its shelter.

It was just as she'd expected.

Thad must have seen the pair, too, because he continued in old-speak. *"And one day, the nymph met a* Pyr, *who was determined to win her heart forever. He called the sparks that flew between them 'the firestorm' and insisted that they were destined lovers. The nymph knew there would be no son, but she brought him back to the Garden of the Hesperides, giving him a golden apple to see if he was sincere in his pledge to stay with her forever."*

"And he was," Aura whispered in the speech of her own kind.

"And he was," Thad agreed. He landed beside the tree with ease, shifting shape in the last moment so that Aura was surrounded by a sparkle of pale blue light. Then Thad was in his human form, holding her in his embrace, his strength against his softness and the heat of the firestorm between them. *"And so she brought him to meet her mother,"* he said, before he bent to brush his lips across hers.

CHAPTER FOUR

The firestorm was blinding in its brilliance as Thad kissed Aura. She reveled in his kiss, not even caring that they were being watched. Finally he lifted his head and smiled down at her, his satisfaction so clear that Aura smiled in return.

She knew what she had to do.

"So she did," she murmured aloud, and changed to a breeze. She flew through the leaves of the solitary tree, making the silver leaves tinkle against each other. They made a beautiful music, more beautiful than Aura had ever heard before, and she dared to believe that her mother approved of Thad.

That was when the man beneath the tree caught his breath. "You tell a story well, my friend," he said, his voice weak with pain. "I can almost hear the music of that tree's leaves. I could believe myself to be there."

"You are there," said the cloaked woman beside him. Aura caught sight of the woman's smile and knew her identity without doubt. She spun around the tree, making the leaves tinkle with joy, suspecting that Hera would reveal herself in a moment.

But the goddess had no chance to fling back her hood. A cold shadow passed over the tree. Aura even shivered in her breeze form, her move making the leaves vibrate tunelessly.

A heartbeat later, a woman with hair the color of a flame stood a dozen steps away from them, her smile so malicious that Aura was chilled. She hadn't been there before, Aura was certain of it.

"Murderer and thief!" she said, her voice dropping low with threat. She pulled a knife and twirled it, then advanced upon Thad.

"I will avenge my sister's death upon your kind, *Pyr*, one dragon at a time."

"She-who-should-not-be-named," Aura said in the speech of her kind and Thad started. She knew from his expression that he didn't fully understand and wished she'd told him what she'd learned from the other nymphs.

He remained calm and spoke reasonably to the woman stalking toward him, and Aura appreciated that he tried to find a peaceful solution.

"Why don't we talk about this?" he suggested. "I don't know your sister, but I'm sure we can work out any misunderstanding..."

The woman laughed, and Thad cringed at the harsh sound. She snapped her fingers and changed shape in a flash of brilliant blue. She became a winged hag with eyes that dripped blood on the ground. She looked like something from a nightmare, but Aura knew this was the truth of her appearance.

Tisiphone's naked body was smeared with blood and perhaps something darker. The smell of her was foul. Her hair writhed, and Aura saw it was composed of glistening black snakes. When she laughed, her rotted teeth were visible. Her fingernails were yellow and her breasts sagged low. She was ancient and withered and should have commanded sympathy, but the fury of her expression and the large bat wings sprouting from her back inspired only horror.

When Tisiphone leapt toward Thad, with all the vigor of youth, Aura feared her dragon would not survive. Thad suffered from no such doubt. Aura saw him change shape and leap into the air in his dragon form, roaring as he lunged at Tisiphone with talons bared, more than ready to fight.

Jorge huddled behind a rock, sniffing. He had a keen sense of smell, keener even than that of the other *Pyr* and *Slayers*. His senses had sharpened when he'd drunk the Dragon's Blood Elixir. Now, he inhaled deeply of the dying pilgrim's scent, trying to identify the man's illness.

It was fierce, whatever it was, a kind of pestilence that was rotting his body from the inside out. It had worked insidiously, leaving the man oblivious to the true state of his health, only revealing itself when there was no hope for him. Jorge admired that kind of stealthy assault.

It wasn't cancer.

It wasn't plague.

It wasn't smallpox or influenza or SARS or ebola. It wasn't any of the familiar suite of illnesses that plagued mankind in the twentieth and twenty-first centuries.

It was, perhaps, something that had been lost and forgotten over the centuries, much as the Dragon's Tooth Warriors should have been.

That intrigued Jorge. He had no doubt it was contagious, given the right circumstances, because all living organisms multiplied to survive. He had no doubt that he would be spared whatever foulness it might do to a body, both because his body was *Slayer* not human, and because he had sipped of the Dragon's Blood Elixir, the source of immortality for his kind. He could recover from any illness or injury, in time.

And if this one took him a while to recover, it just might be worth the price.

Because Jorge knew that the darkfire wasn't done with him. It had some mission, some quest that would ultimately favor the *Pyr*. The darkfire was closely associated with them, after all, and favored their efforts over those of the *Slayers*. He wouldn't have been surprised to learn that the darkfire had swept him back in time to see him eliminated forever, for example.

But Jorge wasn't that easy to eliminate.

Plus Viv Jason was here. He guessed that she had somehow been created in this journey of Drake's *Pyr* to the past, but that meant she had to be flung into the future. He knew her in the early twenty-first century, so somehow the darkfire had to get her there.

Jorge intended to tag along.

In fact, he intended to take a piece of this pilgrim with him when he went. Whatever disease plagued this pilgrim might be just what the *Slayers* needed to exterminate the human race for once and for all.

The remaining *Pyr* would probably die of loneliness.

Jorge couldn't wait. He crept out of the shadow of his rock in his salamander form, watched the *Pyr* fight the creature that Viv Jason had become. He judged the distance to the pilgrim, mustered his strength and waited for his moment.

The hag was strong.

The smell of her wasn't the worst of it.

Thad had known there was something wrong with the red-haired woman, because her scent had seemed off. He'd sensed that she was hiding something, but hadn't been sure of what until she changed shape.

He guessed that this guise was her reality, and she thought it wise to hide this form from casual view. She was hideous and terrifying, the sight of her so horrifying that he'd almost recoiled and taken a blow. In this form, the scent of her was an assault in itself, a horrible mixture of blood and excrement. Thad lunged toward her, wanting to defend the others, even as she leapt at him.

He breathed dragonfire, but the flames didn't stop her. He smelled her hair burning and heard her manic laughter at the same time. She darted through the flames, blood running from her eyes, and jumped at Thad. She locked her arms around his neck, cackling into his face. He was appalled by the feel of her skin. It was cold and clammy, like the skin of a corpse, and when he tried to toss her aside, his talons sank through the soft rot of her body.

She beat at him with her wings, kicked at him with her legs and spat in his eye. It was against his nature to injure an elderly woman, even one so awful as this, but revulsion convinced Thad that she needed no concession from him.

Thad bellowed with fury as he took flight. He guessed this was a fight to the death and wanted this creature away from the others. Even if she killed him, he wanted it to be difficult for her to claim anyone else. He tore the hag free of his neck and cast her into the air before him, exhaling a ferocious plume of dragonfire at her. The flame burned hotter and whiter than he expected and he knew Aura was helping him by fanning the flames.

The hag laughed and turned in the air, flying hard against the wind that would have driven her out to sea. That was Aura again, and Thad was encouraged that together, he and his mate might win the fight. Thad pursued the hag, breathing fire all the while. He heard the screams of the black snakes as they were fried and smelled her skin burning, but she didn't surrender.

She dropped suddenly like a stone, and too late, Thad realized she did it to duck out of the wind. In an instant, she was behind him and latching on to his back. He felt her nails dig in to his shoulders and spun in an effort to shake her free.

"First you, then all the *Pyr*," she vowed. "I'll kill all of you and see your kind exterminated for your crime."

"But what crime is this?" Thad demanded. "We defend the treasures of the earth, the four elements and humankind."

"There are others you slaughter," she muttered and tore at his skin with her nails. The snakes in her hair tried to bite at him, but his scales protected him.

Thad guessed she was trying to rip a scale free, so those snakes could poison him with their venom.

"What others?" He flew a tight somersault, twisting hard, and her own weight pulled her free. He slashed at her as she fell, catching one of her wings with his claw. His talon tore through the leather of her wing and she screamed in anguish. The snakes that made her hair writhed with greater agitation, and she leapt on him again. She had hold of his leg, her grip holding fast no matter how Thad shook.

"Your kind owes me for the death of my sister," she declared.

"I know nothing about your sister!" Thad flew at the mountain and swung his leg hard against a precipice. The woman hit the rock with her back, and blood flowed from her injury as she released her grip on him.

The wound didn't slow her down, though. She was after him again, flying unevenly, but determination bringing her closer. "Ask your friend, then," she whispered. "Ask Damien."

"Damien! You've seen Damien?" Thad held off from striking the hag at this news of his fellow warrior. "You've been to the Underworld? Is he still there?"

She smiled coldly, and he knew she'd keep any knowledge of Damien from him, just because she could. "You show great concern for a murderer. But then, I expected you'd be two of a kind."

"If Damien killed anyone, it must have been in defense of himself or his mate..." Thad began, then caught a whiff of a scent he'd never expected to smell again.

Slayer!

But there were no *Slayers* in this ancient world. The dragon shifters who had chosen the darkness were creature of the future...unless the darkfire had cast one back in time, along with the Dragon Legion. Because Thad knew that scent of rot and decay, a smell that made him shiver even more than the stench of the hag he found. He struck her hard then pivoted in the air, seeking the *Slayer*.

There!

"*Slayer!*" he cried, pointing at the yellow salamander that was racing toward the pilgrim. He scanned the area for Aura, but she must still be a breeze. "Look out, madam!" he shouted to the old woman who crouched beside the dying man. She looked up at him in confusion and Thad knew he had to help her.

It was the creed of the *Pyr* to defend mankind, after all.

The hag's vengeance would have to wait.

He flew hard toward the old woman and the pilgrim, determined to ensure their safety. He felt the hag snatch at the end of his tail, but didn't have time to do more than try to shake her off. He saw the yellow salamander that was the *Slayer* look up from the dirt road. He heard the *Slayer* snarl and saw him swing his tail.

He recognized this *Slayer*. It was Jorge, a particularly mercenary *Slayer* from the twenty-first century.

Thad had time to blame the darkfire for Jorge's presence, then everything happened very fast.

Aura couldn't watch.

She couldn't *not* watch.

Tisiphone fought hard, clearly as determined to kill Thad as she'd said she was. She wouldn't rest until her sister's death was avenged, although Thad's companion Damien probably hadn't realized what he'd set in motion. He probably had been defending his mate.

Maybe Aura hadn't seen a child in her shared future with Thad because Thad didn't have a future.

It was a terrifying idea.

Aura was deeply afraid of the Erinyes and their lust for vengeance, yet she tried to help Thad by blowing against Tisiphone when possible. She fanned the flames of his dragonfire, too, making it burn hotter and whiter. She liked to think she had made some difference, but Tisiphone's thirst for vengeance was powerful.

She saw Thad catch a scent of something, for his nostrils pinched shut and his manner became even more alert. She saw him scan the ground, averting his attention from Tisiphone for a dangerous moment.

She didn't understand why he called the yellow salamander a *Slayer*, much less what a *Slayer* was, but she understood his sense of urgency. He saw the creature as a threat. Thad dove toward the salamander, claws outstretched and fire billowing from his jaws.

The salamander snarled, then shimmered blue.

In an instant, the salamander had become a yellow dragon, just as large and powerful as Thad. Aura gasped as the yellow dragon took flight, meeting Thad part way, and the pair locked talons. They spun end over end in a bid for supremacy, biting and slashing at each other. The contrast between them was striking, Thad's scales so dark as to be almost black with orange around the perimeter and the *Slayer*'s scales brilliant yellow.

Their tails entwined and Aura could see the strength of their grips. Their talons dug into each other and the dragonfire they exhaled burned hot and bright. Aura smelled burning scales and swirled around Thad, trying to cool his burns.

Thad bit suddenly at the chest of the *Slayer*, sinking his teeth deep into his opponent's flesh. The *Slayer* cried out as his blood ran black from the wound. It dripped to the ground and hissed on impact, emitting a plume of steam.

The *Slayer* tore himself free, slashing at Thad so that his shoulder was torn, including the tendon to his wing. Thad's blood ran brilliant red, and Aura guessed this was somehow indicative of the difference between them. Thad's flight faltered because of his damaged wing. He dropped a bit in the sky, and the *Slayer* laughed.

Then the *Slayer* did a strange thing. He hovered in the air, narrowed his eyes and breathed slowly. A moment later, Thad jerked backward, as if he'd been struck in the chest. He faltered again and couldn't seem to keep his eyes open or his wings flapping.

He fell toward the ground, flailing as he tried to regain the momentum of flight. The *Slayer* pursued him, grinning even as he continued to breathe slowly. Aura could almost see a glitter between the two of them, like a tendril of sparkling smoke, but when she tried to look directly at it, it disappeared.

She leapt into the air and blew through the space where she'd glimpsed the tendril. She felt something cool in that space, then the *Slayer* swore and slashed at her. His claws slid through the breeze she'd become, not injuring her at all. Thad recovered a little, but not quickly enough. He hit the earth and didn't move. He was on his back, his eyes closed, his breathing shallow. Aura couldn't believe that her dragon had been felled.

The *Slayer* seized Tisiphone and threw her at Thad. She landed on his chest, and the *Slayer* leaned down to touch the tip of his talon to a spot on the fallen *Pyr*'s chest.

"There," he breathed, and Aura realized with horror that it was the place where Thad's scale had fallen away.

"No!" she cried, shifting shape and landing in human form beside the pair of them. She couldn't be responsible for Thad's death. It couldn't be her fault that his firestorm's promise wasn't fulfilled.

Tisiphone looked up in dismay.

The *Slayer*'s eyes narrowed and he bared his teeth. "Ah, the mate," he murmured with some satisfaction. Aura supposed that was what she was.

"Take me instead." Aura offered her bared arm to the snakes that twined around Tisiphone's hair. "It's my fault he's vulnerable."

The *Slayer* chuckled, as if he found her foolish. "Take them both," he suggested.

Tisiphone looked between the two of them, then smiled darkly. She leaned forward and the snakes in her hair vibrated in their anticipation. She took one in her hand and offered its hissing head to Aura. "Kiss this one," she commanded. "Show me that you mean what you say."

"And you'll let him go," Aura insisted.

"I'll take him if you don't. See if you can satisfy my hungry vipers." Tisiphone made no promise, and the *Slayer* laughed, but Aura had to do what she could. She looked at the snake with its flicking tongue and its gleaming eyes, then bent closer to welcome its bite. The snake opened its mouth, revealing its fangs, and Aura closed her eyes in anticipation of pain.

"I forbid this!" a woman roared, just before the snake made contact.

There came a flash of brilliant blue-green light, like a crack of lightning out of a clear sky, even as the woman shouted.

The moment that the world was lit with that blue-green lasted far longer than an instant. Aura saw the yellow dragon lunge toward the fallen pilgrim. The *Slayer* seized the man's arm in his mouth, tearing it away from his body with savage force. The pilgrim's body was dragged across the ground as the dragon tore the arm free, and blood flowed copiously when it did. The man moaned in agony as his limb was ripped away.

Tisiphone caught her breath and stepped back, her gaze fixed on the old woman who had been huddled beside the pilgrim. That woman had leapt to her feet and flung out her arms. Her cloak had fallen away, revealing that she was young and beautiful.

Hera in one of her favorite guises.

Tisiphone gasped.

The yellow dragon vanished.

The pilgrim closed his eyes and looked to be breathing his last.

Hera pointed her finger at Tisiphone. "Your battle was your own until you dared to threaten a child of mine. I banish you from this age and this realm!"

"You can't banish me!" Tisiphone replied, drawing herself up to her full height. In the strange blue-green light, she looked even more like a nightmare come to life.

Hera walked toward her regally, shaking her finger as she spoke.

> *"Across the centuries and the years,*
> *You will wait and shed your tears,*

Until the darkfire is freed again;
Your vengeance can cause Pyr *no pain.*
I close the portal, for once and all,
To see those I love out of your thrall.
When darkfire will burn once again,
Your sister's death can be avenged.
When daughters of all elements are mates
Then will the dragons face their fate."

"No!" Tisiphone cried, even as she was changed to the woman with hair the color of flame again. She had a moment to glance over herself before there was a clap of thunder loud enough to make the earth shake. The blue-green light faded as abruptly as it had appeared and when it was gone, so was Tisiphone.

Thad was still lying on the ground, his breathing so shallow that Aura could barely discern it. Worse, he was changing shape on the ground before her, shifting from dragon to man and back again, and she knew it was involuntary. He didn't open his eyes and even the pale blue shimmer that accompanied his shift seemed pallid instead of vigorous. He was flat on his back and too still, the blood flowing from his wounded shoulder.

The spot of unprotected skin where he had lost the scale looked terrible. The flesh looked burned, and as if it was festering. Aura feared the *Slayer* had done something that would kill Thad. Aura dropped to her knees beside him, feeling more helpless than she ever had. Even the glow of the firestorm was subdued, no more than a pale glimmer of light when she touched him.

Could it all be for nothing?

Could Thad's dream of a fulfilled firestorm not come true?

Jorge held fast to his prize as he was cast through the air. He didn't doubt that he was being flung through time and space, as well. It was imperative that he return to the future with the pilgrim's arm.

But he had no control over the darkfire, and what it might do. His hatred of that unpredictable force redoubled as he endured the wind and the fog.

Then he was slammed down hard on what had to be asphalt.

Jorge smelled car exhaust. He could almost taste the tar of the road. There was a yellow line painted on the asphalt right beneath his chin.

He smelled the salt of the sea and felt rain pattering on his scales. He heard car brakes squeal and tires smoke as vehicles skidded to a halt all around him. People began to scream.

Jorge sat upright, wondering where he was, besides being in the middle of a road.

Hundreds of astonished people stared back at him, some from behind the windshields of cars, others from the sidewalk. The cars were either very small hybrids or very large SUVs. Jorge's heart skipped with hope. He looked up and saw a tower that had to be the Space Needle in Seattle, and the rain and the sea confirmed his theory.

Then the people turned their cellphones on him, filming and photographing him. Others began to talk into their phones, all of which were models recent to the world he'd left not long before.

Jorge would have thrown back his head and laughed if that might not have cost him his prize. He was back in the future, or close enough to it.

Why not use his weapon now?

He chewed on the arm even as he reared up. He flapped his wings and bellowed without slackening his bite. They filmed him from all sides, some hanging back, others pressing closer. He'd be featured on every news outlet on the planet, which would give fair warning to all the *Pyr* of the world.

Jorge suspected that wouldn't make any difference. He took flight, jubilant that the darkfire had finally turned in his favor. He'd survived so much and now he'd have his revenge. He shook the blood from the severed arm, letting it fall like rain over all the pitiful human spectators. Some of them screamed. Others ran. More of them kept filming his triumph.

This could be big.

This could end it all.

He could be bringing a plague to the world. Jorge wasn't one to admit his limitations, but he knew that he needed the help of a devious mind to ensure that his plan came to full fruition.

Although he feared he might regret his choice, Jorge knew he had to go to Chen. He gave one last triumphant turn over the crowd, then spun in the air and disappeared.

He would manifest in the middle of Chen's own lair.

Tisiphone flailed and howled as she was cast bodily through the air. She couldn't see anything except swirling mist and couldn't feel anything but a buffeting wind. There were occasional flashes of blue-green light in the mist near her, but she couldn't even see the source of the light. It just illuminated the clouds, as if she was in the midst of a thunderstorm.

She was powerless to change her situation, and that infuriated her almost as much as being cheated of the chance to claim the first of the *Pyr*. How dare Hera interfere with her quest for justice? How dare Hera cast her away? If ever she saw Hera again, Tisiphone would ensure that goddess paid dearly for her intervention.

Tisiphone felt herself falling. She tried to stop her descent and failed completely. The sense of helplessness didn't improve her mood. Nor did being slammed into a rocky shore, as if she'd jumped from a great height. She was dazed from her ordeal and bruised from her landing. She heard water lapping a shore close by and smelled smoke in the air. She opened her eyes to discover that it was night and she was on a rocky excuse for a beach. The mist was rising slowly.

She heard footsteps and smelled a mortal. Tisiphone shifted shape quickly, taking the guise of the woman with hair the color of flame. It would be less frightening to a mortal than her reality.

"Hey, there. Are you okay?"

Tisiphone rose to her feet and turned to see a woman dressed in black making her way closer. She had dark hair and red lips, and wore a silver bracelet shaped like a snake.

"It's not that safe down here, especially at night," the woman said. "Are you all right?"

Tisiphone nodded and brushed down her clothing, as if she loitered in such places all the time.

"Do you live around here?"

Tisiphone shook her head, not trusting herself yet to speak. Being divine, she could understand the languages of mortals, but this was a new one for her. She wanted to listen longer before she spoke herself, to be sure she got it right.

"You look like you've had a rough night," the woman said with sympathy. "I can totally relate, but you don't have to tell me about it if you don't want to."

Tisiphone looked down at her feet, as if embarrassed.

"I don't blame you," the other woman said cheerfully. "Men can be such bastards. Look, I'm Viv Jason. I've got a place near here, if you need somewhere to crash or maybe something to eat."

Tisiphone nodded. She was going to make a polite comment, but the mist chose to burn off in that moment. She stared in amazement at the world revealed. There was a massive structure before her, unlike anything she'd seen before. It had clearly been built by man, but stretched taller and straighter than she could believe. It spanned the broad expanse of water that lapped at her feet, providing a path to a glittering city of impossibly tall buildings. She could see rows of lit windows, more than she could count, all glowing with the same intensity. There couldn't be enough candles or lanterns in all the world to make that much light, but it was there before her eyes just the same. The night sky was clear overhead, but the light of the city even obscured the light of the stars.

"Manhattan at night and the Brooklyn Bridge," Viv Jason said with a smile. "It's a sight that stops me cold every time, too." She shivered with apparent delight, then beckoned to Tisiphone. "Come on. We'll find a snack and you can tell me about yourself."

Tisiphone was skeptical that that would happen. She eyed the bridge and knew she was in the future, maybe even at the point in time forecast by Hera when the darkfire would be set free. At the very least, she'd need time to orient herself, to locate the *Pyr* and to discover whether the elemental daughters had mated with the dragon shifters.

Viv Jason might be of assistance in Tisiphone's quest, or she might provide a nice snack herself.

Aura looked up to find Hera watching her.

"You will love him more even than you do now," the goddess murmured.

"Not if he dies! Can you help him, Hera?"

Hera didn't reply, just extended her hand. Aura knew exactly what she wanted, and dared to hope its power would be enough. She removed the golden apple from her tunic and surrendered it to the goddess to whom it rightfully belonged. "I am sorry that I stole it, Hera. I am sorry that I gave him a bite..."

"But you had to know the truth of his heart." The goddess smiled. "I know you would not be cavalier with such treasures, Aura. I raised you, after all."

Aura bowed low. "Thank you for banishing she-who-should-not-be-named..."

"She's not gone, Aura, not really. She is outside of time, waiting for her opportunity. I can't undermine an edict of Hades, but I could delay it. You and your *Pyr* will be safe from her, as will your children and their children, but one day, the dragons will have to answer for her sister's death."

"I understand." Aura smiled at the goddess who had been like a mother to her. "Thank you."

Hera smiled back at her, then considered the apple. She took a bite of it herself, then to Aura's surprise, the goddess knelt by the fallen pilgrim. Aura had thought he was dead, but he moaned softly, apparently realizing Hera was near.

"Great lady, I am sorry that you see me in this state. I would worship you, if I could," he whispered.

Hera removed the piece of apple from her mouth and smiled. "You have shown your true measure in being kind to an old beggar woman," she said quietly. "And by offering the last of your provisions to another." She touched his lip and placed the piece of apple in his mouth. "And here, pilgrim, is your reward."

He closed his eyes and sighed, as if overwhelmed by the taste. "This can't be..."

"But it is. My gift to you, friend. Savor it, and it will see you healed."

A tear slid from the corner of the pilgrim's eye, creating a track in the dust on his cheek. "I knew that only the goddess could save me," he whispered.

"And so she has," Hera agreed, bending to kiss his forehead.

Aura could see the pilgrim's color changing, his skin turning to a more healthy hue even as she watched. She was impatient for Hera to share her gift with Thad, but knew better than to rush the goddess. She waited, hands knotted together, gaze flicking to Thad, and watched.

"Sleep now," Hera bade the pilgrim. "When you awaken, you will be healed."

But he clutched at her hand, apparently amazing himself with his audacity and ability to move. "But lady, I would serve you, wherever you bid me to. You have given me back my life, and I surrender it to you." He gestured to his missing arm. "Whatever I can do."

Hera stood up and looked down at him, her expression benign. "Would you be happy if you worked in my garden?"

"I can't imagine anything better."

"Then sleep," Hera said. "And when you awaken, you will find yourself there." She bent and kissed his brow again, and the pilgrim fell into a peaceful slumber.

Then Hera turned her gaze upon Aura.

She held up the apple, clearly anticipating Aura's question. "It won't help him," she said quietly. "He has already eaten of it and you have seen the sum of its influence on him."

"He can't die!"

"All creatures can die, Aura. Only his own kind can help him."

"But I don't know where to find them, or how to summon them."

Hera watched Aura for a long moment, clearly noting the dimmed glow of the firestorm. "What will you do, Aura?"

"He said we were destined mates. I will stay with him, until the end, whenever that is." The tree shimmered over Aura's head, a sweet melody that made her feel her mother agreed with her choice.

"And what of the firestorm?"

"Maybe the heat of it will help him. Maybe if I stay close, he will remain warm."

"Do you understand why it wasn't satisfied?"

Aura shrugged. "Because I didn't want it to be?"

Hera shook her head. "Even your will isn't enough for that," she said. "Tell me about the firestorm."

"It's the sign that a *Pyr* has met the woman who can bear his son..."

"Woman," Hera repeated, interrupting Aura. "You are a nymph. A woman is mortal. A nymph is immortal. The firestorm is keyed to the connection between *Pyr* and the treasures of the earth they defend."

"Mortals," Aura murmured. "And the elements." She looked up at Hera. "Can you make me mortal?"

The goddess stilled "Are you sure?"

"He wanted the firestorm to be satisfied so badly. Maybe it would make a difference to him."

"It would make a difference to you," Hera reminded Aura. "And it would be no guarantee. You would be unable to find my garden, ever again, for example."

A lump rose in Aura's throat. She considered Thad and knew that if he'd been healthy, the choice would have been no choice at all. As it stood, she was taking a chance. But she remembered the joy of flying with him, the risk they'd taken together and their exuberance when they had succeeded in reaching this place. She thought of his conviction and his sense of purpose, and she knew that even if the chance of fulfilling his firestorm was small, she had no choice but to try.

She would willingly have Thad's son.

She knew that being mortal would allow her to do that, but she didn't want to lose the magic of their flight together. She liked that they were both shifters and they way they had frolicked in the air. She was glad that she'd been able to help him in his battle against Ladon, too. She didn't want to surrender all that she was, even to make his dream come true.

She wanted them both to remain what they were and be stronger together.

Then she remembered Nephele's story. "Those daughters of the elements," she said to Hera. "The ones you included in your prophecy." The goddess inclined her head. "Are there Airdaughters in their number?"

Hera smiled. "Of course. There are daughters associated with each of the four elements, although they are few in number."

Aura got to her feet and met the goddess's gaze. "Would you make me mortal, Hera?" she asked. "Would you make me an Airdaughter, please?"

The goddess took a step closer and framed Aura's face in her hands. She bent to kiss her cheeks, one after the other. "I promised your mother to raise you as my own, and to do my best to ensure you found happiness." She looked into Aura's eyes. "Are you sure?"

"Yes, Hera. Please," Aura said with conviction, then bowed her head.

She felt the touch of the goddess's lips on the top of her head, even as the air cooled all around her. "Blessed be," Hera whispered and Aura felt a strange shimmer pass through her body. It was like the tingle that accompanied her changing shape, but was colder and more vehement. She understood that her very nature was being changed.

And she was glad.

She shivered then opened her eyes, wanting to see the world shift as a result of her changed nature. For a moment, everything was just as it had been. Hera stood before her, her lips curved in a sad smile. The goddess blew a kiss at her, then bent to lift the pilgrim into her arms. He might have weighed as little as a feather for all the strain she showed.

A fine mist was descending, one that obscured the hills and the road and filled the air with moisture. Hera turned and stepped into the mist, her figure lost to view, even as she took the road that led uphill.

"*I'm sorry, Aura,*" whispered Nephele. Aura was glad the shrouding mist was someone she knew.

"*I'm not,*" she replied in kind. "*I never will be, Nephele, although I will miss you all.*"

The tingle slid from the tips of Aura's fingers and toes, releasing a faint shimmer in the mist. Aura didn't know if she would be able to see Nephele or the other nymphs again, or whether they would have to reveal themselves to her by choice. She wasn't sure what would remain of her powers and what would be lost.

But she wanted to explore it all with Thad.

She wasn't really surprised to discover that she was alone on a deserted hillside, Thad unconscious at her feet and the tree with silvery leaves casting shade over the two of them. There was no sign of Hera or the pilgrim. Aura knew that if she followed the road up to the high pass, she'd never see the garden.

A soft rain began to fall, and it made the leaves of the tree tinkle softly, as if in sympathy. Aura fell to her knees beside Thad, who remained now in human form, and kissed his cheek. Their lives were bound together now, whatever came to be.

She knew she shouldn't have been surprised that no spark emanated from the point of contact between them. The firestorm was satisfied, just as he'd desired. She looked at him, letting her fingertips trail across his cheek and lips. Even though the firestorm was extinguished, he was still the most alluring man she'd ever known.

She would have his son.

Aura bent and touched her lips to his, then she twined their fingers together.

She would sit vigil and wait for his kind, no matter how long it took.

Then she remembered his old-speak, how she had been able to hear it and how he had been able to hear the way she spoke to her sisters. Aura closed her eyes and tried to send a beacon to the other *Pyr*.

"The firestorm is satisfied, but the Pyr *has fallen. Help us, please. Come to us, other* Pyr, *and help your own kind, please."*
She broadcast the words, over and over again, Thad's hand held fast in her own, and hoped it was enough.

CHAPTER FIVE

"Good thing it's digital, or you'd wear it out," Eileen said as she walked past Erik with a pile of clean laundry.

The leader of the *Pyr* didn't even look up from the news footage displayed on his laptop screen.

"It's Jorge," he said, starting the clip again. "I'm sure it's Jorge. Spontaneously manifesting in Seattle."

"I wondered when he'd turn up again," Eileen mused. She came to stand behind Erik and leaned on his shoulder to watch.

"You don't sound worried," Erik said, trying to not sound irritated by that.

Eileen pressed a quick kiss to the side of his neck. "I have a personal dragon protecting me."

"But still..." Erik began to argue, then Eileen pointed at the screen.

"What's in his mouth?"

"It looks like a severed limb."

"Nice. With fingers. An arm, then."

On the video clip, Jorge rose on his hind legs, displaying the splendor of his golden yellow scales. Erik peered at the screen, noting that there was a wound on the *Slayer*'s shoulder.

"He fought somebody recently."

"A *Pyr*, no doubt," Eileen agreed. "Those scabs look fresh."

"And we know he heals very quickly because of the Elixir."

"I wonder where he came from."

Jorge took flight and even though he'd watched the sequence a thousand times already, Erik leaned closer so that he wouldn't miss a single detail. Jorge flew a circle over the crowd and looked to be chewing on the severed limb. He shook it over the assembled crowd, dispersing a spray of blood. One drop landed on the lens or phone of whoever had filmed this version and it dripped in a red smear.

"That is gross," Eileen said with disgust and returned to her laundry. "You'd think he'd be able to resist the temptation of doing that."

"And then he vanishes," Erik said, sitting back and tapping his fingers on the table.

"Spontaneously manifesting elsewhere," Eileen concluded. "I wonder where."

"I wonder *why*," Erik said. "Jorge is very deliberate."

"As well as a nasty piece of business," Eileen said, giving an elaborate shiver. "How's our dragonsmoke boundary mark these days?"

"Thick and deep," Erik said, to her evident relief. "Even if he manifests inside it, I'll be ready for him."

"Ever vigilant. That's what I like about living with a dragon."

Erik started the clip again, then caught his breath.

"What do you see?" Eileen asked, and he knew she'd noticed his reaction.

"It's at the very beginning. There's a glimmer of blue-green light, I'm sure of it."

"Darkfire," Eileen whispered. She came back to his side and watched, then nudged him away from the keyboard. She could type so much more quickly than him, and he watched the screen, wondering what she was looking for.

"There have to be more filmed versions. Look at all those cellphones in the crowd. Maybe one starts sooner than the news version."

"Before Jorge appears," Erik said.

A range of search results were displayed on his screen, more versions of Jorge's appearance than Erik could have believed possible. Eileen scrolled down and chose one that apparently started with a flash of light.

Blue-green light filled the viewfinder and when it faded, Jorge was in the middle of the road. He looked dazed, or maybe confused, then surveyed the crowd and seemed to smile.

"He didn't know where he was going to end up," Erik guessed.

"Because it was the darkfire that sent him," Eileen agreed.

They grimaced simultaneously as he flew over the crowd, scattering the blood, then disappeared from view. The crowd was seething with excitement where he had been, many of the people rushing forward to the spot where Jorge had stood.

"Where did he go?" Eileen asked.

"What does it mean?" Erik murmured, but he had no answer to that. They exchanged a glance, then Eileen returned to her laundry and Erik settled in to watch every single second of available footage. If there was a clue, he would find it.

Aura heard the steady beat of wings the next evening, just as the sun was setting. She thought it was her imagination, but the sound became steadily louder. She stood and turned, awed by the sight of dragons flying toward her from the east.

"Here!" she cried, holding up her hands, then repeated the appeal in the speech of her kind. *"Here!"*

They turned with grace and spiraled down toward her. One dragon was just as dark in color as Thad while the other was brilliant gold. They could have been day and night. As they descended, Aura saw that each dragon carried a woman, one of whom carried an infant in her arms. They landed near her and she heard a rumble like thunder. Aura smiled, knowing that what Thad had told her was true.

"It's old-speak," explained one of the women, stepping out of her dragon's embrace and moving closer with confidence.

"The way they communicate with each other. I know. Thad told me."

"Katina," the woman said, then gestured to her dragon. "This is Alexander, who leads the training of the *Pyr* in our time."

"Petra and Damien," the other woman said, lifting her son for Aura to see. "And this is Orion."

"The child of the firestorm," Aura said. "So, you were the Earthdaughter who escaped the Underworld, and your *Pyr* was the one who struck down she-who-should-not-be-named."

The two women exchanged glances of surprise. "You know so much," Katina said.

"I was a nymph, now an Airdaughter. We listen."

"And your firestorm is satisfied," Petra said. "That's good."

They turned to consider Thad, who looked so pale that Aura's heart clenched. "A yellow salamander changed to a dragon," she said and the two dragons looked up at her words. "They fought and his blood ran black where Thad wounded him. Then he seemed to breathe and Thad became much worse."

"Dragonsmoke," Katina said with heat.

"He stole your dragon's life force to feed his own."

The dragons seemed to have come to the same conclusion, for they began at once to exhale steadily and in unison. They were extremely still but Aura could see the glimmer of their eyes as they concentrated. She narrowed her own eyes and thought she could see the same kind of sparkle in the air that she'd discerned before. It was like a plume or a ribbon, one that wound from the mouths of the two dragons, twined together, then touched the wound on Thad's chest.

The two women took her hands and the three of them watched together. "They will give him some of their own strength," Katina said, squeezing Aura's fingers hard.

"Hera said he could only be healed by his own kind."

"They will try," Petra agreed.

"If only he hadn't lost the scale," Aura whispered. "If only he hadn't become vulnerable." She was aware of the way the two women glanced at her, though she guessed they didn't want her to notice. Even the *Pyr* missed a beat in their breathing, their attention caught by her words.

They weren't surprised by what she was telling them, so it was common.

They were expectant. She guessed that she had to do something, or say something.

Aura pulled Thad's lost scale from her tunic to display it to them. "Can it be put back, once he's healed?" she asked, and felt their relief.

"Only by you," Petra said, squeezing Aura's other hand.

"That's what will heal him," Katina agreed.

Aura was fiercely glad she'd stayed with Thad and that she'd chosen to be with him. She watched as the color returned to his skin and his breathing became deeper. The dragons breathed more dragonsmoke, exhaling with power, and Thad's eyes opened suddenly. He looked around, smiling when he saw Aura. He started to sit up and she went to his side, wanting him to take it slowly, but there was no holding back her dragon once he saw his friends.

"Damien! Alexander!" he cried with joy. He was on his feet then, even before the pale blue shimmer of light flashed. In the blink of an eye, two men were embracing Thad. They all had that black dragon mark on their skin, although they wore it in different places. Thad reached up and ruffled Damien's fair hair. "You look like you saw a ghost," he teased.

"Something like that," Damien said, giving Petra an intent look. Aura noticed that their son was fair-haired, too.

She'd have to ask for that story.

Thad turned to Aura and introduced her to his friends. She was pulled into their circle and savored the warmth of their friendship. "We all served in the Dragon Legion together," Thad explained.

"The hunters of vipers," Aura said, closing her eyes with joy when Thad held her tightly against his side.

"The Dragon Legion," Alexander agreed.

But Thad was looking down at Aura with surprise. "What happened to the firestorm?"

"Don't tell me you forgot that we satisfied it?" Aura teased. The women chuckled, but Thad frowned down at her.

"What happened?" he whispered.

"I'll tell you everything later," Aura promised. "It kept burning because I wasn't mortal before. Now I'm an Airdaughter, and mortal just like you."

"And you'll bear my son," he murmured with an awe that warmed her to her toes. "Aura, you shouldn't have given up so much."

"Shouldn't I have?"

"But I'm glad you did," he said with a grin, then kissed her with enthusiasm. His friends began to laugh, and Thad reluctantly broke his kiss. He kept Aura tightly against his side, though, and she was glad to be there. He demanded to know what had happened to the *Slayer* and she told him, as well as the fate of

Tisiphone and Hera's prophecy.

The new arrivals exchanged glances again. "Do you know what it means?" Katina asked Alexander.

"I know it has to do with the future," her partner said. "The darkfire sparked for the first time in eons when we were there. It was what brought us back to this time."

"Maybe it's taken Jorge and Tisiphone back to that time," Petra suggested.

"Hera said we and our children and our children's children would be safe from her, but that one day, the *Pyr* would have to pay the price," Aura supplied.

"What happened to the rest of the Dragon Legion?" Alexander asked Thad. "Are they here, too?"

"I can't smell them," Damien contributed and Alexander nodded agreement.

"They're scattered throughout time. The darkfire took each of us to our firestorm," Thad explained. "Each warrior was left in the time and place of his destined mate."

"The darkfire took care of us after all," Damien murmured.

"It saw destiny fulfilled," Petra said, taking her dragon's hand.

"But what about Drake?" Thad asked. "He was with me at the end and the darkfire took him somewhere."

"He can't be here," Alexander said. "Cassandra has died and Theo is in training with us at Delphi."

"Maybe Drake is further in the past," Katina suggested.

"Maybe he's in the future," Petra said.

"We'll find out if he's here," Alexander said with resolve and the others nodded. "But I think the darkfire must have had other plans for him."

Aura noticed that the three *Pyr* looked thoughtful then, as if they were remembering some experience they'd shared.

"That still leaves the Dragon's Tail wars," Alexander continued. "If the darkfire's gone and we're here, how can we help the *Pyr* in the future?"

"Wait! We already are!" Thad snapped his fingers.

"I don't understand," Damien said, shoving a hand through his hair. "It looks as if I've made things worse for the *Pyr* by being here."

"No," Thad said, pointing to the sleeping Orion. "You had a

son, and he will have a son, and his son will have a son. Because we are here, two millennia before the *Pyr* we came to know, we can build an army for them."

Aura gasped in understanding. "Thad's right! We have time on our side."

Alexander laughed. "It's perfect! We can pass that prophecy along, from father to son, so Erik will learn of it in time."

"And we can mark the flesh of our sons," Damien said, indicating the black dragon mark on his arm.

"That's why the darkfire marked them at Delphi," Katina said with excitement. "It was showing you what to do."

The *Pyr* nodded and Petra spoke. "They'll carry the sign of the Dragon Legion, so that they can recognize each other."

"And best of all, the darkfire didn't abandon the Dragon Legion or the *Pyr*," Thad concluded. "It put everything in motion so the *Pyr* can triumph." The three of them were so pleased that Aura feared they'd missed the point.

There was a new threat against the dragon shifters. Even if she-who-should-not-be-named had been banished to another time and place, she wasn't going to see Thad struck down like that ever again.

"First we have to fix Thad's scale, and we have to fix it now," Aura interrupted, holding up the scale. "Tell me what I need to do."

Drake sat opposite Erik in that *Pyr*'s loft apartment. The kitchen was austerely black and white, the single yellow gerbera daisy in a vase on the table making a bold splash of color. The sunlight streaming through the windows and touching on the daisy was bright enough to make Drake think again of Greece. He had slept and eaten, and he had told Erik all that he knew. He was still exhausted and Drake feared that this weariness would persist.

His men were lost.

The darkfire crystal was extinguished.

He didn't know what the point of anything was anymore.

For the moment, he was content to just sit, to just be. He was aware that Erik watched him closely and that the other *Pyr* saw far more than even most dragons. On some level, he hoped Erik would make a suggestion or give him an assignment. On a deeper level, he wanted this tranquil moment to continue undisturbed.

Erik, however, was not as tranquil as Drake. He got to his feet and paced to the window, moving with a deliberation that didn't disguise the tension within him. Drake watched and appreciated that Erik was tempering his impatience. Dragons weren't always so kind to each other.

"Partial eclipse today," Erik murmured, recalling Drake to the moment.

"Is there a firestorm?"

Erik shook his head, not looking away from the window. Then he stilled, as if listening, then shook his head again. "It is so strange," he murmured, then continued in old-speak. *"I thought you would know more."*

They had been through this several times. Drake couldn't explain the light Erik was seeing, or the sense of impending doom that apparently all the *Pyr* were experiencing.

Maybe it was time for dragons to fade from the world. Drake felt old at that thought and refused to say it aloud.

The silence embraced them again, just the faint tinkle of Erik's dragonsmoke audible to Drake. He liked the sound of it, the comfort of it, the appearance of security it gave him. He knew that he couldn't have slept anywhere else these past days.

The sound of a key turning in a lock made Drake jump. Erik turned as Eileen spoke to their daughter, Zoë. The little girl should be the next Wyvern, Drake remembered, for she was the only female child of one of their kind and the former Wyvern was dead. Drake knew that Erik was impatient for the child's powers to develop, just as he knew that Erik expected no such development until Zoë came of age. Male *Pyr* came into the bulk of their powers at puberty, when their voices deepened and their bodies changed.

He watched Zoë with interest, but saw nothing remarkable about her. She appeared to be a solemn child, with her father's dark hair and green eyes. She couldn't have been four years old, though she was tall for her age. That trait would have come from both of her parents. Drake knew that she went to a daycare at the university, where her mother taught. He never felt much connection with young children, especially girls, so he returned his attention to the yellow daisy.

To his surprise, Zoë appeared suddenly beside him. She could move with her father's silence and stealth, and her gaze was fixed upon him with the same intensity. "I made this for you," she said, then put a large piece of paper on the table before him. Drake was too surprised to speak. Children did not give him gifts. In fact, no one had given him a gift in a long time. She stared at him for a moment, then followed her mother to the fridge.

It was a drawing.

The drawing was clearly the work of a child, but still Drake recognized the location. There was a black oval in the middle with blue spraying out of a block in the center of the oval. Drake knew it was a fountain. There were green curly lines around it, evoking the shrubbery of a park, and the sky was colored in black with yellow dots for stars. Two stick figures sat on the lip of the fountain, and Drake guessed that they were men. One held a blue-green rectangle in his hand and there were rays of blue and green emanating from it.

It was Thad and Drake, just before Thad had felt the spark of his firestorm.

Drake looked at the little girl with shock. Zoë was drinking a glass of milk, more interested in how many chocolate chips were in her cookie than the attitude of her father's friend. Eileen must have noticed his expression because she came to his side.

"It's the park at the university, I think," she said. "We pass it every day." She frowned. "We've never been there at night."

"Who are the men, Zoë?" her father asked quietly.

She shrugged and bit into her cookie. "They wanted to be there." Her gaze barely flicked at Drake, then she finished her snack and went to her room, picking up her pack at her mother's reminder.

"It's Thad and me," Drake said. "This is where the stone brought us the second to last time."

"So close," Erik mused. "But not so close that you could sense my presence, or that I would be much aware of yours."

"Were you?"

Erik slanted a glance at him. "I felt a glimmer a few weeks ago, but it disappeared. I thought I had imagined it, because it was so fleeting. How could you be here and gone again so quickly as that?" He pressed his fingertips to one temple and closed his eyes. "The darkfire is changing everything," he whispered, then grimaced.

Drake was on his feet in a moment, knowing something was wrong but unable to name it. Before he could speak, Erik's eyes flew open and he stared at the door. He crossed the room with long strides, and Drake guessed that he had felt a breach of his dragonsmoke barrier.

There was a knock at the door. Erik inhaled deeply, frowned, then cast open the door.

The corridor was filled with unfamiliar men, young and vigorous men who held themselves with determination. There had to be three or four dozen of them.

They were *Pyr*. Drake stood behind Erik and breathed deeply, not believing his own senses. How could there be so many *Pyr* of whom he knew nothing?

"We are the descendants of the Dragon Legion," said the *Pyr* in front. He tugged up his shirt sleeve, showing a tattoo on his upper arm that was the same as the tattoo Drake and his men had gotten as a sign of solidarity. Drake considered the young man with wonder, liking the intelligence that shone in his dark eyes. "I am named Theo, for my forebear, the son of Stephanos who became Drake," he said, his words startling Drake. "We come to pledge ourselves to the leader of the *Pyr*, Erik Sorensson, as we pledged to our fathers, who pledged the same to their fathers and their fathers before them."

"So this is what I sensed," Erik said, almost under his breath.

Theo offered a piece of paper. "We surrender to you this prophecy, made millenia ago but for these times. We have kept it in trust, preserved it and awaited the moment it should be revealed." He handed an envelope to Erik.

Erik opened the envelope and removed a sheet of paper. Drake could see that it had eight lines of script, though he couldn't quite read the words.

Erik read it in old-speak.

> *"Across the centuries and the years,*
> *You will wait and shed your tears,*

Until the darkfire is freed again;
Your vengeance can cause Pyr *no pain.*
I close the portal, for once and all,
To see those I love out of your thrall.
When darkfire will burn once again,
Your sister's death can be avenged.
When daughters of all elements are mates
Then will the dragons face their fate."

"So, it is time," Erik said aloud. He offered his hand to Theo. "Welcome, Theo. Welcome to you and all your company. Please, cross my dragonsmoke and share your tidings with us." He turned and indicated Drake with a slight smile. "This is Drake, who was Stephanos. He has been weary, but I think you may bring him joy."

Against Drake's every expectation, a son of his line stood before him. Theo smiled and there was a gleam of tears in his eyes. He stepped forward and gave a crisp salute. "I have always dreamed of meeting you. It is an honor beyond all, sir."

"Not sir," Drake said hoarsely. He took Theo's hand and shook it, liking the firmness of this young man's grip. "I would have you call me Drake." And then he embraced Theo, glad beyond belief that the darkfire had brought him this gift.

The repair of his scale was a wonderful moment, and one Thad would remember forever. He couldn't have imagined how any part of it could have been improved.

The sun was setting, the western sky painted with brilliant streaks of orange. He could see the stars overhead and feel a cool breeze from the ocean. He smiled, wondering if it was a friend of Aura's. The tree with the silver leaves tinkled in the breeze, as if to make music to celebrate their bond.

The firestorm had faded, but the weight of Aura's hand in his own still brought a lump to Thad's throat. He was surrounded by friends and comrades, each of whom had found love through the firestorm. He was amongst his own kind and would be with Aura for the duration. He dared to believe that thanks to their efforts, the

Pyr in the future would triumph over every obstacle.

He felt like the luckiest *Pyr* in the world.

"There must be a token, freely given," Katina said to Aura.

"She has surrendered her immortality," Thad said with pride.

"Something tangible," Petra insisted. "Something that is a measure of her link with the elements."

"She is air and I am fire," Thad said.

"But what are your secondary elements? The four must be divided between the two of you, or you wouldn't have had a firestorm," Alexander explained.

Thad met Aura's gaze. She smiled at him. "You must be earth for your practicality," she said and Thad sensed that she was right.

"And you would be water, for your empathy."

Aura's smile turned mischievous. "Or for my love of sensual delights."

The others chuckled at that, but Thad couldn't look away from Aura's shining eyes. He would show her sensual delights, once they had a moment of privacy together. He smiled and she blushed a little, as if she'd guessed his thoughts.

Her eyes widened suddenly and she reached into her tunic. To Thad's surprise, when her hand was revealed again, she held a golden apple. It was perfect, not missing a single bite, and he wondered if she had stolen another one.

"A gift from Hera," she said with a smile. She glanced up at the peak where the garden was hidden. "A wedding gift." She lifted the golden fruit and offered it to Alexander. It looked like it was made of gold, more like a piece of jewelry than fruit.

Alexander accepted it with a slight bow. "I never thought I'd hold one of these myself," he said with awe. "It will more than suffice."

Thad felt Alexander change shape beside him and glanced at the dark dragon Alexander had become. Damien shifted shape next and he nodded acknowledgement of that. The dragon known as the Heartbreaker had changed, and the transformation was more than the color of his scales and of his hair. Damien seemed more focused and less restless. Thad knew it was because he was with Petra, his destined mate, once again.

Thad smiled at Aura, then summoned his own change, reveling in the way it surged through him with such strength. The firestorm had made him more than he had been, Thad was sure of it.

The wind lifted Aura's hair and swept through her tunic as she offered Thad's lost scale to Alexander. Alexander held it in his claws and breathed fire at it. Damien stepped forward and breathed his dragonfire on it as well. It heated to a golden glow before Thad's eyes. They turned their fire on the apple and it turned molten on one side before their surprised gazes. Alexander pressed it into the scale and the two merged together, so that the golden apple sat on the surface like an emblem.

"Fire," Alexander intoned as he pressed the hot scale against Thad's chest. Thad gritted his teeth at the burning sensation of it against his exposed skin. He heard Aura gasp and saw her eyes fill with tears of sympathy.

"Water," Aura whispered, lifting a tear from her cheek and placing it on the scale. It sizzled on contact and evaporated.

"Earth," Thad said, and pressed the scale more deeply into his own chest.

"Air," Aura concluded, blowing against the hot scale as sweetly as a summer breeze. Thad caught her close and spun her around, his heart bursting with pride that she had given so much to be his mate. He swept into the sky and flew around his fellows, then spun to land on his feet, in human form, with Aura in his arms. He bent to kiss her, but she gasped in wonder as she looked past his shoulder.

"Twins!" she said with delight. "Thad, we will have twin sons!"

There was only one good way to celebrate that news, as far as Thad was concerned. He caught Aura close and kissed her soundly, knowing that this particular night would be filled with the exploration of sensual delights.

And so it would be for all their entwined future.

Thad couldn't wait to begin.

READY FOR MORE DRAGONFIRE?

READ ON FOR AN EXCERPT FROM

SERPENT'S KISS

THOROLF'S STORY & DRAGONFIRE #10.

Erik checked the perimeter of his lair, ensuring that his dragonsmoke barrier was woven thick and deep. It was late at night, or early in the morning, depending upon how he looked at it. Zoë had been put to bed hours before and even Eileen had fallen asleep. Drake had departed with the new *Pyr* a week before, revitalized by the opportunity to train a new company of dragon shifters.

Erik had spent the week trying to avoid a sense of pending doom. He couldn't scry the future or see anything beyond the present moment, but he'd had a sense of trouble brewing.

Maybe it was that footage of Jorge appearing, then disappearing, in Seattle. What had the *Slayer* been carrying? It had looked like a severed arm, one that was still bleeding. Erik hadn't thought much of Jorge shaking blood over the gathering crowd, not then, but today's news had changed that.

People were becoming sick in Seattle. Very sick. There was a hum of panic building in Seattle as doctors and hospitals noticed the connections between sudden illnesses and deaths. They hadn't used the word epidemic yet, but the first hospital had put itself into quarantine. They'd already realized that most of the victims had been at the scene of Jorge's appearance.

It was only a matter of time before dragons were blamed.

Erik shivered, remembering the old hunts that had driven his kind into hiding and claimed so many *Pyr* he'd known and loved. Surely it couldn't happen again.

Surely his suspicions were unfounded.

The loft was still, despite Erik's restlessness. He stood at the window and watched the moon ride high overhead, listening to the pulses and breathing of his partner and child. He heard the resonance of his dragonsmoke and felt its icy glitter. The blaze in his mind had quieted, perhaps because he no longer feared it.

The numbers of the *Pyr* had swollen, virtually overnight, thanks to the darkfire crystal and its ability to make reality out of possibilities. The stone remained dark—he had checked it again after Drake's departure—and he sensed that it would always be so. Its task was completed.

His, unfortunately, was not.

Erik knew he should feel optimistic instead of worried. What could he do? If Jorge had a plan, was it possible that the other *Slayers* knew of it? He had never been able to determine how much they communicated with each other, and their alliances shifted like the wind.

Confident that his barriers were robust and his family safe, Erik left the loft and went to the apartment he'd acquired directly below. There the *Slayer* JP was imprisoned, confined by a barrier of dragonsmoke breathed by Erik and buttressed by every *Pyr* who had come to visit since JP's capture.

Erik felt a little bit sorry for the other dragon shifter. JP had been branded by Chen, claimed by that old *Slayer* and held captive by his more ancient magic. He had raved and fought when he'd first been captured by the *Pyr*, venting about injustice and plots. Erik had hoped to learn something about Chen from JP, but he was too incoherent to provide any information of use. Then he'd collapsed into a deep slumber, dozing in his dragon form and seldom awakening.

Chen's sorcery seemed to be killing him. JP's scales became thinner each time Erik visited him. He wasn't sure when the other dragon shifter ate, but he didn't eat much. JP's breathing was becoming shallower and his pulse slower. Worse, the fight had gone out of him. It was such an unnatural state for a dragon shifter that Erik assumed JP would soon die.

It was such a waste. He could never understand why a *Pyr* would turn *Slayer* in the first place, never mind why Chen would enchant another *Slayer* just to let him fade away.

Erik unlocked the door to the apartment, fearing as he did each time that he would make a gruesome discovery. He passed through the cold shimmer of the dragonsmoke, only to find the apartment in darkness. The drapes were drawn but the apartment was unnaturally dark, given the light of the full moon. It should have stolen into the room somehow, as well as the lights of the city itself.

Erik smelled brimstone.

He slammed the door and shifted shape immediately, but even at his fastest speed, he was too slow. A plume of flame illuminated the middle of the main room. It was breathed by a young Asian man dressed in leather, a man with malice and violence in his eyes.

Chen, in one of his human guises.

Erik leapt at him, talons bared, but Chen laughed. He grabbed the inert JP by the scruff of his neck, waved to Erik, then they both disappeared.

Erik landed hard on the bare floor, but his prey was gone. Chen had used his powers to spontaneously manifest in other locations to bypass the dragonsmoke barrier and collect his prey.

Why did he want JP?

What would he do to him?

What else had the darkfire changed? Erik closed his eyes and checked the connections in his mind, following each conduit to one of the *Pyr*. It took him longer, with the influx of new dragon shifters, but he soon realized that one was missing.

Thorolf.

Erik had been angry with Thorolf for revealing himself to humans. There was even a YouTube video of Thorolf shifting shape in Washington, one that was impressive in its popularity. Thorolf was all impulse and powerful energy, but he spent himself in indulgence. That he made such foolish choices was in direct contrast to his impressive lineage. If Thorolf focused, or even tried to hone his skills, he could have become one of Erik's most reliable *Pyr*. He could have replaced Erik as leader. But he didn't try and he didn't seem to care, and when he had vowed to go to Asia to hunt down Chen, Erik had let him go. He'd been sure nothing would come of it, that Thorolf would find a woman somewhere and spend a few months exploring her charms.

That had been exactly what had happened. Erik had checked and checked again just the day before.

But now Thorolf was gone. There was no glowing conduit to him from Erik's mind. There was no link to his spirit, either. He wasn't dead, just missing.

Erik shifted back to human form, impatient with his own failing in this. He should have kept a closer eye upon Thorolf, and he knew it. His frustration with Thorolf had driven his choices, and that had been a mistake.

He turned on the lights, intent upon checking the apartment, on the outside chance that Chen or JP had left some clue.

Chen had. There was a spiral burned into the hardwood floor, a spiral exactly like the mark branded on JP's neck. It was about eight feet across and had been the source of that smell. Erik stepped into it and knew too late that he shouldn't have done so. The spiral drew him forward with relentless force. He was pulled against his will to the very core of the spiral, fighting it even as he saw it begin to burn again. First the mark glowed, like embers, then it was coaxed to a small fire by a wind Erik couldn't feel. In a heartbeat, the flames were burning as high as his knees. He couldn't stop himself from moving closer, even when he heard Chen's laughter echo through the empty apartment.

Was this what had happened to Thorolf? Erik struggled against the force of the spell, but couldn't change his situation. Would he be compelled to join the other *Pyr*? Or did Chen have worse plans for him?

It appeared that Erik would soon find out.

WATCH FOR

SERPENT'S KISS
THE TENTH DRAGONFIRE NOVEL

COMING SOON!

The World of Dragonfire: A Glossary

Every fictional world has its own terminology and that is particularly true of fantasy realms. Here is a glossary of terms frequently used in the Dragonfire novels. Although every attempt is made to include an explanation in context, sometimes a longer explanation is desired. Be warned—if you haven't read the entire series, you may find spoilers here!

Affinities—as custodians of the four elements (air, water, fire, earth), the *Pyr* have a strong relationship with them. Each *Pyr* has affinities to two elements. When any given *Pyr* experiences his firestorm, his destined mate will invariably possess affinities to the two remaining elements. Their strengths and weaknesses are complementary, as a result, which makes a permanent union such a powerful alliance. When the mate gives a gift to aid in her dragon's scale repair (see **Loss of Scale**) that gift often echoes her two affinities.

Airdaughter—an **Elemental Witch** with an affinity for air. An Airdaughter cannot just control the element of air but can become it. Aura is the first Airdaughter introduced in the series: her story (and the link between **Elemental Witches** and nymphs) is told in the **Dragon Legion Novella, Kiss of Destiny**.

Apothecary—the healer of the *Pyr*. The Apothecary is a hereditary position, involving a long apprenticeship and training in the medicinal uses of herbs etc. for the specific treatment of *Pyr*. The current Apothecary is Sloane Forbes.

Beguiling—Both *Pyr* and *Slayer* have the ability to beguile humans, although it is a skill that must be learned and cultivated. The dragon shifter in question drops his voice to a low murmur, speaks slowly, and conjures flames in his eyes. This is usually done while in human form, and generally humans see a flame deep in the iris of the dragon shifter in question. This is so irrational and unlikely that the human looks most closely, then is snared by the dragon shifters' spell. Beguiling is similar to hypnosis, and like hypnosis, yields better results if the suggestion is something the victim already wants to believe. Pyr have used it for eons to convince those humans who have witnessed them in dragon form that they could not have really seen dragons. There is some question as to whether a dragon shifter can beguile another dragon shifter or not. In **Flashfire**, Lorenzo did beguile a *Slayer*, but that *Slayer* was not at his full power or health. Lorenzo is the most adept of the *Pyr* at beguiling.

Challenge Coin—Dragons have a tendency to both fight and to vigilantly defend their honor. If a *Pyr* or *Slayer* tosses his challenge coin at an opponent, he is challenging the other dragon shifter to a fight to the death. If that opponent picks up the coin, the challenge has been accepted. The fight may be interrupted or delayed, but they will fight to death, as a matter of honor. Challenge coins are carefully chosen by each dragon shifter to be characteristic of his nature or background and to be distinctive. Each dragon always has his challenge coin in his possession and carries it between forms.

Clothing—When a *Pyr* or *Slayer* shifts shape, he folds his clothing away quickly and tucks it beneath his scales. It is considered to be particularly important that no one ever witness exactly where the garments are hidden. No shifter can return to his human form without his clothing, so speed with this feat is key to survival. In **Kiss of Fury**, Erik burns the clothing of the *Slayer* Boris while they are both in dragon form; Boris, however, has folded away his underwear, so survives this tactic.

Darkfire—an ancient magic that breeds chaos and unpredictability in the world of the *Pyr*. Darkfire was trapped in three quartz crystals in the past. The *Slayer* Chen broke one deliberately, setting the darkfire free in the hopes of undermining the efforts of the *Pyr* in **Darkfire Kiss**. The location of the second darkfire crystal was also established in that book. In **Flashfire**, the third darkfire crystal was revealed to be in Lorenzo's hoard, until it was given to Drake, the leader of the Dragon's Tooth Warriors. The actions of that crystal feature in the **Dragon Legion Collection** of novellas.

Death Ritual—It is traditional to expose the body of a deceased *Pyr* to all four elements within one day and night of his demise. This was considered to be a ritual of respect and had lapsed from active practice until the **Dragon's Blood Elixir** was formulated again.

Dragonfire—a stream of fire breathed by a *Pyr* or *Slayer*, often aimed at another dragon in battle. Dragonfire burns particularly hot. It will singe dragon scales and can leave a victim disfigured, if not dead. The Smith is said to be able to endure dragonfire, because of his affinity to the element of fire, and can draw power from it, as Quinn does in **Kiss of Fire**.

Dragon Legion—the Dragon's Tooth Warriors who survived the challenge recounted in **Harmonia's Kiss** and were sent through time by the darkfire crystal. They include Drake, Alexander, Damien, Thad, Orion, Peter, Ty, Ashe and Ignatio. Alexander's story is told in **Kiss of Danger**; Damien's story is told in **Kiss of Darkness** and Thad's story is told in **Kiss of Destiny**.

Dragon's Blood Elixir—an addictive concoction that promotes longevity in dragon shape shifters, expedites healing and increases vitality. It also gave the powers of the **Wyvern** to *Slayers* who consumed it over a period of time, particularly that of being able to take a third form (a salamander) and to spontaneously manifest elsewhere. The *Slayer* Magnus found the formula and shared first sips to build a company of loyal followers. He also revived dead dragon shifters with the substance, creating an army of shadow dragons from those dead *Pyr* whose bodies had not had the traditional death ritual. (See **Death Ritual**.) The saga of the Elixir is told in **Winter's Kiss, Whisper Kiss** and **Darkfire Kiss**.

Dragon's Egg—A polished sphere of black stone, perhaps obsidian, which shows the location of a newly sparked firestorm under the light of a fully eclipsed moon. Sophie the Wyvern uses the Dragon's Egg as a scrying glass in **Kiss of Fury**, shortly before it is broken. From that point onward, Erik must learn to scry by using other surfaces, and to develop his ability to feel the locations of all *Pyr*.

Dragonsmoke—a stream of vapor breathed by dragon shifters— whether *Pyr* or *Slayer*—that is invisible to human perception. (Perceptive humans may feel a chill when they breach a dragonsmoke barrier.) Dragonsmoke is not only visible to dragon shifters, but it has a resonant ring when formed into a complete circle. It is used as a protective barrier or boundary mark and will burn any dragon shifter who crosses it without the permission of the dragon shifter who breathed it. This act is called 'setting permissions.' In order to breathe dragonsmoke, a *Pyr* or *Slayer* enters a meditative state and directs the stream of dragonsmoke, weaving it into a barrier that is preferably high and deep. A dragonsmoke boundary will disintegrate over time, and some dragon shifters can tell the age of a smoke ring by its condition. Dragonsmoke can also be used as a conduit between fighting dragons, as shown in **Kiss of Fate**.

Dragon's Tail Wars—The Dragonfire series is set during a period of trial for the *Pyr*, in which they will battle the *Slayers* for custody of the earth and survival of mankind. This test was foretold to commence during the Dragon's Tail, an astrological period believed to be a phase of karmic retribution and rebalance. We are currently experiencing the power of this same Dragon's Tail in real life, which began in June 2006. The moon's node will move back to the Dragon's Head in November 2015, at which point either the

Pyr or the *Slayers* will have been exterminated. The *Pyr*'s prophecy declared that the first three firestorms after the Dragon's Tail commenced had to be successful for the *Pyr* to have a chance against the *Slayers*. Those three firestorms are recounted in **Kiss of Fire, Kiss of Fury** and **Kiss of Fate**.

Dragon's Tooth Warriors—These warriors are a military unit of *Pyr*, charged with hunting down and exterminating those dragon shifters who had turned against men. They come from a time before the evolution of *Slayers* and call their opponents 'vipers.' In fighting one viper, they were enchanted and cursed to take the form of additional teeth for that dragon's maw. They are led by a taciturn general named Drake, and unlike the modern *Pyr*, they are all dark in color in dragon form and almost indistinguishable from each other in either form. They first appear in the series in **Kiss of Fury**. The result of their decision to finish what they had begun is told in the short story, **Harmonia's Kiss**. Their adventures with the darkfire crystal are told in the **Dragon Legion Novellas**, during which they rename themselves the Dragon Legion.

Elemental Witches—women with power not only over an individual element but also the ability to become that element. The first elemental witch introduced in the Dragonfire novels was Liz Barrett, a **Firedaughter**, in **Ember's Kiss**. The history of the relationship between these women and the *Pyr* is explored in the **Dragon Legion Novellas**.

Earthdaughter—an **Elemental Witch** with an affinity for earth. An Earthdaughter can control the element of earth as well as become it. Petra is the first Earthdaughter encountered in the Dragonfire series: her story is told in the **Dragon Legion Novella, Kiss of Darkness**.

Firedaughter—an **Elemental Witch** with an affinity for fire. A Firedaughter can control the element of fire as well as become it. Liz Barrett is a Firedaughter and the first **Elemental Witch** introduced in Dragonfire: her story is told in **Ember's Kiss**.

Firestorm—each *Pyr* will experience one firestorm in his lifetime.

A firestorm occurs when that *Pyr* meets the human woman who can bear his son. Sparks literally fly between the couple, causing an overwhelming sense of attraction and desire. The firestorm is believed to flare the way it does because it marks the presence and approval of the **Great Wyvern**: in her presence, the spark within each *Pyr* is kindled to greater strength and power. The heat of the firestorm builds until the couple's relationship is consummated ("satisfying the firestorm") and this first coupling always results in the conception of a son. *Pyr* only have sons, who come into their shifting powers at puberty. (For the exception to this rule, please see **Wyvern**.) All *Pyr* and *Slayers* can feel the spark of a firestorm and are instinctively drawn to its blaze. Firestorms of particular significance to the *Pyr* tend to occur during full eclipses of the moon. Historically, the firestorm was believed to be a purely biological impulse, but the modern *Pyr* increasingly believe that a partnership of long duration with the "mate" is ideal. (See **Loss of Scale**.) In some instances, the firestorm can be a healing power: in **Kiss of Fury**, the injured Delaney is drawn to the heat of his brother Donovan's firestorm in search of renewal.

Great Wyvern — the divinity acknowledged by the *Pyr*. The *Pyr* swear by the Great Wyvern and attribute radical changes in fortune to her. Their lore insists that the Great Wyvern lit the divine spark within each of them. The **Death Ritual** ensures that the divine spark is fully extinguished when it should be. By this same logic, the blood of *Slayers* turns black because they willingly douse the divine spark in themselves, by turning their backs upon their sacred mission to defend the earth and its treasures. Just as the firestorm is a mark of the Great Wyvern's favor, the sterility of *Slayers* is a sign of her disfavor.

High Council of Seven — a governing council of *Pyr* established by Erik's father, Soren, in the Middle Ages, in an attempt to fight the plan of Mikael Vassily for dragon shifters to turn against mankind. That initiative failed, the *Pyr*'s numbers were vastly reduced, and Mikael became the first *Slayer*. The original High Council included Soren (father of Erik), Gaspar (grandfather of Lorenzo), Lothair, Sigmund (the elder, brother of Soren), Thorkel (grandfather of Thorolf), Rafferty and Erik. At the launch of the

Dragon's Tail Wars, Erik was attempting to locate and gather the remaining *Pyr* to re-establish that council.

Hoard—a collection of treasures kept by every *Pyr*. Although the *Pyr* in question perceives the items in the hoard to be precious, they may or may not be of monetary value: it is as likely that a *Pyr* will keep sentimental trinkets in his hoard—or stock certificates—as gold and precious gems. Some *Pyr* believe that their mate is the most valuable gem in their hoard.

Lair—although each *Pyr* may have multiple homes, his one principle residence is considered to be his lair. The lair is usually where the *Pyr*'s **Hoard** is secured, and is invariably heavily defended by **Dragonsmoke** barriers.

Loss of Scale—a *Pyr* will lose a scale when he loves, particularly when he loves and loses (or fears to lose). His emotional vulnerability is mirrored in his physical armor, which must be repaired by the Smith of the *Pyr*. This is not necessarily a mirror of romantic love: Magnus the *Slayer* lost a scale out of love for himself, while Sigmund lost one over his love for his mother. When a *Pyr* loses a scale due to his love for his mate, that scale can only be successfully repaired with a gift offered willingly by her and the presence of the four elements. See **Affinities**.

Mate—the traditional term for the woman who prompts the spark of a *Pyr*'s firestorm. Most mates take exception to the use of this word, although it does perfectly describe their role as results from the firestorm.

Old-speak—the traditional way in which dragon shifters communicate. Old-speak is gutteral and tends to be terse. It is expressed at a level too low for human ears to understand: humans typically hear the sound of old-speak but attribute it to passing trucks, trains or thunder. Old-speak can be uttered at different volumes: it can be conversational, it can be broadcast and heard at a great distance, or it can be whispered in the mind of another dragon shifter. A very wily dragon shifter can meld his old-speak with the thoughts of his victim so that the two are indistinguishable.

Prophecies—the *Pyr* seem to be particularly fond of prophecies and portents. **The Wyvern** can be a source of prophecies for them, as can their leader, Erik Sorensson, and Sara Keegan, the Seer who is the partner of Quinn Tyrrell, the Smith. See **Dragon's Tail**.

Pyr (or "**true** *Pyr*")—The *Pyr* are an ancient race of dragon shape shifters. Their role is to defend the four elements and the treasures of the earth, and they include humans among those treasures. They are not immortal, but live a very long time. Their senses are keener than humans'—they see more clearly, for example, and hear a wider range of sounds.

Scent—*Pyr* and *Slayers* can detect each other's presence by smell. Each leaves a distinctive scent, which lingers and can be identified, thanks to the keen senses of dragon shifters. *Pyr* with sensitive noses say that *Slayers* have an odor so foul that even if they don't recognize the dragon shifter specifically, they know his alliance by his scent. Erik's son Sigmund knows how to remove his scent from a location, thanks to his diligent research into old dragon lore. Some *Slayers* who have drunk the Elixir develop the ability to disguise their scent willingly.

Shadow Dragons—*Pyr* raised from the dead with the **Dragon's Blood Elixir**. These *Pyr* were not exposed to all four elements within a day and night of their death (see **Death Ritual**) so could be revived by the Elixir. Shadow dragons do not bleed and they fight on, without regard for any sustained injuries. They must be dismembered and burned to ashes to be destroyed, then exposed to all four elements to ensure that they remain that way. Niall's twin brother was made a shadow dragon by Magnus, and that tale is told in **Whisper Kiss**.

Shape shifting—*Pyr* and *Slayers* change shape at will and by choice. His decision to shift form is presaged by a shimmer of pale blue that illuminates his body. When a dragon shifter is wounded, however, he will revert to his human form, whether he is able to choose to do so or not. This may be the result of the *Pyr* living so many centuries in human society. In addition, when a dragon shifter is wounded so severely that death is likely, he will unwillingly rotate between forms. Often the speed of the shifting increases in this situation, until the dragon shifter dies. There is a persistent idea amongst the *Pyr* that it is dangerous for a human to watch the actual transition between forms, and that seeing a man change to a dragon can make a human insane.

Slayers—*Pyr* who have abandoned the mission to defend humans among the earth's treasures. Their blood is black, which is said to be a sign that they have turned away from the light. (The *Pyr* have a saying: "*Pyr* are born and *Slayers* are made.") This historical development is explored in **Kiss of Fate**. *Slayers* also lose the ability to reproduce when they make their choice. It is possible that part of the reason they are drawn to a firestorm is jealousy.

Smith—the armorer of the *Pyr* and the only one who can repair their "armor" of scales. The Smith is a hereditary position and relies heavily upon blacksmithing skills. The Smith has a particular affinity with fire and often can coax a blaze or extinguish it with his thoughts. (See **Affinities**.) The current Smith of the *Pyr* is Quinn Tyrrell and his story is told in **Kiss of Fire**.

Warrior—the Warrior of the *Pyr* can summon the elements to assist the *Pyr* in battle, often in the form of weather as artillery. The current Warrior of the *Pyr* is Donovan Shea, and his story is told in **Kiss of Fury**.

Waterdaughter—an **Elemental Witch** with an affinity for water. A Waterdaughter can not only control the element of water but become it. Katina is the first Waterdaughter introduced in the Dragonfire series: her story is told in the **Dragon Legion Novella, Kiss of Danger**.

Wyvern—the only female *Pyr*. At any given moment in time, there is one female *Pyr*, who has additional powers, including the power of prophecy, the ability to take the form of a salamander in addition to human and dragon forms, and the ability to spontaneously manifest elsewhere. The most recent Wyvern,

Sophie, died in **Kiss of Fate**. Erik and Eileen's daughter Zoë was conceived in that book. All *Pyr* come into the fullness of their powers at puberty, and Zoë's coming of age is told in **The Dragon Diaries** trilogy. The *Pyr* call their deity the **Great Wyvern**.

MEET THE *PYR*

A long-running series results in a large cast of characters. Here's a list of those characters who play recurring roles in the Dragonfire series, including *Pyr*, *Slayers,* mates and children. Note that there may be spoilers in their descriptions, if you haven't read all of the books published to date.

Alexandra Madison—partner and mate of **Donovan**, scientist developing sustainable fuels and the prophesied Wizard. Mother of Nick and Darcy. Alex and Donovan's firestorm is recounted in **Kiss of Fury**.

Alexander—one of the Dragon's Tooth Warriors, **Drake**'s second in command and partner of **Katina**. His story is told in the **Dragon Legion Novella, Kiss of Danger**.

Ambrose—a *Slayer* who tried to steal Margaux, the mate of Thierry and mother of **Quinn Tyrrell**. He vowed to eliminate the line of the Smith after he failed. He plays a role in **Kiss of Fire**.

Aura—mate of **Thaddeus** and an Airdaughter. Aura and Thad's story is told in the **Dragon Legion Novella, Kiss of Destiny**.

Balthasar—a *Slayer*, agate with gold in dragon form, bodyguard and driver to **Magnus**. He first appears in **Kiss of Fate** and is beguiled by **Lorenzo** in **Flashfire**.

Brandon Merrick—a professional surfer, the rebellious son of **Brandt** and partner of **Liz Barrett**. Brandon was targeted by the *Slayer* **Chen** and intended as a sacrifice to build that *Slayer*'s power. Liz and Brandon's story is told in **Ember's Kiss**.

Brandt Merrick—an embittered *Pyr*, estranged from his fellow *Pyr* and separated from his mate, Kay, father of **Brandon**. Brandt and Kay find the spark of the firestorm renewed and make a new beginning in **Ember's Kiss**.

Boris Vassily—*Slayer* and sworn enemy of **Erik**, spectacular in dragon form with ruby red and brass scales and trailing red plumes. He has a large role in the first three Dragonfire novels, **Kiss of Fire, Kiss of Fury** and **Kiss of Fate**.

Cassie Redmond—former paparazzi, professional photographer, partner of **Lorenzo**. Cassie and Lorenzo's story is told in **Flashfire**.

Chandra—a hunter and executor of evil creatures, she first appears in **Flashfire**, when her pursuit of **Viv Jason** leads her to **Thorolf**. An expert in both the martial arts and the mythological creatures, she immediately recognizes **Thorolf** for what he is, as well as the danger he's in, and (unknown to **Thorolf**) takes him under her protective custody.

Chen Lee—a formidable *Slayer* and last of the Dragon Kings (*Lung Wang*) who believes himself destined to be king of all dragons. Chen possesses the secrets of ancient dragon magic, lost to all dragon shifters but him. He is known to have the ability to take six forms: an attractive young Asian woman, an agile young Asian man, an elderly Asian man, a salamander, a snake and a dragon. In dragon form, he is lacquer red and gold. He is manipulative and often underestimated by others. He needs to sacrifice a *Pyr* with an affinity to air to complete his spell: in **Ember's Kiss**, his plot against **Brandon** was foiled, but he entered an alliance with **Viv Jason** to target **Thorolf**.

Damien—a Dragon's Tooth Warrior, known by his comrades as the "heartbreaker" because of his string of short relationships with women. In the **Dragon Legion Novella, Kiss of Darkness,** he has the chance to save **Petra**, the woman who stole his heart.

Delaney Shea—younger brother of **Donovan Shea**, married to **Ginger Sinclair**, father of Liam and Sean. Ginger and Delaney's story is told in **Winter Kiss.**

Donovan Shea—lapis lazuli and gold in dragon form, a former duelist and the Warrior of the *Pyr*. He and his partner **Alex** have two sons: Nick and Darcy. Nick was named after **Nikolas of Thebes.** Alex and Donovan's firestorm is recounted in **Kiss of Fury.**

Drake (aka Stephanos)—commander of the Dragon's Tooth Warriors and leader of the Dragon Legion. Drake finds new meaning in his life in **Harmonia's Kiss.**

Ginger Sinclair—a chef turned organic dairy farmer, married to **Delaney**, mother of Liam and Sean. Ginger and Delaney's story is told in **Winter Kiss.**

Eileen Grosvenor—a university professor whose area of expertise is comparative mythology, partner of **Erik**, mother of **Zoë**. Eileen and Erik's story is told in **Kiss of Fate.**

Erik Sorensson—onyx and silver in dragon form (sometimes described as black and pewter), the leader of the *Pyr*, a pyrotechnics expert who creates large fireworks displays synchronized to music, and the partner of **Eileen Grosvenor**. Erik has had two firestorms, one with Louisa, which resulted in the birth of his son **Sigmund**, and a second one with Eileen, who is the reincarnation of Louisa. He and Eileen have a daughter **Zoë**, who should be the next Wyvern. Erik and Eileen's story is told in **Kiss of Fate.**

Isabelle—adopted daughter of **Rafferty Powell** and **Melissa Smith**. She is human, but the reincarnation of **Sophie**.

Jean-Pierre (aka JP)—a *Slayer*, son of **Mallory**, a renegade, yellow topaz and silver in dragon form. The killing of his younger brother, the *Slayer* Lucien, by the *Pyr* in **Kiss of Fire** made him turn *Slayer* to seek revenge. The killing of his father by **Jorge** turned him against *Slayers*. He was enchanted by **Chen** in **Flashfire** and remained in Erik's custody in **Ember's Kiss**.

Jorge—the most ruthless and mercenary of *Slayers*, yellow topaz and gold in dragon form. He first appeared in **Kiss of Fury** and subsequently became addicted to the Dragon's Blood Elixir. With the elimination of the Elixir's source in **Winter Kiss**, he began to hunt *Slayers* who had consumed it and devour them to get every last drop of Elixir. Seized by Pele in **Ember's Kiss**, he was snared by the darkfire and cast into the past with the Dragon Legion. He makes cameo appearances in the **Dragon Legion Novellas, Kiss of Danger** and **Kiss of Destiny**.

Katina—lost love of **Alexander** and a Waterdaughter. Alexander and Katina's story is told in the **Dragon Legion Novella, Kiss of Danger**.

Liz Barrett—a Firedaughter, marine biologist and mate of **Brandon Merrick**. Liz and Brandon's story is told in **Ember's Kiss**.

Lorenzo di Fiore—three shades of gold with cabochon gems in dragon form, master illusionist and magician, partner of **Cassie Redmond**. Lorenzo is the most adept of the *Pyr* with beguiling and was believed by the *Slayers* to be their best chance of a recruit. Cassie and Lorenzo's story is told in **Flashfire**.

Magnus Montmorency—a *Slayer*, jade green and gold in dragon form, a collector of secrets and foe of **Rafferty**. Magnus re-created the Dragon's Blood Elixir and used it to both enslave *Slayers* and create an army of shadow dragons to serve his will. He first appears in **Kiss of Fury** and meets his match in **Darkfire Kiss**.

Mallory—a *Slayer*, garnet red and gold with pearls in dragon form, bodyguard to **Magnus**. He was given the Elixir when he was badly injured by dragonfire in **Winter Kiss**, but remained disfigured. In **Darkfire Kiss**, he was targeted by **Jorge**.

Marcus Maximus aka Marco (the Sleeper)—nephew of the *Slayer* **Magnus Montmorency** and ward of **Rafferty**'s grandfather. When Magnus murdered his brother Maximilian because that *Pyr* had a firestorm, Maximilian's mate and infant son were taken into protective care by Rafferty's grandfather. The boy was enchanted to sleep until the darkfire burned, in order to hide him from Magnus. The Sleeper awakens in **Darkfire Kiss**. Marco is particularly tranquil and observant and has the ability to both control and anticipate darkfire.

Melissa Smith—a reporter and cancer survivor, the partner of **Rafferty Powell** and adoptive mother of **Isabelle**. Melissa and Rafferty's story is told in **Darkfire Kiss**.

Mikael Vassily—first *Slayer* and father of **Boris Vassily**. His story is told in **Kiss of Fate**.

Niall Talbot—amethyst and platinum in dragon form, the Dreamwalker of the *Pyr*, owner of an eco-tourism business, partner of **Roxanne Kincaid** and father of twin boys, Kyle and Nolan. Niall battled his own twin brother, Phelan, who had become a shadow dragon. Rox and Niall's story is told in **Whisper Kiss**.

Nikolas of Thebes—a Dragon's Tooth Warrior who fell in love with **Sophie**. Their story of forbidden love begins in **Kiss of Fate**.

Petra—lost love of **Damien**, and an Earthdaughter. Petra and Damien's story is told in the **Dragon Legion Novella, Kiss of Darkness**.

Quinn Tyrrell—the Smith of the *Pyr*, sapphire and steel in dragon form, partnered with **Sara Keegan**, father of Garrett and Ewan. Quinn was married centuries earlier to Elizabeth, despite their not having a firestorm, and she was murdered by the *Slayer* Ambrose. He earns his living as an artisan blacksmith. Sara and Quinn's story is told in **Kiss of Fire**.

Rafferty Powell—opal and gold in dragon form, the romantic of the *Pyr*, partner of **Melissa Smith** and adoptive father of Isabelle. Rafferty is the one *Pyr* who has learned to change to a salamander and spontaneously manifest elsewhere. He wears a black and white ring, which is a reminder of the sacrifice of Sophie and Nikolas. Melissa and Rafferty's story is told in **Darkfire Kiss**.

Roxanne Kincaid—A tattoo artist, partner of **Niall** and mother to twin boys, Kyle and Nolan. Rox and Niall's story is told in **Whisper Kiss**.

Sara Keegan—a former accountant turned used bookstore owner, the Seer of the *Pyr*, partner of **Quinn Tyrrell**, mother of Garrett and Ewan. Sara and Quinn's story is told in **Kiss of Fire**.

Sigmund Guthie (born Sigmund Sorensson)—Erik's son by his first firestorm, a *Pyr* with a talent for unearthing lost dragon magic, and a *Pyr* who turned *Slayer*. Author of the rare volume *The Compleat Guide to Slaying Dragons*. Sigmund disappears from the Dragonfire series in **Kiss of Fate**, but makes cameo appearances in the **Dragon Diaries**.

Sloane Forbes—tourmaline and gold in dragon form, owner of a greenhouse and nursery specializing in herbs, and the Apothecary of the *Pyr*.

Sophie—the Wyvern at the beginning of the Dragonfire series. Sophie sacrificed herself in **Kiss of Fate**, and **Zoë Sorensson** was conceived during that firestorm. Sophie makes cameo appearances in the **Dragon Diaries**, the spin-off paranormal young adult series that chronicles Zoë's coming of age as the new Wyvern.

Thaddeus (or Thad)—one of the **Dragon's Tooth Warriors**, his story is told in the **Dragon Legion Novella, Kiss of Destiny**.

Thorolf—the bad boy of the *Pyr*, a former project of **Rox's**, a dragon who enjoys all the pleasures life has to offer. He is targeted by **Viv Jason** and **Chen** in **Flashfire**, an alliance that was shattered in **Ember's Kiss**. They each hunt him alone now. His story will be told in **Serpent's Kiss**.

Viv Jason—falsely believed by **Chandra** to be one of the Liliot, Viv Jason is actually Tisiphone, one of the Erinyes killed by **Damien** in the **Dragon Legion Novella, Kiss of Darkness**. Hades gave her the right to avenge herself upon the *Pyr*, and she has been waiting for the Dragon's Tail wars. She has the power to shift shape into a green serpent. In **Flashfire**, she allied with the *Slayer* **Chen** to trap **Thorolf** but that alliance was broken in **Ember's Kiss** when **Chen** realized her true intent.

Zoë Sorensson—the daughter of **Erik Sorensson**, leader of the *Pyr*, by his second mate, **Eileen**. As the daughter of a *Pyr*, Zoë is believed to be the next Wyvern but (like all *Pyr*) will not come into her powers until puberty. Zoë's coming of age as the new Wyvern is told in the **Dragon Diaries** series.

Deborah Cooke sold her first book in 1992, a medieval romance called THE ROMANCE OF THE ROSE published under her pseudonym Claire Delacroix. Since then, she has published over fifty novels in a wide variety of sub-genres, including historical romance, contemporary romance, paranormal romance, fantasy romance, time travel romance, women's fiction, paranormal young adult and fantasy with romantic elements. She has published under the names Claire Delacroix, Claire Cross and Deborah Cooke. THE BEAUTY, part of her successful Bride Quest series of historical romances, was her first title to land on the New York Times List of Bestselling Books. Her books routinely appear on other bestseller lists and have won numerous awards. In 2009, she was the writer-in-residence at the Toronto Public Library, the first time the library has hosted a residency focused on the romance genre. In 2012, she was honored to receive the Romance Writers of America's Mentor of the Year Award.

Currently, she writes the Dragonfire series of paranormal romances featuring dragon shape shifter heroes under the name Deborah Cooke. She also is writing the True Love Brides series of medieval romances as Claire Delacroix, which continues the story of the family introduced in her popular title THE BEAUTY BRIDE. Deborah lives in Canada with her husband and family, as well as far too many unfinished knitting projects.

SUBSCRIBE TO DEBORAH'S MONTHLY READER NEWSLETTER:
http://eepurl.com/reIuD

VISIT DEBORAH'S WEBSITES:
www.deborahcooke.com
www.delacroix.net

LIKE DEBORAH'S FACEBOOK PAGES:
www.facebook.com/AuthorDeborahCookeFanPage
www.facebook.com/AuthorClaireDelacroix